Free to Fall

A SINGLE DAD, CLOSE PROXIMITY, SMALL TOWN
ROMANCE

AMARYLLIS HERITAGE
BOOK ONE

TRACEY JERALD

Free to Fall

Copyright © 2024 by **Tracey Jerald**
ISBN: 978-1-959299-30-1 (Cover)
ISBN: 978-1-959299-31-8 (Alternate Cover)
ISBN: 978-1-959299-32-5 (E-book)
Library of Congress Control Number: TBD

Tracey Jerald
101 Marketside Avenue, Suite 404-205
Ponte Vedra, FL, 3208
https://www.traceyjerald.com

Editor: Melissa Borucki
Proof Edits: Holly Malgieri, Comma Sutra Editorial
Cover Design by Tugboat Design
Photo Credit: Wander Aguiar/Model: Gianni Militello
PR & Marketing: Linda Russell - Foreword PR

Dedication

To my amazing readers, friends, and family picking up this book.

Don't forget the "ever after" in your fairy tale.

It truly is the best part.

I've been living mine for the last seventeen years.

Playlist

Celine Dion: "Ashes—from Deadpool 2"
P!nk: "When I Get There"
Taylor Swift: "Cruel Summer"
GAYLE: "abcdefu"
Paul Simon: "Father and Daughter
X Ambassadors: "Unsteady"
Miranda Lambert: "Over You"
Ryan Adams: "Desire"
Asia: "Only Time Will Tell"
Dua Lipa: "Levitating"
Enya: "Caribbean Blue"
Chris Stapleton: "Broken Halos"
Little Big Town, Sugarland: "Life In a Northern Town"
Lorde: "Royals"

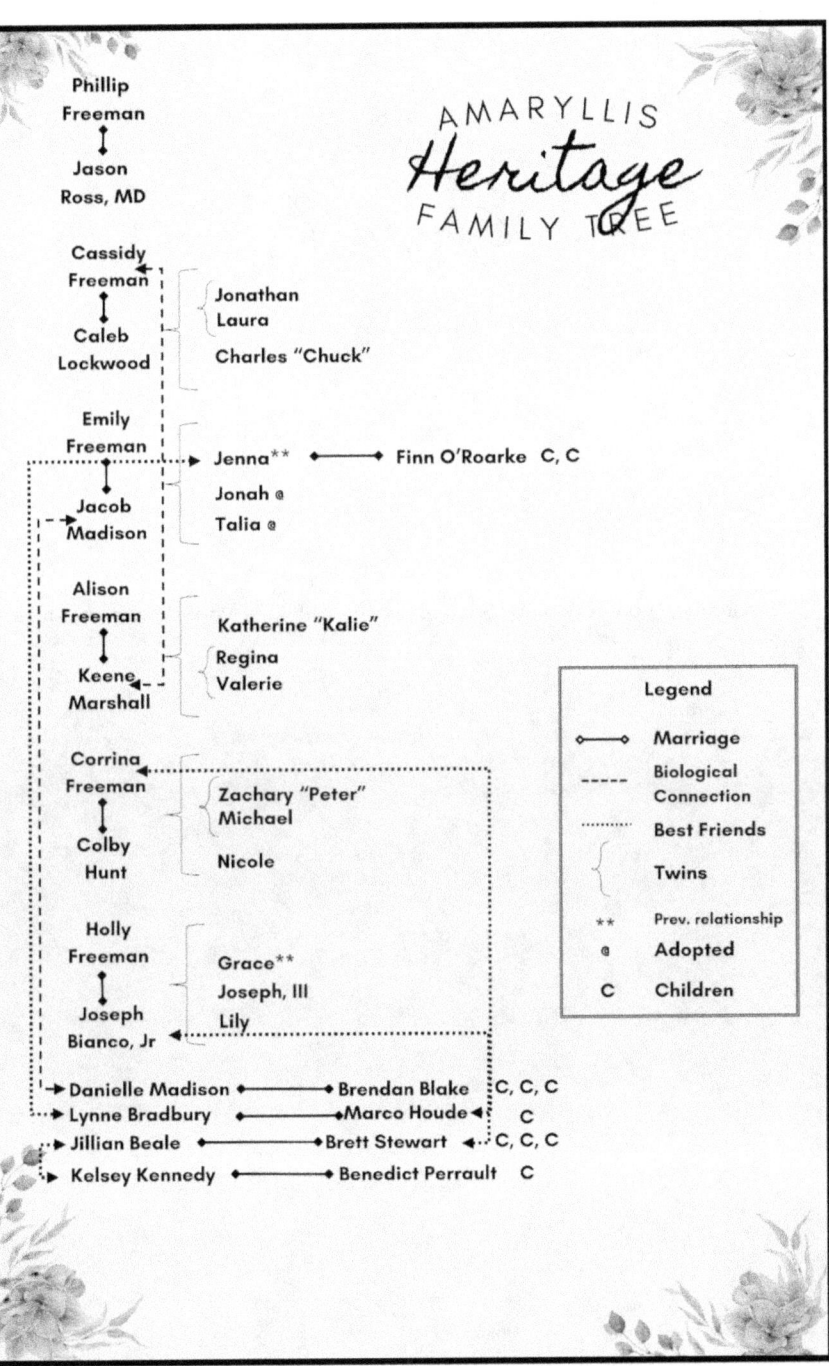

AMARYLLIS
Heritage
FAMILY TREE

Phillip Freeman
↓
Jason Ross, MD

Cassidy Freeman
↓
Caleb Lockwood

{ Jonathan
  Laura

  Charles "Chuck"

Emily Freeman
↓
Jacob Madison

{ Jenna** ←→ Finn O'Roarke   C, C
  Jonah @
  Talia @

Alison Freeman
↓
Keene Marshall

{ Katherine "Kalie"
  Regina
  Valerie

Corrina Freeman
↓
Colby Hunt

{ Zachary "Peter"
  Michael
  Nicole

Holly Freeman
↓
Joseph Bianco, Jr

{ Grace**
  Joseph, III
  Lily

→ Danielle Madison ←——→ Brendan Blake   C, C, C
→ Lynne Bradbury ←——→ Marco Houde ←   C
→ Jillian Beale ←——→ Brett Stewart ←   C, C, C
→ Kelsey Kennedy ←——→ Benedict Perrault   C

Legend

◇——◇ Marriage

----- Biological Connection

······· Best Friends

{ Twins

** Prev. relationship

@ Adopted

C Children

Epigraph

"Sometimes you wake up. Sometimes the fall kills you. And sometimes when you fall, you fly."

Neil Gaiman

From the Journal of Dr. Laura Lockwood

THOUGHTS ABOUT THE LEGEND OF AMARYLLIS

If it wasn't for the indelible strength of my parents at mending the broken pieces within themselves, as well as relationships with their family members as they arose over the years, we wouldn't be where we are now. None of us would have what we do.

By that, I don't mean tangible items like homes, jewelry, or money. I mean items of true worth.

The most important being love.

Until my eighteenth birthday, I believed I was born the daughter of two people who dedicated their lives to accomplish greatness. Technically, that's the truth. Still, there was a price paid for my mother's determination and my father's infatuation. It's a price they never knew they were paying with pain and blood from the time they were both children.

I have a new appreciation for the way I was raised—the bond between our found family means more now that I know its origins. Still, there's no escaping the fact our next generation is ready to assume the thrones they created. Is it really time for the kings and queens of my parents' generation to abdicate their thrones?

Yes and no. They may be ready to hand over the reins, but they'll always be there for us. I know that down to the depths of my soul.

Our family blossomed and multiplied from the ashes of a legend—the legend of Amaryllis. It's one of pride, determination, and radiant beauty. We evolved from the hearts and souls of people who understood the sacrifices necessary to find love and to hold on to it.

Now that I'm older, I appreciate why my parents didn't raise us on Cinderella fairy tales. Their own experiences demonstrated it was necessary to bleed while we're falling in love. Just like the Oracle of Delphi warned Amaryllis when she fell for Alteo while trying to win his heart.

I know the truth. It's burned in my heart and mind. Now, it's inked on my skin as a reminder.

Do I believe in everlasting love? Yes.

Am I prepared to sacrifice for it the way they did?

I hope.

Prologue

Laura

As THE CLOCK ticks toward noon, I feel the unknown future I'm clasping between the palms of clammy hands may just cause my lungs to collapse. That's a virtual impossibility, of course. I should know, I'm a doctor.

But in less than ten minutes, me and the other one hundred classmates I've gone to school with these last four years are about to find out where we've matched to complete our residencies. It was four years of blood, sweat, and tears—most days, literally. Not just my own but the patients I intend to dedicate my future to helping.

A peal of laughter from my right distracts me from the envelope I'm clutching in my fist. My head whips in the direction of my mother, who is snuggling within my father's embrace while laughing at the poleaxed expression on my younger brother's face.

Jonathan, my older brother by six minutes, murmurs amusedly in my ear, "Chuck was just hit on. Then they found out he was your baby brother and backed away with the most horrified expression on their face. What *have* you been doing within Yale's hallowed halls, Laura?"

Loftily, I manage, "Nothing you need to be concerned with, Jon."

His "uh-huh" comes just as I surreptitiously check my watch for the tenth time in the last two minutes.

Eight minutes.

My eyes are drawn to the blank map where I'll soon place the pin announcing my match. It's moments like this that I acknowledge the study of medicine so often reflects the reality of life. Too often, it's a hard-fought battle where the stakes come down to a fight that's over long before it's begun.

Also, like life, nobody said it was fair.

My stomach churns with anxiety as I smooth the envelope against the side of my thigh. My father leans over to wrap his free arm around my shoulders. "No matter where you're matched, it's going to be perfect, Laura."

"I'm certain you're right, Dad." But the truth is, I can't imagine what will happen if I don't get my number one choice—Greenwich Hospital, a key asset to the Yale New Haven Hospital's residency program.

It's not that I wouldn't learn incredible things at Mass General or Stanford, my mind reasons. *In fact, be grateful if you do get into any of those, Laura,* I scold myself harshly. Any doctor here would feel overwhelmed with joy matching with such prestigious programs. But my anxiety boils down to one thing—I'd have to leave. Neither of those programs would allow me to be where I most want to be.

Home.

As the electronic clock flickering beneath the tent set up on Harkness Lawn at the Yale School of Medicine flashes five minutes, the energy ramps up higher. There's eager excitement from faculty, staff, family, and friends. Meanwhile, every single member of my graduating class looks as if they want to find the nearest waste receptacle to release the acid in their stomach.

Same, my friends. Same.

Finally, after an interminable wait, Doctors Brown, Israel, and Aydin make the center of the crowd. Doctor Brown is holding a megaphone.

One minute.

Doctor Brown's voice carries over the substantial crowd. "Welcome to this year's Yale School of Medicine Match Day!"

A raucous cheer erupts as she hands the microphone to Dr. Israel. He amps everyone up further. "You have accomplished so much and every person here is so very proud of you."

He hands the microphone to Dr. Aydin. His voice makes my insides quiver because he seems to speak directly to me when he says, "We hope you have many fond memories of your years at Yale. No matter where you go, know you are a part of the Yale family."

Doctor Brown takes the megaphone back. "Are you ready?"

Hands shaking, I lift my envelope.

I've prepared for this moment for four long years. I've dedicated my life to med school, worked harder than I ever expected, including being accepted into the Medical Coaching Experience. I've functioned on little to no sleep and graduated at the top of my class.

It means nothing as the crowd counts down. "Ten!"

"Nine!"

"Eight!"

"Seven!"

"Six!"

"Five!"

"Four!"

"Three!"

"Two!"

"One!"

"Zero!"

Then, the sound every medical student has been waiting for—the cow bell —rings.

My universe collapses to the white envelope in my hand. For the amount of time I take to inhale, I debate not opening it. Then, as shouts of joy and laughter penetrate through my fog, I slip my finger beneath the seal.

My family hovers anxiously, awaiting my reaction. My eyes burn with tears. I find my mother studying me. Her eyes turn diamond bright even as my smile erupts. I face my father, who's wearing an identical expression of excitement. He demands, "Greenwich?" as if it's a foregone conclusion.

I finally let out a war whoop as I throw my arms around both of them—for everything they were. For everything they are. For everything they gave to me so I could become Dr. Laura Lockwood.

Now, it's time to pay that forward by becoming the newest resident in emergency medicine at Greenwich Hospital—my first choice.

I just hope they're ready for me.

CHAPTER

One

PRESENT DAY

I'M CHORTLING as I describe my shift, concluding with, "Needless to say, there are days when being the chief resident makes our family dinners nothing short of child's play."

My parents, Cassidy and Caleb Lockwood, both burst into laughter on the other side of our video call. My mother, who, if not for the threads of silver in her sable-colored hair, appears to not have aged a day, grins. "Be grateful your uncle hasn't had any new 'illnesses.' He's been moaning on and on about not seeing enough of you at the office."

"Good thing you tacked on the last part or I'd have wondered which one of the family missed me."

My father leans in. "I'm hearing it from your other uncles. Make plans for dinner. Soon. Otherwise, I wouldn't be alarmed if there was a kidnapping in your future."

I chuckle, knowing they're only partially joking. Our immense family—and extended framily—is so close I'm just waiting to be stolen from the hospital one night and whisked away in one of my father's company SUVs to be with family.

Family. Ours started with my mother, her four sisters—Emily, Alison, Corinna, and Holly—and their older brother Philip carving a dream for themselves out of the ruins of nothing. Then the gods stepped in and intersected their lives first between my Uncle Phil and his husband Jason. Which led to my parents meeting as a result of my mother planning my Uncle Ryan's wedding to my Uncle Jared. Which led to Aunt Ali and Uncle Keene reuniting. Then Corinna and Colby reconciled. Emily met Jake. Then finally, Holly's life intersected with Joe's.

Amidst all that, there are numerous tenets of framily that sprang from those relationships.

The Amaryllis Heritage, which is one way we've been described in the media, is a hodgepodge of people whose love is unshakeable. When we love, we love with the intent of forever.

"Oh, sweetheart?"

"Yes, Mama?"

"You should see what StellaNova wrote about you." She names the world's most popular news magazine.

"I'll look at it when I hang up."

"We'll let you go, sweetheart. Love you, Laura," my father calls out.

"Love you both." I blow my parents a kiss and disconnect the call, knowing I don't need to go to StellaNova's site. I know what the tabloids write about me. I've been dubbed the princess of weddings, a courtesan in the Collyer court of billionaires. Then they came up with my personal favorite: the queen of blood and gore.

With a quick glance at my scrubs, I reach out and knock firmly against the table I'm sitting at.

"What the hell was that for, Lockwood?" a stringent voice barks, intruding into my thoughts.

Flashing the all too irritating chief of staff at Greenwich Hospital, Dr. Bryan Moser, a lazy smile which causes his lips to quirk—a rarity that shows why half the staff hates him but still drools over his silver fox gorgeousness. The other half, being any of us who work beneath the taciturn chief and are immune to his superficial charms.

Eager to get the chief's attention off me in case he bugs me again for my monthly financial report, I joke, "It's the cleanest I've been since I started full time in the ER. I've given up counting the number of times I came dressed to work according to our," I air quote. "Documented dress code only to have my clothes puked or bled on within minutes."

Gurgles of laughter all around me let me know my point is welcomed by the other residents, attendings, doctors, and nurses who have a scant few minutes to wolf down a bite of food in between patients. Moser even presses his lips together to keep from laughing aloud, but his shoulders shake beneath his perfectly tailored suit.

Even as I wrap up my fourth-year residency, I know my first-year exploits in the ER will never be lived down within the hallowed halls of this hospital. Then again, they likely softened any antagonism aimed in my direction from previously employed senior residents in the ER because of my family lineage. Mentally, I tell each and every one of those doctors to kiss my ass.

It's now my ER. Just the thought of that sends a familiar surge of pride running through me at what I've accomplished.

My appointment had absolutely nothing to do with the family I was born into. If anything, I think as I study the taciturn chief, being a Lockwood was firmly a black mark against me. Chief Bryan Moser knew I graduated college at nineteen. He also knew I graduated top of my class from med school at twenty-three from one of the most prestigious programs in the country. The bias I was up against was the perception of nepotism due to the fact the last name of varying branches of my family is emblazoned on various walls of the building I stride into every day.

Still, I recall my twin brother's recent teasing when he came to take me to lunch and everyone bursting into laughter at my mentioning I needed to change—again. "What *have* you been doing to make your mark in these hallowed halls, Laura?"

"Let's just say what I did in med school isn't nearly as memorable as what I've done since I became a resident."

"I have no doubt."

Jon's question made me flashback to all my firsts here at Greenwich Hospital. There was Billy French. *My first puker*, I remember with fondness. Poor kid hit the emergency room doors and booted on the first thing in front of him—me. He only doused bile on my Burberry overcoat. Nothing too significant.

Then there was Bernadette Hagen. The sweet cherub hadn't particularly appreciated when I took her temperature rectally due to an ear infection. Her baptism of urine blessed me as well as several peds nurses in her indignant fury. That fountain took out the white jacket with Dr. Laura Lockwood so carefully embroidered on it. My entire family cracked up when I relayed that story at a family dinner, considering it was a gift I received from my parents when I graduated from medical school.

Still, I can't forget Maverick. A street kid, that little beast tried to knock me unconscious just because I was putting pressure on the knife wound on his side. Unfortunately, he still made me trip, causing me to send a trach tray toppling over in the trauma room and slicing my hand open in the process. There went my cousin's silk blouse. Right into the trash.

Grace, despite understanding it wasn't my fault, still made me replace it.

But the pièce de résistance, what finally tore everyone away from the idea that Dr. Laura Lockwood was some kind of pampered princess, was when I split seam a pair of vintage Chanel slacks my Aunt Em bought me while she was in Paris for a runway show of her newest bridal gown designs. I vaulted on top of a gunshot victim who coded within seconds of him hitting the ER doors. The cool air hitting each of my cheeks as my pants tore from crotch to waistband only penetrated once the patient was being wheeled into surgery, and catcalls and wolf whistles followed me down the brightly lit corridor. As I explained to Moser earnestly in his office after he blew his stack over my lack of professionalism, "It wasn't like I meant to show the whole ER my thong; I was saving a life."

His expression filled with resignation. "Get the hell out of my office, Lockwood. Find some fucking scrubs and try to finish your shift without flashing the rest of the hospital."

I backed out of his office, getting my bare ass back to work as soon as possible.

Jon laughed when I drummed my nails against the table as I counted aloud how many times since the staff has asked me how I survived that incident without Moser canning me. "Not to mention where I buy my panties. Christ, Jon. If I wanted to command a commission from La Perla, I could probably get it."

"TMI, little sister."

I rolled my eyes at him in disgust. "You are such a damn hypocrite."

"How's that?"

"You have a problem with me talking about wearing lingerie, but no problem stripping a woman out of it?"

Jon lifted his glass of whisky to toast me. "It's all about context, Gore. I don't want to imagine my baby sister . . ." He pales before taking a slug of his drink. "Nope. This conversation stops now."

I laughed in his face before repeating my earlier comment. "Hypocrite."

"Yep. Now, change of subject, what are we doing for the parents' Christmas gift?"

Flexing my fingers as the titters of laughter continue, I hazard a glance at Moser's again impassive expression. He and I came to a truce some time back. It might have to do with the fact that regardless of whatever has been dumped on me, I haven't let it alter my course—which is to treat the patients that roll up to Greenwich Hospital's ER. The fact I don't give a damn about how awful a patient's odds might be went further than anything in solidifying my position here.

There's no halfway in my ER. Just like there's no halfway in my dedication as a doctor.

Moser must have been told we're receiving new funding for an MRI or something because he snorts with his version of laughter. As he moves away from my table, he taunts, "I give an hour tops, Dr. Lockwood. I mean, Christ. Even the paparazzi know what a mess you create in my house."

I assume an innocent expression. "It could be worse."

That causes him to stop in his tracks. "You think so? What could be worse, *Gore*." He emphasizes my nickname.

Everyone within hearing distance is avidly waiting on my reply. I pause before offering, "I could be Dr. *Bore*. Wouldn't that be so much duller for all of you?"

Like I hoped, everyone—even Moser—groans. "Get back to the ER, Lockwood. Someone there will appreciate your sense of humor. Though likely, they'll have arrived DOA," he snarks with the gallows humor I learned quickly you adopt or you won't make it through your first year in med school. It wasn't too long ago, after we spent a weekend disimpacting patients due to food poisoning, I contributed some flowery prose regarding the odoriferous materials on a clipboard of ass jokes some first-year resident from a decade ago left in the doctor's lounge.

Now, it's an homage, much like my nickname.

The camaraderie at Greenwich Hospital is like no other. When I've traveled to medical conferences, I'm taken aback by the elitism at other facilities. Here, we're not titles; we're a team. Moser walks away, shouting that all department heads had better have their financial reports to him by the end of shift. I shout back, "Can we delegate it?"

"Only if you want your budget cut!" he yells back to a round of applause from the few other heads still in the cafeteria.

None of us are above hard work. Nor are we above jumping in when it's all–hands–on–deck. Just last week, a new first year shouted at me to get more 4x4s when we had a gusher rushed in with their family. The resident in charge of riding herd on their every maneuver simply rolled their eyes and mouthed, "Sorry."

Still, I got the pads, donned my gown and mask, and called out, "What do we have here, people?" right before I chucked them in the direction of the flame-faced first year.

That isn't to say every one of us doesn't take our jobs seriously. It's a necessity, but like I've learned, we need to decompress otherwise there's too much of a chance of failing the people who need us the most because of the long hours and the never-ending pressure to not make mistakes.

Because a mistake here could be the fatalist of falls, it may lead to someone's death.

Standing, I shove the remains of my dinner in my lunch sack before heading out one of the many entrances.

I suppose I should be more shocked than resigned when Moser traps me the second I exit the cafeteria. "Lockwood, a word."

"Certainly, sir." I give him the respect his title is due even though the way he studies me causes my stomach to churn. *What did I do? Forget to call up for a neuro consult?* It's not the first time and I'm certain it won't be the last.

After a lengthy perusal, he stuns me by declaring, "You're a fucking waste in the ER."

Despite Moser hovering on the periphery of stories told by my family since he saved the life of one of my aunts and was briefly engaged to another, it wasn't until a few years ago, after he became chief, that I caught his specific notice. Mentally, I shudder recalling the first time we had a department head meeting he presided over and his cold eyes skewered through me like I was some parasite he was told he'd have to live with.

The head of ontology leaned over to whisper, "Don't worry, Laura. Take it from me. Bryan hates being reminded of his mistakes." She paused a half a heartbeat as he fried her with a similar glare, which she returned with a brilliant smile. This caused Moser to shift the papers in front of him before he aimed his glare at another target. She finished with, "Or the women who have said no to his half-ass offer of a date."

Considering the doctor in question is married to one of the world's most notorious rock stars, I had a hard time containing my laughter. Still, about two years ago, something changed Dr. Moser from being the patron saint of misogynistic pricks—a woman. Hospital gossip ran rampant. Our illustrious chief actually had a heart hidden beneath his bespoke suits. Still, his words infuriate me. I surge forward, barely able to restrain my fury. "Excuse me?"

"A damn travesty."

"Care to repeat that after I have you written up, Chief?"

He crosses his arms impatiently. "Quit the crap." Before I can blast him— head of the hospital or not—his voice softens in a way that's more of a blow than his harsh criticism ever could be. "You've got a gift few have, Laura. It could have been used to make a larger difference than treating MIs, stabilizing GSWs, and treating the indigents you churn and burn."

I don't know what to feel—shock over the compliment or infuriation at his complete audacity that the gifts we've both been bequeathed should be limited to those with the financial means to pay for them. I begin, "It's my passion . . ."

He doesn't let me finish my sentence because he cuts me off. "I've heard it all before, Lockwood. I'm telling you, long term, I'm concerned you'll determine you're too talented to be wasting your gifts in the ER."

You know nothing about us. Not the real us. The thought flits through my mind, along with several insults that could get me fired on the spot. After several deep exhales, where I tamp down my father's gung-ho spirit and channel my mother's inherently soothing nature, I lift my eyes to meet his. I'm not intimidated in the slightest by the scowl he's aiming in my direction. Instead, I question him, "If your own kids were in the same predicament, would you say the same thing to them you're insinuating to me?"

Both of Moser's "kids" through his marriage are talented medical students. They were assigned to me as interns last year. Twins, they're in the same program I graduated from at Yale. Mayer and Bella are coolheaded and dedicated and clearly not related to Dr. Bryan Moser by blood.

Moser preens for a few seconds at the mention of his wife's beloved children—damn, I thought that might derail him—before returning his laser focus back to me. "Don't try to change the subject, Doctor."

"I'm not." I feel a familiar contentment well up inside of me as I recall the long hours I spent contemplating the next step in my career—choosing a specialty. "It was about challenge, about giving back. Emergency medicine offers that."

He glowers down at me before lifting a hand that used to get messy more frequently with people's heads in a whole different way than it does now. A finger jabs in my face. "You were brought to this hospital as a med student . . ."

I wait for the usual reminders about my family's donations to several wings when he shocks the hell out of me. "Because you were the most promising student from Yale. You could have had any specialty you asked for. What made you throw it away? Did the pressure crack you?"

Infuriated he—and possibly the rest of the staff—thinks so little about me, I give him my most ferocious scowl, the kind that my family would recognize as a warning to back off. "It wasn't like that."

"Then tell me what turns a woman from being ready to fly a billion-dollar fighter jet into piloting a crop duster." My lips part to blast him, not caring about the fact he controls whether I complete my residency when he stuns me speechless. Moser lists off my accomplishments since I was an undergrad one by one. Citing journal articles I've co-authored, accolades I've received in different departments during my hospital rotations. As he does, images flash through my mind like a movie, reminding me how each rotation moved me one step closer to my dream. Psych, ENT, OB, Orthopedics, Neurology, Surgery.

I cross my arms over my chest by the time he's finished. All he's done is reassure me of one thing. I'm exactly where I'm meant to be—the ER. "Emergency medicine is the culmination of everything I've learned, everything I've fought for."

"Really?" His voice is derisive.

"There's an energy there I can't duplicate anywhere else in the hospital."

"Thank God," he mutters.

I can't help but chuckle at the snobbery in his voice. "It was the hardest decision I've ever had to make."

"It's not even close to the hardest decision you'll ever make, even in this building. There are others that will make you look back and wonder why even this conversation seemed to matter."

My head whips in his direction, stunned. To hear that from one of the most brilliant brain surgeons in the country is flabbergasting. "Then what's your problem, Dr. Moser?"

The expression on his face is rueful. "Haven't you figured it out, Lockwood?"

"Figured what out, sir?"

"I'm pissed you didn't choose neurology. I wanted you to become my protégé."

"No offense, Dr. Moser, but what you do makes *me* want to vomit."

"You mean the patient who projectile vomited on you last week didn't?"

I give a negligent shrug. "To each their own. You like poking your fingers around in people's brains and making them sing and dance to your own tune."

A wicked flash of humor leaps in his eyes for just a moment, reminding me of why he was, up until a few short years ago, considered the hospital's Lothario. "Singing, Lockwood. No dancing. It would seriously fuck up my procedure if the patient shifted their halo. Maybe you should read my latest journal article on it, just to brush up on the knowledge?"

I lift my watch and tsk with faux regret. "Perhaps later, sir. Look at the time. I'm now officially late for my shift."

Certain I've successfully escaped, I cringe when he calls out, "Lockwood?"

Pausing, I reply, "Yes?"

"You're never going to become notorious being an ER doctor."

I spare a quick thought about my family history and easily fire back. "For me, becoming a doctor was never about becoming notorious."

"Then what was it about?" he challenges.

"It was about saying thank you for being alive. Something we all should be grateful for." Even as the words pass my lips, I immediately curtail the mental chaos he stirred in my mind as I race down the stairs and weave through a maze of hidden corridors to reach the ER. Taking a deep breath to calm my emotions, I use my badge to gain entry to a whole different level of insanity.

Welcoming the burst of the doors opening and the shout of the charge nurse ordering, "Take him to trauma room two! Lockwood, this one is yours!"

I snatch up a paper gown and enter the room. "Someone run it down for me."

"Eighteen-year-old, Caucasian. Hit and run . . ."

CHAPTER
Two

Laura

IT MUST BE A FULL MOON, though I wouldn't know since I haven't been outside long enough to look up at the sky and check.

The ER is wall-to-wall with bodies. I mentally cringe when I realize that's true of both the dead ones as well as those still breathing. Still, instead of losing my cool over what I can't control, I give my attention to the exhausted woman who's running a slight fever with pain in her pelvic region. After the nurse and I step away, I order, "CBC, lytes, pregnancy, cultures for GC and chlamydia."

"You think it's pelvic inflammatory disease, not an ectopic pregnancy?" my on-shift head nurse, Karimat, questions.

"She has differential pain, but nothing that's indicating an ectopic or even appendicitis. Before we slap her with a couple of thousand in imaging, I'd like to try to treat this medically." I scribble some notes on the chart and hand it over. "Let me know the minute those labs are back in."

She holds up the chart. "If you're right?"

"We'll treat her with Ceftriaxone and Zithromax."

"And if not?"

I back away. "Then we'll make her comfortable and prep her for surgery."

"Will do, Gore." Karimat walks straight to the computer to input my orders before she heads back to the patient we just left behind curtain eleven.

I stretch, feeling my lower back crack when the emergency room doors burst open. The EMTs race in calling, "Sixty-year-old gunshot wound victim. Problem."

"Having been shot being the biggest one?"

"We can't find any holes."

"Are you kidding me?" I take off running, shouting for Karimat to follow. Unfortunately for the woman behind curtain eleven, she's going to have to wait. Blood trumps infection in the ER. I order the EMTs, "Take him to trauma room one."

"Will do, Gore," one I recognize, Ostrowsky calls back.

As I lead the patient through the doors, Karimat asks, "What's your name, sir?"

There's nothing but a gurgle in response. I frown over the amount of blood as I'm quickly gowned up and the EMTs lock their stretcher in place. I bark, "On my count, one, two, three."

I immediately spot the wound on the side of his neck buried beneath his black shirt. I demand, "Scissors." They're slapped in my hand and I cut away the wet black T-shirt, exposing a graze caused by a bullet wound. The problem is, after I examine the John Doe, there's too much blood soaking his shirt for such a simple wound. "Where the hell is it coming from?" I mutter.

The patient grunts. I lean over so I'm the only face he sees. "I'm Dr. Lockwood. Can you tell us your name?"

To his credit, he tries. Gurgles just come out of his mouth. I hush him by smoothing a hand over his blood-soaked forehead and over his shoulder where there's a very distinct pucker. Lifting my hand, I see it's soaked in blood. "Shh. Don't worry, everything is going to be fine."

His eyes drift shut, acknowledging my words, giving me his trust. His faith.

I demand of my team, "Start two lines. Get a liter of saline running. Slap an O2 mask on him. Prep the O-neg. CBC type and cross match. Call the OR and tell them to prep a room. They may need to do a laparoscopy. It's possible a piece of the bullet fragmented."

Karimat slips the mask over his face before spinning like the most graceful of dancers to reach the in-house phone to react to my demands.

"Get the rest of his clothes off." I lean over our John Doe's chest as the other members of the ER team slap leads on him once they've cut away unnecessary clothes. Pressing the stethoscope against his neck, I listen to the erratic sound of my patient's breathing. I'm afraid I'm going to have to intubate him very soon. "Karimat, prep an intubation tray."

"Seven and a half?" She calls out to confirm the size of the tube.

"Please. Now, sir? Blink once for yes; twice for no."

He blinks once.

"Does it hurt when you breathe in?"

Once.

"Any pain in your head?"

Two blinks.

"What about . . ." I don't get to finish my next question before I snarl, "Damn it. His pressure's dropping."

Rena, another trauma nurse, calls out, "No sensation radial or medial."

"Give five of morphine. Right away."

"You got it, Gore."

I take precious seconds to scan him, trying to discern where else he could be bleeding. Karimat offers, "Was he shot in the belly?"

"No, I looked. The belly's clear. Unless . . ." It hits me. "Roll him!" Together we roll the patient to his side, and that's where I find a pool of blood the EMTs missed. "Whoa! Knife wound!"

"I thought it was supposed to be a gunshot wound?" Rena wonders.

My fingers graze the serrated edge of a knife wound as Karimat snaps, "Does it matter much now?"

"He's bleeding out. Push four bags of O-Neg, stat." Rolling him back, I snatch up the intubation and call out, "Now, listen up, boys and girls. We're not losing him before he gets to the OR. Get ready to bag him."

I've just inserted the tube when Karimat is there with tape to hold it in place. She places the bag on the side so I can roll the guy, trying to clamp off the bleeder causing him to lose fluid faster than I can order it into him.

It's a bloody ballet, but by the time we rush him out of Trauma One, John Doe has a chance that he didn't have twenty minutes before.

I shove him into the elevator and notice two men loitering in the lobby. Their jaws are rigid and they hold some of the same features as the man lying on my table. Holding their gaze, I blindly slap the button to close the elevator. I don't have time to give them reassurance about their father, brother, son—whoever this man is. Right now, every second counts.

Every one.

Three hours later, I exit the same elevator from where I've been upstairs with my "John Doe." The surgical scrubs I'm wearing have seen better days and I'm spent. Karimat meets me at the elevator with a cup of coffee. "I heard you scrubbed in since Jensen claims you're the only reason he made it to the OR. Come on, Gore. You gave him half a chance of survival."

My eyes fixed on the two men fixated like pillars against the wall. They're waiting exactly where they were when I brought our John Doe upstairs. I murmur, "Someone knew just where to strike to do the most damage. They shot him before sliding the knife upward to ensure there was no hope of repairing the artery."

She frowns. "You think the shot was just to take him down?"

"I'm positive of it."

"What did they take out?"

I run through a litany of organs that were damaged. The elevator doors open behind me and Moser exits with a sharp nod in my direction. He's no longer in his perfectly pressed suit and tie, but in surgical scrubs that match my own. After he passes us, I confide to Karimat something that might not have made it through the hospital grapevine, "Moser scrubbed in at one point."

Her brows wing upward, her only indicator of the shock she must be reeling from. "Why?"

"To see what condition he'd be in if he made it through the surgery. Neuro was slammed tonight. The surgical attending begged."

"I'm impressed. John Doe got the chief."

"It didn't help." I scribble a few notes on a clipboard. "Did our labs on curtain eleven come back?"

She hands me the chart. "I issued the drugs a few hours ago. You were right; it was PID."

I nod as I affix my signature to the chart and instruct Karimat to discharge the patient when she has a moment. She agrees before asking, "What did Moser say?"

"Do you want the translation or the actual?"

"Both."

"Translated? Our Mr. Doe would never be the same man regardless."

"In Moser's words?"

"That if 'He survives this surgery, I'm looking forward to signing off on a night of paperwork from you people. Christ, you're setting this man up for a lifetime supply of a vent—however long that is.'"

She sneers. "Lovely."

"He followed that up with, 'He's lost too much oxygen and I can't wave a wand to make John Doe into an organ donor.'" I slurp some more coffee before my eyes narrow. Placing the cup down, I shift away from the stack of charts.

"Where are you going, Gore?" she calls out.

I don't respond. Instead, I approach the two men I've been studying. Their features so closely resemble my patient, it would be like someone placing me and my brothers next to my parents. My intuition is screaming at me, I just know they're related to my "John Doe." Working up my nerve to deliver the news no one in any hospital anywhere wants to deliver, I probe, "Gentleman? Can I help you? Are you looking for a specific patient?"

The bigger of the two bruisers circles around the back of me while the second one speaks. "It was you—you operated on our Pops."

"I'm sorry. There's been a number of people in this evening. Can you be more specific?"

"You took him upstairs." The man describes the way I escorted my John Doe upstairs, the blood trail that ultimately led to his unfortunate demise confirms my suspicions. They're related to my John Doe.

"I apologize. He didn't have any identification on him. I didn't even know his name."

The smaller of the men clarifies their random statements. "Tiberi. His name was Aldo Tiberi. I'm his son Paulie. That's my brother, Gino."

A shiver ripples through me. Tiberi. Christ. You can't listen to the news and not know who the Tiberi family is. They're only the largest crime family in Connecticut, with ties to the larger ones in New York and Jersey. Still, I hold out my hand to shake the hand of the man in front of me. "Dr. Lockwood. I stabilized your father down here in the ER and assisted in the surgical trauma suite upstairs."

He doesn't accept mine. I let it drop after a few beats. Instead, he demands, "So, how long until Pops can go home?"

The next words are never easy, but right now, with these men, they're causing an unease I can't quite rid myself of. Still, I push it down long enough to ask, "Mr. Tiberi, would you and your brother like to come with me?" I gesture to a small, private waiting room.

The menacing voice behind causes me to jump when he sneers, "We're fine right here, doc. Get on with it. How's Pops?"

Right. Straight to the point. "Your father came in with a gunshot wound . . ."

"I'm aware of that," Paulie interrupts. "That shouldn't have taken more than a few minutes to stitch."

Taking a deep breath, I continue. "During the course of stabilizing him in the ER, we also discovered that he had been stabbed. That was the greater of the two injuries."

I briefly explain the injuries and how I first observed them. A dark, forbidding silence envelops the three of us.

"But he's gonna be all right?" Gino demands harshly.

Carefully, I outline all the organs and nerves that were severed with the upward thrust of the knife wound. Then I circle around to the news no one wants to hear. "Despite our best efforts and a team of three surgeons . . ."

"Don't say it," Paulie warns.

The corner of Gino's eyes begins to twitch.

My heart hurts for these two men despite the unspeakable crimes their associates have committed in the past. Family—however it's formed—is a bond that even death can't sever. Certainly the edge of a knife can't. "I'm deeply sorry for your loss." My head turns and I encompass Paulie in my condolences. "Truly."

Gino stares at me in shock before his eyes move past me to his brother. "Paulie? What the fuck did you do to Pops?"

"Shut your filthy hole, Gino. You just had to tell him, you cunt," Paulie snarls. Before I can take umbrage, he's yanking me back against him as a shield.

Gino's eyes widen before they narrow into furious slits. "Let the doc go, Paulie."

"The hell I will."

"This is between you and me."

"The fuck it is. It's this bitch's fault!" he shouts.

"Fuck you, Paulie. You killed Pops? For what?"

I frantically signal to the hospital security guards for help. They take a step forward.

It's their last.

Flipping open his coat, Paulie yanks out a semi-automatic pistol and takes aim. One shot each, both guards are taken out. That's before he holds the weapon up to his brother and fires. Blood sprays across my face, warm and wet.

He leans over and licks it slowly off my cheek.

A wheezing sound escapes my lips.

"Aww, doc. Now, what are you gonna give me for not fixing my pops? It'd better involve spreading those pretty legs of yours."

I gag and scratch across his muscular forearm with my nails. Cursing my soft-soled shoes, I try to fight him with everything my father and uncles have taught me. I'm rewarded by a burning agony ripping through my shoulder and much to my shock, Dr. Moser falls in front of me.

No. This can't be happening. My head spins even as I try to hold it together.

I won't go down without a fight. I can't.

"Wrong answer, cunt."

Paulie sprays the emergency room with semi-automatic fire. In my head, I hear screams and cries of agony from where one of the bullets ricocheted off the pillar and clipped someone. I let my body slacken in Paulie Tiberi's arms. He flings my weight away, my body hitting the concrete floor. I slowly inch my way across the floor. My hearing is blistered. Are the haunting sounds repeating over and over in my mind made by people suffering over the loss of their loved ones or new suffering being inflicted?

I can't separate them.

Tears track down my cheeks as I listen for someone, something to approach and end all my suffering.

The only thing I hear is agony until the ER doors swoosh open and then closed.

Then there's another stream of fire before silence descends.

I just can't determine whether it's my soul rising up to heaven because I'm dead or Tiberi's gone. Then agony shoots through my shoulder and mind. I recall Paulie's words as I writhe in pain.

Did I do this? Did I get them all killed?

Much later, when I think about the questions the police asked me in my hospital room with my parents safely stationed on either side, I'll remember informing them all, "I'm not certain exactly what happened next. Did someone scream? Other than me, that is?"

"You did your job, Doctor Lockwood," the detective clipped out before leaving me to my parent's ministrations.

But something in the way he behaves tells me I must have fallen down on the job. In doing so, I failed to protect the people I swore a vow to uphold.

At least that's how I remember it.

CHAPTER
Three

Laura

I'm HUDDLED beneath a blanket in the chaise lounge in my parent's backyard in a stage of grief that makes the concept of being numb a goal to attain rather than an acknowledgment of my state of mind.

Whatever pain radiates from the wound on my shoulder is forgotten. Wind whips harshly against my face as if the early spring weather is not-so-gently punishing me for the fact I'm alive and my friends, colleagues, and random strangers I was ready to treat in the ER that night are dead.

Because of me.

What if I'd found Aldo Tiberi's knife wound a moment sooner? I question myself for what must be the millionth time. Could I have given the surgeons a few more minutes to repair the damage to the artery before he died on the table?

Could I have prevented the massacre in my ER?

My hands shake as I replay everything in my head from the moment I walked up alongside Tiberi's body. Worse than any morbidity and mortality review, I pick apart every second I assessed his injuries in the trauma room. Did I take too long trying to reassure him? Was there some small delay in my diagnosis? Why didn't I think of a secondary wound sooner?

The pain in my stomach almost causes me to cry out when I recall gossiping with Karimat. From the moment I stepped away from her and replay how I approached the Tiberis, that's where I was supposed to have full control.

My patient.

My ER.

Emotionally, I feel like I failed them all as surely as if I'd held up the gun and shot them myself. Dispassionately, I conduct an assessment as if I were rating a first-year resident. I was compassionate, but then I question how my words came out. Did I not sound empathetic? Did I come across as dismissive? Weak? Obviously, to men who were hardcore killers, I *am* weak.

Moser, after he got out of his hospital bed from taking the bullet that passed through me, ordered me face-to-face, "Do not step one foot back in my hospital unless it has to do with your mandatory psychological and physical therapy appointments, Gore."

I whispered the God's honest truth, "You don't have to worry about that."

Something in my tone must have set off clanging bells. "Why's that?"

"Because I'm not certain I want to be a doctor any longer," I rasped before turning away, despite him calling out my name repeatedly.

It doesn't matter the police killed Paulie Tiberi. The blood of everyone in that ER is on my hands. He ensured it when he got inside my head.

I just can't manage to work him out.

Lying awake night after night in my childhood bedroom, I fight for the ability to breathe as I replay everything over and over in my mind.

Why me and not them? Why was I spared?

Why am I alive?

Why was I saved?

Why not the mother of two bringing her babies into the ER because of a stomach virus?

Why not the young med student who got his first-choice match?

Why not Karimat, who had just accepted a marriage proposal from the man she was head over heels for?

A tear falls from the corner of my eye and tracks down the inside of my cheek until it brushes against my lips.

Staring blankly ahead, all I can think is I failed. I took an oath to save lives, and I failed.

How am I supposed to absorb that body blow?

No answer topples on me like a ton of bricks nor insidiously worms its way into my thoughts. I am, for all intents and purposes, banished into my own nightmare when I truly believed I'd be helping rescue others from theirs.

It just goes to show what can happen to a lifetime of dreams—they can be shattered in one single night.

Dragging my knees to my chest, I stare blindly over the lake. Due to my state of shock after I was discharged from the hospital, my parents whisked me back to their home. Those first few days, I don't recall much of anything except forcing myself to remain awake for fear awaiting me when I slept. I refused pain medication, punishing myself with physical pain.

If I was going to live, it would be with the reminder of those who died.

Nightmares—when I did sleep—had me screaming, crawling across the floor toward the bathroom to puke. When I finished, I was wrapped up in my mother's warm embrace or my father's strong arms.

Even as I try to control the rapid increase of my heart from taking over, as I try to prevent the arms of overwhelming panic from dragging me down into an abyss only my family can pull me back from. I grab for the nearest pillow and clutch it to my chest, rocking back and forth, sobbing—praying to die. Praying for the pain to ease.

Praying for someone to help me when I know I don't deserve it.

CHAPTER
Four

THREE MONTHS LATER

LIAM

"Daaaaaady! Stop! It hurts!" Bailey screeches.

I immediately still the running of the brush through her hair.

I lift her up from her wheelchair and place her on the vanity so I can meet eyes that are the exact shade as mine—an almost translucent green. Not for the first time, something uncoils inside me when I realize there's very little about Bailey that reminds me of her mother.

I recall the shock of finding out a long-ago affair resulted in Bailey. Because of who I worked for at the time, Ashleigh dramatized to the court I would never be around enough to be a good father—even though I was home every damn night as a forensic accountant. She turned on her undercover agent specialty—waterworks—and the judge ate it up, granting her seventy-five percent custody of our daughter. It wasn't until after she died a few years ago that I became the sole custodian of Bailey, and my lawyer eviscerated the same judge over falling for Ashleigh's tricks.

I heard he's seeking retirement. I couldn't care less.

But the agony of what happened in our past is pale in comparison to what happened when I took her to the ER for an ear infection a few months ago, and all hell broke loose.

In the grand scheme of things, I am grateful for the fact my little girl is whining over something as minor as a hairbrush being pulled too roughly through her dark curls instead of incessant pain from legs that were damaged from shrapnel that came flying off a pillar we were sitting near on the most terrifying night of our lives. A difference of millimeters on either leg and it would have been her arteries severed, Bailey's surgeon grimly told me that night.

Bloodstains are more easily removed than memories. I thought I knew that before, but when it's your child there's no limit to what gives you nightmares. I still wake up covered in sweat recalling the way I instinctively pulled my baby girl out of the chair in the ER waiting room, covering her body with my own. Still . . .

Shaking the memories aside, I zurburt Bailey's cheek. "Does this hurt?"

She squeals, legs in casts kick out in delight, nailing me high in my inner thigh.

Despite the small "Umph" I can't quite disguise, I don't complain. I refuse to bring down Bailey's joy just because she nutted me for the umpteenth time in the last three months. If it earns me her gorgeous smile, I'll sign my name on the dotted line for life as a eunuch.

"How about I put on Dua Lipa to help you get through the agony?" I offer.

My princess beams as I whip out my iPhone from my pocket and play "Dance the Night." Bailey shouts the lyrics at an incomprehensible decibel as I untangle her curls so I can injure my fingers with the devil made inventions called "forever ouchless" hair ties.

Forever ouchless, my ass. Those fuckers hurt when you snap them back on your forehead—especially the ones with the beads.

Fortunately, in my role of chief audit officer of Hudson Investigations, I only had to deal with the ribbing of the owners when I showed up at the office with a *Wild Kratts* Band-Aid at the company quarterly board meeting after Bailey assured me, "It matches your tie, Daddy."

I wore that damn thing all day with as much pride as I once wore my Medal of Honor.

"Let me see how good you look, Buttercup." I leave one hand on her waist and step back to get the full picture of my soon to be seven-year old. I step closer and fiddle with her right pigtail a bit before pronouncing her, "Perfect."

Her lemon-yellow sun dress is cut in a way that shows small scars that make me murderous at a dead man. At a man the police took down with bullets at the hospital that very night. At myself for not recognizing Bailey tugging on her ear all week was a sign of an ear infection so I could take her to her normal pediatrician? At a dead woman whose neck I can't have the satisfaction of wrapping my hands around because she did her best to drive a wedge between me and my little girl?

While these ideas hold merit late at night when I hear Bailey cry out in her sleep, I've learned it's not healthy to entertain these thoughts around my daughter while she's awake.

Case in point, Bailey's face falls. I step closer before lifting her up then lowering her back into her wheelchair. "What is it, Buttercup?"

"All the kids at school are talking about going to the beach this summer, Daddy." Her lower lip quivers.

Knowing immediately where her mind is headed, I remind her of the positive. "Well, we'll see now that you're in your shorter casts. At the very least you can be outside. I'm just not certain about how strong your legs are yet."

"These dumb casts don't let me have any fun." Tears well up in her eyes, making them appear larger than before.

"Hopefully, it's only a few more weeks, Bails."

She sniffles. "I just wanna build a sandcastle."

I hesitate because I don't know what's next in my baby's recovery. "Let's see what your doctor has to say first. Okay?"

"Life isn't fair, Daddy," she mumbles.

Considering everything she's endured, she's not wrong. Worse yet, there's one thing Bailey doesn't know that's going to send her finely ordered world into orbit. I chuck beneath her chin. "Chin up, Buttercup. We have each other."

Her smile isn't as bright as earlier, but she manages one.

As a preemptive strike, I offer, "How about I bring home some cupcakes from Amaryllis Bakery for dessert?"

"Can I have two?"

I pretend like I'm going to argue when we both know I'm going to get her three. I blow out a gust of air. "Fine. But that's because you're you."

She beams at me and lifts her face up. I press a kiss on her forehead. "Okay, now we're officially late. Let's roll."

Bailey wheels out of her bathroom and heads toward the front door. I follow not far behind. Not twenty minutes later, when I drop her off at school, all the worry surges back. The apple cart of Bailey's life is about to be upset yet again.

Our nanny, Mrs. Destry, gave her notice.

Worse, at least for me, I have two weeks to replace her right at the beginning of summer break.

Two hours later, I'm in my office when there's a knock on the open door. I look up from the brief I'm writing to meet the unusually amused eyes of Keene Marshall. Behind him, sporting a semblance of a smile—something I haven't seen on any of the owners' faces in far too long—is Caleb Lockwood. I ask, "What's up?"

"Beckett Miller's attorney called." Keene references the world's biggest rock star, who happens to be one of our largest clients. "His accountant desperately requires an itemized audit of all Hudson charges dating back the last seven years. How quickly would we be able to pull that together?"

I press my lips together desperately trying to keep my expression bland. "Don't tell me . . ."

"Becks is being audited by the IRS? You got it," Caleb rumbles.

Because his amusement is evident, I don't bother to restrain my own snicker. "Now if only Beckett asked us to pull all the data the IRS requires for him, we could close down until Christmas." *Which would take care of my nanny problems*, I think glumly.

Keene can't restrain his bark of laughter as he drops into one of the chairs in front of my desk. "The billable hours could make me salivate in my sleep."

Steeping my fingers together, I contemplate the vast holdings Beckett Miller has and visibly shudder. "As someone who's tracked money laundering, terrorist accounts, traced spies and criminals through their bank accounts, I'd prefer any of those tasks to trying to sift through the financial records of someone as prolifically invested as Beckett Miller. Christ, the man has no pattern to what he buys. I can't imagine the amount of man hours it's going to take the CPA in charge."

Caleb reminds me, "Why do you think his lawyer is involved? Can you imagine someone from the government asking Beckett if he has a receipt for a meal he bought on tour seven years ago?"

We all share a moment of amusement thinking of the piranha Beckett has on retainer likely snapping out that very question. Cringing, I admit, "I almost feel sorry for the auditor."

Whirling my chair around, I open a discrete system only accessible from inside the Hudson office. My fingers tapping a few keys before the data I want appears. Fortunately, Hudson agents are required to maintain strict billing logs just for this purpose. After pulling up Beckett's account and change the default year parameter to seven, I have nothing to do but wait for our financial program to work its magic. Jerking my thumb toward the screen, I remark, "That's going to take a few to download."

"Excellent. Once LLF"—Keene names Beckett's law firm—"signs our waiver and sends it back, I'll send you a copy so you can courier the hard copy and email them the file."

"Perfect. Is that all?"

"How's Bailey?"

One of the things I love about working for Hudson is we're a huge family. Everyone from Caleb and Keene down has been incredibly supportive about ensuring I'm able to care for my little girl. When they found out Bailey had been injured, they immediately adjusted my work hours—even permitting working at night or on the weekend. I've had offers to babysit, to take her to the park, and playdates from the agents with kids. Hell, Sam Akin—who makes my computer skills look like those of a seventh grader earning his first computer certificate—built me a virtual desktop so I could log directly into my Hudson terminal long after Bailey is asleep, allowing me autonomy in my work while still giving me what I need most.

Time with my daughter.

I reach over and grab my cell. Unlocking it, I pull up the latest selfie we took in the car this morning before I dropped her at school. Caleb's face morphs from strained to grinning. Even Keene's cool demeanor breaks when he teases, "I see no damage was caused in the making of those pigtails."

"Bite me, Keene. Those fucking bands are a pain in the ass." I hold out my hand before he slaps the device back into it.

That's when we're interrupted by the executive floor admin, Tony, buzzing through. "Liam? A nanny service just left a message for you."

Please, oh please, I pray silently. "Yeah, Tony. I'm with Caleb and Keene. You can relay the message aloud."

"Sorry. They said no go. They're full up. Said to try a local service since it's late to be looking."

Shit. "Thanks for the message."

Caleb's amusement fades. "What happened to Mrs. Destry?" Since he referred me to her when I took the job, I'm not surprised he remembers her name.

"Quit. Daughter's moving to England, and she wants to go with her."

He rubs his thumb beneath his lower lip. "How much time do you have until she's gone?"

"About two weeks. Why? Have a miracle you can pull out of your ass?" I joke half-heartedly.

Both men exchange an unreadable look. Caleb shocks me when he replies, "I just might. Let me check on a few things and I'll get back to you."

"You're not kidding, are you?" *Please, oh please. Don't be kidding.*

Caleb shakes his head. "No. I just need to wait to find out about a current . . . sit-rep. One of us can let you know for certain the day after tomorrow?"

I hold out my hand. "You'd be saving us, man. Thanks."

He takes it before he leaves my office. Keene stares after him for a few moments before we resume our conversation about Beckett Miller's audit, and while we're cracking jokes at the rockstar's expense, I feel relief.

For the first time since hearing Mrs. Destry will be leaving us, I have a flicker of hope.

CHAPTER
Five

LIAM

ON MY DRIVE to our home in Darien, I think back to what I consider BB and AB—Before Bailey and After Bailey.

There's no question—after Bailey is the only place I want to be, even if during those first few years I had to deal with the bitch I made her with.

Growing up, I was the only child of two upper-middle-class parents who were shocked they had a child so late in life. I loved my family, I did. It's just that what we had wasn't what I have with my daughter. *Like you can imagine your father brushing your hair and being whacked in the face with a hairband.* Just the idea of Nolan Payne doing such a thing forces a grim smile to cross my lips.

Maybe that's why their death in a car crash on the way home from a charity event left me stunned but not devastated. By the time I was seventeen, I was essentially living on my own. Making my own decisions. I felt sorrow, but in a distant way—much like the way they cared for me.

If anything, I was grateful their accountant stepped up to become the mentor I never knew I was missing after their death. Larry urged me to meet before I did something stupid with the millions I inherited between bank accounts, stocks, and life insurance policies paid on people dead too soon.

Over dinner, he reminded me not only did I owe a shitload of taxes, but asked, "What do you want from your future, Liam?"

"I don't know."

"Stick to my original plan. Go to college. Figure out what you want from life. There's plenty of money for you to do that. When you determine what you want from your future, then we'll talk more."

"About the money?"

"About whatever you want."

Since that one meal was more sincere parenting than I'd received in the seventeen years before that, I took his advice. Larry checked in with me quarterly, along with my accountant, to go over my financial portfolio. I found myself fascinated by the numbers they were throwing at me.

Not long after, my future seemed to coalesce in a series of small events. I caught my roommate rifling through his girlfriend's purse after sex to pocket some of her spare cash. After reporting him to the RA, my disgust lingered. I didn't want to stay where I was tagged with the reputation of a "narc."

I also wrapped up an elective in criminal justice that mentioned forensic accounting. After chatting with my professor and learning more about the field, I took an unscheduled trip home and met with Larry to discuss some options.

After wolfing down a fried pork sandwich, something no one makes correctly outside of Indiana, I explained the chain of events leading to my decision about wanting to transfer to Purdue. "I want to become a forensic accountant."

A flash of pleasure crossed his face before it adopted its more serious mien. "You've really thought this through."

"I have." I laid out my course of study.

He leaned forward after setting his own sandwich to the side. "Let me give you something else to think about." That's when he mentioned ROTC to me. Being commissioned as an officer. Going to work for the US Army Audit Agency.

Intrigued, I leaned back. "Is that the route you took?"

"Part of the path." Then he went on to tell me some of the rest. The rest of that discussion led me to where I am today.

My one true regret is Larry didn't live long enough to see where his advice led me. He suffered a massive coronary not long after Bailey was born. Even though he admitted he hated Bailey's mother as much as I did—"There's just something about her that sets all my flags flying, Liam"—I know he believed I would make a good father. "Just love her."

I could easily do that with my daughter. It was her mother there was no hope for.

None.

Ashleigh was as beautiful as she was a deceitful bitch. It made her an exceptional undercover agent, but I'd have claimed she was the worst possible life choice I'd ever made, especially since, after a few nights of fucking, I walked in on her bent over, getting railed by my agent in charge. It immediately put an end to whatever it was I believed we were building, despite her begging to give her a second chance.

As if.

I laughed in Ashleigh's face when she came to tell me she was pregnant. "Do you think I'd believe you considering you aren't exactly known for telling the truth?"

Unashamedly, she agreed while insisting, "She's yours, Liam. I'll give you a paternity test when she's born."

Thank fuck I wasn't stupid enough to tell her to kiss my ass like my former SAC did. One test and my life changed. I was given hope in the form of a tiny pink bundle of my coloring and Ashleigh's smile, which blew tiny spit bubbles.

Still, I hate the damn bitch. I'll never forgive her for taking my daughter with her on a sting.

Ashleigh hid her destructive tendencies. I honestly thought she loved our daughter. But why did she put our baby into that car if she did? She had to have known the danger she was placing Bailey in. If she didn't, I do. I lived through it when the Tiberi's shot up the ER I took Bailey to for a fucking ear infection.

An ear infection that almost cost her life.

Fury still sings through my blood. "It's a good thing they got the man who did this to you, Buttercup. Otherwise, Daddy doesn't know what he'd do."

CHAPTER

Six

Laura

MY THERAPIST, Alice, said something during our session today that has been playing through my mind over and over. "You skipped over anger."

"Excuse me?" At least that's what I would have said if I weren't in the process of shoving a peanut butter cup in my mouth, so it may have come out sounding like the Peanuts classroom teacher on a bender.

She leaned forward and infused me with her strength. "The stages of grief are considered to be denial, anger, bargaining, depression, and acceptance. You went right from denial to depression, Laura. Did you ever consider the fact that you have a right to be angry that this happened to you?"

Immediately I correct, "It didn't happen . . .," but my words trail off.

It did happen to me.

I am a victim of Paulie Tiberi's insanity. As parts of my brain begin firing for the first time in months, filthy words fly out of my mouth. "Goddamn motherfucker!" I scream, leaping to my feet.

Alice shifts, bracing perhaps.

"It was *his* fucking fault. He killed his own brother in cold blood. Right. In. Front. Of. Me!" I scream, letting the nightmare spill out of my mouth as it's been replaying in my mind.

"Yes." It's the only word Alice says and the only encouragement I need.

"I hope he rots in hell. I hope his soul is banished to the seventh circle." Finally, words that as a vowed healer, I should be shocked pass my lips. "I hope he pays the price for his crimes tenfold."

Then, I sink to my knees and sob because I'm the one still paying and I fear for how long I will before I can recover the life I had before this ever occurred.

"Laura, you can't keep these emotions bottled up inside you," Alice chides me gently.

I lift my head and meet her concerned eyes. "Who the hell should I share them with? My family?"

"If you're comfortable."

I scorn her suggestion. "Because that's exactly what I want to do—give my parents more to worry about when it comes to me."

"They'd do anything for you," she reminds me.

I don't reply because I know she's right. Instead, I use the opportunity to try to pull myself together. When I'm done, I'm shocked to find Alice holding out a leather book with gilded edges. I take it. "What's this?"

"Your new journal."

Warily, I ask, "What do you want me to do with it?"

"Whatever you want. Write in it, don't. Tear out the pages, don't. Set it on fire, don't. But live your emotions through it. It's yours, Laura."

My fingers tighten on the pebbled leather imperceptibly. Mine. Something for me to unburden my chaotic emotions to without expectations. I jerk up my chin. "I'll try."

"Good."

That session transformed me.

I'm still learning to accept the things I can't change—death, pain, anguish. I thought I knew how before, but now I accept I was merely an observer. Now, I'm in the thick of the emotions and every trite platitude I've given patients over the years haunts me.

I didn't know.

How could I?

Still, I don't need a crutch, which is what I feel the bottle of pills I clutch in my hand is. "I can do this. I don't need drugs." Pulling open my nightstand, I drop my anxiety medication in the drawer, determined to not use it again.

If I'm going to live, I'm doing so on my terms. I'm no longer hiding behind my pain. My eyes are wide open so I can avoid my triggers. Before this happened to me, I knew the world could be brutal. Now that it's taken a bite of me, I refuse to let it have another.

But one thing I won't give it is my soul, despite it having a thirst for it. That I'm locking away until I know it's safe.

Which may be never.

From the Journal of Dr. Laura Lockwood

The guilt of having survived is more than I can bear.

It isn't manifested solely by thoughts of the ER but by a smell, a taste, a touch.

I feel raw when I smell the freshness of the floral notes beginning to bloom in my neighbor's yards. It reminds me of the fact Karimat was choosing her wedding flowers with Uncle Phil.

It's the taste of coffee, knowing how I fueled myself up with it to power through an extra-long shift. Did the caffeine cloak my fatigue? Obscure my judgment?

It's touch. Pulling on an outfit to go to therapy. Attaching my name tag to access the building—a building I haven't been banned from except by Moser's verbal decree. Feeling tears fall down my face. All small physical acts that amount to one simple realization.

Dead people can't do any of those things. It's as simple as that.

CHAPTER
Seven

My thumbs instinctively rub the two recently healed tattoos inked on the inside of my pinkies. Residing just below a small scar left as a souvenir from one of my early exploits in the ER, my new amaryllis tattoos fit along the arch of my fingers—stitching color against skin. The artist went so far as to have the petals crying tears of blood into the underside of my fingers.

"I couldn't have asked for something better if I had years to design it."

"You asked me to remind you of who you are." Kitty cupped my hands. "There's been bloodshed. The legacy of Amaryllis isn't just a legend for you, Gore. I didn't think you'd want to forget that."

I couldn't reply with words. Then.

To Alice in a later session, I said, "She captured who and what I believe in."

"And that is?"

"I'm a woman, a doctor, and a victim. My heart's going to bleed for what I believe in."

Alice didn't disagree. "Yes, because not only do you throw yourself into everything, you do it with your whole heart."

I rub my fingers over the still tender skin. These remarkable dripping symbols of my life will also remind me of my capability to heal.

"One day at a time," I reassure myself. Healing doesn't happen overnight. Isn't that what I tell my patients?

And most of them don't have the support system I do.

My mother, father, and brothers have hardly left my side. Aunts, uncles, cousins—everyone who could be there physically has been and if they couldn't be, they've only been a phone call away. "But now, it's time to see what happens when I try to move forward instead of constantly looking over my shoulder, waiting for life to happen to me again."

I'm startled from my musings when I hear footsteps on the flagstone. Jolting, a mild twinge of pain I refuse to acknowledge, surges up my back when I find both of my parents staring down at me with open concern, both of them having noticed my flinch. Before they can ask, I automatically state, "I'm fine."

My father holds a large white box in his arms. He chides, "I thought it was only your brothers who used to lie to our faces."

Before I can manage a rejoinder, my mother mimics me, "'Mama, I swear I didn't mean to use your last lipstick on Jon and Chuck'" She tacks on, "'They needed a heart and kidneys, Mama. The steak and chicken were perfect, but they weren't the right color.'"

"How could I forget about Laura playing life-size Operation?" My father's lips twitch.

My shoulders shake with the memory of having my brothers lie on our dining room table, torso's painted in red lipstick and food coloring, and our dinner leftovers placed strategically on their bodies. Relaxing, I tip my head back to receive my father's kiss, reminiscing, "Be grateful I only used tongs to remove the parts. Jon used to taunt Chuck he was going to get a knife."

"Thank goodness you never shared that before your brothers were grown," Mama agrees.

"They're grown? When did that happen?"

"They're out of the house," she corrects herself before crawling to the far side of the chaise and encouraging me to curl up against her. She nods to the box still in my father's lap. "You received a gift."

He hands it over. I pluck at the florist bow for a few before my hands fall to the side, and I ask baldly, "Which cousin sent it this time?"

"My guess? Kalie and Grace. You haven't received anything from them this week." Kalie and Grace are both my roommates and my first cousins. The three of us own a home in nearby Darien—a home I haven't stepped foot in since the night of the shooting.

I pull at the bow and flick off the lid.

Then I scream—loud and long. I'm immediately swept back, caught up in the moment the burn penetrated my shoulder.

My mother wraps her hand around my neck and presses my head into her shoulder.

It isn't until I hear my father holler into his cell phone, "Motherfucker, you have a mole in your goddamned evidence room!" He pauses to listen for a moment. "No, I'm looking at it right now. Now send someone you trust with your damned life to my house," that I realize this is actually happening.

This nightmare isn't over. At least, not for me.

Even though my father whipped it away from me, I have to know what I'm up against. Crawling to the end of the lounger, I'm stopped before I touch it when my father wraps his arms around my waist. "No, Laura."

"Daddy, I need to see it." My words are certain, my voice is void of emotion.

Twisting, still holding me as he used to when I was a child, he lets me get a long look at what was just a glimpse before—something I thought was a cruel joke. Now that I know it wasn't. "That's the scrub top I was wearing the night Paulie Tiberi shot me," I confirm.

My name tag is draped across. Both are splattered with blood—mine and at least Gino Tiberi's. "Who knows who else's is on there?" I mumble under my breath.

Before any of us can say any more, the sound of sirens comes down Farm Lane. My father places me back next to my mother. When the doors open and close, he yells, "We're around back."

"Yes, Mr. Lockwood."

The thundering of hard soles against my parents' flagstone derails any questions.

For now.

"You're still lost in so much pain, Laura."

My mother understands agony in ways I wish she didn't. I nod against her shoulder. "I thought I was healing. Then today happened." The process of healing, whether physical or emotional, is long and arduous. Much like a major surgery with multiple incisions, grafts, and transfusions, my recovery from my own guilt has been slow.

I have been assured I'll make a full recovery. Eventually, whenever that nebulous date is.

My father murmurs, "Sweetheart, I hope you know we'll always be here. Whether for as long as it takes for your nightmares to fade back into dreams or just because you need the comfort of home."

Knowing I can say anything to either of them, I rasp, "But what if my dreams change?" *What if they get worse?*

Mama's wise voice resonates through me, reminding me that the flip side of pain isn't always pleasure but peace. "They're supposed to. Eventually, they'll shift and ease. The pain will drain away. You may not recognize it at first, Laura."

I lift my head off her shoulder and stare into eyes that mirror my own. "When did yours change?"

Her eyes drift past my face and lock onto my father's. Without words, I know the answer—when she had the courage to open herself to love.

When her eyes catch mine again, they're filled with a protective determination to see me through this latest trauma. As if she can see into my soul, she reprimands me. "Stop punishing yourself for something you couldn't control."

I protest weakly, "I'm not."

"You are," my father corrects angrily.

"I can't stand if anyone else gets hurt because of me," I admit.

My father sets me straight on a few facts about the mob. "Laura, regardless of if Aldo Tiberi survived, the same outcome may have happened."

"Wha . . . what?"

"I doubt you've given thought to the fact Paulie Tiberi would have had the same reaction by saving his father's life?"

I suck in a breath, my father's blunt words stealing what air I was able to consume. I manage a hoarse "No."

"What about if another doctor worked on him? Would you have blamed them for the shooting?"

"Of course not," I snap.

He presses a kiss to the top of my head. I feel how charged he is, even if his words are perfectly calm. "You can't control the actions of others."

My mother chimes in, "You can only control how you react to the fear of it."

The words cause a torrent of tears I can't hold back. Angrily, I swipe them away. "It's true."

"What is?" my mother asks as she brushes more than a few drops of moisture off my cheek.

"I've been letting him control my actions and reactions. No more," I declare resolutely.

My father murmurs something harsh under his breath I can't make out. My mother hushes him. She clearly states, "If only the ebb and flow of our pain were that simple. You're going to have good days. You're going to have days like today. Just know we're here."

She opens her arms and I fall back into them.

I let loose a torrent of tears for my mother's past—a past that taught her such wisdom. I cry for the loss of so many due to a soulless monster. And I cry for the last victim, for myself.

This time, I give myself grace knowing I wasn't at fault, but I know I'm not ready to return to work.

Not yet anyway.

CHAPTER
Eight

Laura

THE SOUND of a sharp snap has me leaping from my chair, fear coursing through my veins—an instinctive reaction of a person who had been hurt, hunted.

Oh God! Is that a gun?

Whirling around, my fight-or-flight mode kicks in only to find myself face-to-face with an empathetic Alice. Even as my heart thunders in my chest, I mentally picture myself shrugging on a cool exterior as I try to compose myself. Berating myself, I refuse to give into the combination of embarrassment, fear, and abject terror that's been going on for far too long.

It wasn't your fault. I mentally chant the words everyone's been drilling into my head these last few months. Intellectually, I know that.

But Alice wasn't the one with the emotions riding on the razor's edge as I attended funeral after funeral. I'll never forget the pain in Karimat's fiancé's eyes the moment I stepped into the room to pay my respects. The fear that crossed across the two children's faces who had lost their mother. Moser peering down his nose disdainfully as I fled both services. As if he was disappointed I couldn't hack it.

Who the hell could?

Maybe what I need is to get back to work to heal the mental scars Paulie Tiberi inflicted on me. Repairs are almost complete to the ER and I can't let the ones permanently affixed to me, as much a part of me now as my tattoo, destroy what's left of who I was before that fateful day. Digging deep for the well of strength I took for granted growing up and I refuse to lose ever again, I coach myself, *Don't let what happened ruin your career, Laura. Don't let him have one more victim.*

I'd be a fool to deny I've changed. As much as I believed I understood the invisible chains pain wrapped around a heart, I learned I had no concept of the weight of them. But I square my shoulders and face Alice. I'm determined to turn my pain into power.

Like my mother, my aunts and uncles all did.

To that end, I've worked to locate the fortitude so inherently bred into who I was. Regain my ability to trust without question, my capacity to be open to strangers without reservation. But my biggest fear is will the capriciousness of the events of that day eventually make me a better doctor or continue to terrorize me forever?

Another item arrived at my parent's home last week. This time, it was just a letter. Once the Italian was translated, I wish it hadn't been. It insinuated just enough to spike my anxiety through the roof.

MAY THE DEATH OF THE CONSIGLIERE BE VINDICATED.

A buzz rang between my ears even as my father and Uncle Colby reassured me it was a scare tactic. "Laura, you have nothing to be worried about."

"Right. You don't have a vindictive mob blaming you for the death of their leader!" I shouted.

"Technically, the consigliere is the second in command."

My father turned on him like a hungry dog faced with fresh meat. "Must you get so hung up on technicalities?"

Instead of gracing my father with a reply, my uncle consoled me with the fact, "Laura, do you think I'd let you move back home with Kalie and Grace"—he names my cousins—"if I suspected for a second this wasn't just a scare tactic?"

That, more than anything, reassured me. "No."

"Good. Now go home," he ordered me.

So I packed my bags and returned to my home in Darien with Kalie and Grace. Determined to prevent my family from knowing how truly distraught the Tiberi psychological warfare had been wearing me down, I laid in my bed the first three nights with a kitchen knife clutched in my hands.

In fact, that final night, shaking, I broke down and admitted to myself what I couldn't previously—that I'd never have the same confidence I did before.

I was irrevocably changed. I was one of the people I became a doctor to protect.

A victim.

Before, I believed my family had suffered the worst hell had to dole out. Now, I acknowledge hell is subjective, fluid, with a new level waiting to inflict the most suffering on its patrons. For me, it's not the trauma, per se. It's finding everything you believed—especially yourself—isn't strong enough to survive the fall into the darkness.

I'm snapped back from my woolgathering when Alice flings open her lowest drawer. "Hello, Laura." Inside is access to Willy Wonka's secret garden—the stash of chocolate she keeps to boost the morale of her patients. Without asking my preference, she reaches in and tosses me a king-size packet of Reese's Ultimate Peanut Butter Cups.

Catching them one-handed, I ask wryly, "Am I going to need all four?"

She chuckles. "It's my last pack."

Unwrapping the package, I slide out the first cup and chomp down.

Alice eyes me for a moment before asking me what should be a simple question, but is probably the most terrifying. "How are you?"

I open my mouth to say fine, but what comes out is the truth. "Anxious."

"About what?"

Placing the package of chocolate aside, I lean forward until my head falls into my hands. "Too much, Alice. I don't know where to start."

"Well, let's start with the physical symptoms and then we'll go to the emotional ones. Are you still experiencing pain at your suture site?"

I lift my head and my lips curl briefly before I shake my head. That, at least, is one good thing. "I've been a good little patient and gone to all my physical therapy appointments."

"That's good. Dizziness?"

"No."

"Headaches?"

"Does Aunt Em's singing count?" I half-heartedly joke since Alice has known my whole family for years and appreciates what a disaster it is when my aunt tries to carry a tune.

She snickers. "I'll take that as a no. What about fatigue?"

I surge to my feet and immediately pace. "I'm exhausted."

"You are? You indicated you're getting enough sleep."

The words erupt as if they've just been waiting for the chance to burst forth. "I'm *tired* of waiting."

"Can you expand on that?"

"I'm in limbo. If I'm not waiting for the doorbell to ring and a 'special delivery' to arrive from my favorite psychos, I'm on an emotional spin cycle. I'm *tired* of waiting to go back to a job I trained for seven years to do. I'm afraid at any moment, I'm going to curl up in a corner and have to go through breathing exercises. That makes me *pissed as shit* I'm still not as confident as I want to be before I have to go back."

"Why?" Alice asks curiously.

"Why what?"

"Who says you have to bear the weight of confidence in the ER?" Before I can answer, she holds up a hand. "At least right away, Laura. You endured a major trauma. You were shot in the workplace. You saw people you considered your work family gunned down and killed because you did your job."

Wearily, I flop back into the chair. "That's right. I did my job."

"Everyone agrees you're not responsible for the actions of a psychopath," she reminds me, not for the first time.

"Then why does it feel that way?"

"Because you have a compassionate heart and want to stand before the people you consider yours. It's what makes you an incredible leader, Laura. It's absolutely what makes you an incredible human. But you are just that—human. You're not expected to be Wonder Woman."

"It'd be easier if I was, so I could be certain I wouldn't fail when I return to the ER."

Alice sidesteps my not-so-subtle question. "What do you remember?"

"Christ, Alice. We've been over this."

"What do you remember after the shooting?" she persists.

"I remember crawling and seeing the bodies!" I snap.

She slowly exhales before marking something down on a notepad. "Okay."

"Okay? That's it? So, I'm free to go back to the ER?" I hold my breath while I await her judgment.

Instead of answering my question, she informs me, "You're blocking out memories, Laura."

I open my mouth and shut it. *What?*

I don't realize I've spoken aloud until she responds, "I'm certain it's no surprise I've been speaking with others. They tell a very different account of your actions."

"I . . ." What can I say? What else am I missing? "Did I get someone else killed?"

"Laura, do you really think we wouldn't have worked through that by now if that were the case?" Alice reprimands me.

"I don't know what to believe anymore." My head falls forward into my hands.

"Do you really think you're ready to return to the ER?" Alice probes.

"I think I . . . could be."

"Would you give one hundred percent if you did? Could you be certain you wouldn't make a mistake you'd regret if you went downstairs and back to work right this very second?"

My lips begin to tremble. As much as I want to say "Yes," the "No" my lips breathe is my truth and my shame.

She turns and reaches for a file on her desk before handing it to me. "I'd like to ease you back into the medical environment."

Accepting it, I hesitate to open it and ask, "What do you have in mind?

Alice nods. "I have a patient who could use some one-on-one assistance."

"Go on."

"Her name is Bailey Payne."

I tap the file on my thigh. "What does this have to do with me?"

"Read it and tell me what you think about her medical situation."

"Aren't we violating HIPAA by you showing me this?"

Alice flips around her monitor and I find a non-disclosure statement. I use the electronic pad attached to Alice's computer to sign the statement. Once I do, I immediately flip the file open and am met by the face of a little girl with haphazard pigtails and an urchin's grin. I can't help but be reminded of the plethora of family photos my aunt has taken over the years. My finger taps the edge. "She's adorable."

"Yes, she is."

I scan Bailey's medical history to find she was in an automobile accident two years ago, resulting in her mother's death. Clinically, I note, "Her mother took the brunt of the impact, where Bailey walked away without a scratch. Why does she . . ." My voice breaks off. "She was at the ER the night of the shooting."

"For an ear infection," Alice confirms.

I keep reading. "She was your patient before that."

"Something her loved ones are grateful for daily, let me assure you."

I flip through her file and find out her injuries involved both legs being damaged by shrapnel on top of which the ceiling—shot out by the blast of

Tiberi's weapon—crushed them before her father had a chance to drag her off her chair.

I read aloud, "In each leg, a stainless-steel plate had to be inserted across fracture sites—including the growth plates. Through small incisions in the skin, screws were placed through the plate and bone, above and below the fracture to hold it in place."

I note my former mentor—Dr. Rosenthal—performed the surgery. "She had a guardian angel that night. A difference of millimeters in either direction and her arteries would have been severed as well as her bones being damaged quite so extensively." I keep reading before I note Rosenthal did a second arthroscopy procedure to clean up bone fragments a few weeks ago. Now, I note as I scan Rosenthal's notes, she's in casts while her legs heal. She's also—I wince—subject to his intense physical therapy protocols throughout the summer. I feel for the little girl, even as I agree with Rosenthal. The cure is almost worse than the injury itself—especially to a young child. Overwhelming sessions of pain are emotionally exhausting but are essential to her long-term success in healing.

I should know. Haven't I been doing the exact same thing?

"That's exactly what Dr. Rosenthal told her father."

I wince, knowing my former mentor is an exceptional surgeon but often lacked the people skills at times like those. We talk about the intricacies of Bailey's injuries for a few minutes before I ask, "Why did you want me to read her case file?"

"Because I don't think you're ready for the ER, Laura. But that little girl still needs help."

My eyes drift down at the urchin grinning up at me. "With what?"

Alice surprises me with her response. "She needs a medically trained nanny for the summer."

I'm so stunned that laughter forms in the depths of my belly—something that shocks me because I haven't felt the urge to giggle in so long. *Another piece of my life stolen and given back.* Still, I hold it back to question, "You're telling me I went to med school and completed most of my residency to become a *nanny*?" I close the file so I can hand it back to Alice.

She lays her hand on top of mine, staying my movement. "Bailey's nanny was a trained PA. You actually know her."

When Alice gives me the name, I can't help the curve of my lips as a flood of childhood memories surround me. Memories of when Bailey Payne's same nanny chased me and Jon around the family farm when our parents would go out for the evening.

This little girl and I have more in common than she knows. Still, all I say is, "I see."

"Her residual physical impairments leave her and her father in a difficult situation as Bailey's now on summer vacation. This is a short-term assignment, Laura."

I hesitate. "I appreciate their offer, but still . . ."

"You're going to have to maintain charts, and maybe this will ease you past the psychological roadblocks you're facing as you round the bend in your own recovery. Think back to your first year as a med student. What did you do? Active listening, provide support, reduce feelings of fear and isolation."

The file makes its way into my lap. I rest my hand over it protectively. "True."

"Now, you can do that and push a little girl past her recovery milestones. Just think. Years from now, Bailey will be able to look back and thank you for being the catalyst that changed her life."

"Has the chief cleared this?"

Alice nods. "Moser extended your leave of absence. He agreed to pay your health care coverage out of your hospital salary. Also, you'll be receiving a salary from the Paynes."

I sit up straight. "Now just a darn minute . . ."

When Alice names the amount, my jaw unhinges. It's almost three times my annual salary at the hospital. I gape. "For three months?"

"Like I said, the father's desperate."

I don't give it another thought. "Get the administration to draw up the paperwork. I'll accept their offer contingent on whether the Paynes and I have a good rapport. But you inform Moser I'm on *his* payroll."

Alice's eyes glint. "So to speak."

I shrug my shoulders uncomfortably before agreeing. "So to speak." I haven't taken a dime of the hospital's money since I haven't worked, instead directing my salary to the victim's fund. I advise Alice, *"If* I accept the job with Mr. Payne, he's to do the exact same. I don't want it. You know damn well I don't need it. The families of the victims do."

Alice's smile is beatific. "Deal."

CHAPTER
Nine

LIAM

"I'M HERE to present to you a short-term solution for your nanny problem." Keene saunters into my office without preamble a few days after he and Caleb enticed me with their original offer.

"Does it involve bringing Bailey to the office?"

"If this doesn't work out, that's on the table."

My jaw unhinges. "You're kidding?"

"No, but I'd start by flexing your work hours so you could be home as often as possible with your daughter. You know we believe in family first, whenever possible." Judging by the seriousness of Keene's expression, he means it.

I raise my eyes heavenward, clasping my hands together in prayer over my head. "What did I do to deserve this job?"

Keene rattles off, "You excelled as a CPA in the Army and were considered a forensic accounting savant at Fort Belvoir. Then the Agency recruited you before allowing us to lure you away with offers of copious amounts of money and benefits like a 401k match because our previous auditor had no clue what the fuck he was doing. Not to mention, there's the fact I practically begged, considering I spent more hours doing your job than my own. Does that ring a bell?"

I link my fingers behind my head and grin like the Cheshire Cat. "That's right. You need me."

"Damn straight I do."

"So, tell me about your brilliant idea."

"My niece."

"Which one?" I ask wryly. Keene's wife, Alison, happens to be sisters to both Caleb and one of Hudson's other owner's wives. I was flabbergasted to find out they were three of six siblings who apparently have more branches to their family tree than the one that's strung with lights at Rockefeller Center every Christmas.

"Gore."

"Horrid name. Couldn't you men convince one of the wives to think of something better, or did they nut you during labor?"

Keene aims a look in my direction, riddled with filth. "Gore is the nickname of Caleb's second eldest, Laura."

I do some quick mental digging and recall her age around late twenties. "Isn't she a bit old to be a nanny?"

"Did you notice Caleb's been running the Norwalk office the last quarter?"

I straighten in my chair. "I'm not a frigging idiot. Of course, I did."

"Did you ask him why?"

"I figured you'd loop me in when it was time for me to know."

"That time is now." Keene tells me how Dr. Laura Lockwood, affectionately labeled Queen Gore by the paparazzi, was involved in a mass casualty event in the ER where she works.

I put the pieces together. "The same one where Bailey got injured."

"Yes. During the course of the event, Laura took a bullet to the shoulder, preventing her from returning to work for the first few months."

"I'm so fucking glad that monster's gone."

"We all are."

"If Paulie Tiberi wasn't killed by the police, I don't know what I'd have done," I admit.

"You're not the only one," Keene concurs.

My head tips back as I recall the information I received from the Greenwich police versus what was on the news. Somehow, I always wondered how none of the victims were exploited—now I know. "The victims weren't named because you all put pressure on the media."

Keene's brow quirks. "I don't know what you mean."

I roll my eyes. "Christ, for a while, it was the only thing on the news. I kept expecting news crews on my doorstep. I was grateful Bailey was asleep by the time coverage would come on. The last thing I needed to do was remind her of why she was in her damn casts."

Keene makes a non-committal grunt, his disgust over the media coverage apparent. "It was nothing."

I think about Laura Lockwood before I probe, "I assume your niece has been in therapy?"

"Both physical and psychological."

"Since when?"

"Almost since they finished snipping off the last stitch." Keene leans forward, bracing his elbows on his knees.

"Why hasn't she returned to work?"

"That's between her and her doctor." His steady gaze meets mine, telling me hell will freeze over before he answers that particular question.

"I'll leave that alone if you'll answer this., Do you honestly believe she's in a good enough mental place to be watching over my girl?"

"Yes."

"Keene."

"Fine. Personally, I think she's *been* ready to resume her job."

"Then why hasn't she?" I challenge.

He ignores me, instead choosing that moment to brag, "Laura was rapidly rising to become one of the best emergency room doctors in the country."

"No, that's not family pride talking at all," I drawl laconically.

"It's actually not. It's based on her last four years' worth of evals Sam managed to inveigle from the Greenwich Hospital HR department."

"What's your opinion then on why she hasn't gone back?" I phrase the question differently.

"She watched as her colleagues and patients were gunned down in front of her face." I wince, having lived that experience with her. I know what mental anguish this woman suffered. Keene continues, "Not to mention she took a shot through the left shoulder. Her physical therapist has said she's good to go."

"It's her mental state," I conclude grimly before hesitating only briefly, "I have a right to ask . . ."

"Ask." My gaze whips up to meet Keene's. He shrugs. "What's the worst I'm going to do? Say no? Not answer?"

"What does her therapist think?"

"Physically and intellectually, she's ready, but there's something missing—something that's made her stand out as chief resident."

Impressed despite myself at Dr. Laura Lockwood's credentials, I question, "What's that?"

"Her emotions," he declares bluntly. "She was a doctor who was as comfortable holding a scalpel as easily as she held a patient's hand. I'm afraid for her of what will happen if she doesn't find that part of herself again."

"But she's mentally stable?" I press.

Keene releases a beleaguered sigh. "Would I be here if she wasn't?"

"Speaking of that, why are you here? Why not her father?"

Keene stands. Just like that, he's wrapped his cloak of reserve back around him. "Caleb's in the middle of . . . something. Since I was coming into the office today, I told him I'd speak with you."

Sitting forward, I drum my fingers against my desk as I give the idea some thought. "It would help me out of a massive bind. Mrs. Destry leaves in a little over a week and I'm no closer to finding someone who can help Bailey, regardless of the ridiculous salary I'm willing to pay."

He heads for the door. "Let me confirm Laura is ready for this."

Panic causes me to surge to my own feet. "Wait. I thought this was a done deal."

"The idea is done and the seeds of execution have been planted. Now, it's time to see if they root—on both sides." Keene nods just as a ping indicates I have an incoming email. "You'll need the password 'Delph1!' to unlock the files Sam just e-mailed you about Laura."

"What do they contain?"

"History, background, media, the usual. It also contains her therapist's sign-off for your peace of mind." Knocking on the door frame, Keene disappears from my sight.

I sink back into my chair and pull myself up to the edge of my desk. Turning the discussion with Keene over every which way, the only things that are disquieting to me are what I don't know yet about Dr. Laura Lockwood. Pulling up the email from Hudson's resident hacker, Sam Akin, I pause before opening the file attachment. "Well, at least I have more factual answers in here than whatever family bias Keene might have for his niece."

Typing in the password he gave me, I open the first file and quickly become absorbed in my subject. It quickly becomes apparent to me Keene is right—again, though I'll refuse to admit it, since it just adds to his enormous ego.

On paper, his niece is remarkable, bordering on a wunderkind. I scroll—and scroll—past the number of immediate family relations. Murmuring aloud, I read, "Graduated with top honors from Skidmore at barely nineteen, finished Yale Medical School at twenty-three, earning one of the coveted Yale Medical Coaching Experience spots." My eyes skim over the titles of academic research and journals she's been cited in, awards she's received during her career.

Then, I read a file of news clippings about the night of the shooting—none of which mention Dr. Laura Lockwood as one of the victims of Paulie Tiberi. None of which name my daughter. Thus the power behind the men I work for.

Swallowing to shift the lump lodged in my throat, I "X" out of the profile on Caleb's daughter and open the sign-off from her psychologist. Shaking my head, I murmur, "I guess I shouldn't be surprised to see Bailey's doctor's name here, should I?"

Likely because when I asked for the name of a therapist to help Bailey adjust to living with a father full-time, moving, her mother's death, and—most recently—being the unintended victim of a hospital shooting, I knew I would be given the best. Without question, that doctor is Alice Cleary. I have no doubt, considering her proximity to the main event, the best is certainly what Laura Lockwood would need to work through what happened to her as well.

I flip through the social media articles Sam cultivated, noting which paparazzi blessed her with the nickname "Gore." Now that I understand its origin, I'm amused to know that her family adopted it as well.

I also note the doctor is strikingly attractive. I'd have to be dead not to. Yet, surprisingly, she more often than not is caught on camera alone or on the arm of a family member. More than one member of the press—including the satiric celebrity news magazine StellaNova—notes how "Queen Gore" cares far more about causes than about who she's seen with.

I read aloud from their clipping, *"If the rest of the ridiculously rich and famous acted like the Lockwood/Marshall/Freeman clan—particularly her highness, Queen Gore—real change could happen in this world. Make no mistake, instead of people milling around gossiping about when they should schedule their next martini lunch to talk about scheduling a tea to organize a committee, true action would occur. Maybe they should take their child with a 103 to the Greenwich ER only to end up with a front-row seat to the ballet of Gore dancing between cracking a chest open, calmly soothing this parent as she ran an IV line, and stitching up a wound on an elderly person with interns hovering as she explained the reason she was using a particular suture thread."*

Studying her hospital ID photo, I find myself pulled in by the determination evident on her face. There's something affecting about it, about her. Maybe it's the strength of her character instilled by her family, but there's something about Laura Lockwood that pulls at me.

Or you're just that desperate for a nanny, I berate myself as I close the file.

Leaning back in my chair, I look for any flaws in the plan. Evaluating the pros and cons from every angle, I come to a conclusion. I caution myself, "We're both in limbo and she's not offering forever."

Besides, Bailey will ultimately benefit from such a positive female role model once she gets to know her. That tips the scales and has me sending an email to Keene with only two words.

I'm interested.

CHAPTER
Ten

LIAM

I PACE my office back and forth, expecting her call. When my cell rings at eight precisely, I answer it with a brusque, "Liam Payne."

"Mr. Payne, this is Dr. Laura Lockwood. I believe you've been expecting my call."

I slide behind my desk and focus on the monitor where I'm faced with an enlarged photo of the good doctor's unforgettable face. "Dr. Lockwood, a pleasure to make your acquaintance."

"Yours as well." After we dispel with social niceties, an awkward silence spans between the lines before she breaks them. "Alice indicated you're in need of a medically trained nanny for the next few months."

Her voice is cool, calm, and collected—something I'm used to from having worked with members of her family. It is, however, a complete one-eighty from Mrs. Destry, whose demeanor can be quantified as a grandmotherly sort. Scrubbing my hand over my hair in agitation, I frown. "I am, but I wouldn't say we've reached the critical state." *Yet,* I add silently.

Her doubtful, "Hmm," makes me wonder if someone—perhaps her father —briefed her on the true state of my desperation. But my panic overwhelms me when she proudly states, "If you've already filled the position, then I apologize for wasting both of our time. Have a good evening, Mr. Payne."

Before she can disconnect, I blur out, "Wait!"

There's silence on the other end. She's waiting for me to fill it. Somehow, I know she won't make the next move due to my reluctance. Then I give her the truth. "I think we're more at the catastrophic stage."

A muffled sound transmits over the line. Is that Laura Lockwood's manner of laughing? A sneer twists my lips when I compare it to Bailey's helpless giggles. Christ, I don't want my daughter turned into a soulless socialite in her twelve weeks off from school. Without thought, I state, "Before you meet Bailey, I think we should discuss the offer in person. Nail down any questions you may have."

"I agree."

I pull up my calendar and wince between my work schedule and the number of days I have left before Mrs. Destry leaves. "Would it be problematic for you to come to the Hudson office for the meeting?"

"The headquarters in New York or the satellite office in Norwalk?"

"I work out of HQ."

"What day and time?"

At her crisp return, I frown again. *Am I really doing what's best for Bailey?* Despite my concerns, we agree upon a time to meet tomorrow. "I look forward to meeting you tomorrow, Mr. Payne."

"You as well, Dr. Lockwood."

After I drop my phone back on my desk, I let out a beleaguered sigh. "What have I set us up for, Buttercup?"

But with my daughter asleep in a different wing of the house, she can't answer me.

CHAPTER
Eleven

LIAM

I HOLD up my hands in supplication to Keene. "I agreed to meet her."

Keene rolls his eyes. "It's just a matter of time. With Gore . . ."

"Christ, that nickname," I wince every time I hear it.

"You can thank the paparazzi for it. Specifically, StellaNova," Keene informs me.

"Yeah. No thanks. I'm all stocked up on doing stupid shit in my life. I think I'll leave you to be their target." I've been privy to how much coverage my bosses get in the notorious gossip column.

"You're lucky you can. *Laura,*" he emphasizes, "is going to work out brilliantly for you."

There's a knock on the door just as Keene finishes his sentence. Tony's standing there with a bemused expression on his face. Judging by the slight lipstick smudge on his cheek and the way his cheeks are flushed, little hearts would be floating around his head if he were a cartoon character.

It's a revelation considering Tony's a lethal shot, can terrify agents of this company into organizational compliance, and has better hand-to-hand combat skills than most of our new recruits despite his age. Still, I have to muffle a laugh when his voice comes out dreamy when he announces, "Gore's here."

"Brace yourself." Keene surges to his feet. I do the same, uncertain as to why but feeling necessary to be on equal footing to greet the illustrious Dr. Laura Lockwood for the first time.

Despite her uncle's warning, I wasn't prepared for the impact of her entering my office. Laura Lockwood started overwhelming my senses before I ever caught sight of her.

The clicking of heels announcing her movement.

Then came the subtle hint of sweet spice.

But neither of those two things warned me of my body's reaction when the sharply dressed curvaceous brunette saunters into the room with inbred confidence not even an attempted murderer could strip away. I almost fall back a step at the force that surrounds this petite bombshell.

Now, I understand the invisible hearts floating around Tony—Laura Lockwood is stunning. It's not just her face, which I was certainly prepared for based on the number of photos I studied. Maybe it's her eyes I can't look away from—a Caribbean blue color—a tsunami waiting to crash down on you as you drown in their depths. Even as they fixate solely on me, something shifts inside me—a paradigm of sorts. Perhaps some long-ago buccaneer in my blood came up against a wave of Laura's presence and the magnitude of its sheer presence was passed down via our blood. Or it's just the woman herself. A confidence that radiates off her that screams, "I am who I am. Take me or leave me."

Silently assessing her, I determine if you strip away her custom clothes and subtle accouterments screaming an upbringing of wealth and privilege, this woman would still be a force to be reckoned with. Her formidable power emanates from her, dazzling those caught in its presence the way a well-cut diamond cascades rainbows around a room.

She's a siren, a mermaid. Absolutely not, I think pithily, a woman who deserves the nickname "Gore."

"Uncle Keene," she greets him. It gives me a moment of respite from her allure, allowing me to drag air into my lungs before I'm hit again with the full magnitude of her head on.

This time, I'm prepared. That is until Laura holds out her hand for me to take. "Don't let the blasphemy that persistently drips out of my uncle's mouth influence your decision one way or another, Mr. Payne."

Then she smiles, and it's like being thrown off a dinghy into a tidal wave. Instead, she slides into professionalism as easily as I'm certain as she slid on her eight-hundred dollar heels. She extends her hand. Laura offers me a smile that demonstrates she's not just made-up beauty, but she has a steel core buried in her as well. "Dr. Laura Lockwood,"

"Liam Payne. A pleasure to meet you in person."

I reach forward and grip her fingers. Our hands connect. Immediately, her eyes flick away from mine for the briefest second. If I hadn't been staring at her face so intently, I might have missed it.

As for me, the second our hands touch, I know I'm in for a scorcher of a summer that has nothing to do with blistering heat and everything to do with the woman in front of me. I haven't felt anything like the arc of raw electricity that sizzled up my arm. Ever. Judging by the good doctor's expression, neither has she.

She pulls her hand away and twists her head in the direction of her uncle to tease, "For shame, Uncle Keene. I'm going to have to tell Aunt Ali about you disparaging me to strangers."

He hooks an arm around her shoulder and brushes a kiss to her temple. "I can handle my wife with one arm tied behind my back."

"I'll be sure to let her know that as well," Laura counters.

"That's my cue to let the two of you get better acquainted before I rack up any more demerits." Keene's face softens briefly as he places his fingers beneath his niece's chin. They communicate silently while I scrutinize them. He winks at her. "Love you, Gore."

"Love you too, Uncle Keene."

Then it's just the two of us, and Laura turns to me expectantly. Bailey. Right. The reason this sensational woman is even in my office. "Excuse my rudeness. Please, take a seat." I gesture to the guest chair Keene just vacated.

Laura moves through the space gracefully, as if she's familiar with the setup. I put a mental pin to ask her later how we've never crossed paths in all the time I've worked for Hudson, but that's for later. As she sinks into the chair, she thanks me.

I don't waste time on any platitudes. "It's been a difficult time for Bailey."

"Tell me about her," Laura encourages.

"That might take a while."

She relaxes marginally. "I have nothing but time right now."

I start with the medical, telling her about Bailey's injury, from why we were at the ER that night to the injuries she sustained. Laura interrupts me a few times to clarify a few items before remarking, "I saw she was recently made limited weight bearing to transition to crutches?"

"For things like brushing her teeth and using the bathroom."

"I know Dr. Rosenthal's recovery guidelines well, as I used to be the one explaining them to the families." My shoulders jerk when I hear that.

Laura's lips twist wryly. "Before I ever called you, Uncle Keene mentioned he passed along my CV. You didn't notice one of my rotations was with your daughter's surgeon?"

"Dr. Lockwood—" I begin.

"Laura," she corrects me.

"Laura." I start again. "Your resume reads something along the lines of a Who's Who of the AMA. After I got to page three, I'll admit to it all blurring a bit."

"For your own sake, I wouldn't share that with my father, Uncle Keene, or anyone else who works here."

"Why not?" The question pops out before I can stop it.

She leans forward and cups her hand to her mouth as if she's about to confide something to me. I find myself leaning forward across my desk. With a gleam in her eyes, she stage whispers, "They might wonder if they're not challenging you enough here at the office. Trust me, you don't want that." She shudders in mock horror.

I can't help the snicker that escapes. "I know how to handle them."

"With a whip and a chair?"

"By telling them they're facing an audit."

"Ahh, yes. That would keep them in line." She taps a finger to her lips. "Too bad I can't do that at family dinners. The worst I can threaten them with is a prostate exam."

Chuckling, I ask. "Have to do that often?"

"Threaten my family?"

"Yes."

"You work for them. You tell me," she volleys back.

"I think family dinners must be entertaining, to say the least."

"That's one way to put it."

Curious, I ask, "Are you planning on teaching my daughter how to handle me like you do your family when she gets to be your age?"

"If I have to teach her, she's behind on her coursework. Mansplaining was a preliminary rite of passage in my childhood, Mr. Payne."

"Liam," I correct her again.

"Liam." The way my name rolls off her tongue makes my cock twitch. To cover it, I roll closer to my desk, shifting my legs beneath the well to release the pressure on my strangling dick.

"What are your concerns about the job?" I ask her bluntly to get us back on track.

"What you're offering to pay me," she states immediately.

I'm about to offer her more when she shocks the hell out of me. "If you offer me the job, I don't want a single dime of it. I already expressed my feelings about this to Alice, but I want to make it clear to you. I want you to donate all the money you would have paid me to the fund the hospital established for victims of the shooting. They're the only reason I'm even available to consider taking your offer."

"That's . . ." Words fail me.

She quirks a perfectly groomed brow.

"Incredibly generous," I conclude. Truthfully, what I'm feeling is astounded.

"I'm blessed enough I can afford to be. There are people who are struggling . . ." She swallows and disengages eye contact with me.

"Struggling," I prompt when her voice drops off.

When she reengages, her eyes are like waves as the moisture in them swims but never falls. "To pay for funerals. For home payments. The salary you're offering me would be a boon to relieve them of these concerns. If you decide to take me on, it's not because I need money."

I link my fingers together over my stomach. "Then what do you want from this job?"

Laura gently reminds me, "Temporary assignment. I do have a permanent position to return to eventually."

"Fine. What do you want, if not a paycheck?"

She hesitates before replying softly, "For once, I want to focus on the good of one patient. This one time, I think that may be just as critical as focusing on the good of the many."

"Some would say you have that backward," I counter.

"Some would. Not me. I need to know I won't fall down on the job." Vulnerability flickers in her eyes even as her chin lifts. "To that end, if you choose to hire me, I'd recommend a probationary period before you transition Bailey's care to me full time."

Despite the fact that her words depict uncertainty in her own skills, in my eyes, Laura is already proving Keene right. She's more than ready to return to the ER. But if she wants to spend the summer shoring up her patient care techniques, I'm not about to look a gift horse in the mouth.

Standing, I plant my feet apart to brace myself for the shock of touching her again. Offering my hand, I ask, "Are you interested in the position? If so, I'd like for you to meet Bailey."

Laura stands. Hesitating a fraction of a heartbeat, she takes my hand. Our fingers clasp tightly. If I thought knowing what it would be like to touch her would make it less electrifying, I was wrong.

So wrong.

I don't know what the fuck to do about it except ignore it.

Especially if the esteemed Dr. Laura Lockwood and my daughter get along well enough for her to accept the offer to become my daughter's temporary nanny while recovering from her own mental tailspin.

CHAPTER
Twelve

GRATEFUL I AGREED to a car and driver, I roll up the partition between us before placing a call to the home I share with my cousins Kalie and Grace.

Grace answers, "What's chilling?"

"Hopefully the vodka?"

"It's eleven-thirty in the morning," she reprimands.

"If I'm not mistaken, I just agreed to take on the responsibility for my first patient since the shooting," I declare bluntly.

I must be on speaker because Kalie groans. "In other words, your need for alcohol is imminent."

Grace interjects. "Fine. But let's try to have a little class. Screwdrivers?"

"Deal. I'll be home in about twenty. Get the vodka chilling." I disconnect the call and focus on the trees flying by in a whiz alongside the highway and the blur of cars passing in the mid-morning traffic.

Exactly twenty minutes later, after being dropped off in the driveway of the charming Craftsman the three of us bought by pooling our money together after we each graduated college and came into part of our inheritances, something uncoils inside me that's been wound tightly. "It's good to be home."

All the months I stayed at my parents, I needed their constant comfort. But being back in my own home is another reminder that I survived the massacre set in motion by the Tiberis.

As I approach the front door, I admire the landscaping. Grace's hard work from last summer has paid off as bright orange dragon lilies form a graceful arc amid the other impatiens and annuals dotting our front yard. Kalie and I leave that in our cousin's very capable hands.

The both of us willingly admit we're lucky we don't kill the Christmas amaryllis Uncle Phil sends to each of his nieces and nephews every year. One year, I somehow managed to turn the bright red leaves a sickly yellow color. "Still uncertain about how I did that." But the memory of it causes my lips to lift in a real grin as I jog up our flagstone steps.

Our home is gorgeous—easily comparable to the homes we lived in growing up. Like I said to Liam, I don't need his money. What he may or may not know is I have my own. What only my family would realize is that even if I was eating Ramen noodles, I still wouldn't take a damn dime from someone who was injured during the shooting if they needed help. Sure having money is nice, but it's nothing in comparison to everything else I've been blessed with—a second chance to right the wrongs I made that night.

Truth be told, everyone in my family feels that way. If all our wealth were stripped away tomorrow and all we had to show for our lives was the interwoven connections of love, a set of clothes on our backs, and our varying amaryllis tattoos, we'd be richer than Croesus.

Reaching the top, I find Kalie leaning against the door jamb with a tall glass in her hands. "Are you talking to yourself?"

I snatch her screwdriver from her hands before slugging back a third of the glass and handing it back. "I was just thinking how blessed we are. It has everything to do with the fact we're family and nothing to do with the number of zeros in our bank accounts."

"Amen, sister." She raises her glass against my imaginary one.

I kick off my shoes before following her down the hall. "What are you doing home?"

Kalie flicks her long dark hair, an identical shade to mine. Her blue eyes sparkle. "It's Memorial Day, Laura. Like many people, today is a day off."

"It's Memorial Day?" I blink as my brain assimilates what day of the week it is. Then I shout, "Shit! Tonight's my parent's anniversary party."

"You must be more tired than you thought," she clucks sympathetically because she knows my mother's hyper-organized nature would have sent us at least ten reminders.

"Remember how you felt when you were studying for the bar?"

She chuckles. "How could I forget?"

"That's what I feel like." I shudder in remembrance as we make our way toward delicious smells wafting down the hall.

Grace's head pops up from where she's flipping pancakes on the griddle. "Because of nightmares or something else?"

Sliding onto one of the stools at our kitchen counter, I sip my drink before answering. "Yes? I'm considering taking a temporary position to ease my way back into medicine."

There's not a single sound in the kitchen except the sizzle of the grill. Casually, I lean over and pluck a grape from the fruit salad Grace has next to her. "Better flip those before they burn."

Cursing, Grace begins flipping the golden pancakes one by one.

Kalie immediately begins interrogating me. "Anyone we know?"

I shake my head before giving it consideration. "Actually, you might. I'm not certain about Gracie."

Grace ducks her head to give her attention to the food. "Not another word until we're at the table. I want to hear about this from start to finish."

Kalie hooks an arm around my shoulders before narrowing her eyes. Grace depriving her of her advantage of having me to interrogate. Grateful for the delay, I ask her, "Is there anything we can do to help?"

"Well, since you're so enamored of the fruit, serve that up. Kalie, drinks. We're just about ready."

Kalie drawls, "Can I get Laura a supersize cup? Maybe it will help her loosen her lips."

I reach into the bowl and pluck out a piece of tangerine. I fling it at my cousin's forehead. Instead of trying to catch it with her mouth, she uses Grace's glass to nab it out of thin air.

Grace and I applaud.

"Thank you. For my next act, I pry open safes with just my mouth." She stares at me pointedly.

I do the one thing guaranteed to piss her off. "It's not a state secret. In fact, your father helped arrange it."

Kalie's eyes blaze. "He . . . you . . . tell . . . argh!"

Grace takes the plate of pancakes and contemplates placing them back in the warming drawer. "There's no need for breakfast to get cold while she tries to complete a sentence."

I fork a grape from the fruit on my plate and pop it into my mouth, wondering if Kalie's going to call her father instead of waiting for me to spill the tea.

She whips out her phone. I confide to Grace, "This won't take long."

Grace begins indistinct muttering and serves our breakfast. Sliding a stack of pancakes in front of me, she begins, "You just had to rile her up?"

I speak loudly enough for Kalie's father. "It's payback."

"For what?"

"For Uncle Keene."

"Why?"

"Because in no way was I prepared for that meeting this morning."

The second the words leave my mouth, Kalie's head snaps in my direction and a toothy grin spreads across her face. "I'll tell her, Daddy. Okay. We'll see you tonight. Love you too. Bye." Her voice is a throaty purr when she remarks, "Well, well, well."

Grace sends her a disapproving glare, easily reading the she-cat look Kalie's prone to wear as she's often been on the other side of it. "Kalie, let Laura talk about it when she's ready."

Maybe it isn't that time to heal wounds, but perhaps that time helps create memories that ease them. A spark lights inside of me that prompts me to tease Grace. "You do realize how much you sound like Mama scolding me and Jon when we were kids?"

Grace turns her narrowed blue eyes in my direction, but it softens when my dimple pops out. "Maybe it's because you had time to absorb more of her lectures than the rest of us?"

Grace reaches over to a bowl of fruit, plucks a grape, and tosses it toward my face. "Are you calling me old?"

I catch it one-handed before popping it into my mouth. "I wasn't, but thanks. These are good."

Kalie lifts her drink and toasts my athletic food prowess before teasing Grace. "Impressive sounding like Aunt Cass. Few of us can pull it off."

"A true compliment," Grace agrees before turning off the burner and joining us on the other side of the counter.

"It is." I give my cousin a quick head-to-toe perusal. For not being biologically related to us, she could easily pass as Kaylie's fraternal twin. My lips curve when I recall Uncle Phil's exasperation at our last family dinner. *"Why is it so many of the next generation of Freemans and their progeny look like Marshalls?"*

Aunt Emily was laughing so hard her drink flew out of her mouth. As it was prone to, it landed on Uncle Phil, who shot her an exasperated look. After she managed to calm down, her eyes skated over her oldest, Jenna, where she was cuddled with her husband. The light shone off Jenna's golden hair and that of Jenna's daughter.

Phil waived her off—his trademark move when he doesn't want to be dissuaded from a point. "I mean, look at Grace, Laura, Jon, Kalie, Chuck? And that reminds me. How in the hell did Nicole end up with light eyes? Corinna and Colby both have dark eyes."

Just as I girded myself to fall on the family sword to attempt to explain genetics to Uncle Phil, Mama winked at me before handling him the way only she can. "As head of this motley crew, I would have thought you would have realized the miracle in your exalted presence."

"What's that, Cass?"

"Their eyes are all identical to yours."

Uncle Phil preened even as Uncle Keene's head thwacked the table repeatedly amid the laughter that ran around it. Keene pleaded with his sister, "It's been almost thirty years. Must you encourage him?"

Mama replied, "Of course. He's my brother, just like you are. I encourage both your bad behavior equally."

That's when the howling really started between the generations.

Kalie snickers, "I recall Mama always saying I might look like Aunt Cassidy, but Daddy reminding her we all know who I grew up to act like."

Together we all chime, "Aunt Corinna," before bursting into laughter and toasting the fact we're family.

Even if not all our relations are bound by blood.

Later, in my room, I reflect on the fact of how easily it could have been ripped away with a single bullet.

Even before Paulie Tiberi shot up the ER, I knew I was blessed by family, love, and laughter. Now, each and every moment reminds me I was nursed on it is treasured. I cut my teeth on exchanging quips with my cousins, gaining confidence at family dinners, being surrounded by confidence.

The only difference between then and now is I don't take a single moment of it for granted.

"Family first," I repeat the family mantra as I wander over to the credenza of photos under my window. The pictures of my aunts, uncles, cousins, and all the others create a warmth inside me. They'll all be there tonight to celebrate my parents' anniversary. Every single one—I'm certain of it. Regardless if they're actually related or adopted into our enormous clan, the people tonight are there for one reason. It's not because they're Olympic athletes or reporters. It's not because they're country music or rock stars. It's not because they're famous television personalities, bakers, lawyers, or teachers. Nobody cares if the person is a florist or firefighter, doctor or billionaire, we gather because we love.

And love of family supersedes all.

My lips curve when I pick up an outtake of a photo my Aunt Holly was trying to capture of my brothers and me when Jon and I were six and

Chuck was three. Jon was holding me—at least that's how it first appears. I was actually screaming bloody murder trying to snatch the balloon Chuck was trying to release from his hands. Putting it back in its place of pride, my voice drips with irony when I get a glimpse of the blood on the hem of my dress. "And people were appalled when the press dubbed me 'Gore'?"

My eyes travel up and down the memories. Each one offering me a window into the past, all from the splendor of my sea-inspired bedroom. Glancing around the room, I take in an amber-toned headboard that picks up the striations of the wood tones of the floors, while the bedding is a combination of rich blues. The soothing coastal vibe rejuvenates my soul every time I'm sheltered in this space—taking me as far away from reality as I can get without actually leaving it.

Out of the corner of my eye, I catch sight of a picture of my twin and me on our twelfth birthday. Lifting it, I snicker aloud. "Considering the number of scrapes Jon and I got into at school, it's no wonder Mama said we added more gray to her hair." In the photo, Jon's shirt is ripped, as is the hem of my plaid skirt. Both our knees are skinned but sitting between us is our youngest cousin, Lily. I trace the unmistakable pride on our faces despite torn uniforms and first stains. "It was so easy to stand up to bullies back then," I murmur.

Then why is it so hard to stand up to the demons who are dead?

Placing the photo down with a snap, I get lost in memories of pools of blood, heartbreaking screams, pained moans, and sirens. No longer am I that fearless girl who refused to fall to the bully—the girl who firmly planted herself in front of others. Now, I'm one of the fallen.

A shadow passes over the sun—too long for a cloud.

At least, I think it is.

Is it my mind reminding me again of my weakness? Maybe. Still, before I never recognized shadows. Now, I search for them everywhere.

Refusing to succumb to the fear today of all days, I search for my cell phone so I can reach for my lifeline. Under the guise of confirming dinner is still on for tonight, I press in a number I've had memorized since I was two.

After my mother exclaims, "Laura!" like no matter what happens, I'm going to be the best part of her day, I relax marginally.

Everything is going to be all right. I can crawl out of this backslide.

After all, every once in a while, we all need a day we can take a step forward and not retreat no matter how much we want to.

CHAPTER
Thirteen

LIAM

I CALL HER THAT EVENING. I know it's Memorial Day, but still I want—no need—things settled not just for my sake but so I can begin to transition Bailey's reality.

It rings once, twice, before a laughing voice greets me. Immediately, I glance down at my dick. Yep. I'm rock hard at the sound of her voice. Christ, I'm going to need to get a handle on that. I can't be lusting after my daughter's nanny.

That is, if she accepts my offer. I hear a boisterous noise on her end of the line. I pull the phone away before I confirm, "Laura?"

A pause before an amused, "Yes?"

I lean against the doorjamb of my office, spying on the kitchen where Bailey and Mrs. Destry are making homemade pizza. "Liam Payne."

"I know. I had your phone number programmed." There's a raucous burst of laughter before she asks, "Can you give me a moment to step outside?"

"Of course." I can't help but wonder where she's at.

I hear a shouted, "Laura, they're cutting the cake soon!"

She calls back, "This shouldn't take but a moment. Tell Mama and Dad I'll be right there," before she offers me an explanation when she's in a quieter place. "It's my parent's anniversary party. Unfortunately, I don't have time to talk at length."

"I won't take up too much of your time."

"Thank you."

"I'd like you to come by next Monday and meet Bailey after school."

There's the barest hint of noise on the other end of the line, or I'd swear she'd hung up. "Are you certain?"

Turning away from the very domestic scene in front of me, I let my mind fill with nothing but the woman infiltrating my thoughts all afternoon. My dick is sending throbbing signals to my brain to slam the door on my thoughts. I give her the truth, "No."

"Well, that's honest."

"I refuse to be anything but that."

"That's excellent to know."

"Will you come to meet Bailey?" I send a quick prayer up to heaven she says yes. She hesitates, so I drop all pretense and admit, "I need you, Laura. More than that, my daughter needs you."

Her breath releases in a whoosh. "What time would you like me there?"

"School gets out at two-thirty."

"I'll be there at three."

"Excellent. Thank you." Her name is bellowed. "You'd better go."

"Yes. See you Monday."

"Wish your parents a happy anniversary."

"I'll pass that along," she promises. Then there's nothing but silence, but for the first time in weeks, the sound of silence doesn't terrify me.

It just builds anticipation of what's to come.

CHAPTER
Fourteen

Laura

"I CAN DO THIS," I tell myself as much as Kalie and Grace the day I'm to meet Bailey Payne for the first time. It's the first time I'll come face to face with a victim of the ER shooting who's still alive since the altercation.

Grace captures my hand between hers. I ignore her surreptitiously taking my pulse. "You can. You conquered med school, Laura. Don't go in expecting this to be a regular nanny gig. You're not just some babysitter."

"But isn't that what you're being asked to do," Kalie counters. "I mean, it's not like you can make the kid a pitcher of margaritas and talk about the weather."

Grace gives Kalie an incredulous look before saying exactly what I'm thinking. "Sometimes I wonder if you spent too much time with Uncle Phil as a kid."

"Cute." Kalie's lip is about to curl in the sneer she normally reserves for the courtroom when I swat Grace's hand away.

"Grace, I swear if you try to take my pulse one more time, I'm adding a neon purple nose ring to your next client's nose replacement right before you turn it over," I threaten. As Grace is an anaplastologist, she replaces body parts of all kinds. I can just see one of her elderly clients sporting a neon purple nose ring.

She rocks back on her heels, a small smile lifting the corner of her lips. "If you're making threats, you're not having a panic attack."

"No, I'm not. I'm just . . ."

"What?"

"Wondering what the hell is wrong with me?" I shout, anger superseding all the other emotions I could be feeling. "Other people who were in the shooting are already back at work—including fucking Moser."

"Is that fact or is that the hospital grapevine?" Kalie questions.

"Grapevine, but still . . ."

"Still . . . was Dr. Douche the one who was held hostage?" Grace points out using the nickname I shared with them frequently utilized in the past about our chief when he was a particularly nasty piece of work.

"It wasn't like that," I protest.

"It was exactly that," Kalie confirms ruthlessly before softening. "Laura, no one would blame you if you never wanted to return."

My breathing turns ragged. "I would. I'd blame me."

"Then why not listen to your therapist. Give this a try. See if being a nanny . . ."

I sneer at the word.

"Fine. Call it what you want—does exclusive medically trained home professional sound better?"

"It makes me sound like a hooker."

"You say potato," Kalie singsongs.

"I'd say you'd better run."

Kalie laughs before backtracking with another suggestion. "How about the first nanny educated by Yale University?"

Snorting, I whip out my smart phone and pull up a webpage before flipping it in her direction.

Her jaw drops. "No shit? Yale has a clearinghouse for babysitters and tutors?"

"Yes, they do. So, no, cousin. I don't even have that distinction since each babysitter and tutor is required to be a Yale student."

Grace, living up to her name, just says, "How about you just go in with an open mind and determine who and what you want this to be, Laura? Yes, you need to give that little girl everything she needs, but maybe you'll find you get more out of this than you imagined."

My heart shudders in relief, tired of beating so hard in my chest. Whether that's because the synapses in my brain finally capitulated and kicked in to stop panicking or because it's in agreement with my decision, I don't know.

I'm just grateful the pain has eased up for now.

CHAPTER

Fifteen

LIAM

DING. Dong.

"Just a minute!" I call out. Turning to Bailey, I deflate at the mutinous set of her expression. "I wish there was some other way."

"There has to be!"

"If there was, don't you think I would have tried? Bailey, can't you give her a shot?"

"I want Mrs. D back," she wails.

Striving for patience, I crouch down and remind her, "Mrs. Destry's moving to England to be with her daughter, Buttercup."

Bailey's brow furrows. "How far away is England?"

I begin pushing her toward our front door. "Pretty far away, kid."

"Like how far, Daddy."

I think about the last time I flew over for a case. "About six hours."

"We could go see her on the weekends!" Bailey claps her hands together enthusiastically.

I ruffle this morning's attempt at braids. "By airplane."

"Oh."

"Why don't we meet the doctor Mr. Caleb and Mr. Keene recommended?" I suggest, as we reach the front door.

"But what if I don't like her?" Bailey demands.

"Then I'll listen to your reasons and we'll see if we can work something out," I state practically.

That's when my little girl breaks my heart in two. Just as I jerk open the door, she whispers, "But what if she doesn't like me?"

I barely glimpse Laura's dark, sable curls swirling around the region of my chest height before they disappear. That's because she didn't spare a second to acknowledge me, but crouched down right next to Bailey's wheelchair. "Hi. You must be Bailey."

Bailey's lips press together even as stubborn arms cross over her chest. Christ, even if a DNA test hadn't confirmed she was mine long ago, I'd know it from that expression alone. I'm curious to see how the esteemed Dr. Laura Lockwood handles this.

"I'd like the chance to get to know you, Bailey."

My mutinous child just glares at her. "I don't want to get to know you. I want Mrs. Destry back."

"Mrs. D's the best, isn't she?" Laura agrees.

"How would you know?" Bailey grumbles.

Laura sits down on the ground, barely inside the entryway. I have to prevent my tongue from falling out when her legs twist into a lotus position without thinking. Bailey's face morphs into one of envy. I'd be willing to suffer another audit from the IRS if Laura missed it. Still, I'm not certain who is more shocked when she informs my daughter, "She'd occasionally babysit my brothers, my cousins, and me when we weren't much older than you."

"Really?" The excitement flies out of Bailey's mouth before she can trample on it.

"Yes. I think she went into nannying because we terrorized her," Laura confides.

Bailey cracks a tiny smile but is in no way giving up the war against Laura Lockwood. "I don't want to do any stupid exercises."

"Why not?"

"I'm tired of hurting all the time."

I hold my breath while Laura contemplates Bailey's demand. "It's okay to be tired."

Bailey's jaw flops open. "It is? I mean, you're saying I don't have to do my exercises?"

"Sure." Bailey, now on Team Laura, shoots me a smug look. I'm about three seconds from asking Laura to pick up her perfect ass and leave before she goes on to say, "If you're willing to accept you won't be able to walk or run like you used to."

"I'll be able to! You're wrong! Tell her, Daddy!" Bailey shouts angrily.

Before I can jump in, Laura asserts herself. "In this, Bailey, I'm the expert. I'm not a nanny. What I am is a board-certified emergency room doctor."

"Then why are you here instead of working in a hospital?"

"To help you and your dad out while he finds someone more permanent."

"We don't need your help," she insists stubbornly.

"Hmm. That might be true for everything but this."

I'm about to intervene when Laura speaks to her as directly as Dr. Rosenthal would. Right now, I appreciate her telling me she interned for him. "If you don't do your exercises—with careful supervision—you can harm your future growth. You may not grow as tall. You may not be able to play in the same manner as your friends when you go back to school next fall." But that's where Rosenthal's bedside manner ends and Laura Lockwood's picks up. She reaches over and twists the wheelchair wheel a bit. "You have to build up the strength in your muscles. Don't you want to get out of this thing?"

"More than anything," Bailey admits.

"Why?"

"I want to stop being different than the other kids."

Finally, a breakthrough.

"Then how about I help you?"

Bailey shrugs.

"Look at it this way. What's the worst that happens? If you end up not liking me after a few days, I go back home."

"And what happens to me?"

"You spend more time at the hospital if you want to be ready to play like your friends in time for school."

Bailey makes a face that's a cross between tasting sour milk and sucking a lemon. "No, thank you."

"Physical therapy doesn't have to be a punishment, although I will concede there are days it feels like it."

She frowns. "What does concede mean?"

"Admit something is true." As if she just had the idea, Laura snaps her fingers. "You know, Bailey. You can help me with my own physical therapy."

Bailey scoffs. "What do you need therapy for? You can walk."

"My shoulder was . . . hurt. I have to do exercises every day to ensure I don't lose the range of motion."

As Bailey digests the words, I admire the strength inside the woman sitting on the floor of my hallway who would carefully admit her own vulnerability to earn a child's trust.

Pushing to her feet, Laura says to Bailey. "I'll make you a promise."

Wary, Bailey asks, "What's that?"

"Nobody's perfect, but I'll never lie to you, and I'll do everything in my power to protect you from being hurt."

Without another word to my daughter, Laura turns and heads back toward me. It's then I take in the slim doctor's beauty, her aqua-colored eyes, and determined expression—one I'm very familiar with since I studied her so closely the day we met at Hudson. She holds out her hand to me. "I look forward to hearing from you both."

"You will. Soon, I hope." I take hers to shake and am almost dropped to my knees. Another bolt of electricity runs up my arm that might have felled a weaker man.

She automatically balances herself after letting go of my fingers.

She feels it too. It's not just me.

What god-awful timing to remember I'm a man and not just a father, I chastise myself as I close the door and turn to face Bailey.

But I can't quite get the feeling of the delicate doctor's hand off my mind for the rest of the afternoon.

My daughter is noticeably distracted during dinner that night. Head down, she's pushing her spaghetti around her plate with the fork scraping against the plate. After a few minutes, I lay my hand on hers. "What's wrong, Buttercup?"

"Why can't you watch me?"

I put my fork down and place my hand on hers to still it. "Bailey, there are a number of reasons."

"Tell me," she demands.

I narrow my eyes at her imperiousness. "Watch your tone, young lady."

She grumbles, "Sorry, Daddy."

Lifting my napkin, I wipe my lips, giving myself a moment to consider how to navigate this minefield. Whoever said girls during their teenage years is the roughest time to be a parent obviously hasn't been in a situation like this. I ask her, "How do your legs feel?"

Her face brightens. "Great, Daddy! I was able to do a whole set of my exercises with Mrs. Destry."

"Just one set?" Just like I used to trap criminals into admitting fraud, I lead my daughter to admit the truth.

"Well, then my legs got tired. So, I stopped."

"That matters?" I inject a note of curiosity in my voice. Like I don't know the answer.

"Daddy, you know Dr. Rosenthal said not to . . ." Her hand flies up and slaps her lips.

"Uh-huh. And *you* know Dr. Rosenthal said to do your exercises every day —three times—if you want to be strong enough to walk without crutches anymore," I remind her.

"You're being sneaky," she accuses.

"And you didn't give Dr. Laura much of a chance," I rebuke her gently.

Her face drops. Her little body seems to heave and fall as she lets out an enormous sigh. "I don't like change. Something bad always happens."

Considering since the time she was five, that's all she's known, I can't blame her association. Still, "So, you want to keep using crutches long after you go back to school?"

"No!" Then a tiny, "Will *you* help me with my stupid exercises?"

"Whenever I can," I promise without hesitation. "But Dr. Laura will be here when I can't be."

Her expression turns morose. "Fine." She picks up her fork, fiddles with her pasta, and then drops it back down without taking a bite.

Deciding that unless I want to offer Laura hazard pay, I may need to bribe my daughter into polite behavior—good may be stretching it at first. "Listen, why don't we make a deal."

Her interest piques. "What kind of deal?"

"I was thinking a trip to Amaryllis Bakery for every week you behave for Dr. Laura." She side-eyes me, as she should. I'm outright bribing my daughter to behave for her new nanny. "Come on, Buttercup. I'm trying to do the best I can."

Reluctantly, she caves. "Okay, Daddy."

With those words, I shove back from the table. "Then what do you say? Why don't we seal the deal right now?"

"What about dinner?"

I hear Laura Lockwood in my ear saying it's okay to be tired. Before I know it, I'm pulling her wheelchair back and heading for the garage. "Every once in a while, eating dessert before dinner is okay."

Bailey giggles, and it's the sweetest sound in the world. "I love you, Daddy."

"I love you too, Buttercup." *And there isn't a damn thing I wouldn't do for you.*

CHAPTER
Sixteen

"How are things working out with Bailey?" Alice asks me as she's about to sit in her chair the next day.

I shrug nonchalantly, "I don't know if I got the job."

In all the years I've known her, I've never seen anything shock her—and with the enormity of her patient load, the drama of my family, and the hospital staff, I'd expect she would have heard it all. Yet, my informing her I don't know if Liam Payne has hired me has her missing her chair and landing on her rear.

Fortunately, she lands on the pile of throw pillows she has stacked for her patients to hurl around the office at whim. Getting to my feet, I hold out a hand. "I take it you're surprised by the news."

"Surprised? Stunned. What is that foolhardy man waiting for?" she snaps.

"Aww, Alice. You care."

"Very much."

I flutter my hands as if I'm warding off tears. "Just think. All I had planned for the summer was to sit around my backyard and brood."

She jabs a finger in my direction. "This is precisely why you would be perfect for this role."

Slipping my phone from my pocket, I wave it around. "I don't hear it ringing, do you?"

Like I somehow spelled it to bring Liam Payne into our session by an unspoken incantation, it immediately begins vibrating. Alice cackles. "Do you think his ears were burning?"

I roll my eyes before pressing the option that says *I can't talk right now.* "Coincidence, Alice. That's all it was."

"Few things in life are, Laura. Now, let's talk about your attacks. How have they been?"

I think about the few panic attacks I've had in the past week since we last met. "Manageable. I'm beginning to wonder if they're physiological as much as psychological."

She's intrigued. "What makes you think that?"

"I started doing what you asked."

"And?"

"I started by journaling about what I was doing before the panic attacks triggered." Pulling out my journal, I show her the meticulous notes I've taken. "See? Here? Two of them happened a few hours after PT."

"With another happened after you drank caffeine late at night," she mutters. "That eliminates more than half of them."

"If I can get a grip on those, at least I can *know* when the real ones are coming on."

Suddenly, a message pops up.

LIAM:

When you're free, I'd like to talk with you about Bailey.

LIAM:

She's in agreement, if you're still open to the position.

LIAM:

I apologize for taking a while to get back to you, but I wanted to be certain she was comfortable with the change.

LAURA:

I'm in the middle of something. Can I give you a call in about an hour?

LIAM:

Absolutely. I'm working from home. Call this number.

LIAM:

And Laura, thanks. I really appreciate you getting us out of a jam.

Alice twists her head to the side. "So, what are you going to do?"

"Finish this session with you and then call him back."

She rolls her eyes at me. "You'll tell me what I want to know."

"Maybe in our next session. If you're lucky."

She snatches the pack of peanut butter cups out of my hand.

"That's just cruel."

Alice winks. Redirecting us back to the discussion about my panic attacks, she speculates. "I bet even before that. Do you do yoga?"

Startled by her subject change, I scoff, "Do yoga? Alice, I'm a certified instructor." I became one during my undergraduate years to destress from my compulsive nature.

Alice wheels over to her computer and makes some notes. Sardonically, I ask in a *sotto voice*, "Anything I can know about, Dr. Cleary?"

"I'm letting your surgical and PT team know I want you evaluated to see if we can add enhanced stretching exercises—"

"Such as yoga," I surmise.

"Such as yoga by someone who knows how to do it without injuring themselves," she corrects. "I think you're getting too tense, and this will be a way for you to avoid tightening after therapy, but I want to ensure it won't cause damage."

I give thought to Bailey Payne's last few months spent in a wheelchair. "While you're at it, would you mind tacking on a similar request for Bailey? I think her muscles would benefit from it."

"Sure." Her fingers type rapidly. While she's shooting off orders, she remarks casually, "I knew you'd tell me before you left if you were going to take the job."

Crap. "Just fork over the peanut butter cups and let me sulk for a few minutes."

Without losing momentum, she shoves the pack of open Reese's in my direction.

Sinking my teeth into the first bite, I feel marginally better, though I'm not certain if it's because of the sugar endorphins or because I just agreed to some sort of direction.

Either way, I'm not having an attack.

With that thought, my lips curve briefly as I shove the rest of the cup into my mouth.

I head out to my Pilot in the employee parking garage after the session, my endorphins higher than they have been in months. After confirming to Liam that yes, I will accept the role and the chocolate celebration with Alice, my good mood feels almost tangible.

Maybe things are going in the right direction. I unlock my SUV and chuck my purse into the back seat.

Practically leaping into the front seat, I pull on my seat belt and plug in my phone. I press the Start button.

Then I scream.

And scream.

Even as I dial my father's number, I'm still screaming.

"Laura? Laura! Are you okay?" he shouts when the line connects.

"D-d-daddy."

"What is it, baby?"

"It's taped to the car window. I didn't see it before I got in," I babble, unable to wrench my eyes from the horrific image.

"Laura, sweetheart. Where are you?"

"Hospital. Employee garage."

I hear him open and slam a door. "I'm on my way. Can you tell me what it is?"

Can I? Can I actually verbalize what's attached to my window? "A-a-a . . ."

"Laura Faith. Tell me what it is," he bellows. I hear him unlock his own vehicle. He must be on the run—the same way he was the second he found out I was in the ER bleeding in the aftermath of Paulie Tiberi's bloodbath.

A security photo of which is now taped to my passenger side window.

When I stutter out what it is, his string of curses lights up the air. "I'm going to stop this, Laura."

That's when I admit the absolute truth aloud for the first time. "Daddy, it will never stop, no matter where I go or what I do. It lives inside of me. Don't you realize that?"

Sobs rip through me as my buzz drops me from the highest of highs just a few minutes ago to the lowest of lows as I realize I'm never going to get over this.

Never.

From the Journal of Dr. Laura Lockwood

Few people discuss what happened to me. No, that's not true.
It just feels that way because my family is so sizeable. In truth,
I can speak openly about what happened with my father and
Jon. To a lesser degree with Kalie and Grace.

But none of them understand my guilt.

How can I help others heal again when my own heart isn't
whole?

CHAPTER
Seventeen

THE DAY after my father swore he'd get to the bottom of the nastygram delivered at Greenwich Hospital, I agreed to meet Liam at Amaryllis Bakery in Ridgefield. When we were still in the garage as a team of agents led by one of my father's most senior employees—Al Libert—poked around my car and garage cameras, I informed him I'd meet Liam face-to-face in order to decline the job, but my dad assured me Bailey Payne was safe. "Not only will you have agents shadowing you, Laura, but this asshat only enjoys striking when you're alone."

"Agents? What agents?"

My father nodded at the team around me. At that moment, Al's comforting brown eyes met mine. I felt a pervasive sense of relief flood through me, though I'd be damned if I'd admit it. "What about the box at the house with you and Mama?"

"I spoke with the Collyer police. We're certain that was the Tiberis. But there's no note. The signature on the incident is different, Laura. I'm not certain they're the same person."

"Great, so I don't have one psycho after me. I have more than one."

"Laura." His voice is as pained as mine.

"What do I do, Dad? Never be alone?"

He squeezed my shoulders. "Avoid it for now, if possible."

Now, I definitely needed a damn cupcake.

Located next door to Genoa Deli—an epic business stratagem or catastrophe depending on the day, my cousin Nicole bemoaned due to "The loss of income this bakery sustains by the amount of begging, borrowing, and unofficial DoorDashing Genoa to Collyer!" She shouted at the family during my parents' anniversary dinner.

Nik likes to joke if anyone ever wonders where the bakery's profits went, they could either look down at the scale or at the receipts she saves from Genoa, given the number of times our family calls with an order from their favorite Italian deli to be brought home.

Since I planned on stopping by my parents after I spoke with Liam, it made sense to volunteer to pick up the "Amaryllis Special"—an order so huge it would take the guys at Geona over an hour to put it together.

The minute I pull open the wine-red door, I'm again struck immediately by the fact Nik was able to recreate the atmosphere of the mansion but making it friendly for families. Still, it's the scents bombarding that bakery that sweep me immediately into memories spent lazing around Aunt Corinna's kitchen. Where afternoons after school—and after homework— were wrapped in laughter and sneaking in bites of ganache.

I never quite appreciated it the same way I do right now. Amid all the ugliness in the world, Nik created a piece of home away from home. Walking up to the counter, I order a decaf mocha latte. "But can you double the amount of Colby's caramel?"

"You got it, Laura," Myla, one of Nik's managers, punches in my order. "Do you want it for here or to go?"

Before I can answer, I hear a familiar voice behind me grumble, "Colby has his own caramel?"

I glance over my shoulder and meet Liam's celadon green eyes. "More important, why hasn't he shared with the rest of his poor, beleaguered co-workers?"

Not addressing Liam's male dramatics, I turn and ask Maya, "Can you change my order to two, Maya?"

"Will do, Laura." She rattles off my total.

Before I can swipe my card, Liam is there first, tapping his. "I just hope one of those is for me so I can lord it over him tomorrow."

A tiny smile lifts my lips. "It is."

Liam places a hand at the small of my back, sending fireworks up and down my spine, causing my breath to be left at the counter as he guides us away from the point of sale. I dismiss the action as Liam being courteous when we stop at two overstuffed chairs separated by a small travertine table. Still, my body quakes, missing the warmth of his flesh where the warmth of his hand scorched through my shirt. "Thanks for meeting me here. This way I can pick up dinner for the family."

"Ah, I've heard of this myth at corporate—the legendary Genoa order."

"They talk about Genoa at HQ? Aren't you all supposed to be saving the world?"

"First, the team is investigators, not superheroes."

"Except you."

"I'm the one who keeps them from being audited."

"Ah, you're just *their* superhero."

Liam grins. "Second, I've been in the room when Caleb or Keene has received a directive to show up with food or not to show up at all." Christ, I wish I could lie to myself and say it was just my stomach that clenches at its appeal.

I try for dry to hide my reaction. "Let me guess—wedding season?"

He tilts his head. "Is there a time for your family when it's not wedding season?"

I pretend to give it some thought. Amaryllis Events is the brainchild owned by my mother and her siblings. It's one of the most successful event planning businesses in the United States, if not the world. "Any day that's the thirteenth or April Fools."

"So, your family gets thirteen non-sequential days off a year."

"Pretty much."

Maya brings over our coffees, and immediately I know Nik must be hanging out in the back as they're served with decadent chocolate caramel brownies on the house. Liam's expression morphs into one of salaciousness as he stares down at the sinfulness before him.

I thank Maya and ask her to pass along my thanks to my cousin.

That snaps Liam out of his trance. "Your cousin?"

I nod at the brownie. "Colby's caramel is only served with a side of chocolate caramel brownies for family, Liam. Enjoy the special treatment."

"I'm seriously going to lord this over him."

"I expect no less." I lift the brownie to my lips and take a bite, moaning as I chew.

Liam's hand freezes partway to his mouth with the brownie. His voice is husky when he asks, "That good?"

"Better than good." I nod in the direction of the small treat in his hand. "Try it and you tell me."

He takes a bite and his eyes close as the chocolate and caramel flavors explode on his tongue. I'd be lying if I wasn't a little bit jealous that a bite of brownie brought out his whispered, "Sweet merciful God."

Suddenly, Liam's ecstatic expression turns to a frown. I ask, "Is there something wrong with your drink?"

"I've been thinking about this since the moment your uncle brought it up."

I lean forward. "What is it?"

"How did we never meet before?"

I hold up two fingers and then flip them around. "Two reasons. Medical school and residency."

"The hospital kept you that busy?"

I think back over the last seven years, the family gatherings I sacrificed, the life I led for all of it to shatter. Was it worth it in the end? Then I answer. "Yes. After I graduated early from my undergraduate program, I redirected all that drive immediately into med school. I was selected to be part of the elite Medical Coaching Experience, which began in the spring of my first year. Since then, I have been working on clinical skills, presenting patients, and receiving feedback. So, I'm not surprised we haven't met before now unless Bailey had some reason she was required to come into the ER."

"Not until that night." He takes a sip of his coffee. His eyes widen, lips part. His gaze drops to his cup, gobsmacked at what he tasted.

I drawl, "Now you know why Colby's caramel isn't on the menu."

"No, now I know why you're going to laugh when I tell you I'm scheduling a conference call tomorrow to yell at your uncle for being a selfish bastard."

He's right, I do laugh. The sound comes from deep in my stomach, forcing me to put my drink down so I don't waste any of the precious drops of caramel. Wiping my eyes after, I admit, "I can't remember the last time I laughed."

His gaze bores into mine over the rim of his cup. "Maybe that's something Bailey can help you with over the next few months."

Right. I lean forward. "Let's talk about schedules. There's one day a week I can't help out due to my own appointments at the hospital."

He immediately whips out his phone. "Let's see if they coincide with Bailey's. That would be fortuitous for all of us."

Our conversation immediately turns professional, but that's not to say I don't notice the dab of whipped cream lingering in the corner of his mouth on his perfectly trimmed beard.

I do.

It's just my problem. I want to lean over and lick it clean and maybe spend some time licking down the side of his neck until I get a glimpse beneath his dress shirt. But that's forbidden from this moment forward. I'm now Liam's employee. He's not paying me—ish.

Still, the angel on one shoulder is telling me to go for it. The devil on the other wishes the bullet had taken my damn conscience out because working for a man this sexy for the next two and a half months might push my sanity to the brink.

CHAPTER
Eighteen

LIAM

I TAKE a few days off between Mrs. Destry leaving and Laura taking over full time to be there for the transition, as Laura recommended the day we met for coffee. What I learn in those few days is that Laura Lockwood should sainted.

I, on the other hand, might be headed straight to hell for staring at her ass the way I'm prone to do.

Right now, she's bent over Bailey as they stretch after they've gone through her exercises to release the strain on her IT band. In addition, Laura reminds Bailey, "This will increase the strength of your glute and your quads so when you get these off," she knocks against her lower leg casts. "You'll have better stability."

"What's a glue and a quat?"

"A gluteus maximus and a quadriceps?" Laura's lips twitch in amusement. Then, as if she was sharing a girl's only secret with Bailey, she leans down —Christ help me, even further—and whispers in her ear.

Bailey giggles.

Ava Max kicks into singing about queens fighting. Laura changes the stretch. "You and Mrs. D. did a great job together, Bailey. I'm really proud of your progress."

"Thanks, Dr. Laura."

Laura sits back and suggests, "Let's drop the 'doctor' part, if that's all right with your dad."

Bailey's eyes dart to me.

I nod.

Bailey glows. "Thanks, Laura."

After she helps her back into her chair, Laura hands Bailey a glass of water. Bailey glances at it and then tilts her head, asking a silent question.

"Water flushes toxins out of the body, transports nutrients into the cells, and helps with muscle soreness." To me, she explains, "If you've ever had a deep tissue massage, it's why the therapist is waiting with a glass after you're done."

"That makes sense." But instead of a therapist, an image of Laura's hands digging into my shoulders flashes through my mind, causing parts of my body to awaken. Before my condition becomes noticeable, I shove to my feet and duck behind the couch. Making my way into the kitchen, I call out, "I'll be right back."

Right after I remember this woman—doctor! Stop thinking of her as a woman!—is my boss's little girl. The blood throbbing through my veins and down to my hardening cock starts to ease. Don't forget, Laura Lockwood is here because her father and uncle recommended her. She's your employee. She's . . .

Bailey's giggles erupt from the living room. "Those colors don't go together! Why's your room those colors?"

She's making my daughter laugh over something that has nothing to do with her medical condition.

Eavesdropping like I'm some sort of creeper, I hear Laura clarify, "The sea is the color of my mama's eyes and amber is the color of my daddy's.

When I feel hurt or scared, they're the colors that comfort me the most." Laura leans close to ask, "What's yours?"

I show myself, leaning against the jamb and listening, curious about Bailey's answer, when the evidence on my dining room table suggests there isn't a color she doesn't like.

"Yellow, like a buttercup. Daddy and I go to the park and he holds buttercups under my chin."

"My Uncle Phil knows the meanings of all the flowers."

"Does he really?" Bailey's enthralled.

"Yep. Do you know what it means to hold a buttercup under your chin?"

"That I like butter. Do you?"

Laura's smile is unencumbered, as it so rarely is. It's a smile StellaNova captured on the red carpet in photos taken long before the massacre at the hospital. When she burst into laughter at Amaryllis Bakery at my scheduling a meeting with her uncle to call him a greedy pig. This is the adored "Queen Gore"—the adored unrepentant doctor whose charisma won over colleagues and patients alike.

Every time I think I have it under control, adding joy to the sheer force of her beauty almost knocks me away. I bring up the images of the paparazzi photos in my mind's eye. As good as they are, they don't do her a damn bit of justice. They can't capture her pure aqua eyes surrounded by a long fringe of lashes. Nor do the photos capture the way her hair frames skin that's almost translucent. "Bailey, my aunt bakes with so much butter, we consider it an additional food group."

"Like cupcakes." Just saying the word causes Bailey's glands to have a Pavlovian need for her favorite treat.

It's at this point I inject myself back into the conversation. "Buttercup, I never told you who Laura's aunt is."

"Who?"

I struggle not to give away the surprise when Laura leaps to her feet. "Hold on. I'll be right back."

I'd asked Laura to pick up a cake from Amaryllis Bakery on her way to work. After all, it's Bailey's last week of school and it's been a full week of just Laura and Bailey together. I'm somewhat disappointed to see her return with a plain white bakery box instead of the pale pink box with the bright red flowers along the side—the distinctive Amaryllis Bakery design.

She presents it to Bailey with a flourish. "That was made especially for you."

Bailey reads what's on the lid, and her eyes widen comically. "Daddy?"

I frown before moving behind Bailey's wheelchair and read the top of the box.

> *Bailey,*
> *Congratulations on finishing first grade!*
> *XOXO,*
> *Ms. Corinna*
> *Amaryllis Events*

"I know you asked me to stop by the bakery," Laura confesses. We both swivel our heads in her direction. "But when I stopped to see Mama at her office, Aunt Cori was there. She whipped these up in no time."

Bailey's hand shakes as she lifts the lid. We both gasp at what we find inside.

There are two dozen mini cupcakes. They're cleverly decorated to look exactly like the flowers I nicknamed my daughter after—buttercups.

Bailey's lower lip begins to tremble. From experience, I can tell she's about to dive bomb into Laura.

I barely manage to save the cupcakes before disaster strikes and the dessert Laura likely pressed her aunt into making becomes a stain on my carpet.

As Bailey's little arms reach around Laura, she murmurs something. I don't know what it is, but Laura's words are clear as day. "You've been so brave, Bailey. Now, Aunt Cori wanted me to remind you she can't do something like this every week, but this week was special."

Bailey pulls back. "Why's that?"

"Because it was your last week of school and our first week together. Therefore, that deserves a celebration," Laura replies simply.

Bailey hugs her again. "Thank you, Laura."

Laura presses her cheek to the crown of Bailey's head before gently pulling back. "Unfortunately, I have to go."

Before I can thank her, protest, or suggest she celebrate with us, Laura's already at the front door. She calls out, "Have a good weekend, Bailey."

"You too, Laura."

I follow her to the front door and lay my hand on her arm to halt her departure. "Laura."

"Yes?"

"Stay. Celebrate with us." I glance over my shoulder to find Bailey's wheeled herself over to the box and is enraptured by the decorations world-famous baker Corinna Freeman did just for her.

"I don't think that would be such a good idea."

I'm about to ask her why not when aqua blue eyes highlighted next to flushed cheeks meet mine. "Enjoy your weekend, Liam." With that, she leaves, pulling the door closed behind her.

Later, as Bailey and I both devour the luscious dessert she was surprised with, I wonder if the good doctor makes house calls.

I seem to have developed an ache I suspect only she can heal.

CHAPTER
Nineteen

MY HANDS ARE TREMBLING when I lay yellow roses on Karimat's grave while I tell her all about Bailey Payne. I leave nothing out, including my mixed emotions about why I took the job. Dashing tears away from my eyes, my voice warbles when I admit, "She kind of reminds me of you. She calls me on my crap constantly."

In my mind, I hear Karimat's laugh.

My finger traces over the upraised flowers that adorn her tombstone. "I know why Alice sent me there, Karimat," I admit. "She sent me there because she knew I wouldn't be able to keep my heart closed off from a little girl who was as affected by that night as we were."

A breeze lifts my hair off my neck. A silent acknowledgment from my friend.

My hand presses flat on the stone. "How could she know I'd planned to close it off? I'd only accepted that myself."

A long ago conversation with Karimat comes to my mind.

Alice winks a quick hello to the two of us as she passes by with Dr. Moser in the hospital cafeteria. The two of them are talking in low voices.

Karimat leans in. "Wouldn't you give up your salary to know what they're discussing?"

"Hmm. Probably budget stuff. She is the head of her department."

Karimat flung her napkin in my face. "Come on, Gore. Have a little more imagination. He could be telling her all his deep, dark, dirty secrets."

I snort. "Give me a break. Do you think a man like Moser—no, let me rephrase—a doctor like Moser would lower himself to talk to a shrink?"

"Probably not," she admits. Then she tossed back her tight black curls before she addressed me head on. "But Alice is like a sorceress. She has an innate understanding of where pain sources are and has to fix them. Lost a patient? Alice somehow knows. Rough day? Go talk to Alice. Broken heart? Alice is there ready with her never ending supply of chocolate."

"Do you think it works?"

"If your heart is open to it." She leans forward and beams. "Don't worry, Gore. If you ever have to go see Alice on a professional level, I've got your back."

"Gee, thanks."

"No, seriously. I swear to you nothing will ever happen to cause your heart to die." Her dark eyes bore into mine before they start to twinkle. "Unless Alice runs out of chocolate."

As the echo of my laughter fades in my mind, I'm brought back to the present by the sun moving behind the clouds. I push to my feet and stare down at my wise friend. Wrapping my arms around myself, I rub vigorously even as I make a vow. "No, my heart's not dead, Karimat. I promise. Now, don't tell anyone, but there's a reason it's beating out of control." Then I confess the truth. "Yes, I'm attracted to him. No, I'm not going to do anything about it. Why? I work for him."

In my mind I hear her say, *Only for a few months. Then what?*

Good question.

Really good question.

"Maybe Alice knew exactly what she was doing when she suggested I take this assignment."

The gust of wind that sweeps through the cemetery is as effective as Karimat's laughter. I lift my face and drink it in.

I don't know how long I lay out my heart to my friend. When I'm done, I lean forward and press a kiss to her tombstone. "I'll be back soon."

Gathering my blanket, I make my way to my vehicle. Partway there, I see there's a new "gift" on my windshield. Heart pounding, I call my father.

He answers immediately. "What is it?"

"Dad . . ." My voice is shaking.

My father curses so fluently, I'm certain they must offer a course on this. "Where's your detail?"

I look around and try to search for them. Unable to spot them, I bite my lip before saying, "Umm . . ."

"Don't tell me you can't see them." When I don't respond, he bellows, "They're supposed to be in your sight at all times unless you're in a cleared location."

"I know."

"Where are you?"

"At the cemetery. I came to see Karimat."

"Don't go near your vehicle, Laura. That's an order. I'll be there as soon as I can." He disconnects the call.

Deciding not to waste precious time, I head back to Karimat, where even amid the dead, I feel less exposed.

Out of the corner of my eye, I catch sight of a man in a suit. *Phew. Maybe now Dad won't have a coronary when he gets here. They probably just didn't see me get up and leave.* Spreading the blanket back out, I sit down and think about where to begin. "So, I'm sure you know by now someone's not happy I survived the shooting."

The wind, so comforting before whips around, tossing my hair in every direction. "If I only knew if that meant you were looking out for me or if I was meant to be lying by your side, I'd be better prepared."

Twenty minutes later, my father strides up to me after flinging an infuriated glare in the direction I spotted the agent earlier. Grimly, he shows me a picture of dead flowers as well as that note that reads:

YOU SHOULD BE AS DEAD AS YOUR FRIEND.

"Right. I guess that answers that part of the question."

My father hauls me against his heaving chest. "We're not going to lose you, Laura. Let me do my job."

Giving my trust to the only thing I've ever believed in—family—I nod against his beating heart.

What else can I do?

CHAPTER
Twenty

Laura

"I MET Liam briefly at Hudson shortly after Dad and Uncle Caleb hired him. I swear, the two of them stopped turning gray once they did," Kalie remarks while we walk around the Corbin District the day after I brought Liam and Bailey Aunt Corinna's cupcakes.

I refuse to think about my incident at the graveyard.

"Do you truly think that, or are you just trying to get me to open up about how my temporary job's going?" I ask.

"Both." She's serious as she holds the door for me to follow her into the Darien Sport Shop. "I want you to spill your guts, and I want you to know you're healing."

There's the problem I've been wrestling with all night. Around Bailey Payne, I feel everything I did those first few months as an intern—

excitement, hope, and a touch of anxiety. Emotions I recognize and can handle with one hand tied behind my back. Around her father, I felt unsteady—like I needed something or someone to hold on to.

Preferably him with both legs wrapped around his lean hips.

For a man I know from Bailey's file happens to be twelve years my senior, I'd never would have guessed it. His raven colored hair and beard hardly show any lightness. I was shocked when I discovered he has a tattooed sleeve the first week I worked for him. It drew my eyes almost as quickly as his eyes did the first time we met. It caused my whole body to shiver like the first time our hands connected in his office.

Regretfully, I shove the attraction I feel for Bailey's father aside. *Wrong time, wrong guy. I have a job to do, wounds to heal, not to mention I'd like to be alive for both of those things to occur.*

The sour taste of bile rises in the back of my throat as memories of my stalker surface, because that's what my father called it yesterday when he dragged me to the Norwalk office to grill me with my Uncle Colby present. It was Colby rattling off statistics that scared me shitless. "Over one-third of stalkers have motivations such as retaliation or rage. Another chunk base their stalking tendencies on the need for control. Only about twenty-four percent claim mental illness or emotional instability." He hesitated.

"Give it to me," I demanded.

"Most stalkers are not operating under delusions, although they may suffer under some other form of some kind of mental illness."

"That wasn't what I expected you to say."

"What did you expect him to say?" My father sat on the edge of his desk, arms crossed over his chest.

I wrapped my fingers around the cup of coffee they provided. "I expected you to tell me the last quarter are mass murders."

They exchanged looks, remaining silent.

"You have that look on your face," Kalie taunts, jerking me back into the sports store.

"What look? And by the way? How did Gracie get out of shopping with us today?" I attempt to deflect Kalie by flipping through a rack of clothes I don't see.

The question works. "One of her patient's dog ate their ear. She had to go make a new one."

We hear a gasp and find an elderly couple staring at us in horror. I quickly step in to explain, "Our cousin is an anaplastologist."

The couple appears more terrified than comforted by my response. As Kalie gives them a layman's explanation of how our cousin replaces body parts, I hear my name called out. "Laura Faith!"

I'd know that voice anywhere. In fact, I know for a fact there have been studies done to show it's coded in my very cells. I whirl around and race around racks until I leap blindly into my twin brother's arms. Jon's grip tightens around me as he whirls me around in a small circle. Something inside my heart smooths out when I feel his heart thud against mine. "What are you doing here?"

In my ear, he whispers, "I'm your guard today."

"No. Tell Dad I want someone else."

"No," he whispers before saying loudly for Kalie to hear, "I went by your place and Gracie was just pulling in. She mentioned something about an ear a dog ate as a snack?"

Playing along, I catch him up on what our cousin is up to and like us, he snickers. Loping an arm around my shoulders, he tugs me back in Kalie's direction, who gives him a fierce hug before informing us, "Anyway, she said to let you both know she's headed this way. She's already called in the reservation so we can have lunch together."

Kalie clasps her hands together and cackles evilly. "Good. Now we have time for you to help me wrestle the truth from your sister."

"About what?" Jon's eyes, identical to mine and our mother's, narrow.

"About what she thinks about her new boss," Kalie announces dramatically.

Jon pulls back, frowning in confusion. "You're leaving the hospital?"

"I'm not leaving the hospital!" I exclaim louder than I probably should. Then, in a more reasonable tone, I say, "At least, not for good."

Jon abruptly informs Kalie, "Back in a few," before dragging me to the front of the store and into the fresh, early summer air.

Knowing my twin is on a fact-finding mission, I don't stop him. Even as I earned the pet name of "Queen Gore," Jon earned the moniker

"Steamroller" from the same paparazzi outlet. All of us in the family have been run over by him at least once in his life when he was set on a course he couldn't be deterred from. Once he sets his mind to something, nothing and no one is going to stop him.

Not even his twin, who is younger by a mere six minutes.

"You know, Dad would say to play nice with your sister," I remind him once we're seated on the bench outside the store.

He gives me a crooked smile—one I know is just for family. Unfortunately, when I used to visit him at Harvard, I had a front seat to the one he'd give the co-eds to cause them to drop to their knees—sometimes literally. Jon reminisces, "Then he would threaten to take away my hot cocoa if I didn't. The worst would be if he threatened to take away Aunt Cori's desserts."

I arch a brow in his direction. "Don't make me take away your dessert, Jon. Please leave this to someone else. I couldn't bear it if you were hurt because of me." Of course, that makes me think of Bailey—knowing it was my speaking to Gino and Pauli Tiberi that brought her to the condition she's in. Which leads me to thoughts of Liam. I glance away so my twin won't notice my blush.

He doesn't reply to my angst. Instead, Jon cups my chin, turning my face back to his before declaring, "There isn't a damn thing I wouldn't do for you, Laura."

"The same goes. At least, I'm trying to," I retort stubbornly.

"Do you think I don't know that? Do you think I haven't been briefed on everything that's happened to you? Do you think I don't know how twisted you're feeling inside over all of it?"

I open my mouth and close it, the last comment digging deeper than the others.

He links our fingers. "You're a part of me; I'm a part of you. Of all people, do you think you could hide from me? That I don't know everything you're suffering?"

Rapidly blinking doesn't work. A single tear tracks down my cheek. I brush it away impatiently. "No."

"Then why didn't you just tell me?"

"Jon . . .," I begin before I give up and just rest my head on his shoulder. "Because I brought this down on myself."

"Like hell you did," he snaps.

"Maybe if I'd delivered the news differently. Maybe if I hadn't approached them without security. Maybe . . ."

"Maybe, shoulda, coulda, wouldas."

"You sound like Uncle Phil."

"Laura, look at me."

I tip my head back and find everything I've had from my family the last three months reflected in my brother's face. "It's not your fault. You're one of the best damn doctors in the country. Few would have tried to have save Aldo Tiberi and of those few, even less would have got him into that OR. You did everything right. Get back to work and let us guard the hospital to keep it safe."

I lean my head on his shoulder and whisper, "There's the reason I'm not going back yet."

"Because you feel guilty? Hasn't Alice helped at all?"

"I'm always going to feel guilty, Jon." I hold up my hand to stave off his interruption. "Feeling guilt isn't what's holding me back. It's knowing I can help make up for some of that guilt by working with this little girl."

"That's bullshit."

"That's fact."

He asks the question I've been chasing over and over into the night. "Does Payne know about your stalker?"

I shake my head; fear I'm terrified I'm going to choke on bleeding through my expression. "Dad and Uncle Colby think it's better if he doesn't. They only approach when I'm alone."

"So they're never leaving you alone," Jon surmises.

"Something like that." I give myself a moment to think before sharing, "I'd sooner die before letting someone else become a victim because of what happened that night, Jon."

He gets quiet when he picks up one of my hands with my amaryllis tattoo woven on the inside of my pinky. "I know you won't."

A bell rings above the shop and Kalie steps out with a shopping bag and a wide smile. "Did you get her to spill her guts about Liam, Jon?"

I wince at Kalie's ill-advised choice of words. Spilling my guts is the very last thing I want to happen to anyone involved—my family, the Hudson agents keeping a safe distance, but especially Liam and Bailey.

My brother squeezes my hand. There are some things that have always just remained between us despite the enormous emotional connection our whole family has. I know he won't share what I've told him with anyone, even our father. I don't even have to ask. Instead, he tugs my hair before drawling, "She's a hard nut to crack, Kalie. You know that. We're going to need Gracie in order to break her at lunch."

I roll my eyes. "You both are ridiculous. There's nothing to talk about."

"He's gorgeous and single. Of course we're going to talk about this," Kalie decrees.

Jon winces before asking me, "Will it harm my hearing permanently if I pour bleach down my ears?"

I pat his hand before standing. "Don't worry. It won't be anything worse than Uncle Phil versus Uncle Keene at a family dinner."

He perks up before he gets to his feet behind me. "Oh? Well, if that's the case, count me in."

I shoot him a disdainful look. "There's food involved. I figured you were along for the ride anyway."

He pats his flat stomach. "True."

We walk a few blocks to meet Grace at Bodega Taco Bar, where she's holding our table. For the rest of the afternoon, we stuff our faces as I try to deflect questions about whether I find Liam Payne attractive while answering more serious ones about Bailey's progress. It isn't until Jon kisses the top of my head and whispers, "I think you're going to get everything you need out of this," that I feel something inside me relax.

Something settles inside me. Whether it's the belief in my family, a blessing from Karimat, or my own sixth sense, I just feel like everything's going to be all right. It just might not be comfortable for a while. After all, I still have to face Liam Payne's ridiculously good looks when I walk into his home to care for his daughter.

CHAPTER
Twenty~One

LIAM

No matter where I turn or what I do, I can't get my mind off Laura.

I spent far too long over my weekend wondering who the man was with her when Bailey and I spotted them in downtown Darien. They were so openly affectionate with one another that Bailey even pointed it out. "Look, Daddy! Look! It's Laura and her boyfriend!"

It took all my mental fortitude not to whip my car off the side of the road, park it, and intrude. It was only the blare of the horn behind me to get moving that forced my hand. Still, I crawled as slowly as I could through the traffic filled village of Darien. As I made a right-hand turn, I observed the natural way her body curved into his on the bench outside the sports store. I should have made up an excuse to rearrange our errands for the day and driven us right out of town.

I didn't.

Fortunately, by the time I found a coveted parking spot, they'd disappeared. The pervasive relief I felt was as disturbing as it was short-lived.

As I pushed Bailey into the Bodega Taco Bar, masking my irritation became next to impossible when the same man crowded her against the back of the booth as he attempted to drip queso into her waiting mouth.

Open.

Tongue peeking out against her full lower lip.

Bailey and I sat not too far from them—just far enough to catch glances at the couple but too far away to hear anything except the good time they were sharing with two other women—one of whom I immediately recognized as Keene's daughter, Kalie.

Even amid eating some of the best tacos around and enjoying my time with Bailey, I couldn't get Laura's face out of my mind. Somehow, her laughter rose above the din of the crowd. I intuitively knew each and every time she laid her hand against her man's arm, chest, cheek, and I wished it was me.

It made no sense to my head.

Then I rationalized it. It was the amount of time Laura spent with Bailey every day. We're just becoming attached to one another. Maybe it was some misplaced sort of gratitude for the confidence my daughter was exhibiting. Then I felt the gut kick when Laura tipped her head back and a bellowing laugh escaped at the antics of her cousin and the other woman as they tried to replicate the couple's dripping cheese routine.

All the sense in the world flew out the window when my gut churned with jealousy.

What wouldn't I give to be the man who made her laugh like that all the time? The thought pops into my mind before I can stop it. Even as it did, the man whose face I couldn't see placed a tortilla chip in her mouth. Chewing, she beamed up at him as if his presence illuminated all the dark corners in her soul.

My entire body was strung tight, and I hardly recall eating before ushering Bailey out for the rest of our father/daughter day. Later, after she was carefully drawing at the table, I stood at the window overlooking my backyard. Why do I care if the good doctor is seeing someone? She's young and beautiful; it's to be expected.

My mind conjures up an image of Bailey's birth mother bantering with other agents when we were together on assignment. My stomach muscles unclench at the reasonable explanation. That moment was just a flashback, nothing more.

After all, what else could it be?

Still, I find myself pulling up her photo in my office later and asking her image, "Who was he?"

Unfortunately, much as I had no answers all afternoon, I still don't have one by the time I drag myself to sleep.

CHAPTER
Twenty~Two

PART OF MY "NANNY" responsibilities involve transporting Bailey to and from any necessary doctor and PT appointments when Liam can't make it. I give him credit. According to him, there are a few things he misses. Armed with that knowledge, Liam insisted I drive the minivan his former nanny used. After adding me to his insurance, he handed over the keys at the end of the first week. Monday morning, I decided what was the use of driving to his house in my car when we live just a few streets from one another?

I call my father and ask if my idea is a problem with my current situation. His growly, "You'll wait for an agent to escort you," takes some of the joy out of my intended trek.

Still, I wait until I spy Al and another member of the Hudson team before making my way between my house and his on foot. After giving them both a quick chin jerk in their car, I set off.

Along the way, I admire the garden one of my neighbors put in, laugh at a few kids having a water gun fight, wave at a familiar delivery person. It hits low and hard in my gut, the fact the world is still turning even after the devastation that rocked me earlier in the year.

And amid the turmoil trying to drown me.

The world's still going round and round. I just have to figure out a way to stop my emotions from careening out of control.

Instead of miring myself in negativity, I pull up the antics Jon, Kalie, Grace, and I got into this weekend. A wicked smile breaks across my face instead of guilt tearing like knives through my heart.

Suddenly, something Alice said slams into me, causing my footsteps to falter. *"Laura, life is often a series of unfortunate realities. Doing what you do, you have to accept that. If you don't fight against your present, if you accept things happen for a reason, you'll heal faster, so you're better prepared for your future."*

I murmur, "Maybe I need to stop asking why and be grateful that I'm still here." Even as the words escape my lips, something uncoils inside me that's been wound up since the day of the shooting.

Ringing the doorbell, I take a step back and note the differences between the home I live in with my cousins and this one. Briefly, I wonder if Liam renovated before he and Bailey moved in or after. "Lord knows when we toured it, it was a hot mess," I mutter.

Right before my breath and any form of thought is swept from my body.

In the jeans and T-shirt he sported last week, Liam Payne stirred my senses. Today, dressed much like he was the first time we met in a Tom Ford suit, coordinating tie, and crisp white dress shirt, he makes my tongue want to flop out like cartoons of old. That is if I can pull it off the roof of my mouth to reply to his, "Good morning, Laura. Come on in."

He holds open the storm door, and as I pass by, I get a whiff of his cologne. Christ, did he spray on L'Eau de Lick Me? I recall what Kalie said over the weekend about meeting him and wonder how in the hell my over-sexed cousin didn't climb him like a tree. *Oh, that's right. Her father was standing right there and Liam was likely involved with Bailey's mother*, I think, amused. A bubble of mirth escapes my lips.

He quirks a brow. "Something funny?"

I scan the room for something to redirect my attention to. Fortunately, I spy the collage of photos of him and Bailey and joke, "I hope you covered the holes in the wall behind those."

I realize my tactical error when Liam places his hands on his hips and it stretches his perfectly tailored suit across his broad chest. "Now, Dr. Lockwood, how did you know there used to be holes in the wall near the stairwell?" He shuts the door after me, locking me in and closing the Hudson agent out.

"I could give you some song and dance about magic." I don't realize it, but my lips curve upward.

His eyes flare before they fixate on my lips. Licking them nervously, Liam's jaw squares a bit before he drags his gaze away. Propping his shoulder against the door, he crosses his legs at the ankle. There are some models who pay money to gain the kind of aplomb Liam Payne just has. I should know—one of my cousins told me. He agrees, drawing my attention from his body and back to his mouth. "You could."

"The reality is this place was on our short list of homes to buy."

His jaw drops in a way I really wish I could unsee since I now have a very delicious view of the inside of his mouth and the tip of his tongue. My stomach quivers at how it darts out and glides against his full lower lip. "You've got to be kidding. Were you the one I was bidding against?"

"No. Though I find it interesting that you ended up in a bidding war."

"Where do you live now?"

I point past his west wall. "About a six-minute walk that way."

"What made you decide not to bid on the house?"

"We didn't have the time to renovate."

"We?"

"My cousins and I. Kalie—Uncle Keene and Aunt Ali's daughter—was in law school. Grace—Uncle Joe and Aunt Holly's oldest—was finishing her master's in anaplastology. Then there was me spending more time at the hospital than I was sleeping at home." I turn around and look for the reason I'm standing here. "Where's Bailey?"

His lips twitch. "She asked me to keep you busy out here for a moment. Tell me about the place you and your cousins bought."

I scan the open first floor and remark, "Similar feel. Craftsman, open, airy."

"You're satisfied with your final choice?" He gestures for me to follow him into the kitchen after we hear a shrieked, "Daaaaaady!"

"More than that. We're happy because it's the first home we bought, and we did it with people we love."

"Even though there are three of you, it's still a big purchase. I imagine your families were comforted by the fact you had each other."

I lay my hand on his arm to stop his movement. I tell myself it's not acceptable to pet my boss, despite the overwhelming urge to. Instead, I offer up a simple, "Thank you."

"For what?"

"For not doing what everyone else did."

"Which was?"

"Assuming three young women couldn't afford a home in Darien, Connecticut on their own, or worse yet, assuming our parents bought it for us."

"From what it sounds like, you're three successful professionals who made a wise business investment. Besides, the mortgage insurance must help around tax time."

I can't help but tease, "Watch out. I sense an accountant in the vicinity."

He's about to retort when Bailey rolls up. "Hey, Laura!"

I squat down to be on her level. "Hey, Bailey! How were the cupcakes?"

"Soooo good. Thank you again."

Liam butts in. "We froze some of them. Thank your aunt for the instructions."

Bailey pouts. "I could have finished them."

His wry, "I'm sure you could have," causes all three of us to laugh.

"Well, it was my pleasure. What are we going to do today?"

"I started a 'What to do this summer' list, and I made something for you." She glances up at her father shyly.

"Go ahead and give it to her, Buttercup. I'm certain Laura will love it," Liam encourages, but there's a tightening around his lips I don't quite understand.

"I adore gifts because they come from someone's heart," I reassure her. Then I shudder. "Except Christmas."

Both Paynes shoot me identical looks of shock. "You won't get it unless you've lived through the horror of the annual Freeman Holiday White Elephant Gift Exchange." What had started out as a joke between my mother and her siblings when they were too poor to buy actual gifts has remained one of our most cherished holiday traditions.

And our most feared.

I wave a hand back and forth. "All it will take is me sharing just one of the horror stories about our family Christmas gift exchange. Then you'll understand. That's something you can add to your list, Bailey. You can help me pick something truly terrible out."

"Terrible?" Liam eyes me like he's questioning my sanity.

"You have no idea what the stakes are."

He scoffs. "They can't be that bad."

I nod solemnly. "The power behind the gift has the potential of impacting the mood of the recipient for an entire year."

Liam opens his mouth, but Bailey's little voice holds notes of exasperation as she wheels toward the dining room. "Laura, it's barely June. You can't think about Christmas now."

"With my family, Christmas is like doing homework. You have to study your adversaries, take careful notes, and prepare well in advance for the final exam," I call after her, my voice raising.

Her giggles are my reward.

I slow my steps a bit before murmuring to Liam, "This is so sweet of her."

He slows. "She's a fantastic child, Laura. Between her mother's death when . . ."

Comfortable since he didn't protest before, I reach up and squeeze his arm through his suit jacket, offering comfort. I can't imagine what he must still be feeling after losing Bailey's mother in an accident. I try to put myself in his place, having witnessed the breakdown of such pain in the ER—how broken Liam must feel. "I'm so sorry for your loss. I'm trying my best to understand."

His smile is wan. "I'm grateful there's no way you ever could." Before I can ask what he means, he gestures for me to precede him.

I do, only to find Bailey wheeled up at the table—crayons and papers scattered around her. "Were you drawing, Bailey?"

She glares at her father. "Did you spoil my surprise, Daddy?"

He grins. "Buttercup, if you wanted it to be a surprise, you should have hidden the evidence. Haven't I taught you better than that?"

Her smile reappears instantly. "Oh, right. Here, Laura. This is for you."

Bailey holds up a piece of paper and I'm stunned. It's a fairly crude picture of four people at a table with a big colorful bowl in between them. If I didn't recognize the colors of the bowl, I'd be hard pressed to determine if there were green balloons in the sky or if they were lanterns that float on a string from the patio outside the Bodega Taco Bar. But I'm stunned when I recognize a person in the colored drawing has hair and eyes like mine and she's at an angle next to a man with an arm that looks the length of an octopus wrapped around her.

He's trying to drop something into her mouth.

Her companions who also sport snake arms—God, Kalie and Grace are going to absolutely love this—are hugging each other.

Only half joking, I ask, "Are you psychic, Bailey? This . . ."

"Happened! Daddy and I saw you with your boyfriend and friends. I asked if we could say hi, but he said we should give you some space."

I can't resist. I lean over, press my cheek to the top of Bailey's head, and scrub my face back and forth. "I'm going to treasure this for the rest of my life. Do you know why?"

She grins at me. "No, why?"

"Because you showed the exact moment my brother was making me laugh so hard I was crying, and when I'm sad, I can look at your picture and remember how happy I felt right then."

Her eyes grow wide. "That was your brother?"

I nod solemnly. "My twin brother, Jon, made a special trip from New York City just to see me. Do you know what a twin is?"

"You were born on the same day, right?"

"Exactly. Jon is six minutes older than me."

Even as Liam mutters, "Your poor mother," Bailey shrieks, "That's so cool! Daddy, can I be a twin?"

He runs his hand over his daughter's hair and says in a grave tone, "Sorry, Buttercup. That's a physical impossibility."

She shrugs, not offended in the slightest.

I point to her rendering of Kalie and Grace. "And those friends you saw?"

"Yes?" There's excitement in her voice.

"They're more than just friends too. They're my cousins and my roommates."

"Wow!"

"Bailey, I need you to remember something really super important."

"What's that?"

"You can always come up and say hi no matter where I am or who I'm with."

"Promise?"

I hold out my pinky and vow, "Pinky swear."

That's when I hazard a glance at Liam to find him focused on the two of us during our exchange. But long after he says his goodbyes and leaves for the office, I feel his gaze burning through my body, causing parts of me to throb.

CHAPTER
Twenty~Three

Laura

SHOVING those emotions to the side, I focus on Bailey's list before frowning. "Why don't you have going to the beach listed? Do you not like it?"

Her head drops, and her small fist hits the chair she's still bound to. "I can't do it with my casts."

With an impish grin, I grab an aqua crayon and write "B-E-A-C-H" on Bailey's must-do list. "Nothing is impossible."

I've been reading Bailey's re-named "Summer of Fun" wish list to ensure there are enough indoor and outdoor activities. Despite her concerns about venturing outdoors with her casts, the first item on it makes me grin from ear to ear. "You want to learn to sew?"

She nods emphatically. "I want to make a pillow."

I wonder, "Do they still teach that in school?"

"But not for years and years, Laura, and I need one soon." Her little fist clenches on the crayon so hard I'm afraid it's going to break.

I fold my fingers around hers to settle her frustration. "Why?"

"Because Daddy's always complaining about how bad his pillows are. If I made him one, it would be better for him to sleep on." Her child's logic for something that would likely take Liam twenty minutes of online shopping simply melts my heart.

I remind her, "You know I'm a doctor, right, Bailey?"

She nods. I go on, "Well, I'm pretty good at stitches, so we can practice them."

Bailey throws up her arms. "Yay!"

"Besides, when we're ready, I know an expert who can help us."

Her head cocks to the side. "Who?"

I tap my crayon next to her request to "Feel like a princess" and murmur, "Oh, I know one or two—" Or six. "People who could help us with a few of these items. Now, tell me. If you had to pick one you wanted to do today—right this minute—which one would it be?"

Mournfully, her little fingers trace over the word beach. "Daddy said the doctor was worried about my legs."

I wink at her before slipping my cell phone out of my pocket. "Aren't you glad I have connections?"

"What's con-nessions?

"Connections. Make certain to pronounce the 'T,'" I correct gently before explaining, "It's a relationship—like friends—that is associated with an idea, like going to the beach."

"Like you know someone who could suck up all the sand on the beach and move it to our backyard?" she yells excitedly.

"Even better than that. But before I see if we can do this, how would you feel if you had to wear garbage bags over your casts?"

She scoffs. "I have to do that every time I take a bath."

"Excellent." I press Send. The phone rings once, twice in my ear. When a sweet feminine voice answers, I immediately greet the other woman. "Hey, Aunt Jilly."

"Laura! It's wonderful to hear from you."

"How are you?"

"We're good, sweetheart. How are *you*?"

I want to answer, *I'd be better without the stalker, thanks,* but I don't think my father intended on that as my response when he warned me to keep this to myself. I don't relish the thirty or so people at our family dinners warming up to that thought any time soon. I ignore her question. "I have a favor to ask."

"Anything for you."

"Are you and Cia busy today?" I cross my fingers dramatically so Bailey begins to giggle.

"Actually, no. We were just discussing going to the pool. Why?"

"How would you like to go to the beach instead?" I notice Bailey is holding her breath. I rub her back to force her to release it.

"We'd love to," she exclaims.

"Great. Would you mind bringing Cia's extra beach wheelchair—the one she outgrew that you planned on donating?"

Jillian Stewart isn't an adopted member of our extended clan for nothing. "You're holding out on me, Laura Lockwood. Give it up."

"Nothing but pure intentions, I swear."

"Good. For a moment, I thought you were turning as devious as your Uncle Phil."

"That's blasphemy, Aunt Jilly and I'm going to tell Mama you said so." Her peal of laughter tells me she takes the threat exactly how I meant it—as an empty one. "I'll catch you up when you get here."

"How about two hours? That will give me time to get Cia ready. Wait. Where's here? Are you not at home?"

I rattle off Liam's address. "That's part of the surprise for both you and Cia."

"Well, we can't wait to see you and experience the surprise you have in store for us. Love you, Laura."

"Love you too, Aunt Jilly." I disconnect the call before turning a wide smile in Bailey's direction. "So, where do you keep all your beach stuff?"

Bailey's so excited, I'm certain she could levitate off her chair. "We're going? We're really going to the beach?"

"Yes. Actually, that reminds me . . ." I send a text to Grace in our group chat.

LAURA:

> Can you bring over a bathing suit and cover-up for me? I'm taking Bailey to the beach.

GRACE.

> Absolutely.

KALIE:

> So unfair you get to meet Bailey before me, Gracie.

LAURA:

> Well, if you were working from home today, you both could have come.

KALIE:

> I want a do-over. Soon.

LAURA:

> Let me see how well Bailey does with Cia. Then I'll let the animals out of their cages.

Grace sends a bunch of monkey emojis interspersed with laughing ones.

Kalie just sends ones of the middle finger.

I ping the address and find Bailey's lower lip quivering. Immediately, I think of all the ways I can back out of the plans we've made. I reach up and stroke a finger down her hair. "We don't have to go if you don't want to."

"It's not that, Laura."

"Then what is it?"

"You just do things to make me happy. Thank you." She wheels off in the direction of a closed door off the family room, leaving me stunned in her wake.

While I wait for my cousin to bring me my swimsuit and Jillian to arrive with Cia, I wonder what kind of father Liam Payne truly is. On the surface, he appears to be loving, but how could he miss something I've picked up, having been in his daughter's presence for just a few days.

A desire to return to normal.

Then again, I muse. It might be because like recognizes like. There's nothing I wouldn't give to have a modicum of my old self back before tragedy stripped it from me.

CHAPTER
Twenty~Four

LIAM

KNOCK, knock.

I look up at my door to find a man with a familiar face who shares the unique color of Laura's eyes, giving me a once-over. It doesn't take a rocket scientist to suss this one out. I stand and immediately hold out my hand. "You must be Laura's twin, Jon."

He confirms. "Jonathan Lockwood. I work in Missing Persons and Protective Services. You know, where we *attempt* to find people."

I can't prevent the twitch of my lips as the younger man does his best to try to intimidate me. Still, his eyes don't flicker from mine, so I attempt to curb my humor before asking, "Is there something I can assist you with for a past case?" Normally I only interact with the head of Missing Persons and Protective Services—a cantankerous man, Cal Sullivan, who runs a tight ship—when a past client requires an accounting for legal or tax purposes. Not unlike the one we did recently for Beckett Miller.

"No. I just wanted to meet you face-to-face since I heard so much about you," He pauses. "After all, my baby sister spends so much time at your home."

Leaning against the edge of my desk, I quirk a brow. "First, I wouldn't call six minutes a huge discrepancy in age. Second, she's there to help my daughter."

Jonathan Lockwood saunters into my office as if he owns it, which, for all intents and purposes, I suppose he does—or will someday. Hudson Investigations began as a business created by two best friends who were and are closer than two blood brothers possibly could be—Caleb Lockwood and Keene Marshall. Over the years, as their natural familial ties and business expanded, it became renowned as the premier investigations firm in the United States, with its largest client being the US government.

If there's one thing I don't question about taking the step to leave the Agency and work for Hudson, is that I know its reputation is unprecedented. It's the kind of business that will survive transition long after its founders retire. I imagine it will pass down into the hands of their children—at least those who follow in their footsteps. Much like I imagine the ultra-successful Amaryllis Events and sub-corporations will.

Hell, they'd better. Otherwise, I'll have to cope with a sobbing daughter if she doesn't get her cupcakes from Amaryllis Bakery. Thinking about that circles my thoughts back to the ones Laura brought Bailey as a surprise. It makes me wonder why Laura chose medicine over several lucrative family businesses?

I make a mental note to ask her.

Jonathan reaches over and picks up my most precious photo of Bailey. It's a selfie of the two of us at the hospital after the car accident that took her mother's life. Jonathan morphs from the overprotective brother into a warrior. Head bent, he murmurs, "It says a lot about a person when they're faced with life-altering news and how they handle it."

I fold my arms across my chest. "You ran me." I'm not surprised. I am curious as to how deep.

He continues to study the photo. "Do my father and uncles know about what a bitch your baby mama was?"

"They do."

His eyes lift to mine. "Does my sister?"

"Why would she?" I counter.

"Intellectually, you might not think she shouldn't need to."

"You think differently?"

"For your daughter's sake. Laura's going to be in her life; it's something you may want to discuss with her. She's a doctor." He places the frame down and makes his way to the door.

Just as he's about to pass me, I catch his arm. "What's that supposed to mean?"

Jonathan shoots me a piercing look before he shakes off my grip. "My sister's mission in life is to heal people—everything about them. She took an oath to do just that. It almost got her killed. She won't hesitate to use everything in her arsenal to heal a little girl—especially one who suffered the same trauma she did."

With that, he saunters out of my office. Confusion spiking my temper, I drop back into my office chair and clasp my hands behind my head.

"Christ, why do I have to share with my nanny the circumstances of how Bailey came to live with me full time?" I bitch at the ceiling. I never did with Mrs. Destry.

But Laura isn't Mrs. Destry, is she? my conscience taunts.

Giving myself no wiggle room and no solid answers appearing out of thin air, I return to work. I'm neck deep in pulling the data for a government audit when there's a knock on my door jamb. My head whips to the side, and Tony stands there. He frowns, "You were on do not disturb when I received a call from someone who indicated she's your nanny? Hearing what she said with the background noise was tough, so I didn't recognize the voice. I barely understood you have her number."

Panic crashes over me like a tidal wave. I lift my cell phone up to see that Laura indeed tried to call seven times. "Christ. What could have happened?"

Tony grunts but leaves me to my privacy as I scroll through my contacts for Laura's info. Pressing Dial, I wait for the call to connect. Panic surges through me as I think of all the possibilities. *My baby girl.*

The most precious part of my heart.

Laura wouldn't have called unless something happened.

CHAPTER
Twenty~Five

LIAM

WHEN THE CALL CONNECTS, I recognize the sounds of a crash made by the cresting of a wave and my little girl's giggle. I demand frantically, "Bailey, where are you? Is everything okay?"

Her joyous sounds are cut off. Voice warbling, I hear her say, "I think you'd better tell Daddy where we are, Laura. He sounds unhappy."

Huh? I barely have time to assimilate anything before Laura comes on the line. Apologetically, she explains, "Bailey was so excited to share where we are. I didn't think you'd be upset at us calling."

Trying to get my heart rate under control, I reach up and undo the knot in my tie so I can suck some air into my lungs. It also gives me a moment to not blast my nanny from here into kingdom come for scaring the shit out of me. "I thought there was an accident."

"Why would you think that?" Laura wonders.

"Why would you call seven times?" I challenge. My heart rate slows when I hear Bailey giggle again.

Thank god nothing has happened to her.

The sounds of my daughter's laughter fade as Laura obviously takes a step away from her so she doesn't overhear her next words, which take the wind out of my sails. "Because your daughter wanted to share her joy with you."

Her words make me feel like shit. "Laura, I—"

She goes on to say, "If there was a true emergency, Liam, and I couldn't get through you, I would have called 9-1-1. Then I would have had Tony connect me to a member of my family who easily could have raised the alarm with you without causing an overwhelming amount of panic."

Before I can form a retort to her calm, cool logic, she finishes with a stern, "Check your texts, Liam. Bailey is pleading with me to send you a few photos. We'll let you get back to work."

Jonathan Lockwood's words ring through my head. I was taking my fear of Ashleigh's actions out on Laura without realizing it. *Shit.* "Laura? I jumped to conclusions."

"Apology accepted."

I hadn't apologized, but I appreciate her letting me off the hook with her swift understanding. Raking a hand through my hair, I expound a bit, "For the last year, it's just been Mrs. Destry watching her. I knew what to expect when the phone rang."

Beyond Laura's silence, I can hear my daughter's laughter mingled with another girl's, making me wonder where Laura took her. Her voice softens into a tease when I question her. "Check your phone, Dad. I think you'll be pleasantly surprised in just a minute."

Then she disconnects our call.

That's when the pictures appear.

In the first one, my baby's getting garbage bags carefully tucked around her casts. In the next, she has her butt in the sand with her legs resting on the blanket. In another, she's squealing happily as a wave demolishes the castle she's built and soaking her suit. In every photo, next to her is a girl who bears unfortunate scarring on her skin. As if she knows Laura as well, she too is giving a cheesy grin at the camera. On the edge of the shots are two beach wheelchairs.

Laura gave my baby a gift I hadn't quite worked out how to pull off. Part of me feels enormous gratitude while the other a searing jealousy I couldn't be there with them. Still, pleasure outweighs the pain because I haven't seen Bailey this radiant since before the night at the ER—not even when her legs were taken out of the full-length casts and reduced to ones just below her knees.

I need to call Laura back and thank her. Before I do, I call out and ask Tony to come in. The first words out of his mouth are, "Is your daughter okay?"

I fold my hands across my stomach. "I forgot to tell you, Tony, but I found a temporary nanny for the summer."

He grunts. "Do you have a name for the new one so I know who to put through?"

Just then, my phone pings. I snatch it up to find another text from Laura.

LAURA:

These are better than the first.

Anxious to open the attachments, I absentmindedly answer, "Laura Lockwood."

He chokes on air. "Caleb's Laura? Gore?"

"Yes."

"She's your new nanny?" Tony guffaws.

"I fail to see what's so funny." I'm affronted on Laura's behalf.

"You would if you've known her as long as I have. She looks like an angel with the mind of a steel trap and the demon tendencies most Freemans seem to breed in all their children."

Just then Keene pops his head in as he walks by my open door. He glares down at Tony. "I heard that."

Tony retorts, "Your three are worse than the rest, with Kalie leading them straight to hell."

Keene lets out a beleaguered sigh but doesn't deny the charge. While Tony begins enumerating all the trouble the Lockwood and Marshall progeny got into within the confines of the Hudson offices growing up, I open the new photos from Laura.

These are better. They're close-ups of Bailey's face, and the undiluted joy in her expression makes my heart sing.

Then I get one of Bailey and Laura lying back against the sand, then one of Laura alone that has me willing my dick not to burst through my pants as I study my daughter's nanny in detail. Laura's two-piece bathing suit leaves me with zero doubt her curves are a gift from God. It also sets my mind wondering how her oiled legs would feel wrapped around my waist, how her smooth pussy would feel as my fingers slid over it . . . Recalling who is in my office, I fire off a quick text.

LIAM:

You're right. They're great.

LAURA:

Crap. I meant to send the last ones to my cousins.

I'm not. In no way am I sorry to have these photos. I slip my phone into my jacket pocket so I'm not tempted to tell her I plan on jacking off to the image of her in that excuse for a bikini later.

Keene's phone pings. He whips it out and a grin flashes. "Ahh. I wondered if Laura was going to introduce the two of them."

"Who?"

He holds up his phone. On the screen is a closeup of Laura with a slightly older woman making goofy faces in a selfie. Keene explains, "Laura's Aunt Jillian. I imagine if Bailey expressed interest in going to the beach, she immediately thought of calling her to borrow a beach wheelchair."

"Why would Laura's aunt have beach wheelchairs? Would Laura not just go to the hospital to borrow one?"

"Jillian's daughter is permanently wheelchair-bound," Keene explains.

"So, what you're saying is Gore worked her usual miracles and introduced two little girls who will likely be best friends for life?" Tony injects.

"You got it," Keene concurs.

"I'm obviously not paying her enough," I think aloud.

Keene chokes on thin air. "I think you're paying more than enough. You're paying enough for six nannies, Liam."

I flush. "I was desperate."

"Well, your desperation may be the best thing to happen to Laura. I haven't seen her that carefree in public since the attack on the hospital."

I feel grateful this time it's Tony who lets out the string of curses. Still, "I shudder to imagine what would happen if they hadn't taken care of the shooter."

Keene's eyes narrow. "The shooter should be grateful we didn't get to him first."

"Damn straight," Tony concurs vehemently.

"The police killing him once wasn't enough?"

Keene and Tony exchange complicated glances before Keene explains, "Let's just say, it triggered some old family wounds."

I wonder if what happened to Laura was so traumatic she won't be able to return to the work she was passionate about before. But before I can voice the question, both men leave my office. After all, I know all about actions leaving scars on the heart. I'll never get over what happened to me.

Still, I sit back and scroll through the photos she sent again with a smile curving my lips. Then I respond to Laura's text.

LIAM:

She looks so happy.

LAURA:

She is.

LIAM:

If I overreacted. I sincerely apologize.

LAURA:

Apology accepted.

LIAM:

Will you forgive me if I admit to being a little jealous?

LAURA:

Of what?

LIAM:

Oh, I don't know. Not only did you help Bailey make a new friend, you managed to take her to the beach. It's something she's wanted to do for a while.

LAURA:

Things worked out.

LAURA:

For the record, Bailey's idea was to have a
vacuum deliver all the sand to your backyard.

LIAM:

Thanks for saving my yard.

LAURA:

No problem. See you at home.

Home. I like that word. With Bailey there, and knowing Laura's going to be with her, it has a whole different meaning.

Yes, you sure will.

I can't wait to get there, see her. Reconcile the siren with the doctor.

Part of me wonders what other surprises Laura plans on springing on us.

CHAPTER
Twenty-Six

I HEAR a car slow down outside of Liam's house as I finish polishing Bailey's toenails. The tan on her skin makes her green eyes pop as much as the sea foam color I'm painting with care. She admires my handiwork before saying, "Today was sooo much fun, Laura."

"What number was that?"

"You just finished stroke fifty-one, fifty-two, fifty-three, fifty-four, and fifty-five."

"Great job counting." I blow across her toes before agreeing. "I thought so."

She squeals in delight. "I really like Cia."

I know Aunt Jilly won't mind if I share a little of Cia's background with another little girl who has been through her own trauma. "Cia's one brave cookie."

"Like me?"

"You're your father's brave buttercup," I correct. I remember first time I saw Cia, all swaddled up in the burn unit. "I met Cia when she was about six months old."

Bailey frowns. "I thought she's your niece."

I hold out a hand, and Bailey places her little one in it. With careful strokes, I polish her tiny nails. "My family is enormous, but not everyone is related biologically. Do you know what adopted means?"

The confusion that swamped her features is swept away. "Does it mean standing in front of a judge and agreeing to become a family?"

"That's part of it. Actually, if you're lucky, that's the very best part of it—announcing your relationship to the whole world. For us, for my family, it means finding loved ones no matter who they are or where they come from. Sometimes, it's people you're related to because they have the same mommy, daddy, aunt, uncle, cousin—that biological."

"Like me and Daddy," she chirps.

"Exactly." Then I lean forward as if I'm telling her the most important secret in the world, and maybe I am. "But if you're lucky—if you're really blessed—you'll have people in your life who are family simply because they love you with their whole heart. That's the kind of family Aunt Jilly, Uncle Brett, and Cia are to me." In my mind, I tack on, *Not to mention so many others.*

She purses her tiny lips in concentration, bringing me out of my thoughts. "Has Cia always been in a wheelchair?"

"Yes, sweetheart."

"What happened to her?"

"She was in an accident."

"Like what happened to me?" She glances down at her wheelchair in fear.

"Yes and no. Both of you were hurt because of someone else's actions, but how you were hurt was very different."

"How? I know my bones were hurt, and the doctor said I may have hurt my big mints . . ."

"Ligaments," I correct with a grin. Big mints. God, I can't wallow in pain when Bailey lights me with nothing but happiness.

"My bones broke because of the hospital." Her reality because of my actions, crashes me back to Earth. Then she frowns. "What happened to Cia?"

"Well, Dr. Rosenthal . . ."

"You *know* him?" she blurts out.

"He used to be my boss." *One of many*. I remember my orthopedic rotation before I accepted emergency medicine as my sub-I.

"Really? Like Mr. Caleb and Mr. Keene are Daddy's bosses?"

"Yes." Giving her a moment to absorb that, I blow on her fingers, making her giggle. "Dr. Rosenthal knows when he looks at pictures of your bones if they're going to heal in a few days, months."

She lets out a dramatic sigh that reminds me of Kalie. I snicker when she flings her hand to her forehead. "It feels like a million years."

To a seven-year-old, I bet it does. I pick up my story. "Well, long ago, Dr. Rosenthal looked at Cia's pictures—"

"He looked at her pictures too?" Bailey's grin is obviously because she and her new friend have something else in common.

"He did indeed. But in Cia's case, he had to tell her mommy and daddy she'd never be able to walk."

"Never?" Bailey whispers. Her lower lip quivers.

"No, sweetheart."

Bailey's silent for a moment as I continue to stroke the polish on her nails. "Is she really sad?"

I answer honestly. "Sometimes and sometimes, she gets really angry. Both are normal, healthy reactions."

"I'm going to get out of my chair soon."

"You will," I agree.

I hear a car pull up the driveway and the garage open and close just before Bailey questions, "Will Cia still want to be my friend if I'm not in a wheelchair like her?"

In my time as a doctor, I've had my heartstrings tugged. I always understood being a doctor was more than a career, but a calling. But until this moment, I'm not certain I appreciated that I could fall in love with a heart without listening to it through a stethoscope unless it was with a member of my family. I pass a hand over her silky hair before reassuring her, "I'm certain she will."

Relief fills her face briefly. Then she looks over my shoulder and excitement replaces the worry when she shouts, "Daddy! You're home!"

I twist in my chair to find Liam leaning against the opening to the kitchen. He's lost his jacket, loosened his tie, and rolled up his shirtsleeves so I can see the beginning of the impressive tattoo that runs up his right forearm. His eyes hold mine for a nanosecond. His expression leaves me wondering if I'm reading his face correctly because, in his eyes, I spy more than just a man appreciating a woman for looking after his daughter.

There's a simmering hunger.

For me.

My pulse starts racing. It's one thing for me to admire how gorgeous Liam Payne is. Wondering what he might think of me is dangerous territory for my mind to wander into. Shoving the image of what his face looks like at this moment to the back of my mind for going through later when I'm alone, I refocus on Bailey as Liam approaches us. He reaches down to lift Bailey into his arms when she squeals, "Daddy! My nails! You have to wait!"

"Excuse me, Princess Buttercup. I do beg your pardon." With that, Liam does a fairly impressive impersonation of a courtier as he bows low to his daughter.

I grin hugely at the haughty expression Bailey assumes. I clear my throat and get into the spirit of things. "You, sir, are late."

He gives a smacking kiss on his daughter's forehead before addressing me. "Forgive me, your ladyship. I was caught in traffic." He glances down at Bailey's green finger and toenails. "It seems you two found a way to amuse yourselves."

"Daddy, Laura put on *sixty* strokes of nail polish on me."

"Whoa. That's a lot. Do you think we should ask her to stay for dinner to make up for the fact I was late?" His bright green eyes probe mine.

I fake a yawn and jerk my head to the side. He frowns but nods acceptingly. I excuse myself to Bailey. "If I'm going to be back here first thing tomorrow, I need to get some sleep. This little one wore me out."

Bailey giggles and then yawns herself. "But you're going to miss toasted cheese sammies."

I get to my feet and hold out my right pinky. If I'm promising with an amaryllis, it's a promise I'm going to keep. "Next time?"

"Deal. Night, Laura."

"Night, Bailey." Liam follows me out of Bailey's earshot before I clue him in on her mental and physical state. "As much as she doesn't want to admit it, the little sweetheart is fading after such an active day."

"I could tell from her face she had an amazing time."

"We both did," I agree as we approach the front door.

"Can I ask you a personal question?" He slides his hands into his dress slacks.

"Do I have the right to not answer it?"

"Of course."

"Then fire away."

"You've operated on patients, right?"

"In an emergency room capacity, yes. That's my specialty." *If I ever get back to it*, I add silently to myself.

His head twists until his eyes rest on his daughter. "Why on earth didn't you go into pediatric medicine? You have an incredible way with children."

"That's easy."

He tilts his head back in my direction, waiting for my answer.

"Love."

"I don't understand."

"I simply love children too much to bear their suffering day after day."

His eyes roam my face for a long moment. I can almost feel their brand as they score my flesh. "That might be the most beautiful reason for not taking a job I've ever heard in my life."

My lips quirk. "Dr. Rosenthal thought it was bull."

"Dr. Rosenthal isn't always right."

Silence fills the space between us with shocking intimacy. We don't say anything, but the sparks between us could ignite something I'm not entirely certain I'm ready for.

Not yet.

Blindly, I reach for the doorknob and murmur, "Have a good night," as I slip out into the warm night air.

"You too. And Laura?"

I turn to face Liam once I reach the flagstone path. "Yes?"

"Thank you for making Bailey feel so special today."

I toss my hair and remind him, "That's what you hired me for," before I start down the walk toward the minivan.

I'd swear I heard him say, "Wasn't that smart of me," but I might be mistaken. I know I'm not mistaken about the way the emotions on his face made my heart pound.

Not at all.

From the Journal of Dr. Laura Lockwood

There's nothing ethically wrong with thinking my "boss" looked positively edible today, right? I'm also considering making a donation to fund Tom Ford's next fashion show, but only if they let Liam Payne walk the runway.

I wonder if Aunt Em can arrange that for me . . .

Something to consider.

CHAPTER
Twenty~Seven

"But he's gonna be all right?" Gino demands harshly.

"Despite our best efforts and a team of three surgeons . . ."

"Don't say it," Paulie warns. The corner of his eye begins to twitch.

"I'm deeply sorry for your loss." My head turns and I encompass Paulie in my condolences. "Truly."

Gino stares at me in shock before his eyes move past me to his brother. "Paulie? What the fuck did you do to Pops?"

"Shut your filthy hole, cunt," Paulie snarls. Before I can take umbrage, he's yanking me back against him as a shield.

Gino eyes widen before they narrow into furious slits. "Let the doc go, Paulie. This is between you and me."

"The fuck it is."

Only this time, instead of Paulie reaching for his gun, I'm startled awake when Paulie's toppled before he can brandish his weapon. Knocked over by a barrage of standard and beach wheelchairs, his cries of pain are nothing as the police swarm in to jerk me away.

But what shocked me into waking wasn't the fact my nightmare shifted, nor was it because there wasn't any bloodshed. It wasn't that I emerged physically and emotionally whole from the whole incident. No, it's that in my dream, all the chairs were hurled at him by an avenging Liam Payne.

It was his tattooed arm that picked me up from crawling. He scooped up a bloody crown and set it back upon my head, proclaiming, "You'll be back to being Queen Gore soon. I just know it."

I tip my head back. His green eyes bore into mine. He hauls me against his chest and my heart races as the scent of his cologne mingles with the sweat from his exertion of throwing wheelchairs in my defense.

Just as his head lowers, I snap awake. Snarling, I curse, "Damn, just when I was getting to the good part."

Shifting to the side of my bed, I reach for the bottle of water I keep there and take a long pull, uncertain of what it all means other than the fact I'm obviously attracted to my boss.

A situation I've never been in before.

CHAPTER
Twenty-Eight

LIAM

"YOU'D BETTER GET these leads off of me," I sneer in the agent's face.

Her eyes cut to the technician monitoring my heart rate and my brain waves.

The agent asking me questions jeers, "Mr. Payne, we're sorry about your ex-girlfriend's untimely death, however . . ."

"I need to get to Bailey! What in the fuck makes you think I'm going to sit here doing nothing? Christ, are you even human? Get me the fuck out of here before I do something I'll regret."

Helplessly, she shrugs her shoulders to the person monitoring my session behind the one-way glass. Then his voice breaks through, causing all of us to turn in its direction in shock.

"Pause Payne's session," the agency's director, Parker Thornton, declares. The agent in charge of my questioning jerks up her chin at his next order, "Unstrap him. I'm coming in."

I brace even before I prepare to go up against my boss—one of the most respected intelligence gathering agents of his time.

Just this one time, he has to be wrong. Bailey can't be hurt.

She can't be.

Thorn storms into the room and immediately orders, "Payne, with me."

Not having to be told twice, I follow him through the maze of deep, dark gray stone walls speckled with other agents watching as other polys are being conducted. Thorn takes a sharp left and uses a retina scan plus his voice to open a steel-reinforced door.

As if I'm being led by the Ghost of Christmas Past, I'm pulled through a vortex so instead of being pummeled by the words that changed my life, I'm transported to Bailey's side at the hospital where they fished out the shrapnel and repaired the damage to her legs after the ER incident. Hand trembling, I smooth the tangled hair away from her beautiful, exhausted face.

Only the longer I spend ministering care to her, her image fades. Her hair transforms into dark sable curls. Her lips are fuller. Her eyes, as they flutter open, are Caribbean blue. Her lips part and instead of the childish rasp of "Daddy" I'm used to following me into this nightmare I live through every night, and something else escapes. She rasps, "Do you have something to tell me?"

Her eyes drift shut. Her hand falls out of mine.

"No!" I frantically scan her face. "Laura, come back!"

I'm about to shake her when . . .

I surge awake in my bed, sweating. My heart is throbbing against my rib cage as if I've just sprinted a 10K. Swearing, I reach for the bottle of water on the side of my bed and take a healthy swallow, trying to calm myself down.

"What the fuck was that supposed to mean?" I ask the empty room.

The walls can't talk nor can they make the sun rise any faster so I can stare into the eyes of the woman who just played a staring role in my nightmare.

CHAPTER
Twenty-Nine

I BOUND down to my car, excitement for my plans with my cousins quickening my step. I promised Bailey I'd pick up some pillows for our plans next week, so I told my cousins I wanted to drive separately. Sliding into my SUV, I let out a blood-curdling scream when I twist to place my purse in the back seat.

Immediately, I order, "Call Dad Mobile."

It rings once before he picks up. "Laura."

"Dad," My hands are shaking when I summon up the courage to face what's in the back seat of my vehicle. There's a blanket wrapped around a doll that I'm certain is doused in human blood. "They were here."

"Where are you?" His voice is calm, even if I know he isn't.

"H-home."

"Kalie? Grace?"

"Shopping. I'm supposed to meet them."

He says exactly what I predict he's going to say. "Stay right where you are and stay on the phone with me."

"Dad?"

"I'm on my way."

Relief floods me even as guilt mingles with the fear pumping through my veins. "Shouldn't we tell Kalie, Grace? This is their home too." Knowing I'm sitting in my damn driveway, our sanctuary violated, makes me want to vomit.

I hear the slam of a door, the rumble of his Porsche before he answers. "No. It might scare whoever is doing this to you away."

"But, Dad, Kalie and Grace are smart. They know what to look out for . . ."

"So do I!" he thunders.

Immediately, I fall into silence. His breathing is heavy in my ears. "Trust me, Laura. You have to trust me."

My voice is hardly above a whisper. "Okay, Daddy."

"But I'm installing more security cameras around your property."

"How are you going to explain that?" To Kalie and Grace? To their parents? To our family? I think to myself frantically.

"I'll just tell them the old ones failed. That's not a lie, sweetheart. The old ones *did* fail—they failed to catch whoever thinks it's okay to fuck with you."

I'm silent for a while, trapped in a place where I'm reminded of death in a way I'll never forget. Then I question, "I thought I had agents on me."

"I'll be looking into them," he promises.

The thought of someone from Hudson being my stalker makes my stomach roll. I've trusted Al and his team of men and women to watch over me when I've been alone. "Dad, I'm scared."

"I know you are," he soothes just as I hear the purring engine pull up behind me. He opens my car door before disconnecting the call. It isn't until I'm wrapped in his arms my father admits, "So am I."

CHAPTER
Thirty

LIAM

I wonder what she's doing this weekend.

I wonder who she's with.

I wonder if she's thinking about me.

Slouching down on my couch, my lips curl upward when I recall the startled expression in her eyes the first moment our fingers touched. Would her pulse leap in other places if I kissed her? Touched her?

Took her?

My dick—in a semi-permanent state since I met Laura—presses against the zipper of my jeans. Grunting, I lift my hips and pull one of the throw pillows out from beneath me, hissing when I bump it against the cut on my hand I gave myself when I was slicing fruit for Bailey's breakfast earlier.

Over at the table, Bailey's brushing her doll's hair and conversing with it. "You can grow up to be anything you want. Oh, you want to be a doctor like Laura? Okay?"

With a smirk, I flop back on the couch and give myself a pat on the back. I knew Laura would be a good influence on my daughter. I just couldn't anticipate what she would make me feel.

CHAPTER
Thirty-One

A FEW DAYS LATER, a few more nights with little to no sleep, and Alice handing me a bag of mini Reese's Peanut Butter Cups makes me want to confess everything about what's truly causing my mental strain. I wish it had something to do with why I started seeing her in the first place, but it doesn't.

"So, how does it feel to be Bailey's nanny?" Alice questions.

I unwrap the first one and contemplate my response. Giving myself a moment, I pop the treat into my mouth and moan, "Alice, you must be broke paying for chocolate each month. Please let me give you some money."

"You bring me plenty of 'payment' when you drop by a box of Amaryllis Bakery caramel fudge brownies. Now answer my question."

I swallow the small nugget of goodness and whip out my phone to text my cousin Nik to have her hold a box of them for me. Finishing typing, I answer her question with a mild accusation. "You knew I was going to bond with this family."

"Did I?"

"You're a rapscallion, Alice Cleary."

"One of the many reasons you all love me."

"True." I open another mini peanut butter cup, and before popping it into my mouth, I admit a partial truth: "You were right. I feel more like myself than I have since the shooting." *If I could just be rid of whoever is stalking me, I'd be fantastic. I'd be ready to set my return to work date.*

Alice is visibly relieved. "I hoped it would remind you as to *why* you became a doctor, Laura."

"I never forgot that, Alice. I remember why every time I look in a mirror."

Alice jerks her chin to the wall where a mirror hangs. "Go look into it now. Tell me why you want to remain a doctor."

I toss the bag of Reese's on the coffee table and stand. Staring at my reflection, my eyes meet those of the woman in the mirror. I did something similar when I was eighteen, a junior at Skidmore back after a holiday break. I'd recently learned about my family history—our true history. The history of Amaryllis—a history based on lies, deceit, kidnapping, torture, and found family.

A history I channeled into empathizing with the patients in the ER until life was shot out in front of me.

How many of them face what you're going through every day? An insidious whisper worms its way into my thoughts for the first time. How many patients have I treated and streeted who face that kind of fear and channel it. Becoming stronger from it.

Like my mother did.

I once looked in a mirror and believed one day, I'd be able to give my talent to people who were victims of trauma the way my mother was. Now, as I face my reflection, I stare down the woman I've become, the doctor I still am. I don't hesitate. "Because one day, someone who hasn't come into my ER is going to need the help only I can give them by having lived through this experience. My change is going to affect their future." *And I don't just mean living through the shooting.*

"What's changed?"

Life since the shooting, including my stalker, flashes through my mind. "Maybe I'll have more compassion because I've lived through their fears? Maybe I'll understand their anxiety because I, too, have that? Perhaps I'll take the time to appreciate every miracle for what it is instead of lambasting what could be."

I meet Alice's eyes and what I don't say is almost more important than the words I speak. "I'll always grieve the loss of my friends, my colleagues. But I'm not to blame for what happened."

"No. You're not."

"It feels good to finally believe that."

She gestures me back to my chair. "Tell me if you've been having any episodes while you've been working with Bailey?"

"None." I walk Alice through a normal day of how I'm Dr. Laura Lockwood first, including Bailey's dreaded PT.

She cackles when I tell her about how I presented Bailey with miniature buttercup cupcakes. "I'd have let you torment me through PT for those as well."

"Alice, it's a wonder your teeth don't rot out," I remark dryly.

We both guffaw, knowing it's the truth. After our laughter subsides, she asks, "What do you do after?"

"Then Dr. Laura fades away and nanny Laura kicks in for the rest of the day."

I explain the "Summer of Fun" list, how I took Bailey to the beach, and some of my ideas for her other items. When I finish, Alice switches gears.

"No problem with the patient exchanges?"

"None," I assure her.

"No problem charting?"

"No."

"No problem—"

I interrupt her. "Alice, I'm not kidding. Everything is perfect. Except . . ."

"Except?" she probes.

I flush.

"What?"

"My dreams have been changing."

"Changed how?"

"They start out the same."

"What's different?"

"Liam rescues me by throwing all the wheelchairs at the Tiberis before the guns start firing." The words fall out of my mouth without thinking.

I should have known she'd pick up on that faster than she snatches one of my aunt's freshly baked brownies when I bring them to her. "Liam? Are you seeing someone?"

My eyes narrow at her deliberate obtuseness. She knows who I'm 'working' for. "Liam Payne. Bailey's father. Late thirties. Gorgeous. Single widower."

"He's not a widower," Alice corrects me.

Confused, I cock my head and argue, "That's not what's in Bailey's chart."

Now it's her turn to look dumbfounded. "It's not?" She wheels over to her computer and pulls it up. Exasperated, she flips her screen around to show me. "Laura, it's right here. Father—single."

I stand up and move toward her terminal. Pulling her mouse away, I scroll down a few pages and point out the area from Dr. Rosenthal's intake. "Father—widower."

She frowns. "I'll put in an interoffice request to get that rectified. Bailey's parents were never married."

Even as Alice types, my skin does that tingling thing the same way it does when we touch. I didn't want to acknowledge it, assuming he had just lost his wife in the same accident that had caused Bailey's injuries. Then I scold myself. *So what, Laura? They may have been engaged. Or what if he just abhors the idea of marriage? She still may have been the love of his life? Just because you have some chemical reaction to a man doesn't mean he reciprocates it.*

When she turns back to me, she asks me what else has changed about my dream finally ending up with the questions I know she's bound to ask. Do I remember anything new from that night and do I want to return to work yet?

This time, my answers are different, which also surprises her—no and not yet.

Maybe Bailey isn't the only one healing as a result of our time together.

CHAPTER
Thirty-Two

Laura

"DADDY'S HOME!" Bailey cheers.

Behind us, the door to the garage opens. For a split second, Liam's penetrating green eyes bore into mine via the reflection in the microwave before his face morphs into the most tender smile I've ever witnessed— that of a father's love for his daughter. Not uttering a sound, he immediately goes over to Bailey and lifts her from her chair.

I quickly turn back to cooking to offer them privacy. Sliding tray after tray of homemade meatballs into the oven, I mentally calculate the cooking instructions I need to leave with Liam so dinner will be ready by the time father and daughter have had their moment together.

Knowing that Liam will be taking Bailey to see Alice in a family session tomorrow, I want to spend a few moments updating her charts with the additional information I received from her physical therapist today. I shift out of the kitchen to offer the Payne's privacy as well as to give myself time to do just that.

Pulling out my cell phone, I dial the hospital's central recordkeeping number and recite my authorization numbers before I rattle off Bailey's patient ID. "Copy Doctors Rosenthal and Cleary.

"Bailey Payne is a seven-year-old female who, as a result of a being caught in the crossfire at Greenwich Hospital's ER, is in the final stages of recovering from multiple breaks to both legs as a result of flying debris including a partial ceiling collapse while in chairs during the events of the ER dated"—I give the date—"Patient was at the ER due to a severe ear infection. Additionally, there was shrapnel that embedded itself in the patient's skin, missing her inferior medial genicular artery and inferior lateral genicular artery respectively. Patient sustained transverse displaced fractures of her left tibia and a transverse unstable open fracture of her right."

I launch into basic charting. "Patient has undergone one surgery to repair the damage and a second to remove latent bone fragments. Four months after initial injury, patient's blood pressure is one hundred over sixty. Resting pulse, seventy beats per minute. Temperature is thirty-six point six degrees Celsius when taken at seven fifty-five am."

Pausing a second to gather my thoughts, I continue, "Patient continues to receive ongoing surveillance at the request of her primary caregiver due to her age and the extent of her injuries. Agreed upon by ortho due to significance of growth plate. Well documented frustration with physical limitations as a result of the injuries sustained, which is not unusual considering previously documented activity level prior to accident.

"Due to recent at home transition where patient lost previous caregiver, a unilateral decision was made by patient's care team, at the request of this doctor, to scale back the patient's at home therapy exercises to build a level of trust with Lockwood, Laura F." I hear a sound behind me. I whirl around to find Liam's eyes blazing into mine, questioning my last statement.

Smoothly, I continue, "While this may set her back physically at most a week, it was done with her psychological well-being in mind. Regular at home therapy was resumed the following week and is to be reevaluated after appointment with Cleary, Rosenthal, and PT. Recommend scheduling new X-rays after session with Cleary to determine advancement of whether the knitting of patient's bones permit removable cast and or casts."

At my last comment, Liam's dark brows shoot skyward and a hopeful look takes over his face.

"Request for copies of all continuity of care documents dated"—I give tomorrow's date—"To be copied to Lockwood, Laura F., MD." Ending the call, I study his face before remarking, "Do you have any questions?"

He leans against the side of the couch. "About Bailey's progress?"

"Alice mentioned she was going to drop you an email about the easing in her therapy during transition."

"She did. She just never mentioned it was your idea."

I slip my phone into my shorts pocket before wandering to the picture wall. Unseeing the photographs cataloging Liam and Bailey's life together, I ask, "Do you know a study performed by NIH showed the average wait time in an ER for a child is fifty-six minutes? That's before they're taken back, meet a strange doctor, have all sorts of poking and prodding performed."

"That has to be frightening."

"For them and for us. There's a burden when you hold someone's pain in your hand." *Or you're responsible for the pain of everyone else because you mishandled a situation.* To cover my discomfort, I bow my head before mumbling, "I hope you like Italian."

He steps forward. "I love it."

"That's good."

"I didn't come in here to question your decision, Laura. I trust and respect my daughter's doctors too much. They all sang your praises."

My head snaps up and I blush when I meet his translucent green eyes. But it's not only unwavering support I find there; there's more. So much more.

The question is, am I ready to find out what it means?

My body quivers.

His eyes darken.

The tension between us grows until it bleeds into the air between us. He takes a step forward, eyes blazing.

I take one back.

He stops his forward momentum, uncertainty filling his handsome features.

Meanwhile I'm giving myself a good shake. While Liam Payne's been slaying my demons in my dreams, I'm here for two critical reasons—to care for his daughter and to regain my confidence. Not to crush on my boss. I stammer out, "Oh."

Amusement lightens his expression. "'Oh?' Is that all you have to say?"

"Thanks?"

His lips twitch. His body shifts and the scent of his cologne fills my senses. I want to drown in his scent, bury my nose in it. I find myself swaying slightly before I plant my feet and ask, "Was there something else?"

"I actually came to see if you'd like to join us for dinner. Apparently a meatball fairy landed in my home today."

I raise my fingers and pinch them together. "I might have got carried away showing Bailey how to make them."

"Then come enjoy them with us."

"I did promise Bailey."

"That you did."

Liam gestures for me to pass him. My stomach clenches when our bodies brush up against one another.

We both still at the close proximity to one another. His hand slides upward from my hip to rest at the side of my waist. My skin is on fire, my heart is pounding when he licks his lips. Then, "Laura."

That's it, just my name.

"Yes?" I rasp.

He opens his mouth to reply, but I'll never know what he was going to say because my voice is said a second time. Actually, it's bellowed by a seven-year-old. "Laura! Stay!"

I pull out of my Liam stupor to realize my hands are hovering over the rock-hard wall of Liam's chest—as if they were deciding whether to rest against the muscles or push him against the closest flat surface to have my way with him.

His husky voice murmurs, "Bad timing."

You could say that. I thought I used my inner voice, but I obviously didn't when his rough chuckle comes out.

Still, my body protests at the kind of meat that's for dinner when I feel Liam's courtly hand on the small of my back guiding me into the kitchen. "Look who I convinced to stay for dinner."

When he moves in front of me toward the stove and I get a good shot of his ass, I suck in a breath. Yeah, meatballs are on the menu, but they're definitely not what I'm craving.

Cursing myself for not making my escape while I had my chance, but I can't let Bailey down since she cheers. Hiding my reaction to Liam behind a blinding smile for his daughter. "Who's ready to eat?"

At Bailey's exclamation she is, I shoo Liam out of the way to resume dinner preparations.

CHAPTER
Thirty-Three

LIAM

DOCTOR ALICE CLEARY *has enough degrees on her walls to intimidate her young patients and enough chocolate in her desk drawer to frighten the parents of her little ones*, I think with amusement as Bailey and I get comfortable the next day.

Alice immediately hands Bailey a bag of peanut butter cups and offers me a cup of coffee. "How are things working out since I last saw you?"

Before I can get a word out, Bailey chatters away about "Laura braided my hair" and "Laura did my nails." For a good ten minutes, my jealousy spikes as Bailey describes their "Summer of Fun." But I trip over my own stupidity when I hear how they've had a Dua Lipa dance party. I open my mouth, and "How? You have casts on" just flies out.

Alice and Bailey swing their heads toward me. Alice's face is amused, and Bailey's is insulted. With a huff, she explains, "Laura got on her knees and danced in front of me."

All the air escapes my body. I hope I didn't make a sound because the idea of Laura Lockwood on her knees dancing in front of me conjures a very different image in my mind than the one my seven-year-old is painting for our therapist. Despite the way I knew I'd be impressed by the doctor based on the file I read about her, I had no idea of what the woman herself would do to me. Laura Lockwood is quite simply the entire package—compassionate, brilliant, and beautiful.

And in the next two months she's going to be in my house. It's entirely possible she's going to take away what's left of my sanity.

I want to howl at the moon and fall to my knees in agony. This—she—wasn't what I was looking for. I wanted a nanny for my daughter, not a woman to tempt me every moment I see her in person and every night I dream. *What kind of sweet torment did I sign myself up for?*

I find myself reeling back when Alice snaps her fingers under my nose. "What? Sorry. I was thinking about a work . . . problem."

"I was asking if Bailey's had any more memories of the accident?" Alice enunciates.

Ashleigh. Fury singes through my blood as I listen to my daughter painstakingly pick through her memories. How she was in the back seat—good. How Mommy was texting—bad. Was she using voice text? No. *Damn bitch.* Then Alice goes somewhere I wasn't expecting her to. "Do you remember if she ever talked about Daddy before the truck hit your car, Bailey?"

Bailey thinks about it before finally, she nods—for the first time. "She showed me a picture."

"What did she say about him?" Alice nudges her gently.

My daughter's face gets that timid, frightened expression on it like it normally does before she's about to lie. I'm about to call her on it when Alice holds out a hand to stop me. "I don't remember."

Frustration eats at me, but Alice lets her get away with it. "That's okay. One day, you'll feel well enough to remember."

Bailey relaxes visibly.

Alice turns to me. "How is Dr. Laura working out for both of you?"

She's making sleeping next to impossible. On top of that, I might be chafed. But that's not the answer Alice is looking for. "She's terrific." I go on to explain the routine we've established from my perspective.

Alice looks at her tablet and contemplates something before broaching my daughter's least favorite topic—physical therapy. As expected, Bailey groans piteously. Alice smothers a chuckle. "Laura has ordered new X-rays. She's hoping you might be able to switch to a synthetic cast."

"What's the difference?" Bailey's pout grows to mammoth size at the word cast.

"Well, for one thing, you can take them off to bathe," Alice shares.

Bailey perks up. "Really?"

"Truly. But it comes with a price," Alice warns.

I deliver the bad news. "Laura needs to up your PT, Buttercup."

Bailey's face is conflicted. She hates physical therapy—the fatigue and weakness she's left with afterward when all she wants is to feel normal. I pluck her out of her chair and onto my lap. "Listen, it could be worse."

"How?" she wails.

"Instead of Laura helping you, you could have more appointments here," I point out.

Bailey, trusting now that I'll protect her, leans back and throws her arms up in the air. "Yay, Laura!"

My mind flashes with an image of the gorgeous doctor as Bailey yells her proclamation to the ceiling. Not long after, we're wrapping up our appointment and heading down to X-ray.

I shoot Laura a text:

LIAM:

We're off to X-ray.

LAURA:

That's exciting.

LIAM:

For you. Bailey was less than thrilled to know you're going to up her PT.

Laura's next text comes through and it makes no sense.

LAURA:

I'm soaked!

Yes, even between my cheeks. It's not funny!

LIAM:

???

LAURA:

Oops. Sorry, Liam. My watch picked up. . . never mind.

I give myself a second before I give in to temptation enough to ask.

LIAM:

But now I'm curious. Come on, doc. Spill it.

LAURA:

She already did!

LIAM:

Oh?

LAURA:

My cousin. A drink. Right down my back.

LIAM:

Ah.

Even as little blue dots move, I picture Laura's clothes molded against her. It causes a tightness behind my jeans. Just then, Bailey's name is called. Regretfully, I type to Laura:

LIAM:

We're being called back.

LAURA:

Let me know how it goes!

How it goes is that we're at the hospital for another three hours as we're sent up to Dr. Rosenthal's office so Bailey can be cut out of her casts. Despite the very interesting manner our texts were taking earlier, I wouldn't trade anything for the beaming smile on my daughter's face as they cut her out of the fiberglass and fit her for the synthetic casts. Her legs have healed.

But it's nothing in comparison to her heart.

A porter is pushing Bailey along and I shoot off a new text to Laura. It's a picture of Bailey in her new "Boots, Daddy! It's like I'm wearing big gray boots!"

What I get back is:

> LAURA:
>
> Congratulations!
>
> LAURA:
>
> One of Dr. R's nurses called me earlier.
>
> LAURA:
>
> There may be a surprise waiting when you get home.

We drive back to the house after a day that ended up being infinitely more exhausting than we expected—both emotionally and physically. I'm carrying Bailey in from the garage when I stop short.

There's a bouquet of yellow balloons tied together with little lights on green strings. They're resting on an Amaryllis Bakery box. And there's not one, but two notes.

I lean over Bailey's shoulder as she reads hers where Laura encourages her. As I slit the envelope holding mine, my heart thumps against my ribs when I read,

Liam,
You deserve as much credit as Bailey does. This hasn't been easy on your emotions.
Congratulations on this next milestone.
Soon, this will just be a bad memory.
Laura

As awful as my daughter's pain has been, it's brought this compassionate woman into our lives. Tapping the note against my palm, I'm not entirely certain I want to forget that.

CHAPTER
Thirty~Four

LIAM

I'M WORKING from home today since I have a call to take with all the Hudson principles about our upcoming quarterly audit figures. Since we're coordinating three offices, Keene proclaimed, "It doesn't make a damn bit of difference for you to haul your ass into the city if this is the only pressing thing on your desk."

"It is."

"Then keep your ass home. Spend time with your daughter. Free my niece for the day."

Yeah, I'll do everything except the last.

As I wait for the call to connect me with the five owners, I watch as Laura navigates Bailey's wheelchair to the flattest part of our backyard where she's spread a couple of blankets. I frown wondering what the two of them are up to.

Spying on them from the safety of my home office, I see Laura go through the normal physical therapy exercises. Then she grins as Bailey when they assume the same position. Their knees are bent, feet together—in Bailey's case, as best as she can, hands crossed one in front of the other, shoulders back.

"They're doing yoga," I murmur aloud.

"What did you say, Liam?" Caleb's voice comes through my speaker.

"Your daughter is teaching mine yoga."

There's a pause before he chuckles. "She became a certified instructor when she went to college."

"Really?

"Yes."

Keene chooses then to come on the line. "What are you saying yes to, Caleb? We never agree to anything when it comes to audits."

"Hold on to what's left of your hair, Keene," the other man snarls even as I guffaw. Caleb explains, "I'm telling Liam that Laura's a certified yoga instructor."

"Thank Christ she is. She's helped reduce the therapy bills around Hudson simply by teaching a few classes."

"You're kidding."

Caleb acknowledges. "Keene's right."

Colby logs in. "Must you say something so odiferous so often?"

Keene chuckles. "All kidding aside, yoga offers a combination of movement with mental focus, in which individuals are taught good posture, self-awareness, and self-care along with relaxation. It's not just for injuries, but for people who do repetitive work like our computer techs."

Colby clues in. "Oh, is Laura planning another class soon? I have a team of agents *very* interested in taking it."

Caleb's dry, "I'm sure you do," is what sets me off.

I manage to keep my voice even despite the fact Laura shifts into a move I know is called downward facing dog. *Christ, her ass is perfectly molded in those pants.* "Sorry. Right now, she's too busy conducting private sessions."

"Aww, Bailey's getting some lessons?" Colby wonders.

"Yes."

"Guess my guys are going to have to wait a while," he cedes.

I don't want to offend him, but if I have my way, Colby's agents are going to have to find a new yoga instructor. Permanently.

Caleb blows out a breath. "Can we get to the point of this meeting—not that I have a problem with discussing my daughter's incredible talents."

Just then, Laura shifts her legs from being parallel to the ground to raising them in midair. Her shirt falls down, revealing her toned abs before she lowers her legs halfway and lifts them straight in the air again.

I might have just swallowed my tongue. I wonder if the good doctor can find it for me or if I need to call 9-1-1 for that?

"Maybe there's a special form of mouth-to-mouth she can teach me," I mumble.

"Liam? What did you say?" Keene snaps.

"Yeah. Sorry. Faulty connection."

"No worries. Now, let's get this discussed. Caleb's got a lot on his plate today."

"Right." I have to reach down and fist myself to relieve the pain caused by the images of my nanny, but after a few moments, I'm fully focused on the figures flashing on my screen. But I've got a good memory.

I'll bring them out later when I'm alone.

CHAPTER
Thirty-Five

"Laura." Liam's voice stops me from slipping out the door. "Could I have a minute?"

"Of course. Is something wrong?"

"No." His face is a study in frustration as he stares down at the card he's holding. "What do you know about the annual Greenwich Hospital fundraising event?"

"Before or after the paparazzi field day on the red carpet?" The words slip out of my mouth before I can stop them.

His obvious agony causes my lips to twitch. "I take it you're not a fan of black-tie events?"

"Like most men, I'll suffer having a tie choking the crap out of me when it's for a good cause."

I blurt out, "But you always dress so sharply for work."

His head raises. Like a gazelle pinned in place by a tiger, I'm frozen in place by the ferocity of his gaze. "You think so?"

I mentally berate myself for admitting I've checked him out. Instead, I pluck the *very* familiar invite out of his hands. I have it memorized since not only have I RSVP'd myself, but I also wrote most of the enclosed pamphlet information for my mother before my life was taken under siege.

Handing it back to him, I coolly state, "Like I said, it's for a very good cause."

"Do you plan on attending?"

This is the million-dollar question I've been asking myself—and being asked—since the reminder came up for my gown fitting earlier today. When I answered my mother's call, I never expected it to be a reminder of my fitting with my Aunt Emily.

I froze before managing, "So soon?"

"It's been almost five months, Laura."

Swallowing down the panic of bullets and blood swirling in my gut, I confirmed my appointment. Now I just need to decide if I'm going to keep it. Still . . . "It's an amazing event."

He crosses his arms, his tattooed sleeve prominently displayed. "Convince me."

"Are you for real?"

"Absolutely. If I have to don a monkey suit for the night, I want to know it's for a worthwhile cause."

I roll my eyes at his blatant audacity before ticking off, "Amaryllis Events donates their services. Because my family is obviously made of miracle workers, they somehow manage to get the venue, food, music, and auction items donated. One hundred percent of the proceeds go to the hospital, which is unheard of when it comes to charitable events of this size."

"Is the dessert donated?"

"*That's* what you're concerned about? Your sweet tooth?"

Then he gives me a panty-melting smile before his next words wrap my heart in a fluffy cloud. "Hell yeah, I am. If I'm going to smuggle it out for Bailey, I hope it's one of your aunt's creations."

"Then, yes, the dessert is donated by Amaryllis Bakery, and so are the takeaway boxes."

"This event sounds more and more appealing by the second."

Knowing the department receiving the funds this year is the ER, I whisper my biggest fear aloud. "I don't think I have a way to get out of going."

His eyes narrow at me. "You don't want to attend?" He waves the card. "I would think you'd want to be there."

I blurt out, "For what purpose? For my colleagues to judge me? So they can see how much I've let them down by not returning to work the minute the ER reopened?"

He steps forward and cups my cheek. "For them to see their leader needs to be healed so she can help save everyone else."

I'm not certain how long I absorb his words into my soul. Finally, I blurt out, "If I go, I can't babysit for you so you can."

His thumb caresses the underside of my jaw. "I know a few people willing to watch Bailey for the night—Hudson employees." A slow smile creases his cheeks. "See? Then I don't have to run a background check on them. It's already done."

I can't help but chuckle.

"I like hearing you laugh."

"It doesn't come as easily as it used to."

"That just makes it that much more precious, Laura."

His fingers draw down away from my face and he steps back, giving me space. His lips curve wryly. "Maybe when you get a load of me in my monkey suit, you'll laugh so hard you won't stop."

After I've crossed the threshold to head home, I let out the breath I hadn't fully released. "Somehow, Liam, I doubt that."

I very much doubt that.

"You should just ask him to go with you as your date," Kalie shouts the next morning over breakfast at The Coffee Shop. She joined me for something to eat before my fitting with Aunt Emily.

"Yeah. That would be a great move." I twirl my spoon around my cup of coffee—the *tink, tink* sound both comforting and driving me insane.

Zane—Ava and Matt's nephew glares at us over the counter he's wiping. "You two are taking up space that can be used by customers."

Kalie, proving exactly why she went to law school, smiles sweetly in his direction. "But Zane, we *are* paying customers."

He grunts at her, showing he gives exactly zero fucks about customer service. Kalie winks at him and he snarls at her before tossing the rag in our general direction and disappearing into the back.

I observe, "He seems to despise you."

"Oh, it's not me."

"Liar."

"No, really. It's Daddy."

"Uncle Keene? Why?"

"Because he has some serious hots for Reggie? Val? One of them. Anyway, Daddy—how do I say this? Ah, yes. Interrupted his 'Me man, you woman, let's fuck' approach to asking one of them out?"

Fortunately, I was out of coffee or it would have ended up all over Kalie's suit at the way she interchangeably discussed the dating life of her twin sisters. "Are you kidding me right now?"

"Not in the slightest. Now that I think about it, it had to have been Reggie. She was pissed and didn't talk to Dad for a week."

My brow wings upward. "That's huge."

"She'd been waiting forever for him to make a move. Much like your Liam, who is taking his sweet time to dip his fingers into your honey pot."

"First, he's not my anything. Second, if I want him, I'll make my own damn move."

"Good. Now that you've shown you have your big girl G-string on, pull it out of your crack and ask him to escort you to the ball."

I completely fell into that trap. Kalie holds up her hand. "Laura, all the bullshit aside, do you like him?"

I open my mouth to tell her it's none of her business, but what comes out is, "Yes."

"And it's not residual because you're falling in love with his daughter."

"No."

"Then, for the love of all that's holy, ask him to escort you to an event you're already going to. Let the rest of the night figure itself out."

"All right! Fine! I'll do it when I see him tomorrow."

"You swear?" She holds out her pinky.

Crap. I know if I swear with my pinky—lined with amaryllises—she's going to hold me to it. Resignedly, I hold up my finger, red ink on full display. "I swear."

She slides out of her seat and drops cash on the table. "Good. Now, let's go get your gown fit. It's gorgeous."

From the Journal of Dr. Laura Lockwood

Did I seriously allow myself to be goaded by Kalie into asking Liam to the ball?

I did.

I am a mature woman. I'm a doctor. I feel pressure stronger than this when a patient is wheeled into my ER. And yet, my cousin taunting me to ask out the man I'm wildly attracted to flung me off some invisible ledge.

And I fell for it. Hook, line, and sinker.

But now, it's an honor thing. I hope I haven't misinterpreted the intent in Liam's eyes.

CHAPTER
Thirty-Six

LIAM

EVERY MOMENT I spend in Laura's presence is driving me slowly mad.

When I first met her, I likened her to a siren, and I wasn't wrong. Without effort, she's alluring—calling me to her in ways I haven't ever experienced before.

Maybe it's the way she's with Bailey. Maybe it's her natural beauty. It could be the small things—the way she always makes certain there's a warm meal waiting for me and Bailey at the end of a long day, the way she curls next to my daughter when they're plotting something, or simply the way she pushes her long dark curls away from her face when she doesn't realize I'm watching her.

Which I do quite a bit.

Today, Laura brought over a stack of magazines and a neon pasteboard, and they made a collage of Bailey's summer adventures. Laura teases her, "Don't forget to leave room, Bailey."

"You mean if I ever run into Kensington? Like that's ever going to happen." Bailey rolls her eyes at Laura, obviously used to Laura teasing her about running into the infamous DJ.

Laura chuckles. "Hey, you never know. Her family has a place not too far from here. It might happen at a grocery store . . ."

Bailey lays down her scissors and demands we go shopping when I know we need absolutely nothing. Laura and I both crack up over the normal childish behavior we endured when she stuck her tongue out at both of us.

Laura asks Bailey to give her and me just a moment. My brows shoot directly into my hairline when she leads me out of the kitchen and into the living room, outside of Bailey's hearing. Her arms cross beneath her breasts. She takes a deep breath before releasing it. "I may have misunderstood something the other day and if I did, I'm going to feel really foolish."

I lean against the back of an armchair and wait for her to continue.

I don't have to wait long.

She drops her arms and clasps her fingers together, twisting them anxiously. "It came across . . . I don't know. I might have misunderstood. Maybe you were just looking for some information, but . . ."

I straighten, giving her my full attention, hoping against all hope she's talking about what I think she is.

She blurts out, "Were you trying to see if I was interested in going to the charity ball with you?"

"Yes." The word is succinct and immediate.

She continues on, obviously not hearing my answer. "Because if you weren't, that's okay. I'll see you there—if you're going, that is."

I step forward and press a finger to her lips. "Laura, I said yes. That was my out-of-practice, very lame attempt to ascertain if you'd be interested in going to the ball with me."

Her lips pucker beneath my finger. I don't want my finger in the way; I want to capture her lips beneath mine.

Still, I can't prevent mine from twitching. I lift my finger away and ask her solemnly. "Dr. Lockwood, I know your family is running the event, and your presence is probably mandatory, but I'd truly enjoy the pleasure of your company to an event I believe means a great deal to both of us."

That's when my heart stops. Laura smiles fully at me. Not because of the fact we're sharing a moment about my daughter or we're laughing about the antics of her family.

She's smiling at me because of me. My heart notes every muscle movement, every crinkle of skin around her eyes.

Christ, she's magnificent.

"I accept. I would be honored to attend with you." Then she laughs a full-throated laugh.

I cock my head to the side. "What's so funny?"

Long sooty eyelashes lower. When they raise, her eyes are sparkling with laughter. "I'm just wondering if this counts as 'asking' you to the ball. Otherwise, my cousin is going to demand a redo at a later date because I boggled the job so completely."

I grin down at her upturned face. "You completely boggled it."

Her words are slightly breathless. "Why don't we see how the first date goes?"

With that, she turns to head back into the kitchen, back to Bailey. I stand there, motionless, watching the sway of her movement. *Oh, I know how the date is going to go.*

It's going to be perfect.

CHAPTER
Thirty-Seven

LAYING IN BED THAT NIGHT, I can't escape thoughts of her—the way her dark hair swished against her T-shirt as she walked away, the way her shorts clung to perfect legs. Her adorable way she was trying to determine if I was interested—as if there was a man foolish enough on the planet who wouldn't be?

But what's completely snuck up on me is her caring nature. The amount of small things she does to show Bailey she cares for her, for me, is something neither of us has experienced.

My parents might have loved Bailey differently than they loved me, but that's something neither of us will know. Even Larry, who I'd consider the closest thing to a father figure never had the chance to love Bailey. Then there was the crap Ashleigh pulled—leaving Bailey almost as wary of bonding as I was, which is why she took Mrs. Destry leaving so hard.

Never before have I had someone to share small moments with. Then, I met Laura. And almost immediately, everything changed in the best kind of way. She's shown both Bailey and me that it's not too late to open our lives and let others in. Something I might have said was an impossibility before her.

I chuckle aloud in the silence of my room. If she only knew the amount she infiltrates my thoughts at night. I stare at the shadows on the wall. They shift in such harmony, all I can think of is how her body would move with mine. Would our shadows move just like that if I were to slide my hand into the back of her hair? Pin her body against mine for a kiss?

My hand drops beneath the sheets and I grip the base of my cock hard so I don't spill my seed. Shifting my boxers down to my thighs, I begin lazily stroking my cock, drawing harder on the upstroke until a small bead of fluid appears.

Another stroke, two. I lazily swipe my thumb over the head, spreading it around to lubricate myself.

I shift my legs apart, wondering what Laura would think if she knew she had me so tied up in knots, I was jerking off to thoughts of her.

My hips thrust upward as I remember the feel of her sweet body pressed up against mine the night I asked her to stay for dinner.

Then there was yoga and the way her body bent. My other hand joins in on the occasion, squeezing my balls on my next pull. I shudder, knowing I'm not going to last long.

I close my eyes and recall her lips against my finger and how much I wanted to drag that finger down over her neck to one of her perfect breasts. Play with the nipple until it budded beneath my fingers.

I release my balls to fist the sheet next to my hips, which are now pistoning as I stroke hard.

My hands gripping her hips.

My mouth lowering to hers.

My dick sinking into her warmth . . .

My cock explodes onto my stomach and hands as my breath rasps harshly in the empty room. I stretch my arm to the side and grab a wad of tissues to clean up the majority of the mess. Once I'm certain my cum isn't going to drip on the floors, I make my way into the bathroom and wipe myself down with a warm washcloth.

Staring into the mirror, I know I've only taken off the initial ache. Until I have Laura spread beneath me, fulfillment is going to be empty. Making my way back to my bed, I flop back onto the mattress, cursing my pillows viciously.

"I really need to do something about those before Laura sleeps here," I mutter aloud, allowing my thoughts to travel to how well Laura would fit curled against my side. Hell, she fits beautifully with both of us—Bailey and I as a unit.

There's something healing in her touch. Her touch, which has only barely skimmed mine, has dug down deep. The good doctor trying to mend broken pieces of what's left of my heart? Maybe.

Jonathan Lockwood's words float through my mind. *"My sister's mission in life is to heal people. She took an oath to do just that. It almost got her killed."*

A surge of protectiveness wells inside me. The rough edges of my heart, which haven't fit together correctly in years, try to align themselves but can't quite do it. They need someone to smooth them.

Could she be the one to do that? Or maybe she doesn't see me as a man, just as Bailey's father. I scowl. What has she done to show me I might mean more than being a patient's father?

On that less-than-cheerful thought, I punch my hated pillow and try to find sleep.

I welcome when Laura follows me there.

CHAPTER
Thirty-Eight

My knees are tucked against my chest as I sit up in bed in my room. I wrap my arms around my legs and stare out the window into the night, resting my chin against my knees.

I'm not afraid of sleep, nor was I woken by panic.

It was something completely unexpected—an undiluted desire for Liam Payne.

When he infiltrated my dreams tonight, it wasn't to save me. It was to tempt me. His smooth hand over my bare shoulder, slipping the thin silk strap of my camisole off my shoulder before his mouth trailed behind it.

His mouth slipped over one pebbled nipple before his tongue pressed it against the roof of his mouth and he suckled.

Hard.

I moaned aloud, jerking myself awake. Holy hell, it wasn't just my heart throbbing. I could almost feel his heart synchronizing against mine, the power of the blood rushing through our veins.

Desire.

I'm not so foolish I haven't caught the occasional glances he's tried to hide from Bailey, from me. The banked heat in his gaze when I've turned my head and caught him admiring my body.

But what has me awake is the fact there is more than my own pleasure at stake. There's the trust of a seven-year-old girl on the line and the fact the last time I didn't do my job properly, someone got hurt.

So for now, I'll ignore it. I care too much about Bailey's happiness and well-being for what could be nothing more than an inappropriate lust for her father. I just need to let the quivers racing through my body caused by my dream pass. Then I'll try to capture a few more hours of sleep before I face them both again.

I'm just uncertain how much longer I'll be able to hide how I'm beginning to feel.

Then, just as I'm about to be lulled back to sleep, I scream.

And scream.

An hour later, I'm being held by my father even as I confess to Uncle Keene, "I've never been so grateful Kalie and Grace are out for the night with dates as I am right now."

That's because when I was home alone, a dark-haired doll, dressed in scrubs, meticulous down to the tiny hole in the upper left shoulder, was lowered down to my window.

It had a noose around its neck.

My stalker hasn't gone anywhere. They've just been quiet.

Waiting.

Uncle Keene glares at my father. "What the fuck is going on?"

My father stubbornly remains silent.

"Speak. Now," Uncle Keene orders.

Reluctantly, my father does, starting with the incident at the house before I returned home. My uncle glares at him. "You're now just telling me about this?"

"Colby knew."

That enrages Uncle Keene more. "And you didn't bother to tell me? Are you crazy, Caleb?"

"I'm trying to keep my daughter safe, and you damn well know you'd do the same thing."

That freezes Uncle Keene's fury for the moment. His eyes narrow on my father before he hisses, "Do you have any leads?"

But my father is too busy comforting me to answer. As for me, I'm too busy being terrified to do more than beg my father to make them go away.

He swears it's almost over.

I hope, for both our sakes, it's the truth.

CHAPTER
Thirty~Nine

LIAM

"DADDY, WHAT ARE YOU DOING?" Bailey wonders.

Drinking a mug of coffee, I lift it in her direction.

She giggles. "It looks like you're waiting for Laura."

Busted. Placing the mug on the counter, I assume a serious expression. "Maybe I just want to know what you two are doing today?"

"No!" Bailey shrieks.

"Hmm, now, isn't this interesting. Are you two planning on letting monkeys into our house?"

Bailey giggles. "Nope."

"What about building a swimming pool?" Pretending to be affronted, I jab my hands on my hips. "Are you tearing down the house today?"

Bailey is outright belly laughing when I spy Laura coming up the walk. Pretending a nonchalance I don't feel, I say, "Well, if I can't get it out of you, I'll get it from your partner in crime."

Instead of waiting for her to use her key, I fling open my front door before Laura can open it. She's carrying an enormous backpack. I frown even as she sidesteps me. Hurt and confusion drip into my blood until I see her wink at Bailey, who giggles. I drawl, "That's a mighty large bag, Dr. Lockwood. Going somewhere after work?"

She swings it off her shoulder. It almost floats to the floor like a bundle of feathers. My frown snaps into place. It didn't make as much noise as I thought it should.

Laura replies, "Actually, it's holding the key element of today's Summer of Fun activity. I just needed a bag large enough to get it here."

I give the backpack a once over. "You know I'm dying to see what's in there."

That's when I'm given an unexpected gift to send me on my way to work —Laura Lockwood's full-throated laughter. She holds up her three fingers in a Girl Scout salute. "I promised on my honor I wouldn't tell you a thing.

Now I'm really curious. My lips purse. "What shenanigans are you two up to?

Laura rolls her eyes, clearly not intimidated in the least. "The only thing I'll assure you of is there's no water involved in today's activities."

Stalking her around the room, I manage to get her body pressed against the wall. I lean my forehead against hers. "Good morning."

"Hi." She smiles at me.

I cup her cheek, noticing the fatigue beneath them. "Did you sleep okay?"

"I had some . . . interesting interruptions."

"Dreams?"

She shrugs. "You?"

My cheeks catch fire. "I'll tell you mine if you tell me yours."

Her eyes flash. "Well, that sounds interesting. I'm game."

I'm about to start grilling her when we hear the squeak of Bailey's wheelchair. Laura and I spring apart just before Bailey rolls up. "Laura! Does that have everything?"

"Most of it."

Bailey glances up at me anxiously. "You didn't tell Daddy, did you?"

Laura casts her sea-colored eyes at me in a smoldering look that makes my dick hard as a rock. "You said you wanted it to be a surprise. Of course, I didn't tell him."

While I love the fact Bailey is getting along so well with Laura, I feel I need to interject, "Do I need to approve this project? I mean, there's no Devil's Dust involved?"

Bailey snickers before translating. "He means glitter."

Again, I'm rewarded—this time with her unencumbered smile. "Since that's a banned substance in everything but our holiday gift exchange—"

"I really want to hear more about this gift exchange," I interrupt.

She kisses the back of her fingers and rubs them against her shirt. "I can explain better than the others."

"Oh, you think so?" I challenge—hell, who am I kidding. I'm outright flirting in front of my daughter.

"Well, since I've won the last four years in a row and have no plan on losing anytime soon, I'd say yes." Her voice holds a smugness I want to wipe off any way I can—preferably with my mouth.

Still, I reiterate my most critical criteria for today: "No glitter."

She vows, "I swear, no glitter—that I'm aware of."

"That you're aware of?" This is not reassuring.

"Bailey's taking the lead on certain aspects of today's adventure," Laura informs me.

Bailey, meanwhile, is bouncing in her chair in excitement, leaving me with no choice but to give one last warning. "Don't hurt yourselves. Have fun. Stay out of the ER."

Laura moves next to Bailey before lifting her amused eyes to meet mine. "You do realize you hired the ER to be Bailey's companion?"

Bailey nods furiously. "Still, we promise. We'll be too busy working on—"

"Bailey," Laura stops her from spilling the secret.

"Right. Bye, Daddy."

Laura smirks. "Bye, Daddy."

With a wink at both of them and praying to God I can walk without spraining my dick, I leave them to it. Still, from the moment I start my car's engine and back out of the driveway, I mentally count down the hours until I can get back to find out what this huge surprise is.

CHAPTER

Forty

I WAIT for the garage door to close before I reach for my backpack. Confidentially, I share, "I bought three kinds of pillows."

"Can I see them?"

"Sure. We need to let them fluff a bit before my aunt gets here." I pull the backpack closer. I'm grateful I knew I'd have another use for it someday since the last time I used it was when Jon graduated Harvard, and I had a few weeks off after my first year of medical school. The two of us left everyone and everything behind touring Europe together, cementing our twin bond as we experienced European history, hit the bars, all while traveling on the Eurail.

"How did you get three pillows in there, Laura? It's like Hermione's bag."

Loving the Harry Potter reference, I explain to her the trip. Wistfully, she looks down at her legs before looking at the bag. "That sounds like a lot of fun."

"What? A vacation?"

She nods.

"Have you ever told your dad you want to go on a vacation?"

"No."

"Why not?" I ask, reaching inside for the first pillow.

That's when she throws my heart into a tailspin about the man I've been becoming more and more entranced with. "What if he decides he doesn't want me around all the time anymore? He can't send me back home to Mommy, Laura. What will I do?"

My insides curdle and my voice is icy. "Excuse me?"

She frantically tries to explain. "I . . . I didn't mean to say anything, Laura."

I pull her out of her wheelchair and into my arms. "You can talk to me, Bailey."

"Do you have to tell Daddy?"

"I might." *And I might have to kill him if he doesn't reassure me*, I think viciously.

Bailey's expression is panicked.

"But it's only to help you, Bails."

Her eyes well with tears before she whispers—as if she's confessing something. And maybe she is. "S-sometimes m-my M-mommy u-used to scream at me."

I smooth a hand up and down her back. "What kind of things?"

"T-that I r-ruined her l-life."

What kind of woman was Liam Payne in love with? Fury surges through my veins when she goes on in a broken voice, "I-I n-need to s-show h-him I-I'm a g-good girl."

My heart is struggling so hard to beat, I wonder if I'm about to trigger an arrhythmia. *How did Liam end up creating such a beautiful child with such a complete bitch?*

Knowing I've been "let in," I tread carefully like I would with any ER patient. "You don't want me telling Daddy?"

Her head shakes frantically.

"I need to share this with Alice though, Bailey. Plus, I think your daddy would be sad if he didn't know you were going to be talking about it first."

Her lower lip quivers. "You *certain* he won't want to g-give me away?"

"How about if he does, you call me?" *I'll take care of you.*

She nods imperceptibly. Instead of forcing the issue or upsetting Bailey's precarious trust, I hold on to her while I try to resume our normal activities. *Screw PT. Mending Bailey's heart is much more important today*, I think furiously. Tugging out the third of the three pillows and laying them out on the couch, I explain why I got three. "Since I didn't know what kind of pillow he likes, I got a soft, a medium, and a firm." Before she can ask me any questions, I push to my feet, lifting her back into her chair. "Bailey, I need to make a quick phone call before someone gets here. Why don't you feel how squishy they are and tell me which one *you* like best?"

"Okay, Laura!" she agrees, some of her natural joy returning now that I've let the subject drop.

I stride into the attached sunroom, close the door so I won't be overheard, but also to keep an eye on her, before I dial a number I know by heart. I leave a message with Alice's PA for her to call me back as soon as possible. Then I dial a second number—one he made me memorize immediately after I learned my home telephone number. The second ring doesn't even process before my father picks up. "Everything okay, Laura?"

"Hey, Daddy." My voice sounds broken even to my own ears.

"What's wrong?"

"I need you to answer something without thinking and without details."

"You know I can't agree to that unless I hear the question," he scolds me gently, his breathing coming easier knowing I'm not about to tell him my stalker has escalated.

"Fine. Does Liam Payne love his daughter?"

"As much as I love you."

Warmth steals through me at those words. "That's all I needed to know."

"You do plan on discussing the reason behind that with the individual himself later?" His hard tone brooks no argument.

I spy Bailey as she hugs one pillow after another to her chest. "Yes, Dad. It was just something she said that hit me the wrong way." *A very wrong way.*

"I suspect I have an idea of what that might be about. Have that conversation. Sooner rather than later."

I pause before I read between my father's ambiguousness. "Liam's right there, isn't he?"

"You're so smart; it would be scary if it wasn't used for good."

"Dad?"

"Yes?"

"I love you."

"I loved you first."

"I know. I've always known that. I was just reminded—again—how blessed I was growing up knowing that all of us knew love."

Before he can say anything else, I hear the peal of a doorbell. "Let me let you go."

I dash my fingers beneath my eyes and call to Bailey that I'll get the door. On the way to open the door for my Aunt Emily, I think about my family's past. Because of their sacrifices, I grew up with love. I was surrounded by family. I knew there wasn't anything we wouldn't do for one another.

It wasn't just them who was cursed, apparently.

After peeking through the peephole, I open the door and find my arms filled with a beautiful woman with corkscrew blond curls.

Even as I'm being squeezed to death, I call out, "Bailey, my Aunt Em is here."

Bailey wheels up to us to find the ever-stylish Em next to me. She beams. "You're going to help me make a pillow for my daddy?"

"Right after you tell us what colors the pillows should be," I confirm.

"Green. The color of Daddy's room is green."

Like his eyes? I wonder, but I don't say that aloud. Instead, I keep silent when Em proclaims, "Then let's go out to my van to pick some green fabric."

Bailey's gaze flits between the two of us. "How will I know if it's right?"

I think back to all the gifts of pottery, drawings, and bracelets I've made for my father over the years that he's displayed proudly. I give her the truth. "How could it be wrong if it's coming from you and made with love?"

Bailey beams and Emily nods her approval. The three of us make our way to Emily's van parked in Liam's driveway to pick the green Bailey likes best from the selection Emily brought with her.

"Does your father have any special nicknames for you, Bailey?" Emily casually asks.

"Buttercup." Bailey goes on to explain what she and her father do in the park with the buttercups that blossom all over the fields in Connecticut.

"Hmm. What would you think if I did this?" Emily pulls out a notebook and sketches a simple flower that no one would mistake for anything but a buttercup.

Bailey frowns. "Do you draw it on the pillow with crayons or markers?"

Emily's smile blooms as bright as the yellow flowers. I interject, "I think she means she'll stitch it on, Bailey."

"Using a needle? But won't that take a long time?"

Emily picks up a piece of light wool that caught my eye earlier. I had been debating asking Emily if she'd make a dress for Bailey, but this has so much more meaning. A little girl will grow out of an Emily Freeman Original, but a father will never let go of a pillow that reminds him of his little girl.

Never.

Not if he loves her the way my father claims he does.

Emily quickly threads her machine with green thread shades darker than the material and gets to work. All the while, she entertains us by chatting about her granddaughter Hannah's latest exploits. Hannah was the first grandchild born in any branch of our family tree. Now fourteen, she laughingly jokes, "I don't know what I want to be when I grow up. A doctor, a lawyer, or chief executive officer—like Aunt Cass."

"Do you know what you want to be when you grow up, Bailey?" I ask.

Her brows pucker before she gives an answer that has Em discreetly wiping her eyes before she focuses on her embroidery. It's the best answer of all. "Happy. I want to be happy."

My own voice raspy, I acknowledge her plans. "Excellent. After all, why would you want to be anything else?"

"Exactly."

After lifting her foot off the pedal, Emily's navy blue eyes catch mine. In them, I find approval for the lessons I'm imparting to Bailey, but there is lingering worry for me. After all, like the rest of our family, she knows the hardest emotions to recover from are the ones we treasure the most—the basic human right to safety and trust.

CHAPTER
Forty~One

LIAM

"That was Laura?" I ask Caleb.

He lays his cell phone down before gesturing for me to sit. "You overheard everything I said."

"I did."

"Then you should also know my daughter's question to me was, 'Does Liam Payne love his daughter?'" Before I can fly off the handle between the hurt and betrayal coursing through my veins, Caleb lifts his hand and pins me into my seat with his tiger's eyes. "Her voice was breaking when she asked. That leads me to believe Bailey said something in casual conversation to Laura that has her protective instincts in an uproar."

Goddamn you, Ashleigh, I think not for the first time in the last two years. Even as my blood pressure drops with regard to Laura's curiosity, I have to admit it springs from a place of caring. *Unlike Bailey's bitch of a mother.*

My senses have been telling me something is going on with Bailey for a while, but even my constant love and sessions with Alice haven't been able to inveigle it. If Laura managed to, I'm not certain what I'm going to do—punch a wall or kiss her.

Maybe both.

Caleb speaks. I tune back in to listen. "She's not jumping to any sort of conclusion. All she wanted to know was if Bailey was loved. If she knows you love your daughter the way I love mine, she doesn't need the gritty details."

I surge to my feet and stare out the one-way glass at the analysts operating in the Norwalk office. "What could Bailey have said to her, Caleb?"

He holds up his hands in surrender. "That's between the two of you to discuss."

Great. Something to look forward to when I get home, I think sarcastically.

"For now, explain to me what you found out about the Tiberis money and how it relates to Hudson Investigations." Caleb's voice hardens.

Uncertain if Caleb receiving the information will compromise any chain of evidence we may eventually have to provide to the DA, I move my chair forward and begin doing what I do best—analyzing facts and figures and coming out with the correct conclusion with little to no emotion. "There's money being deposited from the Tiberis into an account of a man named Alfredo Tiberi."

"Why the fuck do I care about that?"

"This is a picture of the man identified as Alfredo Tiberi." I open a folder and slide a photograph I printed out across the table.

Caleb's face notably pales as he stares down at the image. Then he shocks me by ordering, "Get out."

"Excuse me?"

"I have to contact Keene. Now."

My breath releases when his words right my unease. That makes sense. As Hudson Investigations corporate lawyer, Keene Marshall will fricassee anyone trying to mess with what he considers his.

Especially someone who might be hiding in plain sight within our own Missing Person and Protective Services Division.

The sun is just beginning to set when I pull into my garage. I lay my head on the steering wheel, trying to gather the strength to face the inquisition I'm certain is waiting for me, not that I haven't endured a day of hell of Caleb's follow up questions.

How did you trace this? How do you know for sure it's him? Will it be admissible in court?

Finally, I snapped, "If you think you can do it better, Caleb, do it your damn self."

He backed off. Now, I'm about to face the man's daughter.

What am I supposed to say? The truth? Other than the polygrapher, Parker, and the team at Hudson, the only other person who knew the truth about why I never met my own daughter until so late in life is dead.

The rest just believe I didn't have sole custody of Bailey until she was five, I think wearily.

Not a lie, not the full story.

I open the door between the garage and the kitchen and expect to face the Spanish Inquisition. Instead, I'm assaulted by smells that cause my stomach to rumble rather loudly. Two females burst into giggles. Ruefully, I walk straight to Bailey and hug her. "See what happens when Daddy misses lunch?"

"Your tummy makes super loud noises?"

"They're actually called borborygmi," Laura educates us both.

"Borogami?" Bailey tries to repeat.

Laura winks at her from where she's stirring what I can only assume is dinner on the stove. "Close enough, Bailey. You'd be impressed, Liam. She worked hard today."

I loosen my tie. "Oh? What was your Summer of Fun project today?"

Bailey's face becomes anxious. She darts a glance in Laura's direction, who sends her a reassuring one in return. "Go on, Bailey."

My daughter blurts out, "You said you didn't like your pillow."

I slide a hand down Bailey's cheek before confirming for Laura's sake. "She's right. I hate my pillows."

Laura turns away from us but still asks, "What did we do today, Bailey?"

I crouch down until I'm at eye level with my daughter. "What did you do, Buttercup?"

"We made you a new pillow!" Bailey announces triumphantly.

I'm stunned. "You did?"

She bounces in her chair. "Surprise!"

I look around, expecting to see it wrapped. When I don't, I ask, "Where is it?"

That's when Laura answers. "Your room. Bailey wanted it displayed on your bed, so I carried her up there so she could put it just where she wanted it."

I ruffle my daughter's hair and announce, "Then why don't I run upstairs, change, and check out this amazing gift?"

Bailey lurches forward and presses her lips to my cheek. "I love you, Daddy."

My heart swells. "I love you too, Buttercup."

I stand, and without a word to Laura, jog up the stairs. The doors to the master suite are partially closed. I push them open and come to a dead stop.

Because I can't believe what I'm seeing.

Over my hated king-size pillows are new dark green covered standard pillows. There are cards in Bailey's handwriting that read "Soft," "Mediums," and "Firmy."

But those aren't what my fingers dance over.

In the middle is an enormous square pillow made of wool. Embroidered on it is a buttercup. Beneath it is the word "Love."

Tears burn my eyes.

I guess Caleb was telling the truth earlier. All Laura wanted to know was if Bailey was loved and once she did, she wanted to show me how much my daughter loved me in return.

No judgment.

No questions.

Instead, it's replaced by an overwhelming need to make her understand.

Quickly, I shed my clothes where I stand, not giving a damn about hanging up my suit. I tug on jeans and a T-shirt and head back downstairs, ready to give answers to any questions she asks and to ask a few questions of my own.

CHAPTER
Forty-Two

LIAM

I'M in trouble when Bailey grows up, if the way she's playing Laura is any indication.

"Oh, pleaaaaaase?" Bailey pleads, full drama. I wouldn't be surprised if there was a tear or two watering up in her eyes. Bailey throws herself forward, her head landing on Laura's breasts. The image the two of them make causes my heart to twist.

Her eyes meet mine over my daughter's head.

For a heartbeat, an eternity, no words are spoken between us. I hold her gaze steadily, trying to communicate without words what I want and what we need.

Her. Just her.

Laura's gaze doesn't waiver, even as she smooths Bailey's hair away from her face.

I could live in this moment feeling more emotion surging through me than I had in years—except maybe the first time I held Bailey days after Ashleigh gave birth to her and I knew she was mine.

Finally, Laura relents. Her lips curve into a smile. "Okay. Fine. I'll stay for dinner."

"Then during it, you'll tell us all about your family's elephant gift?" Bailey barters, confusing a story Laura and her aunt must have been telling her earlier today while they were making my pillows.

Laura's body rocks with suppressed laughter. "Yes, but I refuse to give up my secret to winning."

"No one expects you to. Right, Buttercup?" Hell, I'd agree to anything at this point.

Bailey obviously feels the same way. "Right."

I sputter my wine into my glass. "You make the poor fool who loses display whatever piece of trash they're stuck with in their home for a whole year?"

Laura's eyes twinkle with mischief. "Prominently."

"What does that mean?"

"It can't be hidden, nor can it be obfuscated. The item has to be in a place of prominence so any of us—or any visitors—can see it." Devilishly amused, she recalls, "The best was last year when my father and Uncle Keene ended up with the same entry because they both were too busy to shop."

"How did that happen?" I'm intrigued, despite myself.

Laura adopts an angelic face. "Both of them asked me to pick up something for them."

"You sabotaged your own father? What happened to family loyalty?" I howl at the idea of Laura pulling a twofer and taking down both powerful men in one fell swoop.

Her face adopts the fiercest expression I've ever seen. "We're all loyal to one another."

"I didn't mean . . ."

Then it smooths out before she teases, "However, just because we love each other doesn't mean we're not competitive. It's war, and no one is safe until Christmas is over."

I chortle into my wine, holding her captivating gaze even as Bailey's laughter wraps around us. It's a moment in time so perfect, I want to memorize every second of it. Especially when a light blush spreads across Laura's cheeks, bringing more attention to her incredible eyes. My voice is husky even to my own ears when I quote, "'All's fair in love and war?'"

That's when the earth shifts, or maybe it's just my world. Her voice rings true when she lifts her own glass and takes a fortifying sip before acknowledging her call to her father without saying the words. "Love, if it's true, involves loyalty, strength, and courage. Therefore, by definition, all love is a war. If you're not fighting for it, you should be fighting to hold on to it, to cherish it." With that declaration lying between us, she turns to a wide-eyed Bailey. "How about you wheel into the kitchen with your dishes and bring back the cookies we made yesterday for dessert."

"Okay, Laura." Appeased, like most seven-year-olds are with the concept of dessert, Bailey wheels off to do as Laura asks.

She twirls her glass around in her hand before saying, "My call to my father before didn't mean I was jumping to conclusions about you, Liam."

"Then what was it about?"

She pauses a moment before admitting, "I've had to stick my hand in a person's chest and manually push the blood through their heart to keep loved ones alive."

I sit up straighter. "Laura . . ."

Her fingers tighten on the stem of her glass. "I've also been shot by a man because I told him his father died. In between, there's a constant war between love and hate, life and death that consumes—consumed—my every day. I couldn't bear the thought of Bailey . . ."

"Of Bailey?" I prompt when she trails off.

"Of her not feeling the same level of love I had growing up after everything that she's endured. Because she was hurt in the crossfire of me telling two men their father died." Laura moves to shove away from the table, to escape the emotions swimming inside her eyes. Instead, I stop her by stretching my hand across it and clasping her wrist to stay her movement. The second I do, her pulse leaps beneath my fingers.

Our eyes meet.

Hold.

There's an inhale—*hers*.

An expulsion of breath—*mine*.

The room shrinks to the distance across a farmhouse table. My thumb grazes the silken skin of her inner wrist and I watch her face as the blood thrumming through her sends an electrical surge through my body.

Her lips part but what she says is lost when there's a squeak of rubber on the floor. By the time Bailey rolls out with the tub of cookies in her lap, Laura's hands are tucked safely in her lap and mine is wrapped once again around the stem of my wineglass.

　　　　　　　　　　　✧

As I lay in bed that night on "Firmy," I think about my whole day from beginning to end. Unsurprisingly, it all begins and ends with Laura and Bailey. I scrub my hand over my face and beard when I realize I was about to kiss Laura without any consideration as to where Bailey might be.

Okay, yes. We have a date to go to the charity ball.

No, Laura isn't the she-bitch who birthed Bailey. Thank God. But still. She's entrusted with my daughter's well-being. Part of me wants to howl in agony over the moment that was interrupted, but that's the part that takes the backseat to the father.

Because after Ashleigh, no other woman should ever come first in my heart.

Still, Keene's words about his niece having a gift flit through my mind. It made me realize despite whatever trauma led Laura into our lives, we'll never be the same people after she returns to her regular job.

I wonder if her regular patients feel the same way, is my last thought before I drift off to sleep.

CHAPTER
Forty-Three

"You like him—Liam. And not in a 'he's a good dad' kind of way," Kalie concludes after I've caught her up on everything while we're getting a mani/pedi at Shimmer in preparation for the ball. Unfortunately, Grace had to bail on the pampering due to another patient losing a body part to their pet. "It's a nose, guys. Sorry. This is going to take a while since I have to make sure they can attend the ball with some dignity."

I scowl at Kalie. "How do you deduce that from the fact I just spent the last thirty minutes talking about his daughter?"

Smugly she points at the bottle of polish being applied to my toes. "Your normal summer color is You Got Nata On Me. Now you're wearing Mod About You."

Damn it. I didn't even realize I'd subconsciously made a different selection. Part of me wants to ask the esthetician to change the color but I don't. There's just something a little brighter about the color that appeals to me. I inform her loftily, "It has nothing to do with Liam."

She singsongs, "Of course not. So you won't mind if I drop by and ask him out."

Quickly, I snarl, "Don't you dare." Then, to cover my reaction, which has Kalie's eyes widening, I remind her, "You're the one who said you're not certain you want to be tied down."

Her laugh is practically a purr. "Depends on the man and the manner of which I'd be tied."

Knowing I've fallen into her trap, I resort to my best argument. I stick my tongue out at her, which just sets Kalie hooting.

"Just admit it, Laura. You like him."

I think about the dream last night, more vivid than any other, and I shudder. I more than like him if my subconscious is to be believed. Still, putting that kind of ammunition into Kalie's hands is dangerous. I decide distraction is the better course of action. "I do."

Her face immediately takes on a serious mien. "Now what?"

"Now, I go get my dress fit and figure out how to knock Liam Payne's socks off."

"I want to help."

"Of course." After all, despite her protests, Kalie's inherited the need to meddle from our Uncle Phil. Keeping her out of any scheme is impossible.

After we left Shimmer and drove over to the mansion that houses Amaryllis Events and Company, we both sit in my car for a few minutes admiring the business our parents built up with dedication, hard work, and an eye to the fact they never wanted to return to the place they'd come from.

I run my thumbs along the insides of my pinkies even as Kalie rubs her instep against her calf together—the place where her tattoo lies. I muse, "How much do you think they're going to go overboard during this dress fitting?"

"On a scale of one to ten?"

"Uh-huh."

"Nine hundred and sixty-seven," Kalie deadpans.

I burst out laughing, shocking us both.

Silence falls in between us until Kalie reaches for my hand. Squeezing it hard, she says, "I just want to say this before we go inside."

"What?"

"I don't care if it means a banging affair with Liam Payne, driving to the moon, or playing dress up with a child. I will do whatever it takes so you laugh the way you used to." Before I can reply, Kalie slips out of the vehicle.

I swiftly follow, catching up to her on the wraparound porch. Before we enter through the mahogany door, I wrap her in a tight hug. "I'd be a whole different me without you, Kalie."

I push open the door inlaid with a stained-glass amaryllis just as our Uncle Phil deposits a vase of fresh flowers onto the grand entryway. Seeing Kalie with tears in her eyes, he immediately panics. "Cass! Ali! Your daughters are here! Kitchen! ASAP!"

A slow smile lifts my lips. I was right. Just like Kalie, Uncle Phil can't keep his nose out of anything.

⁂

We're huddled in the kitchen eating what Uncle Phil decreed as, "Emergency cake! Cori, after all these years, knows she has to keep one of them around."

Corinna mutters, "No, don't worry, Phil. That wedding tomorrow didn't need that top tier."

He smiles beatifically before causing us all to wince when he cut into the top tier with a serrated knife, decimating it in seconds. Holly perched on her favorite spot on the counter and immediately began taking photos, asking, "Where's Gracie?"

I answer, "A dog ate a nose," as if that explained it all.

Which it does to her mother. She lowers her camera long enough to order Phil, "Make sure you save a piece for my daughter."

Phil flaps his hand at her as he cuts another slab out of Corinna's masterpiece. Corinna lays her head on her arms. I pat her back as my mother, Alison, and Emily saunter through the kitchen door.

Mama comes up short. "Philip. Tell me that isn't the top of the Beaumont wedding cake you're desecrating."

Corinna's shout of "Yes!" overrides his "Uhm . . ."

Mama's eyes narrow into slits. But before her wrath can explode, he says, "Kalie's been crying!"

Alison gapes at her daughter before she rushes over and slips an arm around her shoulders. "Who does your father need to maim?"

Kalie points at me.

Everyone's jaws fall to the floor. Mama turns on me and demands, "Laura Faith, what did you do?"

Kalie sniffs. "Nothing, Aunt Cass. It's just . . ."

"What, sweetie?" Alison prompts.

"Laura . . . god, I feel so ridiculous for crying again." Kalie buries her head in her mother's shoulder.

Mama approaches me, concerned. "Honey? What happened?"

I stomp my foot. "It's nothing. I laughed. Okay? It's not the first time—"

"It was for me!" Kalie wails.

"Kalie said something funny and . . ."

The next thing I know, I'm being mass hugged by my mother and our family. I think Emily's boob is jamming one ear shut. The other one is right next to my mother's lips. I can hear her clearly as she whispers thanks to her mother for answering her prayers to watch over me.

I'm about to ask for a little breathing space when we all break our little huddle. Corinna shouts, "Right, so this deserves eating the whole damn cake. I'll bake a new one. Phil, this time, give *me* the knife."

He's too busy dashing into the walk-in cooler for the rest of the three-tier cake to answer.

Mama smooths a hand over my cheek and presses her forehead to mine. "You laughed." The choked emotion in her voice makes the heated sting behind my eyelashes worth it. It isn't just me Paulie Tiberi damaged. It's my loved ones.

Knowing I survived, that I lived, is better than any punishment he could have tried to enact that horrible day.

Or any I've been subjected to since.

CHAPTER
Forty~Four

LIAM

Two days before the ball, I corner Laura in the kitchen. Before I open my mouth, her cheeks pinken.

I can't say I'm disappointed by her reaction. Leaning forward so my body brushes against hers, I feel a surge of power rip through me when her body trembles against mine. Casting a glance at the entrance to make certain Bailey's not around, I lean my body against hers so she can feel the length of my attraction to her.

Just as she shivers, I lean down and brush my lips against the shell of her ear. "What color is your gown?"

"G-gown?"

"Gown? Ball? Date?" I take a quick nip of the lobe, causing a tiny gasp to pass her lips.

She tips her head back and I feel like diving into the pools of blue reflecting heaven up at me. "Blue."

I lean down and nuzzle my nose against the side of hers before a thump alerts me that Bailey just drove her wheelchair into the wall. Backing away, I take in the picture of Laura flushed and flustered. Winking at her, I remind her, "I'll pick you up at seven."

Mutely, she nods before turning and bracing her hands on the counter.

I can't say walking away from her is easy, not when I have her so close to being right where I want her.

With me.

CHAPTER
Forty~Five

Laura

"ARE YOU ON YOUR WAY HOME?" Kalie demands. "I'm hangry."

"What happened?" I immediately ask. My cousin doesn't get hangry.

"I had to go into court today and some jackass ran me over. I mean literally ran me over. I swore I almost broke my ankle, so instead of eating, I had to have a medic check to make certain I didn't jack up anything."

"Are you okay?"

"I'm pissed. Other than that, I was told to rest. Now, I want comfort food."

"You just want someone to feed you because you don't cook."

"Well, there's that too."

"I have to run to Corset. I didn't want to take Bailey with me to a lingerie store," I tell her with more than a touch of amusement at the questions I'd be fielding from a seven-year-old if I did.

"Good call. Hey, mind picking me up some more thigh highs just in case I run them?"

"I'll grab some for Gracie too. I won't be long," I promise before disconnecting.

In fact, I'm in and out of the store in twenty minutes. The problem is what's waiting in my car when I do.

It's a doll with a bloody body—its throat having been sliced.

It's in a blue ball gown.

I call Kalie and tell her, "I have a flat. Eat without me."

She immediately agrees, hanging up before I can finish.

I try to find my Hudson team and can't even as I place the call to my father.

This time, he and Uncle Keene show up. Both, I note with more than a touch of fear, are armed. "What changed?" I press.

"What do you mean, Laura?" my father hedges.

"You're . . ." I flick my fingers toward his holster.

Uncle Keene runs a hand up and down my arm. "Don't worry about it, kid. It's a precaution." Still, his eyes roam above my head as if searching for something.

Or . . . someone?

I wait for them to gather what they're looking for and make their calls before I press on with the question I need an answer to. "What aren't you telling me?"

They exchange long glances and my father's gaze meets my eyes, barely, before skipping away. "Laura, if there was something to tell you, I would."

I remain silent even as I shift my weight slightly. My every sense is telling me my father just lied to me. He knows more than he's telling me.

The question is, why isn't he sharing?

CHAPTER
Forty-Six

Laura

It's the night of the Greenwich Hospital Annual Fundraiser. Liam is due at my house at any moment. Kalie and Grace have already gone ahead in a car sent by Amaryllis Events. Despite my offer to arrange transportation, Liam flatly refused, telling me he'd take care of it.

I'm standing downstairs in our living room waiting for Liam to arrive, my anxiety beginning to swirl. *What am I thinking trying to attend an event like this with the threats against me? Especially with Liam Payne? He has a child!* A wave of nausea hits me just as I hear the doorbell ring. I catch sight of my image in the beveled glass mirror above. Despite the deep blue of my gown, my skin is almost waxy.

No. Not now. I can't have a panic attack when Liam's about to come up the steps at any moment.

I try a few deep breaths to calm my racing heart.

Inhale. Exhale.

Inhale. Ex—

Ding. Dong.

Shit. The doorbell. Hand shaking, I reach for the handle and step back. Then my breath leaves my body for an entirely separate reason.

I've seen Liam in jeans and T-shirts. I've watched as he's sauntered out the door in a thousand-dollar suit. Nothing could have prepared me for him in a custom-made tuxedo holding a small bouquet of flowers I recognize from long days slaving in the Amaryllis Florist workshop as a kid. In fact, the bouquet is wrapped in the distinctive paper Uncle Phil uses for his custom orders. Liam steps forward and holds it out to me. "Laura, I'd say you look magnificent, but that doesn't even come close."

My lips tremble when I gently touch a finger to the stem of each bloom. "You brought me roses, lavender, and jasmine wrapped in eucalyptus."

A flag of color sweeps his cheeks. "I didn't want to presume anything, but I thought it might help ease any last-minute tension you might feel about attending an event some of your colleagues will be at."

Clutching the bouquet in one arm, I wrap my hand around his upper arm and press my lips to the underside of his jaw. Letting them linger for just a moment, I murmur, "I'm not certain how you knew what I'd be feeling."

His fingers dance delicately over my cheek. "Probably because I'm feeling the same way, and I don't have half the reason for it you do?"

Remaining close enough so my body absorbs the warmth of his, I ask, "Why could you possibly be nervous?"

The pupils of his eyes expand, eclipsing the green for just a moment as they roam me from the tip of my upswept hairdo to the hem of my dress. His fingers curl in slightly, setting off a whole different set of butterflies in my stomach. No, his response isn't verbal, but it settles something inside me I didn't realize was wound up so tightly.

Liam gestures at the flowers. "If you want to put them in some water, we have time."

I clutch them tightly, not willing to leave them behind. "I actually want to take them in the limo."

A slow smile spreads across his face. "Then do you need to get anything? We really should get going."

"Let me grab my clutch." Turning my back to him, I hear his hissed breath when he gets a load of the dramatic plunge to my dress.

Happy my back is to him to hide my smile, I'm fervently grateful to Emily for convincing me to go with such a striking design for this year's gown that was in the making long before I met Liam Payne.

After I pick up my gold clutch, I whirl around. His green gaze is no less fiery when I saunter toward him. "I'm ready."

He holds out his arm and before long, we're seated in the car for the short ride to the event.

As we wait for our limo to slither forward, I note, "Looks like the paparazzi are out in full force tonight." Not that I expected any differently. The Greenwich Hospital Annual Fundraiser at Lord Thomson Manor is considered one of the preeminent events of the year.

Liam reaches across the armrest and removes my fingers from where they've been clutching the flowers he gave me. He takes my hand in his. "It's just me and you, Laura. And if you give me the word, I'll ask the driver to pull straight past, and we'll drive around for hours. Listen, we can go to McDonald's and grab a cheeseburger."

I glance down at the deep royal blue silk emblazoned with sweeping white amaryllis flowers Aunt Emily designed before nodding solemnly. "Totally screams the ball pit. Maybe we can get a kid's toy in our Happy Meal?"

"That's what the paparazzi feels like."

"The Happy Meal?"

"The kids toy."

"Some of them are actually quite charming."

Liam leans back and gives me the once over to make certain I didn't turn into an alien on the ride over. "Who are you, and what did you do with Dr. Laura Lockwood? Wherever she is, I'd like her back right now."

I burst into laughter. His slow, devastating smile is my reward. I twist a bit and lean forward until I'm close enough to his ear to whisper. "Can I tell you a secret?"

I'm also close enough to watch his Adam's apple bob up and down. "You can tell me anything you want."

My lips brush the shell of his ear. "I really enjoy StellaNova."

He groans. "They're the worst. I hear they're the ones who gave you the *nom de plum* 'Queen Gore.'"

My lips curve against his ear. "That's because the owner, Arek Ronan, has a weak stomach. His wife was too busy laughing at him when he turned a lovely shade of green as I gave a *very* detailed description of what it was like to disimpact a bowel."

"What?"

"Liam, I, we, the whole family, is *very* friendly with StellaNova's owner and his entire family."

"You've got to be kidding."

I shake my head, a few loose curls brushing my neck. His eyes follow the dancing strands before fiery green eyes lock onto mine. His reaction causes my heart to pump faster, distracting me as the car inches forward to the glare of lights we're all too quickly approaching "Thus why . . ." My voice trails off.

"Why what?"

"Later," I reply faintly. The limousine has stopped and the driver is hurrying around the car. I squeeze Liam's fingers one last time for strength before the driver opens the door, waiting for him to ascend. "It's show time."

He doesn't move. "Last chance. I have no problem with a quarter pounder with cheese."

I give him a gentle nudge. "Not if you want to bring Bailey home dessert."

His eyes soften before he slips out of the car. Holding his hand back, he waits for me to put mine into it. Just as I'm about to alight into the shouts and noise, he leans back in to whisper, "Tonight's already been the perfect first date, Laura. Anytime you want to ask me out on the second one, I'm game."

So, it's with an enormous smile I exit the vehicle and make my way down the red carpet.

CHAPTER
Forty-Seven

LIAM

SHE'S beautiful as she poses for pictures on the red carpet. Her sweeping halter neck gown with its deep backless plunge is striking. But it isn't until she stops right in front of StellaNova's call out of "Gore! Hey, Gore!" I realize how magnificent she is.

Slipping an arm through mine, she guides us to the well-lit area where she answers question after question about the event and how it benefits the ER. "In a year where we've lost so much, to have our community surround us is the cushion after the fall. Day after day, they've kissed our healing cuts. We appreciate those who have donated everything from the venue, goods, services, and, above all, their time to support Greenwich Hospital." She takes a deep breath and continues, "But there's always more to do. We're not the only organization that needs help. Send Me An Angel—chaired by the incredible Ursula Moore—is one such organization. If you're looking for other ways to help, I'm certain StellaNova will have their information included on their website tonight, as well as ours."

After she's done, the lights dim and to my shock, the cameraman lowers his camera a bit before winking at her. She returns the gesture.

From behind him, a dark-haired man steps forward. Ignoring me completely, he hooks an arm around my date's shoulders and pulls her in for a quick hug. "Thanks, Gore."

"Like you weren't going to figure out some way to work it in yourself?" she counters archly.

I clear my throat and Laura pulls me forward. "I'm sorry. Liam, this is Arek Ronan, owner of StellaNova. Arek, my date for the evening, Liam Payne. Liam is the Chief Audit Officer for Hudson Investigations."

"Laura, did you just admit to a reporter on the record you brought a date to an event?" Ronan chides her.

"No comment," she sasses before she bites her lip. "Is Sula inside?"

His face morphs from reporter to friend instantly. "Yes, and about a hundred other people you're related to in some way. All of whom have your back. So, walk in with your head held high, sweetheart." Arek Ronan's green eyes pierce into mine. "I sincerely hope you're the kind of man worth being at Laura's side, Payne. Few have been."

"Arek," she snaps.

"Just calling it like I see it, Gore." He holds up his hands as if he's surrendering to her viperish tone. But the cool, assessing look he shoots me as we move past tells me he wasn't joking. At all.

Well, shit. There goes remaining off this man's radar.

Still, I am the man at Laura's side and I don't foresee a time I won't be.

"Is that who I think it is?" I lean down to whisper in Laura's ear hours later as Brendan Blake strides out with a guitar slung over his shoulder.

The audience hushes as if they know what he's about to say before he steps up to the microphone, including Laura. Her lips curve. "It is."

Up to this moment, we've spent hours navigating our way amid the higher ups of the hospital administration as Laura glad handed her bosses with the appropriate amount of deference. There was one—a Dr. Bryan Moser and his wife—whose reaction to Laura's presence I clocked. The wife's lip trembled while the chief of staff stared intently at Laura.

As if he was trying to force her to look in his direction.

Needless to say, I think we were both grateful when I steered us over to what she amusedly dubbed the "Amaryllis Section" which to my shock includes Arek Ronan and his wife Ursula "Sula" Moore. I hiss in Laura's ear, "How did they become such good friends with your family?"

"Oh, that's a long and complicated story."

"To say I'm curious is probably an understatement."

"You and most of the world," she mutters before she presses her lips to each of Sula Moore's cheeks in quick succession.

I'm shocked when Ronan comes over and shakes my hand. For someone who makes his living exposing secrets of celebrities and the uber wealthy, I would have thought Laura's family would have stayed far away from the media mogul. Yet, Ronan is surprisingly easy to like with an at ease personality and satiric commentary that more than once almost has me choking on my drink. Still, the one impression about him that stands out above all others is the adoration dominates his features when his eyes rest on his wife.

"Maybe that's why you get along so well with the men married to Freeman women," I speculate after I share what I was thinking.

He roars with laughter. "That's one of the reasons. Certainly none of them have ever hidden the way they adore their wives."

He eyes me speculatively. *Yeah, take a good look, buddy.* As the relationship between Laura and myself has been evolving, maybe I'm not doing such a great job of hiding my own emotions if the wild amusement in Arek's eyes is anything to go by. Then Laura's voice brings me back. "Uncle Brendan always tries to make an appearance."

"*Uncle* Brendan?" I emphasize. Arek does a piss poor job of hiding his snicker next to me. I desperately want to flick him off, but this is a high-class event.

Sula's lips flirt with a smile. "You mean you didn't notice the world's most famous fashion model milling around?"

"Who?" I ask in confusion.

"Oh, come on, Liam. Danielle Madison is just over there." Laura rolls her eyes.

"She's here?" I'm dumbfounded.

Laura points to her left and my body jerks in shock at seeing Danielle Madison standing between two of Laura's aunts, laughing uproariously. I'm stunned. "I truly didn't notice her."

"Because Alice talking your ear off after we ran into Dr. Douche robbed you of your senses?" she teases.

"No." I slip an arm around her waist and block her view of the stage, forcing her to focus on me. "Because I lost the ability to feel anything but awe from the moment you opened your front door."

She's struggling to respond. Either that or Ronan's "Aww" has her ready to throat punch him when Brendan Blake's voice washes over us.

"There's been many nights at this fundraiser where I've stood on this stage and dedicated a song to one of my best friends—the woman who dragged me on national television and helped me win some money decades ago. It started a friendship that morphed into our families becoming related through marriage. Every year, I've thanked the lord for that moment in time when our worlds intersected—and a long-ago day when she browbeat me to become functionally competent in the kitchen long enough to raise the money for my nephew's cancer treatment. I will never be able to thank you enough for that, Cori."

There's a loud burst of applause from the people surrounding me as I put together a piece of the puzzle—Brendan Blake is related to Laura through some family member's marriage.

Holy. Crap.

He actually is her "uncle."

Then he goes on. "But tonight, there's something else I think we all need to recall—that we can rise from the tragedies forced upon us. A different kind of strength and beauty within my family was almost lost to us earlier this year." He plucks a few notes on his guitar and a familiar song echoes around the room.

Laura's voice breaks, "Oh G-god . . . t-tell me h-he isn't g-going to do what I think he is."

I tuck her against my side firmly and hold on. She grips my waist as if she knows she won't be able to remain upright if she doesn't. The lights dim until Brendan's only lit by a single spotlight. Even illuminated, Brendan knows exactly where she's standing. "Tonight, this song is dedicated to my niece, Dr. Laura Lockwood. I'm not going to drag her up on stage, but I have a special message for her."

With that, Brendan Blake's rich baritone starts singing "Ashes" from the *Deadpool 2 Motion Picture Soundtrack*. He immediately paints a picture of a person who has walked through fire—someone who lived through heartbreak, loss, and struggle, yet refuses to be defeated.

In other words, he serenades Laura with a song that could have been written for her.

When Brendan hits the refrain, his powerful voice belting out the call for beauty to find its way out of the remnants of ashes, chills run up Laura's arms. I know this because I'm holding her body up with every ounce of strength in mine as hers is wracked in sobs. Especially when the Amaryllis section lifts their cell phones—a light to guide Laura out of the dark.

The action is quickly picked up around the room until the space is dotted by bright diamonds of light. Unwilling to break the magic of the moment, Brendan repeats the refrain, staring right into the space where his niece stands.

As Brendan's final note fades away and cell phones begin clicking off, I know we have seconds before the houselights come back up.

The core of Laura's devastation has been laid open. Now, it's up to me to piece it back together while I hold her close to my heart.

Without a word to anyone around me, I sweep her into my arms and stride for the nearest exit. Her cheek presses into my shoulder as—what I hope are cleansing—tears fall on to my jacket.

Once I have her safely within the confines of the limo, she snatches up the bouquet I gave her earlier and buries her face in it. I order the chauffeur to drive back to my home before raising the window between us and him. I start, "Laura . . ."

Her cell phone rings. She holds up a finger before answering it with a warbly voice. "I had to leave . . . no, I'm fine. I'm with Liam. Too much, Daddy." There's a pause before, "Tell Uncle Brendan I loved it. I love him. I love all of you." She disconnects the call before admitting, "I'm so mortified."

"You have nothing to be embarrassed about."

She lifts her tear-streaked face and I swear, she's never looked more beautiful with her heart exposed for me to explore. I push tendrils of hair stuck to her cheek away and whisper, "Do you want to know what I'm feeling?"

Laura hesitates briefly before whispering, "Yes."

I lean over and brush a kiss very near her lips. I feel a tremor shoot through her at the contact. "I feel like the luckiest guy who was in that room."

Her head tilts to the side in confusion, which is swept away with my next words.

"I already know the answer to what Brendan was singing. The right beauty not only can be resurrected, it should be." I lift her fingers to my lips to trace their fullness.

I let my finger fall away before asking her, "Now, would you like to come over for a nightcap so I can check in on Bailey? Then I'll have the driver take you home?"

She lifts her fingers to her mouth, touching her lips right where my fingers were seconds ago. Then she responds with a simple, "Yes."

CHAPTER
Forty~Eight

LIAM'S HAND guides me up his front steps. He unlocks the door and ushers me inside before speaking to a familiar Hudson agent whose name I can't place right now. After, the agent nods in my direction before leaving us alone.

Together.

While Bailey's asleep down the hall in her room.

Liam's hand smooths up my back. "What would you like to drink?"

I tip my head up and meet his hooded eyes. "Whatever you're having is fine."

He drags his fingers down my back before stepping away. "Give me just a moment."

With that time, I walk over to the windows overlooking the backyard and stare into the dark, letting the night absorb my reflection as if that can also take away the wild emotions rioting through me.

My fingers clutch the sill as I contemplate the events of the evening from the moment I opened the door to find Liam standing in front of me with a bouquet of armor. My fingers smooth along the richly sanded wood as I recall the confidence with which I navigated the red carpet.

Joking, like always, with the StellaNova team. A private smile lifts my lips when I think about the number of connections we have to them. "I wonder if Liam picked up on the wink," I murmur.

"From StellaNova's cameraman? Of course I did. You'll find I don't miss much."

I look over my shoulder and find him holding two cognac glasses. He lifts one to his lips and takes a sip before remarking, "I didn't put it together until just now. He looks too much like you to not be a relative."

"My younger brother, Chuck."

"Ahh."

"He's worked for them since college." I can practically see the wheels turn in Liam's head if that's why we're so comfortable with the media outlet owner. "We're a complicated family, Liam. You're not going to figure us out in one night."

He holds out my drink. I step forward to take it when he captures my other wrist. "Then let's drink to that."

"To what?" My voice is raspier than normal.

"To complications—wherever they lead us." He lifts his glass and holds my gaze.

My heart is racing in my chest, but it isn't anxiety making it dance. It's the irresistible lure of the man standing mere feet in front of me. I tap my glass against his. The ping rings clear around the room before I repeat, "To complications."

We both sip and the fiery burn of the sweet and spicy liquor slides over my tongue as it makes its way toward the back of my throat.

I'm about to lift the glass to my lips for a second drink when his voice stops me. "Laura?"

I lower my glass. "Yes?"

"Your family isn't the one that's had me lying awake at night trying to figure them out." He steps closer. "Who are you, Laura?"

My lips part when he plucks the glass from my hand and places it on the windowsill. In the shadow of the moon, he rasps, "Why are you becoming so vital to me? To us?"

In the dim light of the living room, Liam's green eyes glow as they lock onto mine. My breath comes out in short bursts as a magnetic force pulls us closer. Despite the clanging alarm going off in my head about Bailey asleep only a few rooms away, the air between us electrifies. The tension is so incendiary I feel as if my blood could catch on fire. I try to justify it may be the sole sip of liquor, but I know better.

It's him.

It's me.

It's whatever this is between us.

Knowing there's an equal desire I've been suppressing, I don't stop Liam when his arm snakes around my waist.

When he hauls me up against his chest.

When I feel the drum of his heart pounding against mine.

Still, I fall for him even more when he hesitates, torn between the sizzling desire arcing between us and the responsibility of being Bailey's father as he casts a last glance toward the hall leading to Bailey's room. *It's possible I might want him less if he didn't*, I think to myself as my arms twine around his neck.

His hand comes up to slide into the thickness of my hair, fingers clenching the bound curls tightly before tugging my head back until my eyes meet his.

My breath catches at the emotion leaping from his when he admits huskily, "You're special to me, Laura. Listening to that song tonight . . ." He doesn't finish his sentence.

He lets his kiss speak for him when his lips cover mine.

But if he thought he would own this kiss, he's in for a big surprise. My lips part beneath his. I feel his start of surprise before his lips slant over mine, confirming what I already suspected. His kiss is just like him—scorching hot, intense with a hint of softness he shows to too few people.

Also, as I expected, kissing Liam Payne could be my downfall.

All from a single kiss.

Well, that and the way the banked fire between us springs into an inferno the moment we released it.

"Laura," he whispers as his arm bands around my hips, freeing his hand to roam the bare skin of my back, to slide around to cover the silk encasing my breasts. God, I've never been so grateful for the wonders of Aunt Emily's miracle construction. The feel of his hands molding my breasts elicits a moan from me I can't restrain. I'm going to pool into a puddle of couture silk soon; I just know it. It's all because of the way Liam Payne drives me insane.

My arms start slipping from around his neck, but he catches them. Wrapping them tighter, he smirks down at me. "I love being able to touch you."

"Kiss me again," I plead breathlessly.

As his head lowers between my raised arms, he murmurs, "With pleasure."

The feel of the skin of his neck will be forever imprinted on the pads of my fingers. If—when—I go back to wearing medical gloves, I'll always bear the mark of Liam's skin as a barrier between my fingerprints and the harsh latex. Where before, the tips memorized a human body for the purpose of saving lives. Now I blindly focus on committing every millimeter of the skin above his shirt collar to memory. The way his close-cropped hair dips between my fingers. There's a tantalizing spot where his skin meets his tux shirt that I fight with so I can slip my hand beneath his collar to do as much exploring of him as he does of me.

Just then, his fingers dip beneath the sides of my gown. His rough voice rasps my name. I suck in an enormous breath as he tears his lips away. His eyes are wildly dilated as he stares into mine. But his focus is on the nipple he's now flicking slowly—too slowly. Enough to keep me riding the edge, but not enough to fling me over. "Liam," I moan.

"I know," he growls. His lips descend, wreaking havoc as they run up and down the side of my neck. I arch into his arms, pliant.

His.

Willing.

Prepared to take this next step if he's ready to be the man who wants me.

As if he can sense my capitulation, he fuses our mouths together. My lips part immediately, tasting his as he glides his tongue over mine. It's a dueling, a mating dance as old as time. Woman to man—ready for the ultimate culmination of joining.

After cheating death, I refuse to hold back on life. I want this. I want him.

I need Liam with a certainty I've never experienced before.

Whimpers I'm unable to restrain feed the hunger inside him. He breaks away long enough to drag me to the sofa. Falling back, his hands slide down to urge me to straddle his hips, which I do so eagerly. In this position, I can stare down into his remarkable eyes.

Our passion explodes, and kisses and touches are urgent as we desperately try to communicate with touch what words don't seem to convey. I frantically fumble with his bowtie, then the studs of his shirt, so I can drag my fingernails across his pectorals.

Meanwhile, Liam shoves my gown up and over my hips. Then he tests Emily's sewing skills as he strains the sides until my breast falls into his waiting hands while the dress forces them around the compressed silk. But I'm not worried about stitches for long. It's barely a breath before his lips surround my areola and he suckles me, distracting me from my endgame —which is to drive him insane with lust.

Rocking forward and back on his ironhard dick, I moan, "I might come just from that alone."

"Good."

"Don't stop."

He flicks me a look so raw I feel stripped bare before lowering his head again. "Wasn't planning on it." He resumes suckling.

I lean into his mouth and press against his cock. I'm heedless of anything but pleasure, life, and Liam.

I'm not certain how much time passes, how much passion cloaks us in her nebulous ability to forget time and space. That is until we hear a familiar squeak on the wood floor echoing in the hallway.

Even as our lips cling together for a last impossible second, neither of us moves. It's as if our souls are unwilling to part. Still, Bailey's arrival reminds us of the person we are both willing to put above ourselves and these tumultuous emotions.

Liam rolls us upward and brushes his nose against the side of mine, leaving a taste of what could have been if we weren't interrupted. His promise of "Later" sends shivers through my body before he heads off to intercept Bailey so I can right myself.

CHAPTER
Forty~Nine

LIAM

AFTER I'VE LAID Bailey back in her bed, I quickly use the opportunity to get her a glass of water and wash my hands, which are still shaking from having just touched heaven on this side of dying. I'm asked the question I've been waiting for from the moment she almost wheeled herself into a scene she may not quite have understood. "Daddy, was that Laura I heard?"

Brushing her tussled hair away from her forehead, I lean down and press my lips against it. "It was."

Bailey sleepily smiles up at me before snuggling into her pillow. "Do you think—" She interrupts herself with an enormous yawn.

"Do I think what, Buttercup?"

"Would she tuck me in too?" There's a light in her eyes that causes me to pause. Bailey's eyes, so much like my own, are reflecting hope. It makes me wonder if my eyes give away my emotions just as easily.

Disconcerted, I brush some stray hairs off her face. "I'll go ask her."

"I think . . ."

"What, Buttercup?"

Then she blurts out, "I love Laura, Daddy."

Her words still my fingers. I knew the two were getting closer, but to hear words reserved for me solidify my growing feelings for Laura and cause a flurry of trepidation. Shoving the latter aside due to the newness of it all, I resume skimming my fingers through her hair.

Her sleepy smile lets me know she might not make it until Laura makes it into her room. "Thanks, Daddy. Love you."

"I love you, Bailey. More than anything." Stepping back, I dim her light and make my way down the corridor to find Laura.

The second she hears my shoes on the hardwood, she whirls. "Is everything all right?"

"Bailey's fine. She is, however, asking if you wouldn't mind saying goodnight."

Laura moves swiftly in my direction. Just as she's about to pass, my hand snags her wrist. Her head snaps up and our eyes meet. Every second we burned like fire in each other's arms leaps between us. Heat flags her high cheekbones and I know she's reliving every kiss, each touch between us.

It's enough to let her go for now. Releasing her, I urge, "Go. Before she falls asleep."

"I'll be back." Then, with a swoosh of her gown, she makes her way down the hall.

I head over to the table where I left my drink and throw what's left of it back. The burn down my throat doesn't begin to relieve what I really want—her.

Laura.

In my bed.

But more important than the need to feel what it's like to slide my cock deep inside her, I need to think. More importantly, so does she. Bailey asking for her tonight reminded me there's too much at stake here for me to give into my baser instincts. There's a bond of trust that's entwined three ways.

So, what happens after Laura and I give in to what this is between us?

Part of me bitterly regrets what Bailey interrupted while a small part of me is relieved. "I will never do anything to deliberately hurt her."

Laura's voice comes from behind me. "Time and again, you've shown that."

My head twists, and I find her casually leaning against the wall, studying me. "How long have you been standing there?"

"Long enough to recognize you regret what occurred here between us." She waves her arm to indicate the general room.

"Regret's the wrong word."

"Then what's the right one?"

I hold out my hand for her, one she steps forward and takes without hesitation. Wrapping her back up in my embrace, I rest my head on the crown of her head. "How was Bailey?"

I feel her smile against the skin still exposed by my open tuxedo shirt. "Almost asleep. She mumbled something about a fairy princess right before she went down for the count."

I pull back and stare down into her face. "She must have been trying to tell you how exquisite you look tonight."

Laura's lips quirk to one side. "Flattery will not get you back to the place we were at before your daughter came looking for you."

"Good, because that's not what I want." Even as the words come out of my mouth, I know they're partially a lie.

Laura knows it too, if the way her brows arch is any indication.

"Not right now, at least." I smooth a hand over her cheek. "Laura, I never planned on meeting you."

"Is that a bad thing?"

"No." My eyes leave her face and drift across the room to the corridor toward Bailey's. "It's just . . ."

"Liam." Her fingertips applying gentle pressure to my cheek capture my attention. "If you loved your daughter any less, I wouldn't be as attracted to you as I am. Fatherhood is very appealing on you."

My chest rises and falls with the force of my exhale. Laura continuously surprises me. She quickly summed up my concerns and still managed to amp up my desire. *She's willing to take me as I am.* Christ. It's more of an aphrodisiac than her luscious body or incredible brain.

She's openly displaying the heart her uncle sang about tonight—the stunning compassion that eclipses even her beauty. A miracle that managed to resurrect itself after the trauma she survived.

My heart tumbles over and over when I clasp her back against me. All night, I've been wondering what's so different.

It's her.

It's the realization I'm falling for her as easily as my daughter is.

CHAPTER
Fifty

I'M LYING in the sun in my backyard thinking. My thoughts are racing through my mind, chasing one another as much as I tried to chase passion the other night.

Much like my night with Liam ended, I can't find satisfaction.

It's been two days and nights since the ball, since I felt Liam's touch. Since I learned the truth about Bailey's mother and my heart broke for both of them. Instead of staying, which had been a real possibility before Bailey woke up, I laid my lips against his cheek and murmured, "You need time."

He walked me to the door that night and embraced me one last time before causing a fissure in a heart I'd only just repaired. The thing is, his words repaired it just as quickly. "I wouldn't be the kind of father I promised myself I'd be if I didn't take into account that whatever happens between us will have a lasting effect on Bailey. She loves you, Laura."

"I love her too."

"I just want to make certain what I want isn't going to deprive her of what she needs."

I rode home in silence, clutching the bouquet he gave me earlier that night, bombarded by everything that had happened since I first walked out my front door and falling for the man who gave it to me with every second we were apart.

Turns out we both needed the time albeit, for very different reasons.

After getting home, I was startled to find another doll waiting for me—this one carrying a bouquet mimicking the one I was holding. Shattering my illusions about my stalker easing off, I whipped out my phone and contacted my father.

Within minutes, a team of agents swarmed my home. Not long after that, my father stormed up my driveway. He took one look at the doll and declared, "This ends soon. They need to get the evidence."

"Daddy, do you know who it is?"

"I have an idea." His voice is calm and steady.

"Because if Liam or Bailey is in danger, I have to let them know . . .," I began, but he whirled me to him.

"Laura, you can't share with anyone what's occurring. Not even your cousins."

For a moment, instead of the safety of my father's embrace, I'm hurled back into the arms of Paulie Tiberi. I scratched and clawed to escape the man who has treasured me since I was seconds old. My voice was hysterical when I shrieked, "Let. Go. Of. Me!"

He released me immediately and I stumbled back. Guarding myself from my father, my pain. I'm not entirely certain. I reframed my question. "Are Liam and Bailey in any danger because of me?"

His "No" was emphatic and immediate.

My shoulders drooped in relief.

"You still can't tell him, Laura."

"Why not?"

Days later, a niggling continues in the base of my skull. Something that feels off. With the single-minded determination that got me through college and med school with a perfect GPA, I swear to figure it out because, as my father reminded me the other night, "It's not your fault."

It's not, but protecting Bailey and Liam is.

Liam. I close my eyes, and his face immediately appears behind my eyelids. I writhe on the chaise recalling the passion that clouded his bright green eyes. The way his hands felt against the skin of my body. The way his lips closed over the tips of my breasts.

I moan aloud and then yelp when I hear, "I hope you're thinking about me."

My eyes fly open and there he is. Hands in the pockets of casual pants, his black T-shirt molded to his chest. Knowing my cousins are out for the day, I lift a hand and ask, "How did you get inside the house?"

His eyes trail from my toes up my body, lingering at the juncture of my thighs, the dip in my waist, my breasts before meeting my gaze. "Hmm?"

"How did you get in?"

A lazy smile twitches his lips. "I haven't . . . been inside yet."

I press my lips together to keep my own from smiling. "No?"

"We were interrupted," he reminds me, wagging his brows.

I laugh before sitting up and gesturing for Liam to take a seat. "So we were. I was just thinking about that."

"I've been thinking as well." His finger trails across the top of my foot.

I feel the throb of his touch everywhere. I want him to stop. I want him to slow down. I want him to strip before driving into me so I forget where he begins and I end. Clearing my throat, I remind him, "You wanted to consider Bailey's feelings."

His hand slides up the inside of my calf. "I have."

"Oh?" Did that squeak come from me? It must have because Liam stops trailing his fingers at my knee. He leans forward, resting his chin on top of my joints.

"Yes. She and I sat down this morning. I told her I liked you very much."

Anxiety swirls in my stomach. "To which she said?"

"'What took you so long, Daddy?'"

I throw my head back and laugh because it's quintessential Bailey. When I'm done, he continues, "I told her Laura would always love her for her, but that I wanted to see if you liked me for me."

"Oh." This time, the word comes out breathless.

Then I jump. His other hand slides up the back of my thigh until his hand is gripping my ass—much like it was when I was straddling him the other night. Casually, as if he expects I'll take all the time in the world to answer him, he asks, "So, do you?"

"Do I what?"

"Like me?"

Deciding actions speak a lot clearer than words do, I shift. Liam slides back until I'm kneeling on the lounger. Gripping his T-shirt in my hands, I pull him forward and ask, "How about for our second date, I give you a tour of the house?"

"How about you give me a tour of your room and we can see the house later?"

"I love how you think." Just as the last word crosses my lips, his mouth crashes down on mine.

CHAPTER
Fifty-One

Laura

As SOON AS our lips connect, I press my body against his, picking up where we left off the other night. Liam's mouth opens beneath mine and my tongue swipes inside to tangle with his. My fingers dive into his hair to hold on tight as he shifts my body, to once again have me straddling his lap.

But with the excuse of a bikini I was wearing to sunbathe, when his hands roam my back and thighs, there are no yards of silk hindering his fingers from encountering skin.

My skin.

And good Christ, the way his calloused fingers feel against it makes me want to feel the rest of him.

Ripping my mouth away, I tug at the edge of his shirt. "You're wearing too many clothes."

Liam grips me beneath my ass and stands. "I'm thinking the same thing, but I don't want an audience. Tell me how to get to your bedroom."

Trailing my lips up the side of his neck, I reach his ear just as he lets out a harsh growl. "Through the doors. Up the stairs."

Liam immediately begins walking. The second he does, I angle my hips so I feel the length of his cock rub against my clit. Now it's my turn to groan as the friction burns through me—every hard part of him gliding against the parts of me that are softening in preparation for him.

My head falls back after he starts up the stairs with me in his arms, every knee bend rocking me against him. "Faster."

His hand, which had been supporting my back at that point, slides into my curls. Bracing me against the wall, he orders, "The first time you come will be with my fingers and mouth. The second time will be with my cock buried deep inside you, Laura."

My sanity takes flight and I tug his lips down to mine for an impromptu make out session. "Then hurry."

He bounds up the stairs until he reaches the landing. "Where the fuck is your bedroom?"

I drag one hand from where I'd been clutching his muscular arm and point at the door just beyond the stairs.

Liam immediately resumes his hasty movements.

The second the door closes behind us, I unwrap my legs from around his lean hips and let my body slide down the front of his. As I do, my hands immediately reach for his T-shirt. Breathlessly, I inform him, "One of us is overdressed."

He arches his tattooed arm behind his back and rips the offending garment off with one hand. "I agree. Strip."

I can't. I'm not certain if I can force my lungs to inhale as I stare at a body God must have created on a day she realized orgasms were necessary for humans to live.

My mouth waters as my eyes roam from his eyes down over the scruff of his beard, down the cords that define his neck. My eyes flicker across broad shoulders I must have dreamed up in a fantasy. Then over his pectorals, where a sprinkle of hair leads to his six-pack. Down further to where his hip bones jut out just slightly, making the waistband of his jeans gap just a bit.

I reach for him and my hand slides into that gap. I yank him toward me. I want to feel Liam's body against mine, with as much skin touching as possible. "Let me help with this last little problem."

He rotates his hips and my eyes almost roll back into my head. "Little?"

I back away from him, leading him to where I want him—in my bed. Along the way, he undoes the button and lowers the zipper of his jeans before toeing off his shoes. Sweet merciful heaven. When we stop by my bed and his pants fall to the floor, I'm facing a primordial male whose predatory gaze tells me he's intent on one thing.

Sex. Sex with me.

His arms wrap around the back of me and with a few flicks, my bikini top drops to the floor. Judging by the way a dark ring wraps around his light green eyes, he not only feels the pebbling of my nipples against his chest but he's as turned on by it as I am by everything that's him. His hands come up to cup my breasts. I protest when he moves me back a step, but that transitions to a moan when he bends forward and takes a nipple into his mouth.

Sucking and licking, his lips worship one breast while his fingers roll the other nipple. Then—yes!—he switches to the other as his ministrations with his finger and thumb resume. He releases my breast with a pop before saying, "Christ, Laura. I could spend a whole day just worshiping your tits."

"Later," I pant. My hands skim down his back. "I want you."

His head lifts and he topples me backward until I'm sprawled across the bed in a diagonal. "I believe I made you certain promises on the stairs." His hands reach for my bikini bottoms.

My hips lift as he drags them down over my ass. Then I am exposed to his touch, his mouth.

Whatever he wants to do with me.

A whisper of a flutters distracts me. I eye the condoms he tossed onto the bed with an amused glance. "Think you have that much stamina?"

"I fucking hope so. I'm not leaving here until I've used them all."

"Bailey?"

"Is at a sleepover. We have all night." He crawls up my body until his naked torso is perfectly aligned with mine. That's when I realize he's shed his boxers. Wrapping my legs around his, I rub my pussy against his lower stomach in anticipation of how it's going to feel when he finally thrusts his cock deep inside of me. Liam's head crashes down onto mine. "Don't be so impatient."

I huff out a laugh that's abruptly cut off when he slides down, pressing kisses down the center of my body as he goes.

Eventually, Liam props himself in between my thighs. One of my hands is threaded through his hair, the other is clutched in my duvet cover and all he's done is touch me. Now, he glides his fingertips around my clit in slow circles, causing my body to quiver. "That's what I want."

"More," I beg.

"You'll give it to me," he snarls. His fingers drag down to my saturated entrance before he notches them inside my opening.

"Please. Oh, please."

Then he slides a finger inside.

My body bows, especially when he begins thrusting before lowering his lips to my clit and sucking on it. My head thrashes back and forth, my thighs quiver. Liam, proving he's a man of his word, keeps up the pace, adding a slight curl as his fingers hit my core.

I'm right on the edge. I lift my head and blindly, I search for an anchor. Instead, I find Liam's eyes and fall over into rapture. The throbbing of my core tightens around his fingers. I'm certain my wetness must drench his beard, but I don't care.

All I care about right now is not stopping until I feel him connected to me.

Liam straightens from his position on the floor. He uses the lubricant from me to stroke his cock. Any exhaustion I felt from my own orgasm falls away. I struggle to sit up. "Let me."

His eyes gleam with interest and agreement. "Next time. If you wrap those lips around my cock, I won't last."

I lean back, bracing on my elbows. My legs fall open. "Then what do you want me to do?"

He snatches up a condom and rips it open, stroking it down his length. "Sit right there. Just like that." The second he's sheathed himself, his hands move to my ankles. He slides his palms up over my calves, making room for his hips as he crawls back up in between my legs.

I wrap my legs around his hips as he coats his cock in my remaining wetness. Every time the head of his cock bumps against my still humming clit, I grind myself up against him. I'm about to roll him over and take him deep inside when his cock probes my entrance. "Are you ready?"

I lift my hips in response.

His answer is to drive into me in one single push before he stills his body over mine.

My breath escapes with a gasp. "Fuck me, Liam."

Liam gives me a second to adjust to his size. Then he begins thrusting. "With pleasure."

In and out, long strokes that have me clutching his shoulders for purchase as my thighs clasp his hips. Liam rotates his hips in a tight circle as he flings us to the cliff where we're intended to fly.

The second orgasm bowls into me quickly, my inner muscles clamping down on his cock. I moan his name and wrap him up as he continues to pound into me. Then, three, four strokes later, his fingers clenched on my hip as he shatters. His body stills before his hips shunt forward, jerking as the orgasm rips through him. He gasps my name, "Laura," before he collapses on top of me.

In that moment, I absorb everything. My hands run up over the barely leashed muscles of his back, down over his taut ass. I smell his aftershave mingled with the scent of sex, us. I hear his harsh breath in my ear.

And I know I didn't just fly.

I fell off a cliff.

One where I might be falling in love.

CHAPTER
Fifty~Two

LIAM

LAURA ROLLS over my chest and places a bottle of water on the nightstand. After she does, she runs her hand up my tattooed arm. "Tell me about your ink. I have to say, it doesn't scream chief audit officer."

I finish chewing the last bite of the sandwich she made for me. Originally, I fantasized aloud that she should be naked until she pointed out that "Kalie and Grace could come home any minute. I'm not so certain I want them to have the image of your cock, Liam." At that, I slid into my jeans before tossing her my tee.

Now we're finishing our snack in my preferred state of undress. "It started when I was in the Army." I point to the complex design on the main part of my forearm. "This was the design my unit wore."

"Were you forward deployed?" she asks as her lips trace the outline.

I point to a different set of ink. "Not until I went to work for the Agency. There, everyone saw some time in the field—even if we were just support staff." I take a deep breath before I point to a final set. "And this is what I got when I realized Bailey was mine."

She cocks her head to the side, spilling her sable-colored curls over one creamy shoulder. "What do you mean when you realized she was yours?"

Tonelessly, I tell her about Ashleigh, about how we were together. What I walked in on. How I demanded a paternity test. I don't know what to expect.

I shouldn't have wondered. Not with Laura.

She lets out a snort. "I'm a doctor. There are questions about implantation dates from couples who have been together for years. Of course you'd have questioned it. So what happened after?"

I pass my hand through her curls and lift her lips to mine. After a long and drugging kiss, in part to thank her for having my back so unconditionally, I realize I don't want Ashleigh here. Not tonight. I summarize the story with a brief, "Bailey was shuffled between two parents until Ashleigh passed away in a car wreck."

Laura's face drops. She's an ER doctor. She knows far too well what that means. And right now, I can't bring myself to share with her what a complete fuck up Bailey's mother was.

Later, I tell myself. We have all the time in the world for me to share this.

Instead, I ask, "What made you choose emergency medicine?"

She groans before her face crashes into my chest. "Don't tell me you're going to say I should have done something else with my life."

I frown. "Why would I say something like that?"

"Because I hear it from my chief of staff—Dr. Moser."

"Isn't that the same guy you refer to as Dr. Douche?" I recall from the gala.

"One and the same."

"Then why do you care?

"I don't except when he corners me on the way to my shift to remind me I should have become his protégé in neurology." Laura's curls dance across my chest as she shakes her head negatively. "No, thank you."

I pull back a bit. "The chief of staff wanted to mentor you?"

"Yes."

"I read your CV, Laura. I know you're ridiculously intelligent. Are you that good of a doctor?"

Her head lifts and her eyes stare straight into mine. "I'm probably better."

Holy crap. "And you're nannying for me. Why?"

She props her head on her chin. "Because somewhere along the way, I forgot something that made me such an exceptional doctor."

Concerned, I cup her cheek. "What's that?"

"How to care. I was afraid if I let people back into my heart, they'd wind up hurt."

I piece the puzzle together. "Just like with the Tiberis."

She nods. Then she bites her lip before a determined look drifts over her face. "Liam . . ."

I roll her to her back before kissing her breathless, stopping her words with my lips. My hand rests on the space between her bare breasts. I lean down and kiss the scar left over from her bullet wound. The pounding of her heart is reassuring, knowing how close she actually came to dying. "You, Laura Lockwood, have an enormous heart. I'm just grateful you found your way into our lives."

Her face softens before a devilish gleam enters her eyes. "Is this your way to butter me up so I suck you off?"

I shrug, but I can't deny the hardening of my cock at her earthy words. God, the idea of her kissable lips wrapped around my shaft has brought me to full erection. "Maybe."

Laura pushes at my shoulder. "Then maybe you should let me take a closer inspection of your condition, Mr. Payne. After all, I am a medical professional."

As Laura brushes her lips down the center of my body, I whisper, "Apparently you're excellent at your job."

I don't know how true my words are until her mouth wraps around me and I end up shouting her name while she drains me with her lips, her hands massaging my testicles. Just before I doze off, Laura wrapped up in my arms. I can't help but wonder if what I endured in Bailey's early years was so I'd be grateful for this.

For finding Laura.

Otherwise, I'd be afraid of doing something to screw us up.

From the Journal of Dr. Laura Lockwood

If being in my life is dangerous, loving me would be sheer idiocy. I can only imagine what the threat is for those I love.

I should run, leave my family, Bailey, Liam . . .

Did I just write that?

Oh, God. I did.

I love them.

I need to protect them.

I need to talk to my father. He has to understand. I can't leave them unaware, in danger.

He'll protect them.

I know it.

CHAPTER
Fifty~Three

Laura

IT'S BEEN weeks of this, of uniting what I feel for Liam with what I feel for Bailey. Of falling in love with each of them individually and together as a family.

Of finding that special place my mother always told me she found the minute my father came through her front door the first time they had dinner together in the house I grew up in.

Home.

In the warm glow of the kitchen, with the lasagna cooking in the oven perfuming the air, I couldn't help but let the happiness we've been living bubble over me.

We've been together every night, Liam, Bailey, and I. At first, my cousins were concerned with the speed with which this relationship was progressing. But then they were included in our outings and gave me two thumbs up a piece—or in the case of Grace since she had a spare one in her purse, three.

Bailey found that a riot, so Grace let her keep it with the promise she'd help out on Bailey's Halloween outfit this year.

Liam's "Just don't give her an extra eye or something, Grace. They might freak me out too much" not only told me he was cool with my family, but he, too, saw us together at Halloween.

And hopefully well beyond.

Stirring the extra sauce, I think of each of our weekend adventures. We explored a famous Connecticut seaside town, laughing over the feral way Bailey became obsessed with blue crabs. We taught her how to tell the difference between a good and bad clam. We wandered in and out of seaports, museums, and stores.

We played with Bailey in parks during the day and at night held hands sprawled out on blankets beneath the stars to enjoy outdoor concerts.

When we wanted alone time, Grace and Kalie stepped up. It not only gave us freedom as a new couple, but allowed my cousins the opportunity to get to know Bailey—something my heart rejoiced in.

My favorite was when Liam and I did nothing more than take walks along shell-filled beaches while my cousins offered to cook dinner for all of us. Hand in hand, we'd stop and pocket shells to commemorate each new stop we'd been to as the sun painted the sky with hues of orange and pink. But even as the fiery sun set, it was nothing to the way I'd lose myself in the burning green of Liam's gaze when he pulled me close to kiss me.

I marveled at the bond we'd created. It was unlike anything I'd ever experienced with my family, even my twin. It was the very essence of life.

Which is why I was quietly terrified.

Every couple of days, I persistently questioned my father about if I was placing them in any danger. "Should I tell Liam, Daddy? He works for you. He won't say anything."

"No, Laura. My team has this under control. Do you not trust me?"

"Of course, I trust you. It's just . . ."

"It's just you're falling in love with Liam," my father concluded grimly.

Unable to deny it, I replied, "Yes."

"Laura," he pleaded.

"Daddy, I love him and I love Bailey. I will not let them be harmed. I'd sooner die myself."

His growl did nothing to intimidate me. Flatly, I gave him an ultimatum. "You have two weeks to figure out who is doing this to me or I'm telling him."

He swore savagely. "I will yank you away from Liam and Bailey so fast, your head will spin. Do not think I won't hesitate to put you in protective custody."

"Dad, nothing has happened." Silence from the other end of the line makes my antennae quiver. "Or has it?"

"We'll talk about it in person." Then he hung up without his normal "I loved you first," setting my mind whirling.

He has three more days before I tell Liam everything. A dark cloud passes over my thoughts, causing me to stir the sauce too fast and fling it all over the counter. The laughter in the air comes to a halt when I let out a weak, "Oops."

Liam slips his arms around me from behind. "We're not trying to feed the seagulls this time, sweetheart."

My head swivels to the side and I shoot him a glare. "They almost took my hand off." When we went to visit a local lighthouse, I held up a piece of bread to break apart and the next thing I knew, a seagull swooped in and nipped it from my fingers.

Liam nuzzles my ear. "Hmm. Now that's a good memory." He presses his lips against the side of my head before murmuring low enough so Bailey can't hear. "The chocolate."

My body melts against his when I recall Liam slathering the melted chocolate onto my nipples and feasting on them for a snack before I returned the favor. He presses another kiss in my ear. "Who knows? I may want seconds using your red sauce."

I spin around, the spoon in my hand, sauce dripping all the way down to my wrist. I accuse, "You're terrible."

He lifts my wrist and licks it off. "Hmm. Definitely seconds."

I blush to the roots of my hair before replying tartly, "If you want firsts, you'll stop distracting me."

Liam roars with laughter. He rips the spoon from my hand and hauls me against the length of his body. "Sweetheart, I don't care if dinner goes up in flames. All I care about is you and Bailey, you know that."

My breathing quickens. Even though we haven't said the words, I feel them emanating from him, which is why this subterfuge my father has me engaged in is killing me every minute. "I do."

His lips quirk. "I like those words." Then he mutters to himself, "At least coming from you."

Wait. What? Just as he's about to move away, I grab the back of his shirt and haul him to me. "What did you say?"

He affixes his work face. God, that expression makes me so damn hot. I want to lick him up and he knows it. My cheeks burn and Liam gives me a potent stare. Grumbling, I mutter, "I blush like a Roma tomato."

He presses his lips to my forehead before murmuring, "It's one of the things I love about you, Laura."

I turn to stone in his arms. Did he just say? Does he mean?

At my stillness, he pulls back and his eyes dilate when they search mine. "I didn't mean to freak you out. I thought you knew?"

"That you loved me?"

He nods.

"No."

"They're my feelings, Laura. You shouldn't feel pressured . . ."

Slapping my hand across his mouth, my heart is trembling when I admit, "I love you too. I just thought it was too soon."

He shoves my hand away and gives me a relatively chaste kiss. "Nothing is too soon if it's right. Now, that will have to hold you over until tonight."

He spins me around and pats my ass. I give a quick check to see if Bailey's watching. She's instead coloring. Crooking my finger at him, I murmur, "I can't wait."

After making certain the sauce isn't ruined, I let my mind dream of a life doing just this—loving Liam and Bailey. That's when I make my decision.

My father can be pissed at me from now until eternity, but he has less than three days.

I refuse to lie to the man I love, and that's what it feels like at this point. Especially when I hear laughter echoing in the kitchen of the house I consider my home because of the people in it.

CHAPTER
Fifty~Four

LIAM

SPEARING them both with speculative glances, I reach down to press a kiss to Bailey's cheek. What I didn't realize is with how close Laura's standing next to her, my face would be within inches of her long, bare legs.

Legs I spent hours memorizing with my lips, worshiping with flicks of my tongue.

Before I reached heaven at the juncture between them just the night before.

Christ. If I inhale deeply enough, I can pick up the rich scent, reminding me of that very moment over the sweet scent of my daughter's skin. Now that we've been together for some time, I can differentiate between the two. The scent of Laura brings up memories of heat filled nights exploring her body, knowing what to do to make her moan and tremble in my arms.

It's not enough.

A month has gone by and I know how I feel.

I'm head over heels in love with her.

Jerking to a standing position, I find myself irrationally infuriated by the fact that I seem to be the only one affected. Perhaps it's just the persistent proximity between us that has me noticing her sheen of sable curls that cascade down her back. Or the way her sea-colored eyes focus exclusively on the person she's speaking with. How the dimple in her cheek pops out when she's happy or excited by something—as she is right now.

What I sure as fuck shouldn't be remembering when she's around Bailey is how the slim, muscular shape of her thighs feel wrapped around my waist as I sink my cock inside of her. What it feels like to grip the curve of her hip, her tight ass, or to mold her high rounded breasts in my palms as I push inside of her tight pussy. When her internal muscles contract all along my length.

What it sounds like when her breath hitches right before her body spasms as she comes.

I groan, causing her head to snap around. There's a flush on her cheeks that belays her disinterest. All I want to do is make up some excuse to drag her inside, pin her against a wall behind a locked door and find out if we're as good together vertically as we are horizontally.

Just then, my phone rings. Slipping it from my pocket, I feel the blood drain from my cock by someone who can kill a hard-on worse than my daughter—Laura's father. For fuck's sake, I need my little brain to catch up with my big one. The only problem is I'm not certain which one is calling the shots anymore.

She's my boss's daughter, my daughter's nanny, and neither of those things seem to matter anymore. All that matters is ensuring she knows she's mine.

Gesturing to the phone, I answer, "Hey, Caleb. What's up?"

Laura rolls her eyes before letting them drift downward. She snickers at my obvious problem. My shaft throbs, that's for damn sure. I'd be apt to tell her how I want to take care of this problem if not for the fact I know I have very precocious eyes watching.

And apparently listening. I focus on Caleb's words. "Listen, I need you to come to the Norwalk office tomorrow. Is that going to be a problem?"

"No. Not at all, since I have Laura here to watch Bailey."

He sounds distracted when he repeats, "Yeah, Laura and Bailey. We . . . See you in the morning, Liam."

I shove my phone back into my pocket, wondering why he didn't just text me. Pushing aside all thoughts of Laura's father into a box and throwing away the key, I entertain myself by imagining all the ways I'm going to touch Laura's body later tonight.

All the ways I plan on dragging my fingers across her smooth skin.

Pleasuring her with my mouth.

In fact, I'm so dedicated to the job, I convince her to stay when she had planned to sneak out and head back to her home.

We both sleep past my alarm the next morning. With that mistake, there's no chance of Bailey not finding out Laura stayed the night as she thunders down the stairs while I get dressed. Still in my towel from our quick shower, I hear Bailey squeal, "Laura! You had a sleepover."

"I did, Buttercup." Laura's voice is clearly cautious.

"Did Daddy sleep well?" Bailey's innocent voice asks.

Oh, shit. Instead of us talking to Bailey together, Laura's getting hit with the difficult questions without me. She coughs repeatedly before I hear Bailey whale on her back. I blatantly eavesdrop to hear Laura force out, "He did."

I smirk. When I slept, that is.

Laura probes. "How do you feel about that?"

"About what?"

"Me being here when you woke up?"

"Can you wake up here every morning?" Bailey asks.

"Oh, sweetheart," Laura's voice murmurs.

"Besides, now Daddy has new pillows. You can take the best one."

Laura outright laughs at this point. "What if he doesn't want to give me his favorite?"

"Then he has to learn to share," Bailey reasons.

My daughter's absolutely right. I'll need to learn to share more than "Firmy." I need to learn to share Laura with Bailey, her job, and her family. My smile fades when I realize what the changes at the end of the summer will bring—less of this special time when we're all wrapped up together as a family.

What will that do to all of us?

I quickly dress, eager to be downstairs, spending as much time with the two most important women in my life before I have to go to work. Grateful I only have to drive from Darien to Norwalk instead of to Manhattan, I have a few minutes to linger before I leave. The second I enter the kitchen, my glance ping-pongs back and forth between Laura and Bailey.

Bailey beams at me while Laura can't quite meet my gaze. A huge grin spreads across my face as I press a kiss to the top of her head. Just to drive the point home, I do the same to Laura.

Her cheeks flame even as Bailey laughs and points out, "Laura, your face is as red as a tomato."

Bailey announces she's going to get dressed. The second she's out of the room, I tug Laura close. "Take care of her today."

She smiles up at me, smoothing the lapels of my jacket. "Of course. We don't have much going on. I'll text you our plans."

"Any possibilities?"

"Swimming. Cookies, maybe."

I lean down and press my face against the juncture of her neck I know gets her riled up. "I love your . . . cookies."

She swats my waist. "Rude."

"That may be true, but you know what else is?"

"What?"

"I love you, Laura," I openly remind her in the light of day.

She smooths my lapel even as her eyes hold mine. "I don't care if it's fast. I love you too, Liam."

I press my lips against her forehead and then her lips. "Have fun with Bailey. Later, we'll drive you home so you can pack a bag."

Her body freezes. *Crap.* "Are you moving me in?"

"Let's start with you staying tonight," I clarify quickly.

"That works."

A whoosh of breath rushes out of me. Then she alleviates all my fears that I might be pushing too far too fast when she admits, "It's not that I don't want to be here with you both, Liam. It's that I want to give Bailey time to adjust to you and me. I want everything with you."

I'm about to reply when I hear Bailey shout, "Laura? Can you help me?"

She pulls back and I miss her in my arms already. "Coming, sweetheart!"

"And with that, I'm out."

"Have a good day. Save my family from some unholy audit."

"Well, since you asked so nicely." I wink at her before I head toward the garage.

If I had known that was the last thing I'd have said to Laura coherently, I would have reminded her to take care of Bailey.

I'm certain of it.

CHAPTER
Fifty-Five

Laura

It STARTED as a quick errand to my house. Bailey pleaded with me to see Cia again, so I contacted Jilly for another beach day. Unfortunately, I didn't have my suit with me. Knowing Kalie was in court and Grace was fitting someone with a new hand, I didn't want to disturb my cousins. I sent Liam a quick text.

LAURA:

Bailey and I are running to my house. Need to grab my suit.

LAURA:

We decided to go swimming with Cia and Jilly.

LIAM:

:) Be safe. I love you both.

LAURA:

I love you too. Wish you were here.

LIAM:

Me too. Your uncle is a sadist.

LAURA:

Tell me something I didn't grow up knowing.

LIAM:

LOL! I'm telling him you said that.

LAURA:

Wouldn't be the first time ;)

I just parked the minivan behind my Pilot before asking Bailey, "Want to see my home?"

Bailey frowns down at her casts. "How?"

I tug one of her braids. "Well, now that I can carry you, I can pick you up and bring you through the front door. Then you can wait for me while I run upstairs."

Bailey lets out a happy gurgle of agreement.

I shut off the engine and dash around the back of the car. Opening her door, I wait for her to climb onto my back. Once I have a good grip on her legs and her little arms are tight around my neck, I bound up flagstone steps similar to the ones that are in front of Liam's home.

Seconds later, I regret the decision.

I regret everything.

⁂

"She can't stand," I shout.

The feel of the smack across my face comes as no surprise. My head whips to the side. I manage to hold in my shriek of pain, but Bailey cries out. The bitch who has one arm wrapped around her waist grips her by the chin brutally. "Shut your fucking trap, brat," before she flings her face away.

There are red marks where her fingers were, but as much as they hurt her, I'm being savaged by the pain in Bailey's eyes.

The same bitch snarls, "Get me a chair to strap this brat to. And who the fuck didn't realize she'd have a kid with her?"

No one volunteers.

"Who did the research on the good *doctor*," she sneers.

Out of the ten or so people in the room, two raise their hands.

Seconds later, two shots are fired. I jerk beneath my own captor's grip as the two men fall with bloody holes between their eyebrows. But Bailey? My sweet Bailey can't be blamed for not keeping it together.

She screams, "Nooooo!"

All the oxygen leaves the room when the monster holding her twists her and shouts, "Did I not say to shut the fuck up?" Only this time, she uses her gun to thump the side of her head next to where her braids begin.

Silence immediately descends on the room, like someone lifted the needle off a record. Bailey's lip quivers and her eyes roll back in her head before she faints. There's a thunk when her head hits our hardwood floors because the whore doesn't bother to catch her.

Instinctively, I leap forward to grab her, but I'm hauled back by the chokehold the behemoth behind me has on my neck. "Please, let me go to her."

A silver circle arcs in my direction. "Fine. While you're checking out your 'patient' you can also tape her up for us."

Knowing my options are limited, I catch the tape one handed. Dully, I agree. "Fine."

A chin jerk from cunt to asshole releases me. Once I'm released, my knees give way. Crawling over to Bailey, I check for a pulse and lay my head on her chest to make certain she's still breathing. Thank the lord, she is. She's just passed out from shock and pain. As carefully as I can, I begin to bind her two casts together.

Then I feel it—cold carbon steel pressed against the base of my neck. I still. The cruel voice dictates, "Unless you want her screaming to necessitate her death, Doc, I suggest you start with that fucking loud mouth of hers. I don't want to hear another fucking sound made by a voice that isn't yours. You got me?"

Even as I rip off pieces of duct tape, I demand answers. "Who are you? What do you want? If it's money, I'll get it for you."

She leans against the side of my sofa. "Well, isn't that accommodating, Doc. You're much nicer than your daddy, aren't you?"

I try to bluff. "My father? What does my father have to do with this?"

Instead of answering, she thumps over and crouches down until her body is right next to Bailey's. I balance over hers. If I have to, I'll throw myself on top of her, sacrificing myself to save her for Liam. I love him, I love her.

I won't let another trauma ruin their forever.

"Maybe I should introduce myself," she muses. The roar of rusted laughter that erupts around the room reminds me of that scene in *The Mummy* where the mummy swallows Brendan Frasier's plane—like it's the gateway to hell if you're not strong enough to endure it.

I pause, hesitating to place the first strip of tape on Bailey's mouth. Every second the one in charge holds out, my fear increases. The threat for both me and this little girl I cherish reaches a new peak. Then, her eyes narrow just before her hot breath heats the side of my face. She murmurs, "Olivia Tiberi. Paulie should have shot you through the heart, Doc. But my husband always was a bit of a moron. Now that he's dead, it's my job to avenge him. We'll never have our own little girl to pamper, which is why I so loved leaving those dolls I'd been collecting for you."

I feel the blood draining from my head as the room begins to spin. It can't be. My nightmares should be over, not coming back to life. "You . . ."

She sits back on her haunches, waving her gun carelessly over Bailey's still unmoving form. "We're all Tiberis—some blood, some bonded. And you, Doc? You're going to die for what you did and what your daddy's tryin' to do. That's a promise."

Then she aims the gun right at Bailey's heart. "Now, get to fucking work."

Without a moment's hesitation, I do. I've experienced first-hand the lack of mercy these people have. The best chance I have of getting Bailey and me out of here alive is to comply with their orders.

I lay the first piece of duct tape across Bailey's beautiful bow lips, hoping I'll have the opportunity to see them pucker into a smile at least one more time before I die.

After finishing taping Bailey up, I am swiftly bound to lie next to her. Unlike the half-assed job I did—for which the Tiberis took great pleasure in kicking me in the ribs with their steel-toed boots. Al— Christ, my hope of getting out alive dwindles seeing his normally soft brown eyes void of emotion—does a much better job focusing on his task. Every piece of thick silver tape he lays across my skin not only prevents me from moving, it increases my fear factor as well as raises the level of desperation in the air.

"Please," I beg. "Leave my fingers free. If she wakes up, I can hold her hand. Keep her from being too frightened."

Olivia sneers before conceding. "She's right, Al. Just their fingertips. Make certain neither of them have anything in their hands or so help me God, I'll see you in hell."

The second my fingers are free, I grasp Bailey's fingers with one hand, entwining her little fingers next to my Amaryllis tattoo. Praying I won't get shot, I watch as they stand guard—as if they're waiting for something.

Or someone.

"What the fuck are we doing, Liv? We just going to sit here waiting for her father to come looking for her?"

She props her booted feet on my back. "Nah. See, I took a picture and sent it to fucking Lockwood. He knows you got his little bitch."

"You stupid cunt. We could have popped her and been out of here for him to find," Al breathes.

Olivia kicks me in the hip when she surges to her feet. "Bastard shoulda kept his fucking nose out of our shit! Why didn't you fix it?"

"You wanted info on Hudson Investigations! How the fuck was I supposed to do that and keep my cover?"

"Fucking asshole. Had to go poking his dick in our crap instead of his wife when Paulie lost his temper."

I'm not certain if I want to puke or grab his gun and shoot Olivia myself, despite my oath to heal. My teeth grind together with the desire to scream, *Lost his temper? He killed innocent people.* But even if the duct tape wasn't slapped across my mouth, I wouldn't.

I want to see my father kick his ass for me and for Bailey. I sure as hell wouldn't mind if Liam took a few shots at this bitch too.

Then I tense when the house phone rings once before it disconnects.

In my head, I rationalize it could be a wrong number. But I also recall the lessons my father taught to me, Jon, and Chuck when we were younger. He warned us, "The largest fear your mother has is you'll be kidnapped."

"Dad—" Jon started to scoff until my father's eyes blazed into his. I'd never witnessed my father so deadly serious before or since.

"Jon, one day, you'll understand why. In the meantime, listen to my instructions." My father released a sigh. "If you are ever taken, we'll make a noise. Then we'll wait thirty seconds."

Then two noises. Knowing my mother endured the kind of hell no one ever should and that she did indeed want to LoJack me, Jon, and Chuck, I count down to one before the phone rings again.

Ring, ring. Then it disconnects.

I slide so my body partially covers Bailey's. Olivia shouts, "Who the fuck is calling?"

One of her minions picks up one of the cordless handsets and checks the caller ID. "The first time, it was the cable company. The second time, spam."

He relaxes.

In my head, I'm counting, *twenty-seven, twenty-eight, twenty-nine,*

Our house phone rings again.

By the time the third ring happens, I'm rolling on top of Bailey as the front and back doors are kicked in by the SWAT team.

Olivia opens fire, her semi-automatic assault rifle spitting out bullets at a rapid pace. Realizing how fucked she must be, she makes a tactical error.

She turns her head away from the imminent threat and searches for a hostage—me.

I'm far enough away that it gives enough time for a laser to light up both her forehead and the center of her chest.

The glass shatters. The force of the bullets slams into her. I'd swear she isn't dead by the way her feet keep moving if it wasn't for the gray matter that explodes out of the back of her head.

I close my eyes and try not to vomit. *Bailey, just think of Bailey. You have to get Bailey out of here safely.*

CHAPTER
Fifty-Six

Laura

"LAURA? ARE YOU OKAY?" I hear the second most beloved voice in the world—my father's. He spots me lying across Bailey and spits out, "Shit." Rushing over, he calls out, "Tell RA to pull up immediately."

"On it," one of the SWAT guys repeats the order into his headset. Across our front yard I see the Darien Fire Department pull up with medical kits and an ambulance not far behind.

My father winces before he peels back the tape from my mouth. Immediately, I order, "Dad, Bailey. She's been out too long. That bitch clocked her, and she went down hard."

Quickly, he uses a knife to cut through the duct tape and peels back the piece covering her lips. As he takes care of her, another Hudson agent approaches. He lifts his mask before familiar blue eyes penetrate mine. Jon says, "Laura, turn over."

I do, and with a few strikes of my brother's blade, he removes the duct tape from me as well. I snap at him, "Get my stethoscope out of my bag. Hall closet."

My brother frog leaps up to do my bidding even while I do a cursory examination of Bailey's legs, praying I hadn't caused any damage.

"Fuck all of you Lockwoods!" Al screams as Darien's finest lead him out of my home. Olivia's still splattered everywhere.

I'm not paying attention to anyone or anything but Bailey as I've just slipped the earbuds in so I can listen to her heart and lungs. My hands tremble as I feel for the knot on her head. Just as I'm about to check her pupils, the EMTs arrive. "We have it from here, Dr. Lockwood. You need to get checked out."

Stubbornly, I refuse. "I'm staying with her."

"Laura," my brother argues.

"Jon, Bailey is *my* responsibility. Don't even think about trying to separate me from her."

My father struggles with his feelings for me and understanding my emotions for the little girl being threaded with an IV. Love. It's a circle that begins and ends with love. "Let her go with Bailey, Jon."

He doesn't argue with me. Despite how much I want to hurl words of fury at my father, there's something far more important to deal with right now and I need to get her to the hospital. Struggling to my feet, I snatch up my purse and place a hand on the board to jog with the EMTs as best as I can with legs that feel like the muscle and bone were removed in the last hour. "Where are we taking her?"

"We're closest to Darien West," the one EMT begins.

"Is she critical?" I demand.

"No, ma'am."

I override the order. "Then take her to Greenwich ER."

"Ma'am, that's outside our district," the other EMT says.

"But it's not outside mine. That's *my* ER. And it's not ma'am, it's Doctor. Dr. Laura Lockwood. I want her treated by the best. If she's not critical, take me there and have your damn house send me the bill."

The two EMTs exchange glances before lifting Bailey into the back of the bus. I climb in after and immediately resume listening to her heart and lungs.

"You're going to be just fine, Buttercup," I promise. Then I pull out my cell phone and make a call—a favor I never in my life thought I'd be asking for.

Within seconds, he grants it before saying, "Now, get off my phone, Gore. I have to let your ER know you have a patient coming in."

An agonizing eighteen minutes later, we pull up to my ER. Just like Moser promised me, they were waiting. All of them.

All my team—from the attending to healthcare housekeeping services— each and every one of them are lined up and waiting.

Like a damn honor guard.

For me. For my girl.

The bus doors are pulled open and Anna—today's day shift chief nurse— demands, "Give us the rundown, Gore."

"Seven-year-old female was a victim of a home hostage situation." I wait for the initial rumble to subside as I toss my purse to one of the med students loitering around. Let them figure out what to do with it. If they're not smart enough to figure it out, then they shouldn't be in my hospital. "Patient's name is Bailey Payne. Patient is recovering from a hostage situation just under six months ago that occurred in this ER. Records are available in the hospital system."

"Take her to trauma room two," Anna orders.

I jog alongside the gurney, stroking Bailey's precious face. Anna catches sight and challenges, "Gore, are you going to be able to run this?"

"No one touches my girl except for me," I hiss. We align to the bed, and I grab the handle on the board before calling out, "And on my count, one, two, three."

Like I never left, the choreography comes back to me. We lift Bailey from the EMT's board to the hospital bed. Even as leads are being attached, I lean over and press a kiss to her cheek, "Don't worry, Buttercup. Everything is going to be fine. I've got you."

Then I hold out my arms to be gowned up. "Patient was clipped by the butt of a gun. She hit her head again after fainting during a hostage situation. I want to know where the fuck Moser is."

One of the nurses snorts out loud. "Good luck getting the chief to come down, Gore. I get this is your first patient back but—"

Her words are cut off when the man himself strides through the door in scrubs like he's one of us. The room goes static when he barks out, "What's the read, Gore?"

I order my nursing staff, "I want a CBC type and cross match her blood despite what's in her chart." Then I inform Moser, "I don't think we're going to need blood, but I'm afraid after I order scans I might find a clot because of the way those assholes had me tie her up."

The room gasps. Ignoring them, Moser agrees. "Get the scans. Expedite the wet read. Tell them I gave the order if anyone down in Radiology gives you a hard time. Rosenthal is her primary for her legs?"

I jerk up my chin since my voice is lost somewhere in the echoes of fear I'm beating back.

"I'll get him to come down and consult after you get her imaging back. If you even suspect she's throwing a clot, bring me in. I'd rather push meds than operate on a seven-year-old girl unless I absolutely have to. Do we have a plan, Gore?"

"Yes, sir." The second he turns, I rap out additional orders for Bailey's imaging.

No one is surprised when Bailey is immediately rushed from the room; we're making the hospital grapevine burn. Not only is the chief resident of the ER back, but the chief of the hospital is consulting on her first case. I lag behind a brief moment, my mind still partially left back at my house in the nightmare we just lived through. Still, I hear Anna shout, "Gore! Let's go!"

"Right."

I shove my guilt to the side so I can take care of my first patient back in my ER—the most important one of my life.

Mingling with the rhythmic beeping of the medical equipment surrounding her, I struggle with guilt and responsibility of this being my fault.

I knew a stalker was out there, but I let my father assure me he had everything under control.

My emotions are as raw as the wounds I dressed on Bailey as I try to anticipate what's going to happen, not just between me and Liam but to Bailey, who has already suffered so much in her brief life. I've already placed an emergency call into Alice, the weight of what happened lending credence as to why she needed to come to the ER. Now.

Regardless of whatever else she has going on.

She's on her way.

I feel the barest pressure on my fingers, which are clenched around Bailey's. My eyes fly open and meet hers. "Bailey?"

Her lips open and close. Her brows lower. Intuitively, I know it's because, despite the IV, her lips are parched. Standing, I grab a moist swab and wipe it around and inside her lips.

Her rosebud lips pucker before she whispers, "Hero. Love you."

Her heart rate evens out as she slips back into sleep.

The noise outside of Bailey's cubicle recedes as I sob out a mixture of love, gratitude, and guilt. "Oh, baby. I love you too. So much."

CHAPTER
Fifty-Seven

LIAM

KEENE'S AMICABLE EXPRESSION DISAPPEARS. In its place is the man who served his country under a shroud of secrecy for years. His voice is icy when he reveals, "Caleb's been hunting the Tiberis."

"Is he crazy?"

"What would you do if it was Bailey?"

The words are out of my mouth without hesitation. "It was Bailey, or did you forget that?"

His mouth tightens.

"You should have told me. I'd have helped him set the world on fire and roast marshmallows as it burned to the ground."

"Exactly."

It's a matter of time until these fuckers go down, I think not without some satisfaction. "Why are you telling me this now?"

"He was coordinating a team out of Norwalk, throwing resources behind the local police to get them whatever evidence they needed." His head drops. "Something happened."

"What?"

"You."

Ice crystals form in my blood, freezing it instantly. "What do you mean?"

"That audit you did for Caleb. You found the link—the reason we couldn't nail the fucker down immediately."

"The mole in Hudson reporting back to the Tiberis. You confirmed it wasn't a mistake?"

"No." Keene releases his breath. "One of our own betrayed us. Al Libert's mother was the stepsister to Aldo Tiberi. That's the link."

Keene's phone rings. He answers it with a brusque, "Caleb? Status?" His head is turned away, but his body tenses. "Right. Ten minutes." He disconnects, and his face is a bit paler than it was a few moments ago.

I resume my questions. "What intel did he give them?"

Keene's jaw tightens. "Enough."

"What do you mean?"

"I need you to keep calm."

My mouth feels like someone's wedged cotton into it. "What happened?"

"They—the Tiberis—broke into Laura's home."

"Al?"

"He was with them." Keene's face is grim. "Plus someone Cal trusts implicitly who's been undercover with them for ages."

I feel smug. "Good."

"Then went down hard. Eventually, I'll have to go bail our agent out of jail." He hesitates.

"What?"

"There's something else."

"Keene, man, spit it out."

"I don't know how to say this. Christ, Liam. It's a fucking mess."

He lifts tortured eyes to mine, and the fiery burn of satisfaction is melted away by my fear. "Spit. It. Out."

"They were there. Laura and Bailey."

I shove back from my desk. "You motherfucker. Bailey was there? Those should have been the first words out of your mouth."

Keene grips my shoulder. "They're on their way to the hospital. We need to go. Caleb's meeting us there."

I shove his hand off me. I don't want comfort. I want revenge.

Someone tried to take my baby girl from me today.

It's not the first time.

But it sure as fuck will be the last.

That I can guarantee because no one is getting the chance to harm her ever again.

No one.

CHAPTER
Fifty~Eight

IN THE AFTERMATH, after dealing with the emotional turmoil of being rushed by ambulance to the ER, of waiting for tests to confirm there was nothing wrong with Bailey that rest and a few counseling sessions with Alice won't heal, I lean over her trying to avoid waking her as she finally rests after waking for those precious seconds to offer me reassurance I don't deserve.

Pressing my stethoscope to her chest, I'm relieved her heart rate has resumed a steadier rhythm of sleep and that nothing else happened today to cause it to turn into a terrified staccato.

A war of gratitude and fury is waging inside me. *How could my father not tell me the Tiberis were still after me?*

I'm so shaken at what could have happened to this precious light in my life that my legs give out beneath me. My hand flies back, and I grip the hard plastic chair, forcing my body to sit. Hand trembling, I lift my hand to smooth her hair away from her face when the curtain is ripped almost clean off the rings. Immediately, I launch myself to my feet, placing myself in between Bailey's body and whatever danger may be facing us.

Then my soul relaxes when I realize there's no danger. It's my reward. Liam's here. Immediately, I turn in his direction, ready to rush into his arms, desperate for his comfort.

But instead, all I get are two words that freeze my blood.

"Get out!"

CHAPTER
Fifty~Nine

Laura

"LAURA."

Just my name, but it's broken.

Exactly how my heart feels.

I don't turn around to face him. He doesn't deserve my forgiveness, not right now. Not when I trusted him to protect me, us, them. To know the first man I loved, my father, kept something so critical from me is almost worse than the icy daggers Liam hurled at me. "You swore to me there was no chance of them being hurt."

"Sweetheart." I hear the plea in his voice, the desperation.

It shatters the remaining parts of my heart that are still intact after Liam bulldozed over them. Slowly, I face him to find my Uncle Keene a few paces behind him. Their expressions are equally devastated and horrified at today's turn of events.

If I cared to look into a mirror, I imagine mine would be similar. The only thing keeping my heart from calcifying is knowing Bailey's safe. That's it.

There's nothing else keeping me breathing.

I can't dredge up even the slightest remorse even as my hands dig into my purse. Finding what I'm searching for, I pitch the keys to Liam's house and car into the air toward Uncle Keene. He catches them one handed before asking, "What are these?"

"Since you arranged for me to work for him, you can give them back to Liam with a message."

"What's that?"

"I quit." With that, I head straight for the exit.

Before I reach it, my father catches up to me. He grabs onto my shoulder to stop me. "Laura. Please, sweetheart. Let me explain."

Stepping away from the touch that got me through dealing with my "stalker" these past few months, I say coldly, "What is there to say, Dad? You lied to me. You said you would protect me and them, but you had your own agenda."

"Protecting you was my agenda!" he shouts.

"Was it?"

He rears back as if I've slapped him. "I can't believe you'd ask that."

"And I can't believe you didn't tell me Olivia Tiberi was after me. That Al was part of her family! You knew. You knew and you didn't give me the chance to protect myself or the people I love!" I scream, finally releasing some of the pressure valve inside of me. I point my finger back in the direction of the ER. "You're the reason that little girl is lying in that bed."

"No, Laura, Olivia Tiberi is."

I step back, the automated doors opening behind me. I need to get out of this hospital, away from my father, away from Liam. Away from everything. "Maybe you're right. But you're the reason I feel like my heart's dead inside me. Live with that."

Spinning on my heel, I sprint away from the man I grew up knowing would always protect me. *If I had known it would be him who had let me crash to the ground, maybe I wouldn't have fallen in love with a man just like him,* I think, as I slide into the back of the Uber.

The driver takes off and I don't look back.

I can't.

I'm certain I'll die if I do and I won't give a dead Olivia Tiberi that satisfaction.

CHAPTER
Sixty

Laura

The Lockwood Industries corporate pilot, Claire Hastings, welcomes me, Kalie, and Grace on board with a respectful, "Dr. Lockwood, Ms. Marshall, Ms. Bianco," and firmly shakes each of our hands. Her voice barely penetrates the haze I've been living in since yesterday when she advises us, "Flight time to San Diego is estimated to be a little more than six hours. Take your seats. We'll be cleared for takeoff shortly."

Kalie guides me to my seat, ensuring I'm secure much like Grace did when she packed what little belongings I had from our hotel in the middle of the night—both of them fueled by fury and unwavering loyalty—so we could beat a hasty retreat away from Connecticut. Their voices cocooned me like a protective shield, berating Liam for his inappropriate cruelty. "He loves you!" Kalie exclaimed.

"How could he treat you like this after everything you've been through?" Grace seethed, her loyalty burning bright.

I didn't say a word when they started discussing a plan to get me as far away from where my father or Liam Payne could be as fast as they could.

I didn't protest. I wouldn't have even if I had the energy to.

In fact, if I could have asked Grace to build me a new heart in her lab of prosthetic body parts, I would have. Even having something as synthetic as a heart that didn't feel emotion was more appealing to what mine was experiencing right now.

Despite the luxury and space Uncle Ryan's jet has to offer, Kalie and Grace don't give me any. Crowding me—one on one side, one across—we taxi toward the runway with the speed of a snail when all I want to be is hurling through the sky, placing time and distance between me and what happened yesterday. I manage through dry lips, "Did someone let the authorities know where we would be if they need my statement?"

Kalie replies, "Yes. I called my father. If they need you in person for a statement, we'll be able to go to a local precinct or fly you back for all the evidence and processing they're going to need to do."

Grace squeezes my fingers even as she snaps, "Kalie!"

Kalie has the good grace to blush. "Right. Sorry."

But I appreciate her update, her lawyer's mind trying to ensure my safety by arresting as many of the Tiberi family for attempted murder and kidnapping as possible. Still, I can't think about it too much because if I do, I'll be forced to recall what happened.

Then I'll end up a broken shard of nothing on the floor.

Captain Hastings announces we're in position one for takeoff. Seconds later, we're racing down the runway, defying gravity as the plane lifts and climbs through the clouds.

After ordering only a water from the steward, I stare out the window at the puffy clouds as the heavy silence tries to push the plane back down to earth. As I look out over the cumulous clouds dotting the bright blue sky, I'm surprised there's not a tailwind of red behind the jet—my lifeblood draining away.

More to myself than them, I wonder, "Maybe the gods didn't believe I paid my price for what happened at the ER."

Kalie hisses, "Don't. Do not let him take you back to where you were when this all started."

Grace chimes in, "He had no right to hurt you, Laura."

"Didn't he? After all, if it wasn't for me—well, me and my father, Bailey wouldn't have been caught in the crossfire."

Their anger over my words is so enormous it fills the confined space, likely suffocating the steward, who warily approaches to deliver their drinks. Grace's voice is filled with an unusual venom. "He said he loved you."

"And?"

"Did you mean the words when you said them back?"

My throat closes. "Yes."

"Then you damn well know love in this family means promises of respect and trust. It means passion, fidelity, and faith."

I smile sadly before reminding her, "That's just the problem, Gracie."

"What's that?"

"He's not a member of this family. For a short time, I wished he was. Now, I wish I'd never met him. At least Bailey would have been safe."

Kalie unbuckles her seatbelt before leaning forward to wrap her arms around me. Within seconds, Grace's arms join her. Their murmured assurances they won't let Liam hurt me anymore are just words. They can't get to where it really hurts—my heart.

I know this pain is going to last forever because I love him. The wound he inflicted is raw and bloody. But as devastated as I am right now, the emotions I'm feeling will scar over.

I know it.

So I don't worry my cousins, I reach for my purse. Fumbling around, I feel inside it for a container, extracting a small green pill. In my head, I repeat a mantra I haven't needed for a while.

Inhale. Exhale.

Every breath feels like it's choking me even as my heart thunders against my rib cage. Laying two fingers against my wrist, I shudder at the racing of my heart. It's not getting any better. There's logic knowing it's panic and the emotional pieces of my heart galloping out of control. Any second, I expect I'm going to scream because the spaces between my heartbeats are being eliminated as it pounds more rapidly . . . again . . . again.

I toss the pill in my mouth and swallow it with a swig of water.

That stops Kalie and Grace immediately. Grace's fingers slide upward and I slap at her. Tucking my wrists beneath my armpits, I reject her capable hands from checking my pulse, which I already know is out of control.

"Maybe this wasn't such a good idea," Kalie whispers.

"Laura, how bad is it?" Grace asks bluntly.

"I just took breakthrough anxiety meds for the first time since the shooting. I'd say that's a good indicator of how bad it is."

"He's not worth getting this upset over," Kalie rallies behind me.

I meet my cousin's eyes head on. "In the last twenty-four hours, I've had my life threatened, had them threaten the life of a little girl I'd give my own for because my father kept his investigation of a traumatic event I was *finally* beginning to recover from a secret, and the man I'm in love with brutally dumped me and announced to anyone listening all of the aforementioned. Excuse me if the foundation of my world is rattled just a bit."

Kalie lets out a rough sigh. "Yeah. Want a gallon of margarita to chase that?"

Grace slaps her leg. "You know better, Kalie! Laura has to moderate her alcohol intake when increasing her anxiety meds."

Oh, but I wish I could. Maybe I could finally put an end to this agony. I lay my head back while Grace and Kalie talk softly about the person whose home we're invading once we touch down in San Diego.

Kalie snickers. "For his sake, he'd better hope he's alone. Last time, it was more embarrassing for him than it was for us trying to prove to his girlfriend of the hour we weren't her replacement."

Despite my pain, the part of my heart always reserved for my family glimmers with humor at the memory Kalie resurrected. It gives me the faintest hope there's a reason worth living.

I might heal.

But I'll never survive the loss of Liam and Bailey.

After Kalie and Grace fall asleep, I pull out my journal and pour my emotions into it.

It's the only safe space I have left.

From the Journal of Dr. Laura Lockwood

I'm not certain there's a speed fast enough to carry me away from my pain. No, pain isn't quite the way to describe what Liam did to me tonight.

He murdered me right in the middle of my own ER.

He slaughtered me, accusing me of deliberately placing Bailey in danger. But there was no way I could have known going to my home would have done this. And Al? How was I supposed to know he had changed sides—turned traitor to my father and family? How is that my fault?

His voice bellowed at me, how if I was in danger I should have stayed away from him and his daughter.

Pain kept me frozen in place, accepting his words as my punishment for listening to my father when, intuitively, I knew better. I should have said something. Still, I felt myself back down, so great was his fury. I trembled in the face of it, even though I had faced off against a mob faction earlier in the day and succeeded.

Is love supposed to make us this mortal? This weak? What

happened to love raising us up to feel as strong as gods, becoming unconquerable in the eyes of the world? No, that's not the kind of love I found. The security I thought I had ripped away.

It boiled down to one thing—trust. I'd given Liam mine, and he believed I'd handed him nothing but lies while I cared for the most precious piece of his heart. No matter what I tried to say, none of my words penetrated through the cloud of fury surrounding him.

I finally ran—past him, past the chief. Past my father, who had betrayed us both.

Still, as much as I love, is there any way to erase the feeling of desolation I feel when I think about how I tried to tell Liam I loved him and he said, "Don't finish that. Don't you even dare say that to me or to Bailey. Not now, not ever again. Get out."

I knew words could hurt—my mother taught me that a long while ago—but this was a bludgeon, a sudden agony that left me feeling nothing.

Maybe this was less painful than an actual death. Maybe not.

CHAPTER
Sixty-One

LIAM

THE ER RESIDENT on duty coolly reassured me Bailey was fine after she regained consciousness. "Her stress is keeping her under, Mr. Payne. I suggest you follow up with one of our therapists."

"Yeah, she sees one for the first incident she had in this ER," I explained acidly.

"Hmm. Fine. I'll discharge her to *your* care." I winced at the emphasis on the word, knowing I'd royally fucked up with the ER staff by maligning their precious chief. Still, while I was completing paperwork, several of Laura's co-workers came by to say goodbye to Bailey including Dr. Rosenthal, who reminded me of Bailey's appointment next week, Alice, who dropped a packet of peanut butter cups on my baby girl's lap, and the chief of staff—Laura's Dr. Douche. He ignored me, focusing solely on

Bailey. Delivering a teddy bear dressed in scrubs to her, he murmured, "That's not from me, it's from Laura."

Bailey immediately hugged to her chest before asking me a question I couldn't answer. "Daddy? Where did Laura go? She was holding my hand before."

Almost like they were like rats on a sinking ship, all the medical personnel left me to field my daughter's inquiry. "I-I don't know, Buttercup. I'll text her when we get home."

I tried to find Laura's whereabouts, only to realize no one would disclose dick to me. My screaming had made the rounds and if it weren't for Bailey, I'd be persona non grata here.

I need to apologize. I hope she'll forgive me. God, knowing it was the Tiberis after her with Bailey caught in the crossfire, I couldn't keep a hold of my temper. My mouth went into fucking overdrive.

I immediately start texting her.

LIAM:

Where are you? Bailey is asking for you.

Even now that Bailey and I are safe at home, and having sat next to Bailey as she sleeps, I can't feel relief. I fucked up.

Huge.

Around two a.m., I text Laura again.

LIAM:

Sweetheart, just let me know you're safe.

I don't move from my position even as the sun rises. Every minute that passes causes my stomach to cramp. It's not because Colby called earlier to let me know Hudson agents would be patrolling my property. It's the overwhelming sense of knowledge that I blew Laura and me up.

My phone calls are going straight to voicemail. My texts remain unanswered. Like a swift swipe of her scalpel, I'm somehow cut off from the woman I love. Still, I try to remain rational as I rule out possible scenarios. Maybe she's with the police, but could it really have taken this much time?

LIAM:

Laura, come over as soon as you get this. Please, we need to talk.

Still, she's not a suspect. She would be able to answer her phone. That's when the insidious voice inside my head taunts me, *If she wanted to.*

When my front door slams open just after sunrise, pervasive relief floods through my system. I'm ready to wrap Laura up in my arms for hours before I school her on answering her phone in the middle of a crisis. An even larger part ready to drop to my knees and sob my apology against her warm skin after I've stripped us both naked and we're curled up in my bed together.

Only it's not Laura standing there.

It's Caleb and Keene. Their faces are neutral, but as I approach them, I recognize the barely banked fury in their eyes. I feel the blood leach from my face.

"What are you two doing here? Where's Laura?"

My eyes drift away from theirs, my lungs seizing when I recognize what's dangling from Caleb's fingers. It's the keys to my house and my car. I don't have to guess how they got in. Between the fact she's not picking up her phone and their possession of them, they're making a statement.

A clear one.

My mouth feels like I was just forced to consume a cup of sawdust but I manage to say, "They're locked up?"

Caleb takes a step forward, quivering with rage. "I don't know who to blame more, you or me."

I confront what I believe to be Caleb's issue with me head on. "Come on, Caleb. You had to know I'd be pissed."

"Pissed is what Keene was, but he was fucking rational!" Caleb roars. He flings the keys at my feet.

I ignore the clatter they make against the hardwoods and focus on the man. "I love her. I'll make it up to her."

"Like hell you will," he retorts. He lifts his chin. "Laura gave those to me right before she—"

"Caleb, shut up." Keene snaps at his brother-in-law. Then he snarls, "Laura's condition is need to know and Liam has no right to any information about Laura. Not anymore."

"I love her," I say.

His smirk is laced with such contempt I want to punch it off his face. "Charming the way you demonstrate it. Accusing her of deliberately trying to get Bailey killed, was it?"

"How dare you?" Caleb hisses.

"Like you're one to talk?" I snap, my rage that he knew about her stalker and refused to tell me rising to the surface.

Before my eyes, his indescribable fury deflates to roaring anger. "You're right. For that, I'll apologize. But only that. You desecrated my little girl, Liam."

I scrub my hand across my forehead. "She lied to me."

"No, I lied to you. I'm the one who forced her to keep everything *that she knew about* quiet." Caleb snarls at me like a rabid wolf. It takes Keene leaping in front of him, slamming a hand against his chest to forcibly restrain him.

"You?" My heart bleeds a second time in less than twenty-four hours. The first time was knowing Bailey was injured. Now, it's knowing I unjustly wronged the woman I love.

"Yes, me. So, take your best shot. I dare you. Repeat every word you said to my daughter to me. Then lie to me. Tell me you wouldn't do the same thing, execute any and every fucking maneuver to protect your own little girl if it meant the choice of her life or death. Try to tell me you wouldn't lie to whomever you needed to, even if it meant losing her . . . forget it." Before my eyes, Caleb's indignation deflates.

Keene steps in and tells me the actual happenings of what went down inside her house and at Greenwich Hospital before I arrived. Hearing it, I feel smaller than a bug that's been swashed inside the gum beneath someone's shoe.

I misread the situation completely. Laura didn't endanger Bailey. She tried to save her, even to the point of putting herself in danger. "What did I do?"

"You fucked up, and it cost us all the most precious thing in the world— my daughter," Caleb hisses.

"She loves you." Of course Laura loves him.

"Laura hates me right now and it's all because of you," he spits.

To myself, I whisper, "What? No."

Keene answers, "You might as well have finished the job Olivia Tiberi set out to do."

My legs give way. I clutch the back of the couch to remain upright.

Keene's voice is flat when he informs me, "Laura's gone, Liam."

Caleb nods at the keys lying between us like the Maginot Line. "She asked Keene to formally resign on her behalf. She won't be coming back."

Bile is trying to force its way out of my throat.

Laura's gone.

She won't be coming back.

The agony welling up in my chest causes a fissure that splits my heart in two. "Dear God. What did I do?"

For the first time, Caleb admits his own culpability when he mutters, "What did we do?"

"That's for the two of you to figure out, but neither of you are to show your face around the office until you do," Keene reprimands us both. He's equally pissed at his brother-in-law as much as me. That much is obvious.

"I'll add stay the hell away from my daughter while you figure out you."

"Are you planning on doing the same?" I sneer in contempt. Fucking hypocrite.

"Laura needs to focus on putting her life back together . . . again." Caleb tacks on roughly.

Knowing the hell me and her father have put her through, I bob my head. Voice cracking, I agree to Caleb's request, "I will."

At that, my bosses make their way to the door. Just as the two men I've known and respected for years are about to walk through, I stress, "For *now*. Until I can figure out what caused me to attack the woman I love." The woman who risked her life to save my daughter.

I don't even react when the two men slam out my front door.

All I can think about is Laura, and with that, the events of the night catch up to me.

I fall to my knees and break down in tears over knowing Bailey's safe.

And Laura's broken, all because of me.

CHAPTER
Sixty~Two

LIAM

FEAR ISN'T EXCLUSIVE. It doesn't give you a license for anything. It certainly doesn't give you a right to take your emotions out on the people who love you—a lesson I've learned well in the time since Laura disappeared from my life. I've also learned the woman I love has more courage than half the people I work with. She essentially used herself as a body shield for my daughter, kept a hostage situation as under control as it could be, and still managed to limit my daughter's injuries.

In other words, she was just Laura.

With this knowledge, I spend my days with a morose child who misses Laura as much as I do. At night, I work. I don't sleep because I'm chased by one of two very different nightmares—one where Caleb doesn't save Bailey and Laura and the other where Laura walks away.

Both terrify me because they're so vivid in their reality.

Dragging my knees up, I brace my elbows on them as my hands thrust into my hair. "Where are you, Laura?"

I don't know what I'm going to do if I can't get her back.

Get her to talk to me.

I need to apologize.

CHAPTER
Sixty-Three

Laura

Two weeks later, I stretch my legs out and let the warmth of the California sun relentlessly beat down on them. Tipping my head back, I sigh, "I should show up in the middle of the night more often."

The devastatingly handsome man lying in the double lounger next to me reaches over and tugs at a lock of my hair. "You should. I've missed your face despite the fact it's looking a bit beat up, love."

Turning to face my cousin Zachary Peter Hunt—known around the world as heartthrob Food Network television host Peter Freeman—I somehow manage to tip one corner of my lips up for the briefest of moments. "Better?"

"Hardly," he drawls. Tipping his mirrored sunglasses down his nose, his gold-colored eyes meet mine. "I hope my father and Uncle Keene fillet the bastard and squeeze lemon juice over his bloodied skin before grilling him over an open flame."

"Pete, this isn't a rerun of *Cutthroat Kitchen*. Dining on him won't help," Kalie mutters from Peter's other side, where she's sharing a lounger with Grace.

Peter's expression is appalled. "Kalie, you should know by now I don't eat second rate trash. But if the family doesn't want the wet work, I'll happily demonstrate what I can do with a meat tenderizer."

As heartbroken as I am, I still manage a sardonic, "I bet you I can still wield a scalpel better than you can a chef's knife."

Peter smirks at me, giving me a smile that used to drive me, Kalie, and Grace insane as teenagers because it's so sanctimonious. Now, that same smile causes hordes of women to whisper more than their favorite recipes in his ear. "Oh, darling. Let's have a cook off tonight and let me prove to you how wrong you are."

Haughtily, I lower my own glasses. "I never said I was a better cook, Pete. I just reminded you I have better knife skills."

Grace yawns before reminding Peter, "Even your mother says so."

Peter's golden eyes spike with brown, exactly the same way Aunt Corinna's do when she's infuriated. He jabs a finger in my direction and challenges, "You, me, and wagyu beef tonight. We'll put this to rest once and for all."

Kalie immediately declares, "I'm on Team Laura."

Grace grumbles. "Why do I always get stuck on Team Pete? He doesn't let me do crap except clean up his mess. I'm not one of his damn minions."

Being the good sport he is—at least with family—Peter grins at Grace before conceding, "If Laura kicks my ass tonight, I'll do the dishes for both of us."

Kalie taunts. "We know that's going to happen, Pete."

Grace scoffs, "And that means what? You'll put in a 9-1-1 call to your maid service?"

"What's wrong with that?" he wonders, truly bewildered.

My cousins laugh at him. Grace flings a towel in his direction, which he easily catches. "Come on, Gracie. Like you expected something different?"

"Nope. We know everything about you," Grace taunts.

"To your detriment," Kalie adds.

The three of them snicker before I wonder aloud, "What do I get *when* I kick his ass again?"

Peter brings my hand to his lips in a courtly manner. I wonder if Colby or his illustrious grandfather, a former US senator, taught him. "A perfectly cooked meal crafted by yours truly."

Kalie snarks, "In other words, same shit, different visit."

Peter doesn't try to rein in his amusement at Kalie's remark. The sound of it causes a trio of women to whip their heads around from where they're lying ten yards away.

Kalie shouts, "He's already got a harem today, ladies. Go scout out some other celebrity."

One of them, a buxom blonde in a barely there string bikini, flicks Kalie off.

"Christ. I missed you three." Peter's amusement is evident.

She rolls her eyes. "Like I said on the flight out here, it would be more embarrassing for Pete if we showed up."

His voice turns fierce. "Never embarrassing, Kay. Family first. You know that."

Peter speaks no less than the truth. Every time we visit him or when he manages a trip back home amid his hectic filming schedule, it is the same —family becomes the center of his world. He relishes our tribe the same way we do. Certain traditions must be upheld, including—inevitably— Peter challenging me in a knife-off. Every time I remind him, I honed my professional skills on mammals with still-beating hearts. Peter's competitive edge and his distinct lack of ego with those he loves make the exhibition a riot for all the family.

However, this time, it's different. The simple pleasure of being with people who would do anything to ensure I don't backslide after this most recent attack causes tears to slide down my cheeks.

Peter reaches over and brushes them away. "None of this. What happened isn't worth any more of your tears."

I sniffle but don't correct him. *No, but the fact I fell in love with a man who would savage me in such a way is,* my broken heart counters. Instead of saying the words aloud, I reach up to grab hold of his fingers.

He flips his hand around in my grip, lacing our fingers together. "I have a surprise for you. It should be here soon."

"Ugh. Tell me you didn't arrange a party tonight," I groan. The last thing I want is some Hollywood shindig that will be reported in all the tabloids.

"Of sorts." Peter's voice is completely unapologetic.

"And you invited them for dinner? *Family* dinner?"

"I actually asked if they wanted to stay with us for as long as you're here." He relaxes back in his chair after dropping that bomb.

Grace's head pops up like a prairie dog coming out of its burrow. "Are you dating someone? Is it possible we're getting a scoop before TMZ?"

Peter's face whitens beneath his tan. "No, Gracie. Hell, no."

"No to the scoop or no to the dating?" she challenges. Even Kalie raises her head, interested in what's unfolding.

"So, if it's not a woman, would you consider them a friend?" I question. Despite my lack of interest in anything, I'll help Kalie and Grace. After all, they set aside their lives to resurrect me in the last two weeks. The least I can do is pretend I give a damn.

"You know me, Pete. Bring over all your hot banging-eligible friends." Kalie fans herself.

"Pretty certain you can't call a cousin 'banging-eligible,' Kalie," comes a voice from behind us.

Peter relaxes against our lounger as I leap from beside him to race across the sand and jump into my twin's arms. He rocks me back and forth even as tears I swore to Kalie and Grace I'd stop shedding the second we stepped off the jet in San Diego drip beneath my sunglasses. "What are you doing here?"

He snorts. "Because the East Coast is such a fun place to be right now?"

"Mama and Dad?"

"Don't ask. Let's just say there's no punishment you, Chuck, or I endured combined as teenagers equals how furious she is with him." He lifts my glasses up and stares down into my face before quirking a brow. "Besides, there's our twin thing."

"Jon," I reprimand.

"You need me here."

"You should be back in Connecticut." What I leave unsaid is supervising our father so he doesn't go off the rails between our mother's fury and his inability to reach me since I blocked him from calling after the first day.

He hasn't stopped trying to reach out to Kalie and Grace, who calmly just ignore him.

Jon clasps his hand over my mouth. I glare at him. He leans forward conspiratorially, informing me, "Connecticut is a four-letter word this week."

I mumble, "Issasmoresanfoursetters."

"What did you say?" Jon lifts his hand.

Glaring at him, I enunciate, "It has more than four letters. Technically, it has four syllables."

Loping his arm over my shoulders, he leads me back to my lounger. "Same difference."

Before I can formulate a response to the man who argued with his Harvard professor for two hours on the finer details regarding the importance the *USS Lassen* had in rescuing hostages from a passenger cruise ship, he taunts our younger cousin. "Besides, it's not like I could trust Mr. Hollywood to take care of you."

"I was doing a fucking fine job of it before you arrived."

"Tuck your dick back in your board shorts, Pete. No one here cares about seeing it," Kalie snarks. Her head flops back down since the surprise isn't some hot celebrity she can hook up with.

Peter winces. "You girls are getting more vicious as you age."

"See what happens when your species turns on us?" Grace's smile is feral.

"Is it time to start day drinking yet?" I wonder.

"It's five o'clock somewhere," Kalie warbles the infamous line from the old Alan Jackson/Jimmy Buffet anthem.

"Christ, Kalie. Are you taking singing lessons from Aunt Em drunk at a karaoke bar?" Peter sneers.

"Are you disparaging my singing?" she asks sweetly.

"No, I'm questioning if anyone in a twenty-mile radius is now deaf," he volleys.

Kalie isn't about to take an insult like that sitting down. Quickly, I duck behind Jon as Kalie unscrews her thermos of ice water and dumps it right onto Peter's lap before he puts together what she's doing.

Jon chortles even as he pulls me down onto the dry part of the lounger. Peter leaps up to chase Kalie. "You're threatening the continuance of the Hunt line! Christ, that was cold, you pain in my ass!"

"More like a pain in your balls, Pete. I thought you passed biology in college."

"Watch your smart mouth, Kalie." He catches up to her and scoops her off her feet. Stepping over to his pool, he simply walks off the edge, ensuring Kalie takes the plunge with him.

"Oh, good. I got here just in time for the good stuff." Jon grins.

I scrub my face against his shoulder. "No, you got here just in time for me."

He presses a kiss against the crown of my head. "I'll always be here for you, Laura."

That causes my heart to flip painfully in my chest because another man who I loved also said that to me. Just turned out to be a lot shorter time than I expected.

From the Journal of Dr. Laura Lockwood

Since we left Connecticut (a four-letter word, according to my brother), I willingly gave up my capability to communicate with anyone. I needed to distance myself from all but a select few. Although I find myself needing to tell you a few things. This is the only way how.

It's the only place I feel safe.

Right now, I love you and never want to set eyes on you again. How is that possible when it wasn't two weeks ago, we were laughing in your kitchen as I made too many meatballs—again. Making Bailey laugh while doing her PT on a weekend. Loving each other as the moon followed us across the sky?

Your words shattered my heart. How could you make love to me that morning, tell me you loved me, then hurl such debasement at me? After I did my best to protect Bailey?

I'd have died for her, and you know it. Or maybe you don't. After all, you never knew about my stalker.

It wasn't a choice, but advice from my father that led to that decision. And while the excuse of "But Daddy said not to" *wouldn't fly in most circumstances, we both understand who and what my father is—to us both.*

Late at night, while lying here in Peter's guest room, I still accept the blame for not telling you. Even if my father is considered one of the best investigators in the world, you're a father. You deserved to know, to make your own decisions.

Because I found out my father hid pertinent details from me—details that when I found them out, absolutely changed my mind about sharing what was happening with you. In the end, he? Me? We endangered your daughter. I can never forgive myself for that.

Maybe you can't either.

CHAPTER
Sixty-Four

LIAM

THE ROOM IS LIT by only a little table lamp when I pour a small snifter of liquor. Tossing back the cognac, I grimace as the taste hits the back of my throat.

It reminds me of her. Everything does.

At dinner tonight, I had to let Bailey know that Laura wouldn't be returning. Her plaintive "Why?" is seared on my soul almost as much as the despair when I told her I'd said and done things to hurt Laura when she was in the ER.

"But, Daddy, you love Laura."

"I know." The words were torn from me.

"Then apologize." Her logic was simple. It's what all the adults in her life taught her—you do something wrong, you say you're sorry. How in the hell do you explain to a seven-year-old that some things are so awful, an apology just won't cut it?

I tried. Lifting Bailey's hand, I placed it against my chest—where my whole heart should have been beating. "When I did what I did, Buttercup, I hurt this." *Hurt? You apparently destroyed her, you jackass,* I berate myself.

My daughter glares at me before yanking her hand away. "Why?"

"I wish I knew."

"Daddy? Laura loves me, right?"

"Oh, baby. She absolutely loves you. She didn't leave your side." *She wouldn't have left mine either. She'd still be here except for me making her.*

Her eyes dulled. I recognize it because I've seen it in every reflective surface I've passed over the last forty-eight hours. "I'm sad by what you did, Daddy." Then she teetered out of her room, down the hall, and closed the door.

Closed me out.

So am I, Buttercup, I think now, more than a healthy mixture of self-disgust and loathing pouring through me.

It isn't just the silence in the room where, for weeks, there was none. It's the knowledge I drove away any chance of Laura using her key to open that door. I slide my hand into my pocket and finger her keys. My fist closes around them as I recall how they were hurled at my feet.

As if I was nothing—apparently the same way I treated his daughter.

I sink onto the couch, haunted by the realization I drove her away. And now, Bailey's refusal to speak with me—even after I let her know it was time for dinner—intensifies the silence permeating the room.

I reach for my phone and pull up the text string with the photos Bailey's been sending me since the beginning of summer. Laura had no idea how often my daughter had taken random photos of her as her love for her grew. I can't prevent the pain-laced chuckle as I stare at her "oops" face Bailey captured as Laura dipped her spoon into the cookie batter. Or the time they were sewing my pillows and Laura scowled down at her stitches. When I asked about that one, Laura laughed and reminded me, "I'm much more proficient on humans."

Which had me scrolling through the photos I had on my own camera from the night of the hospital gala. Laura's graciousness as she greeted one donor after another and finally the picture that bleeds my heart—one her father took just before Brendan Blake sung to her. Laura was wrapped in my arms as if it was the only place she wanted to be. Even then, I knew it was a moment out of time I never wanted to let go of.

Just like I can't let go of her.

Desperate, I begin typing.

LIAM:

> I was wrong. All of this is entirely my fault. There aren't words to convey how sorry I am, Laura. But this isn't how I want to apologize. I want you to read the remorse on my face, knowing I'll never hurt you like this again.

I hit Send and there's no response.

Hours later, nothing. Not that I can blame her. I shut her out first. I just didn't realize it would be so damn painful to be on the receiving end of it.

CHAPTER
Sixty~Five

LIAM

I<small>T'S</small> <small>BEEN</small> three weeks since the hostage situation and I've done little more than take care of Bailey and mope around my house trying to figure out a way to reach Laura. But the time for penance—at least where it pertains to work—is up. I'm only mildly surprised it's Caleb, not Keene, who orders me into the office. "With or without Bailey. There's information you need that can't leave the office."

Subdued, I reply, "It will have to be with. School doesn't start for a few more weeks." I don't have to remind him I no longer have a nanny.

I can barely think about the reasons myself.

Laura hasn't replied to a single one of my messages or voice mails despite the fact that I've been leaving them daily. "We'll be there in the morning."

"Fine. See you then."

LIAM:

Laura, please. Let me tell you how sorry I am. You didn't deserve what I said to you. Let me apologize.

Within minutes of wheeling Bailey onto the executive floor of Hudson Investigations, she's whisked away by Caleb and Keene's wives to go shopping around Rockefeller Center. I was about to protest when I find myself blindsided by Laura's eyes reflecting back at me in her mother's face. My words disappear, and shame washes over me when fury crackles behind them. It's a catalyst for me, causing me to recall Laura's eyes flashing in much the same manner any time she mentioned her odious chief of staff.

I lift my hand, rubbing my chest as the snatch of memory causes it to ache. Wearily, I thank both women.

"You're welcome," Cassidy carefully modulates her voice around Bailey.

It isn't until after the women leave that I'm herded into Keene's office. Even as I settle at a small conference table, Keene uses his iPad to engage the room's soundproofing. "Did something happen?"

Caleb shoots a file across the table in front of me. "Read those, then sign them."

Lifting the first one, I realize it's a specialized NDA on Hudson letterhead. I frown. "Are we under some kind of special audit? What the hell's happening?"

Keene's eyes crinkle in the corner malevolently. "They say I can murder you in cold blood if you speak of anything we're about to share with you without explicit authorization."

I scan the document quickly. "Authorization only comes from one of the senior partners—you two and Colby?"

Caleb's chin jerks up. He doesn't look much better than I feel.

I continue signing document after document, a total of twenty, all of which Caleb countersigns and Keene witnesses. Finally, Keene glances at his desk before meeting Caleb's eyes, and he walks out the door. "I'll be in your office."

Caleb walks over to Keene's desk and lifts a hefty file from it. "You'll have to forgive the dramatics, Liam. There's only been one other man who was read in without approval."

"Read into what?"

"What we're about to share with you." He drops the folder onto the table, resting his hands on it. "None of what you signed means dick until the talking starts. So, I'm going to ask you one last time, did you mean what you said? Are you in love with my daughter?"

"Don't you think that's between me and Laura?"

"No. Not if you want a half a chance of fixing it." His jaw tightens. "What you said that night . . ."

I surge to my feet. "I didn't mean it, Caleb."

"I believe you, even if no one else does." A male voice I don't recognize injects himself into our conversation.

"Who are you?" My irritation fades even as recognition sparks in my brain. "Wait. You were in the Amaryllis section during the gala."

Caleb gets up and gives him a manly back slap. "Jake, brother. Thanks for coming in."

"No problem. I was happy to when Cassidy called." The man holds out a hand. "I'm Jake, Laura's uncle."

Caleb jerks his head at the other man. "He's the person who can probably most relate to you right now, Payne."

Growling, I bite out, "Why's that?"

Jake's smile drops from his face. "Because I've been *exactly* where you are."

"I doubt it."

He lifts his hand and ticks off his fingers. "Blamed your woman for hurting your child?"

Ashamed, my head drops. "Yes."

Caleb snarls in my direction before asking Jake, "What is it about making spectacles at hospitals?"

Jake flips him off before flicking another finger forward. "Can't get her to talk to you?"

Uncomfortably, I nod.

"Drove her away."

I scrub my hand over the back of my neck before admitting, "Yeah."

"The entire family is against you?"

I catch Caleb's lethal glare out of the corner of my eye. "So, it appears."

"Hi." Jake holds out his hand. "Jake. Founding member of this particular club. Hate you screwed over my niece to join it, but I wish someone was willing to give me advice when I became the founding member."

Warily, I take it. He grips it firmly before remarking, "You and my niece appeared happy at the gala. So, wild ass guess here, you're spinning your wheels trying to figure out how to take it all back."

My gaze pings back and forth between him and Caleb, and I say the only thing that comes to mind. "Fuck, are you clairvoyant or some shit?"

Jake deadpans, "No. I'm a high school music department head."

Caleb, slightly less inclined to kill me now that there's a neutral party with us, gestures us back to the table. "Now, let's talk."

"She cut me off." My voice is morose.

"You're not the only one." Caleb's voice is just as depressed.

Jake's lip curls in disgust. "I'd at least have thought you'd both be ready to beg on your knees by now."

Caleb and I exchange looks of shared wretchedness. Then we face the teacher, ready to learn.

Jake clasps his hands together. "Well, there's no time like the present. Let's get started." Then he points at me and jerks his thumb at the table. "Both of you, sit the hell down. Class is in session."

✧

We're a good three cups of coffee in when Jake encourages me to set up individual therapy sessions. "You've got to figure out what triggered your behavior."

"If she'll ever talk to me again?" Pieces of my heartbreak spill on the table between us.

"See, that's the thing right there." Caleb points a finger in my direction. "It isn't just about figuring out what's wrong for *Laura,* but for you and Bailey as well."

I frown. "I can't imagine hurting Bailey."

Jake nods emphatically. "Could you imagine *ever* screaming at Laura?"

My head gets light. "No."

"It may not be an issue now because Bailey's still little, but Caleb knows, and you can trust me. My oldest daughter and I had enormous communication problems. Until my wife, I had no idea what they stemmed from."

"Do you mind if I ask?"

Jake and Caleb exchange covert glances before Jake gives me a non-answer. "I haven't ducked a single question you've asked, Liam, but this one I have to. I don't want to influence your therapist's path." He takes another drink of coffee. "Do you have one?"

"A therapist? I suppose I could go to Alice Cleary since she also works with my daughter and I know she's treated Laura."

Jake leans forward, expression intent. "This is the hardest step. You know why?"

"Why?"

"Because down to your bones, every instinct is screaming at you to chase Laura down, and to do everything possible to get her to listen to you."

"Yes." The word escapes on an exhale.

Jake gives me a meaningful look. "The problem is, if you don't know why you're crawling, what good will being on your knees do?"

Something in the way he says that makes me wonder if he means his words literally. But Caleb derails my train of thought. "Have you ever read the legend of Amaryllis?"

"No."

He jerks his chin up. "Go to my wife's website. It's there."

Pulling up the Amaryllis Events and Company page on my cell, I scan the explanation of Amaryllis, Alteo, and the Oracle of Delphi. Confused, I'm about to ask Caleb what this has to do with Laura when he braces an arm on the table. "That's why Laura left."

"Because of a legend?"

"Because our arrows landed directly in her heart. She's bleeding out. It's up to us to decide if we want to take the necessary steps to stop it from being a death sentence. I've already made my decision."

Caleb rises, Jake following. Intuitively understanding they've given me all they're going to, I hold out my hand to Jake first. My "Thank you" is heartfelt.

His lips curve. "I take payment in the form of inspiration."

My head cocks to the side. "I'm sorry. What?"

Caleb rolls his eyes. "You and your cousin-in-law do not need to win another CMT off my baby's heartbreak."

I'm confused, and it shows. Jake clasps me on the shoulder. "Don't worry. If you're lucky, one day Laura will show you our family tree."

God, I hope he's a prophet as well as a high school music teacher. Leaving Caleb's office, I find my baby holding a new doll—one that looks remarkably like Laura. She's cradling it against her heart and telling it how much she loves and misses it.

Yeah, I need to fix what I did.

Jake's right. If it means being on my knees, I'll gladly crawl.

CHAPTER
Sixty-Six

LIAM

I LIE BACK on the couch, throwing the stress ball into the air and catching it.

Over and over.

As if on my next catch it will release something in my mind that tells me why I lashed out at Laura.

This is my fourth individual session with Alice. I've laid everything out from my perspective, from when I met Ashleigh and our relationship, to how I found out about Bailey—though I had to edit out the classified aspects, to needing a new nanny, and meeting Laura. The first spark from when she came into my office, how her direct manner of addressing Bailey's concerns seemed to be exactly what my daughter needed. Then how I admitted my attraction to her.

Today was tougher as we discussed the more intimate aspects of my relationship with Laura as it progressed—what I felt as I observed my daughter falling just as I did. The moments at the hospital gala, our first kiss, and waking up with her in my home.

Now we've circled around to the moments in the ER and how I lashed out at her after the Tiberis attempt at retribution. For a moment, when I speak of Laura and what I shouted at the ER, there's a flash of something on Alice's face, but it's quickly masked. "You know what happened," I voice in a low tone.

She doesn't deny my accusation. "Most of the hospital does, Liam. If only for her sake, I hope the speculation dies down before she returns to work."

I wince as the ramifications of my actions hit again.

Alice studies my face before reminding me, "After all, your words assured her she wasn't important."

Automatically, I correct her, "That's not what I said."

She adjusts herself in her oversized chair. "What did you say then?"

My stomach twists. "I don't know if I can repeat it."

Alice doesn't let me off the hook. "Why should a woman as smart and intelligent as Dr. Laura Lockwood return to a man as brokenhearted as you claim to be if you won't discuss the reasons behind why you acted the way you did."

I lurch upward and shout, "I don't know why I did it!"

Her eyes meet mine levelly. "Yes, you do. You're just afraid to say the words aloud."

"Of what?" I snap.

"Your fear."

"Of course I was afraid. My daughter was beaten and bruised."

"And it brought back a lot of ugly memories for you, Liam," Alice counters.

Denial fights to be let out, but residual fear surpasses it, leaving me with nausea swirling in my stomach. I can't say anything. Instead, my breath just heaves in and out.

"You have to admit how colossal your fear was because if you do, you'll admit the rest."

"What do you mean, admit the rest?" I snarl.

"You'll admit why you targeted your anger at Laura."

A chill runs through me at her words as a pounding throbs in my head. I croak out, "Go on. "

"Love is the most fertile ground to breed hate. It's also the easiest channel to release extreme emotions because there's a presumption that our partner will always be there for us. Instead of reaching out to Laura, sharing your anger at her father with her, you substituted her as your target."

"No," I immediately deny.

"Yes, Liam. You did. The whole ER heard you." Alice loses her notorious patience and snaps. She takes a deep breath and releases it before flinging open her own drawer of chocolate and reaching for a bar of Godiva. "I need a moment."

"You have to help me," I beg.

"I need a moment."

"Alice," I plead.

"Don't I have a right to a moment, Liam?" she hisses.

Just that quickly, the words I hurled at Laura come spilling out of my mouth and take me back to the ER and my conversation with Laura.

"You don't have any right to touch her, Ash. Not after what you did to her." To me. Taking her on a sting operation when all she had to do was call me? Completely unfathomable.

"Liam, please. I didn't do anything."

"Didn't do anything?" Christ, how was it I worked with this woman undercover for over a year and never knew her to be such a selfish bitch.

Her voice is a rasp. "Yes."

"And you did so with no security to protect you?" No backup. Nothing. I had to find out about Bailey's condition from my boss.

Just like the last time.

"I didn't know we would get hurt." I'm immune to the tears dripping down her face, I'm so furious at Ashleigh. I shout something else in her direction, causing her choked, "I had no idea, Liam, Believe me,"

Barely any of her words penetrate. All I can see is the blood on Bailey's face from the car wreck. Christ, how can this manipulative liar be allowed to mother my daughter?

I need to vent this anger or I'll never be able to have a future where Bailey won't be threatened. "The only thing I believe is you're a selfish bitch. You're a danger to Bailey just by existing."

I'm incredulous when she tries to plead, "Liam, I love . . ."

"Don't finish that. Don't you even dare say that to me or to Bailey. Not now, not ever again. Get out."

"Just like that," Alice murmurs after my outburst. There's no judgment in her voice, but I feel like I've shattered my life into a million broken pieces.

"How did I look at Laura and see Ashleigh?"

Alice's eyes drift shut in agony. "Do you want me to answer as your doctor or as a woman?"

Realizing the extent of the pain I caused to Laura, my voice cracks when I admit, "I think by the time this is over, I'll need to hear both."

Alice leans forward and meets my eyes squarely. "Now, let's go back to talking about Ashleigh."

Hours later, I'm driving toward our Norwalk office. My voice was dead when I called Keene to inform him, "Incoming."

His brusque, "I'll tell Caleb," netted me a meeting at the end of my boss's workday.

Before he hung up, I had copies of my therapy session records from Alice sent over. They at least deserved to know why I attacked the person I loved with such a determined viciousness.

As I take exit 1 to Route 7, the way I screamed at Laura reverberates in my mind. Worse, the way she pleaded with me before stoically absorbing my blows. As if she deserved them when the only thing she deserves is love.

Entering Hudson Investigations, I head straight into the elevator for the executive floor. After using my badge, I'm dumped out right outside Caleb's office. The hallway is empty of random passersby. Still, my stomach knots as I lift my hand to knock.

Keene swings the door open to reveal an exhausted Caleb. It strikes me that I've seen that face before—in the mirror. A flash of insight hits me. Even as much as he hates me, he hates himself more. This is why he's trying to help Laura, help me. I recall the frosty reception I received from Laura's mother and realize she isn't likely only furious with me, but with her husband for daring to hurt her child.

Caleb's in the same lifeboat as I am for the same reason. Knowing that still doesn't help either of our situations, but it makes me resent him less when I step into his office. Spotting Keene, I wait for the first attack of words, knowing I deserve them. When neither man speaks, I don't say anything.

I wait.

And wait.

Finally, it isn't me Caleb addresses, but Keene. "It's annoying as fuck Liam grounded my guns by having Alice send over her reports on his sessions."

"Liam is often annoying as fuck," Keene retorts before he approaches. The older man comes up next to me and drops into a chair.

I take a chance and apologize to both of them. "I'm so fucking sorry. I never meant to hurt Laura."

Much to my surprise, Caleb asks, "Now what? What are you going to do now that you appreciate the damage you did, Liam?"

Feeling the weight of my brutality resting on my heart, I still know one thing. "I can't live without Laura in my life. But I . . . I need your help."

Caleb studies me, his gaze unwavering. The tension in the room is palpable. I stammer, "I messed up, Caleb. I've been trying to apologize without realizing what I was trying to say I was sorry for."

Keene snarls, "So, what? You want to have a clear conscience?"

"No, because I'm so in love, I'm falling apart without her," I snap back. A hushed silence descends on the room. "I love Laura, Caleb. How do I fix what I broke when she's not here?"

Caleb opens his mouth, but it's Keene who injects, "Keep doing exactly what you're doing, Liam. Fix yourself first."

My head jerks to the side as a feeling of helplessness washes over me. Then, because I can't hold the question back, I rasp, "Is she coming back?"

"Eventually."

"Eventually isn't a date I can plug into my calendar, but even if it's years from now, I'll still be waiting."

Keene's voice is like battery acid. "You've shattered my niece's trust, Payne. You expect us to believe you had this epiphany—as good as Alice is —and suddenly we're expected to believe you're never going to hurt her again? You're never going to take out your emotions about your ex on my niece?"

These men—my bosses, my friends—have every right to challenge my word. I outline the commitment I made to myself—not to seek Laura out until I resolved my issues with Bailey's birth mother.

"And what about Bailey? How are you handling that?" Keene challenges.

"One day at a time." My head hangs down between my shoulders. "As you might imagine, I'm not her favorite person right now."

Caleb grunts at that. "You've caused a lot of pain, Liam. So did I. If I'd listened . . ." His words hang in the air between us before he finishes. "She wanted me to tell you."

"How long before?" I ask.

"Almost as soon as she started working for you, she asked if it was safe. I read Caleb's notes," Keene confirms.

Almost from the beginning. Another shaft of pain lances through me when I realize the accusations I hurled at her and how utterly wrong I was.

Caleb laughs bitterly. "I have no leg to stand on here, Liam. I owe you an apology as much as I owe my daughter one. She gave me an ultimatum."

"When?"

"I had two days left when she went to her house. I was furious with her, thinking she would have endangered her life further because I worried Al would have given that information to Olivia Tiberi. That somehow, we'd have been protecting three of you instead of just her. Instead, we almost lost your little girl. I should have trusted you. That's my cross to bear." His expression is bleak.

"Two days and Laura would have told me herself. I fucked up because of forty-eight miserable hours."

"You fucked up because you have issues," Keene reminds me. Then he encompasses both of us in his next statement. "Both of you have a lot to make amends for. Keep working on it."

With a brusque nod, I agree. Until I can apologize, I'll carry the weight of my mistake as well as the determination to prove I'm not going anywhere.

To my employers.

To Laura's family.

And especially to the woman I love.

CHAPTER
Sixty~Seven

LIAM

"DADDY, did you find out from Mr. Caleb when Laura's coming back?" Bailey asks as I tuck her in.

Dinner, a silent affair I've grappled with since Laura left our lives, is done and over with. Bailey has PT early in the morning. With luck, we'll find out if she can move to crutches. *Maybe that will give her something to be happy about*, I think morosely as I shake my head.

Her lower lip quivers. "She won't be here tomorrow for my appointment?"

"I'm sorry, Buttercup . . ."

I don't get to finish. She rolls over, turning her back to me. Despite my daughter's frustration, I lean over and press my lips to the side of her head —a head Laura had one of the best neurosurgeons in the country check on.

Softly, I murmur, "Sweet dreams."

With no response, I slip from her room and head into the empty living room. It's the last place I kissed Laura. Just standing here, I can call up the memory of her aqua eyes.

Now that I know the truth about what Laura knew versus what Caleb withheld from her, I don't blame her for clinging to her self-respect and cutting us out of her life. Still, I rub my hand against the pain in my chest. It hurts.

Like someone severed a lifeline I never knew I needed.

Pulling up Laura's text string, I send her a flurry of messages.

LIAM:

I just put Bailey to sleep and all I want to do is cry because she's angry. I'm not upset she's angry with me. I'm grateful for it.

I know, that sounds odd. The truth is, there's two reasons behind it.

The first is I'm grateful she's alive, and that's because you saved her. You, Laura. No one else. You put your life on the line to save our girl.

Yes, you read that right. OUR girl.

She thinks of herself that way, would be my guess. She's not speaking with me because I can't figure out the way to bring you home.

I'm asking for the chance to explain the reason for what happened in person.

Please. Just a chance.

Every time I hit Send, I wait for the dots to move, for her to write back. Instead, the lack of response left an even more indelible mark—one of despair.

I grapple with what to do next as I relive each moment I spoke with her, touched her, tasted her, searching for a clue I knew must be there. It isn't until the alarm goes off on my phone that I realize I sat there the whole night trying to piece together something that may not be able to be fixed.

That's when desperation sets in.

Later that afternoon, after Bailey receives the news she can come out of her casts and use crutches to be weight bearing, I place a call.

"Amaryllis Events and Company, this is Cassidy. How may I help you?"

"Mrs. Lockwood, this is Liam Payne."

Her polite Southern charm falls away. She hisses, "Yes?"

"I'd like to make an appointment to speak with you at your earliest convenience."

There's a long pause before, "And should I refuse?"

My voice breaks before I beg, "Please."

I hang up terrified because I have an appointment to speak with Laura's mother in three day's time. Now, what the hell am I going to say?

CHAPTER
Sixty~Eight

LIAM

IF I EVER WANTED TO KNOW WHAT Laura would look like as she aged, I'm facing her right now. I'd bet my life she'll be as exquisitely beautiful and just as determined to take my nuts at the slightest offense as Cassidy Freeman-Lockwood is at this very moment.

Her icy demeanor almost does the job of shriveling my balls enough for them to fall off when she drawls, "If Laura had wanted us to meet in more than the professional capacity you work for my husband, I'm certain she would have introduced us before she . . . departed."

Still, I find it hard not to admire her. She's one pissed off mama bear I chose to greet in her den after I terrorized her cub. "It's my fault Laura left."

"Oh?" It's said from queen to peasant with an undertone of *No shit, Sherlock.*

I shove to my feet before moving restlessly around her meticulously organized office. I come up on a photo that stops me dead in my tracks. I instinctively raise my fingers to touch it. It's Laura and her brothers, one of them holding her, the other a balloon. My head cocks to the side as I study it more intently. "I've seen this photo somewhere else before."

"Men are so intuitive about some things and so plain dumb about others." Cassidy's remark startles me from a closer study of Laura as a child. But her voice has lost its hostile edge—in fact, it's kicked up several degrees. Her fingers reverently touch the frame. "You'll figure out where you saw this photo one day."

"Maybe by then it will be easier to fix what happened between me and your daughter."

"You can't change what you said to Laura, Liam. She's never going to forget it. That's not the kind of woman I raised her to be."

If her voice had been laced with fury, I'd have thought it was bitterness talking. But the wise words edged in sympathy make me want to howl in pain. My lip trembles, but I firm it up so I can rasp out, "Bailey misses her. If . . . if you could let her know. I'll . . . I'll make arrangements if . . . if she . . . Laura, that is . . . if she wants to spend time with . . ."

I can't even finish stammering out my request for Cassidy to pass along to Laura when I feel a painful punch against the side of my arm. I gape in astonishment before I lift my hand to my biceps. "I'm a little embarrassed to admit that hurt." *A lot.*

"I intended for it to. I said you can't change the past, Liam, but what about your future? Do you want to change that?"

I shake my head.

Her eyes narrow to slits.

"I don't know what the future holds. All I know is I want Laura in it."

"Then sit down and tell me what happened—all of it, starting with that woman who gave you such a beautiful child."

"You sound a lot like Alice."

Her face softens. "A compliment. You're capable of them. That's good to know."

Still a little stunned over the fact a woman the size of a pixie managed to nail me with a solid hit, I repeat my story—something I'm surprised Caleb hasn't shared. From the moment I met Ashleigh to when Laura rightfully left. I unburden myself to Cassidy. When I'm done, she leans back in her chair and asks, "What would you do differently?"

"I wouldn't have attacked Laura," I declare immediately.

"Really?" She tilts her head to the side.

"Yes."

"I wonder about that." I'm about to defend myself when Cassidy continues. "Love is a gift, but the price we pay for it is the ability to hurt and to be hurt."

"Your husband made me read the legend of Amaryllis."

Cassidy's eyes flash at that. "Did he?"

"Yes." I wet my lips before admitting, "I'd like to think I'd I wouldn't have attacked her."

"Maybe you wouldn't—at least not in the same way." Cassidy concedes. "After all, Laura had just had a gun held to her head—literally—for the second time. And the one person she relied upon to be by her side wasn't there for her. The only advice I can offer is to give her time, Liam. As her mother, as a woman, all I can advocate is patience and time. Laura will come around if and when she's ready."

Knowing my time's up, I thank her and leave before I do something desperate like throw myself at her feet to try to find out something more. Some secret key to unlock the deep freezer Laura's hidden her heart in. It isn't until I've been escorted outside of the mansion behind me I ask, "But when that doesn't work, what do I do?"

There's no answer. No one whispering secrets in my ear on how to win back Laura's heart. But I know if it ever shows signs of defrosting, I plan on melting it the rest of the way.

No matter how long it takes.

CHAPTER
Sixty~Nine

After returning from California, I make an appointment to meet with Dr. Moser, bypassing Alice all together. I don't need her playing mind games with my head right now. What I need is to reclaim the part of myself Liam tried to destroy. Still, I'm not going to lie to myself or put patients in danger. I approach Moser with a solution—one which I think he might like.

"I'm considering changing my specialty—leaving the ER—if you're not opposed to it."

He studies me from behind his massive desk before asking, "Why? The last time we spoke about it, you were determined to become the champion of the wronged, Gore."

I shrug, trying desperately to convey a negligence I don't feel. "I would have thought you would support this decision."

"I would if it was the right one."

My jaw falls open before I sputter, "It wasn't that long ago you lit into me because I didn't choose neurology as a sub-I. Now, I come to you for advice and you're—"

"About to convince you not to let those bastards take away what you were born to do, Laura." His voice is feral when he says, "And I don't just mean the ones with the guns."

I'm not certain what shocks me more, his words or the use of my given name. While I'm regaining my hard-fought composure, Moser pushes out of his chair before rounding his desk. He opens his mouth and what comes out freezes my vocal cords. "You're not stupid. You had to realize I was going to read my medical report from the night the ER was shot up at some point."

I'm truly confused. "What does that have to do with me coming to talk to you about studying a different form of medicine?"

"If it wasn't for you, I'd have died on the floor of the ER—your ER, Laura. But even amid your own pain, your own personal and physical agony, you didn't let me. You refused to let a patient go."

My chest rises and falls as I try to breathe through the weight of Moser's words. Alice's question comes back to the forefront of my mind.

"What do you remember after the shooting?"

Apparently, a great deal. I meet Dr. Moser's eyes and don't say a word as memories begin to drift in.

The pain as the bullet rips through me.

The same bullet taking down Moser.

A spray of bullets dance around me as he spins like a top in every direction before I'm abruptly released. People move slowly, fearfully shifting as if they're worried the gunfire is going to start again.

I hazard a glance behind me and quickly turn away from the now faceless man. I yell, "Triage, people. Now!" Realizing those who could, were moving, I clutch my pain-filled shoulder and stumble a few steps to the left before I spot him lying there motionless. Releasing my wound, I drag a cart filled with medical supplies with my good arm. I drop to my knees and roll Moser onto his back so I can assess the damage.

Shit, his face is chalk white.

Snarling, even as my father sidles up next to me to try to get me to stop, I bite out, "No! I have to help him."

"He'll get it, Laura."

"Stop. Leave me alone, Dad. This is who I am, who you raised me to be."

I tear open a package of 4x4s with my teeth. Cursing, my father rips open more, passing them to me. I stack them and press them against my chief's wound. Moser groans, eyes fluttering. I snarl, even as I ignore the pain in my own shoulder to accept more from my father. "He's saved more lives than I can begin to count. I have to do everything."

My father pressed a kiss against the side of my head. "Laura." Just my name, but it's filled with pride and riddled with lingering fear.

Finally, I shake my head as that dark void finally fills in. My eyes meet his and I declare with all the haughty confidence I can muster, "It must those Freeman genes."

His lips quirk. "I should have guessed. None of the women in your family have ever backed down in all the time I've known them—especially when they band together to take on a common foe."

Without thinking, I blurt out a question I've wondered for most of my life, considering there was once a possibility of this handsome man being a relative. "Why did you hurt my aunt all those years ago?"

He looks away. "Because I made a catastrophic mistake."

"What's that?"

"I didn't trust my instincts. When I fell in love with your aunt, and then she and your Uncle Colby became involved—"

I gasp.

"Weren't expecting complete honesty from me, Gore?"

"Not really, sir."

His gaze takes on a faraway look. If I had to guess, he just transported himself back to my childhood. "I left my position at Hopkins so I could be near her. I assumed, wrongly, I could swoop in and Corinna's and my friendship would naturally lead to . . . well, let's just say I thought I could play my mind games, as you've eloquently called them."

"When that didn't work out . . ." My voice trails off.

"I made myself believe I could make things work with her sister and almost ruined your other aunt's life in the process."

Since the family opinion is exactly the same, I don't reply. I'm barely able to process what my chief has admitted to—loving one sister while being engaged to another. Some might call it heartless. I just think it's horribly sad so many years later because for my aunts, they ended up with their true loves.

"I know what my reputation is—was—around this hospital before I met my wife, Gore. I admit there was a lot of truth to it. Then again, I was just trying to find my third—and last—chance." He lets out a rough breath. "Do you know you're only the second person I've shared that with?"

"Your wife?" I guess. My jaw drops again when he shakes his head in denial.

"Not the details. She knew I fell in love once before her." His eyes bore into mine. "And she knows I was engaged once before. She also is well aware it was wholly my fault for how poorly it ended."

I want to ask him so badly who the other person who knows is. Moser must be able to read it on my face before he admits, "Alice."

My eyes bug out, not expecting that.

He grumbles, "What? You think I don't need someone to talk to? Why do you think I send my patients to her before surgery?"

"She must have a field day with you." The words fly out of my mouth before I can stop them.

His lips twitch. "She . . . appreciates me."

"I'm sure she does."

"Why do you think I approve her chocolate budget each month? If I'm going to sit in her office and subject myself to her intrusive questions, I want there to be some decent choices, for fuck's sake."

"On behalf of every person who has sat on that couch and endured *her* particular mind games, thank you."

He reaches down and squeezes the opposite shoulder to where I was shot. "You, Laura, have thanked me any number of times without knowing it."

I want to laugh it off. I really do. But instead, my lips admit something entirely different. "It hurts so badly."

"Your shoulder? Still?" He frowns immediately, a surgeon through and through.

I shake my head vehemently.

"Ah." Moser moves away from the desk and sits in the chair next to me. "Your heart."

I can't stop the trail of hot tears from pouring down my cheeks. "I thought I was improving until . . ."

"Until the Tiberi crime family decided to take further revenge by holding you and Bailey Payne hostage bringing you back to the ER almost the same way you left it."

I sigh in relief. "You get it."

"More than you know. Let me ask you a question."

"Shh-go ahead." I almost said *shoot*. I'm not so certain I can be cavalier about my words again. Certainly not about three little words, eight letters, that together once held together pieces of my now broken heart.

"Before that night, were you ready to return?"

I nod before admitting, "I wasn't afraid of the ghosts any longer."

"I should have known it was something like that."

"Known what?"

His head bows. "Known that when it's a matter of life or death, you're not afraid to fail. But now, you're terrified you're going to fall." He lifts his head and his eyes bore into mine. "No one here is going to let you down, Laura."

"But it was . . ."

"If you finish that sentence with 'all my fault,' I'm calling your parents to tell them I'm paying for you to get a tattoo that says 'I love Moser'— placement to be determined."

A giggle escapes over Dr. Moser's whimsical threat. He snickers even as I try to control my blatant laughter that feels so wrong in light of the heartbreak I'm dealing with. Once I have myself under control, I concede mentally. There's just one thing left to deal with. "I'm still dealing with some latent anxiety."

"Laura, are you addicted to your medication? Taking more than the prescribed dosage?" My face must reflect how appalled his words make me because he continues, "Yeah, I didn't think so."

"Then what's your plan?" I ask, knowing he has one.

"I want you back two days a week to start. You'll continue to see Alice once a week to be evaluated."

"What if I have an anxiety attack when I'm working on a patient?"

"Then use the damn brain that got you your job here. Get one of your other highly trained staff members to come into the room. Increase your appointments. For fuck's sake, what do you want me to say?"

"That it won't hurt?"

"I can't guarantee that. Half the days here cause heartache of one kind or another."

It's time, the voice in my head encourages me. I knew it in my heart, but my mouth says something different. "It's not that easy."

"Why?" He pushes.

"Because I'm scared! What happens if—"

"If another lunatic comes through the doors with a gun? What happens if you're shot again?"

"Yes." It feels good to share the burden with someone else who understands.

"That may or may not ever happen. I can't predict that." He lets out a shuddering breath, his own fears riding close to the surface. "What I can guarantee is there's eventually going to be another little girl who is hurt. She's going to need a sympathetic doctor to examine her. Maybe there will be someone who was brought in for a knife wound, but he was really shot. That's when they're going to need the best. That's you, Laura."

"You make me sound stronger than I am."

"You are." He rolls his eyes before admitting, "You stand up to me all the time when everyone else—except Alice and Paige—pussyfoots or genuflects around this place."

My lips quirk. "I had good teachers."

His eyes meet mine before he admits begrudgingly, "You were taught to care by the best, and it started from the moment you were born."

"You're really pulling out all the stops, aren't you?"

"Like you said, I like playing mind games."

"Dr. Moser," I begin.

"Let me put it this way. I may be one of the best neurosurgeons in the country, but if you force me to work in your ER another night, I'm going to lose my damn mind. I don't know how you do it."

"It's not an easy job."

"No. It's not. Right now, I'm honored to say I have one of the best doctors in the country working in mine."

I swallow hard to move the lump his words cause.

"Are you ready to resume your job—finish out your R4 and take back your damn ER?"

It's then I capitulate. "I'll start back next week."

Moser pushes to his full height. Holding out a hand, he shakes mine when I place it in his. "Welcome back, Dr. Lockwood."

The pressure in my gut releases even if I know the pain in my soul never will. "Thank you, sir."

"And Lockwood?"

"Yes?"

"If your family, the hospital grapevine, or my wife ever hears about what I shared with you, I swear I'll have you suspended so fast, your head will spin."

I reach his door before I turn and quirk my brow. "I don't know what you're talking about. After I came in, all you did was badger me. Right, Dr. Moser?"

He smiles. For just a moment, I stand there and contemplate what my life would have been like if either of my aunts had actually married him.

Yeah, no.

Shuddering at the very concept, I yank open his office door. Exiting, I know I've found some purchase on my riotous emotions instead of free falling through my heartbreak. It's a small comfort to know I found my way back to one of my homes.

Because the other one I'll never walk through the door again willingly.

Never again.

From the Journal of Dr. Laura Lockwood

I'm back in Connecticut now. In preparing to return to my ER. I see Alice regularly. In fact, she's mad at me. I went to talk with Dr. Douche before coming to see her. I finally have closure on what happened and feel at peace—at least about the first run in with the Tiberis. But it's you and Bailey I truly need to thank for returning to me my humanity. Somehow between delivering the news of a patient's death and the first cry of agony, it was lost.

In the grand scheme of life, knowing one of those injured caught hold of my soul just before it was lost is a gift I will always treasure. The journey I took with both of you that gave me the desire and fortitude to make the decision to return to work. So, you may never see this, but thank you.

CHAPTER
Seventy

I SHOULD HAVE KNOWN BETTER than to have announced my return to work at a family dinner. Immediately, my mother's older brother, Phil, yells over the furor caused by my announcement, "This calls for a celebration, little girl."

I glance around multiple farm tables packed to the gills with family and close friends and groan. "Do we have to make such a big deal out of this?"

A resounding "Yes!" was vocalized by everyone, including my mother. Shit. There was no way I was getting out of it.

Phil whips out his phone, shouting, "Thanks to Cass, I can see who's in town."

My mother rolls her eyes. "You make it sound like I invented our family calendar last week. It's only been up for close to thirty years, Phil."

That sets off a wave of raucous laughter around the room. My father leans over and presses his lips against my mother's temple. She leans into him, obviously having forgiven him. He studies her face a moment before brushing his nose against hers and pressing his lips to hers in a gesture so ingrained and intimate I have to look away.

It hurts. While I wasn't with Liam long, I recall our little intimacies—when he'd come lean against the stove. Picking shells up along the beach. The way he'd trail a finger across my skin.

It wasn't a lot, but it felt like it had the potential for everything.

Now, I'm left with less than nothing.

Nothing but a whole bunch of useless words apologizing to me. What good are words when there's nothing to back them up? What's to stop Liam from doing the same damn thing again? What . . .

Yanking me from my anguish, Phil shouts in excitement, "It looks like we can manage it tomorrow night. Everyone—and I do mean every member of our family. Good thing you flew back, Peter, or we'd have sent a jet."

Peter lifts his glass of wine in a toast to our uncle, appreciating the call out. "Always happy to accommodate your shenanigans, Uncle Phil."

He beams at him before setting an event, trigging a massive amount of pings and ringtones to go off around the room. "Tide Pool, tomorrow night. Seven PM."

Emily's husband, Jake, calls out, "I've got music covered."

Corinna declares, "I'm on cake duty."

Phil glares at her. "Of course you are."

Holly doesn't bother to reply. From the safety of her husband's arms, she's already documenting our family, taking the pictures that have made her a household name.

Mama's on the phone. "Jess? It's Cass. We're descending tomorrow night. Do you want to close down, and we'll pay you to rent Tide Pool out?" There's a pause before Mama stresses, "All of us." Pause. "Right. That's what I thought." She asks Jake, "Live music?"

His fingers are typing. "Yep. Absolutely."

"Yes, Jess. We'll need the stage. Thanks. I'll send you the deposit in a few minutes." Then Mama chuckles. "No, some things never change." My mother leans back into my father's arms before giving Phil a thumbs up.

I open my mouth to indicate I don't need a back to work party. Frankly, I'm not certain I'm up to something this grand when Kalie leans forward and tips a wine bottle in my direction as if it's a pointer. "You have to remember something, Laura."

"What's that?"

Grace wraps her arm around my waist and hugs me tightly. "They're not just celebrating you going back to work. They're celebrating the fact you're well enough to do so."

I twist and stare at my parents. My mother is animated in a way I haven't seen her since before Olivia Tiberi took me as a hostage. As for my father, his face is still lined with guilt, grief. I lift my wineglass in his direction and mouth, "I love you."

His features soften. He mouths back, "I loved you first" before he salutes me with his whisky glass.

Twisting to face my cousins, I throw the rest of my glass back. Then I demand, "Who else can we invite?"

Together we whip out our phones. I send a text to Alice, Paige, and Austyn —all of whom confirm yes, they're in. Kalie invites any and all members of the Amaryllis Events staff who isn't scheduled to work tomorrow. Grace? She hesitates before placing her phone face down.

I know who she was going to text but I'm certain Uncle Brendan will take care of it. Now, I wonder if he'll have the guts to show up and face his biggest regret—losing my cousin's adoration.

By the time we leave, I'm exhausted and ready to crawl in between my sheets to try to sleep. After all, it's exhausting trying to hold my facade of happiness when the real person I want to invite is the absolute last person I want there.

From the Journal of Dr. Laura Lockwood

I'm not certain I can handle what my family's doing. They want to celebrate my return to work. I'm almost one hundred percent positive this isn't a good idea. But the temptation to smile, to laugh, for the first time since losing you and Bailey, is appealing.

CHAPTER
Seventy~One

LIAM

THE MESSAGE I received earlier from my bosses had me rushing to find a last-minute sitter. Apparently there is some kind of Amaryllis event occurring at Tide Pool in Collyer that every member of their family—extended and otherwise—is planning on attending.

> CALEB:
>
> I'm not saying she's going to talk with you.
>
> KEENE:
>
> If she does, I'll be impressed.
>
> CALEB:
>
> $50?

KEENE:

You're on.

LIAM:

You're both assholes. But I appreciate the intel.

CALEB:

Wear body armor.

KEENE:

You might need it.

I slip in the side door at Tide Pool, expecting to find Laura huddled at a corner table drinking amid her siblings and her cousins. Then I could slip over and ask her to take a walk with me so we could talk.

I couldn't have been more wrong.

"Fuck off!" The entire room explodes just as I show the bouncer my cell phone with the QR code Caleb told me I'd need to get in. Maybe I should heed their warning, turn around, and try approaching her on a different night.

That is until I capture Laura in my sights. Then I'm immoveable as I can't process what I'm seeing.

Every person who could call themselves a member of Laura's extended tribe is on the dance floor, including—my eyes bug out—Caleb and Keene. But that doesn't compare to the fact the woman I'm in love with is rocking right alongside my daughter's idol—Austyn Kensington. The two women are harmonizing to Gayle's infamous "ABCDEFU."

If Bailey was here right now, she'd squeal louder than the music.

There isn't an ounce of heartbreak visible on her exquisite face. As a spotlight catches her, the natural highlights in her sable locks shine. Laura smirks at the other woman as she sings. Long legs encased in form fitting leather pants and high-heeled boots, saliva pools in my mouth at the sight of her after having no contact with her the past six weeks. The way her body undulates in time to the sadistic anthem makes me want to rip off that excuse for a shirt and feast on her perfect breasts.

You're a long way from that, I caution myself as I lurk in the shadows.

Kensington takes the lead, and Laura takes a swig from a bottle of champagne a handsome man hands up to her. She hands it back to him. Shit, there's no way I'm going to escape without blood being shed. The guy she just handed it to knows how to use knives way to well for my liking. I easily recognize Peter Freeman, even from a distance.

Off to the side, I see my "friend" Jake hanging next to Brendan Blake, and my asshole twitches a bit when I realize why security's so tight.

Beckett Miller.

Great. So not only do I have to face off with the woman I love's family, but this place is also just crawling with Hudson Investigation bodyguards who are likely authorized to take someone out on a simple kill order. I'm pretty certain the sweat dripping from my balls makes me look like I've peed myself, but that's okay.

I'm ready to face Laura.

The crowd roars the refrain alongside Laura as she raises her mic for the bridge. Her fist raises in the air with the tempo as she calls out the song's title. "ABCDEFU!" Her family shouts it back like it's some kind of anthem —Cassidy is more enthusiastic than the rest, I note self-depreciatingly.

Despite the few times Caleb's pleaded with his wife to watch Bailey, or since Cassidy and I spoke in her office, I'm pretty certain I'm still on her shit list.

A hand clamps down on my shoulder. My head whips to the side. Even though I could likely have a fair fight with her twin, my balls have now turned into ice cubes due to the frigid expression Jon's aiming at me. Before I can speak, he squeezes. "I hope like hell you're not going to crash her celebration party."

"Her what?"

Jon forces my attention back to the direction of the stage instead of on him. That's where I spy the banner hanging over the musicians that reads "Congratulations, Laura!"

Congratulations? On what? Then it hits me that I wasn't there for the biggest moment in her recovery, unlike all the milestones she's been there for my child. Dully, I say, "She's returning to work?"

"See, that's why you aren't the right man for my sister." Jon relishes telling me.

"Why's that?" I challenge.

"Because you were damned determined to make sure this night never happened."

"That's not true."

"No? Then why couldn't you look past the fact what happened to your daughter wasn't her fault?"

"I don't have to explain myself to you," I snarl, pissed he struck at the heart of the matter. But he has no right to know I never really blamed her. Laura does.

If she wants it. If she believes it.

God, I hope she does.

"Why don't you shove that stick further up your ass and leave us in peace so we can celebrate her overcoming the worst thing to happen to her, to us." Jon backs up, still facing me. "You know what your problem is, Payne?"

"I assume you're going to tell me."

"You're such an ass, you'll never let yourself truly fall for the one person who already loves you." With that, he spins on his heel to rejoin the foray.

CHAPTER
Seventy~Two

Laura

AUSTYN HIGH-FIVES me even before she calls into the microphone, "My girl should give up medicine and come on the road with me."

Her words are met with cheers from the music contingency and loud boos from most of our family. Throwing me a wink, she goes on, "There's this incredible parallel between music and medicine. Did you know that?" Austyn places a lingering kiss on my cheek before heading to the back of the stage, where a drum kit is being set up.

Peter shouts, "Nice girl-on-girl action there, Austyn!" A hand—seemingly out of nowhere—reaches out and slaps my cousin upside the head. I crack up, realizing it's Austyn's husband who just pummeled him.

Catcalls come from all the cousins over Peter taking a rightful beat down. He accepts it good naturally, fist bumping with Austyn's man while I'm lifted from the stage. Peter wraps an arm around my waist. Seconds after, instruments are moved into place even as three gorgeous men bound up to take their positions.

Austyn loops her arm around her father's waist when rockstar Beckett Miller leans into his microphone over a keyboard. "All of us hope and pray when our loved ones are hurt that they get a doctor as dedicated as my Paigey and our own Dr. Laura Lockwood."

The crowd cheers. I find Paige in the crowd and place a finger on my nose while pointing directly at my mentor. Sitting alongside the wife of Beckett's lead bodyguard, she does the same back at me.

Then Uncle Brendan tacks on, "Or that we receive good news from medical diagnoses." He kisses the tips of his finger and points it toward the back of the darkened bar to a man sitting in the shadows.

My eyes find Grace in the crowd. She claps, but the shrieking madness that's consumed me, her, and Kalie all night temporarily disappears from her face. Gah, now my list of men I want to nut is growing.

Austyn slips behind the drum kit, and Uncle Jake winks at me as I take a slug from my champagne bottle. "Which is all a lead up to say, who's heard of the expression, 'only time will tell?'"

He lifts a horn to his lips and begins the intro to the famous song from Asia. Then Austyn kicks in with drums. Brendan with lead guitar.

Finally, Beckett begins to croon the first stanza of lyrics.

Within seconds I'm getting serenaded by two of the world's most famous musicians and the man who writes many of their song lyrics—not that anyone but family knows that. Paige makes her way onto the dance floor and I can feel the way Beckett's eyes kindle from the stage. On our other side, my parents are dancing, oblivious to everything but each other.

That's the way love should be, I think with sudden clarity. Love should be a seduction, a comfort, a warm embrace amid chaos. It should be a fury, a storm, and a haven. What love shouldn't be filled with is accusatory, distrustful, riddled with never-ending pain.

Maybe love isn't Liam. At least loving Liam isn't meant for me.

Maybe that's what time is trying to tell me.

Peter deliberately bumps into me as the song approaches the refrain and shouts, "Look up!"

I shoot a quick glance at my mentor only to find her staring at her husband biting her lip. Beckett winks down at his wife before he shows off, spinning around and nailing his next chord. He then grabs the mic from the holder and moves closer to Jake. So does Brendan. All three men have a foot propped on an amp and lean forward to sing together in a perfect three-part harmony.

Meanwhile, Austyn—musical prodigy that she is—keeps wailing away at the mid tom and high hat.

I lean over to Peter and shout, "If we weren't related to two out of the four of them, I might give up being a doctor and become a professional groupie. I mean, that shit's hot."

His laughter peals out. "I'm going to tell them you said that at the next family dinner."

"Go right ahead, it's not like you haven't . . ." My voice trails off as Peter's smile fades.

Tingles, which have nothing to do with being serenaded by three gorgeous men, start at the base of my spine. I shouldn't be surprised when my hair is brushed from the side of my neck and Liam's voice shouts in my ear, "Can we talk, Laura? Please?" But I am.

I'm frozen in place until I see Peter lunge for him. I whirl around and back my body into my cousin's to prevent him from spilling blood. I stare into Liam's eyes for a long moment. Finally, because I'm a doctor and sworn to heal and don't want his death on my hands, I nod.

I know there are too many people here who could easily snap him in two and are more than willing to volunteer for the effort.

Liam has a grip on my hand I can't break. As Austyn calls out a break, he drags me out the back door onto the dock behind Tide Pool.

Coming to a stop, Liam's face is filled with remorse. He opens his mouth to speak, but I lift our joined hands before he can. "Can you please release me?"

"Will you give me a chance to talk before you walk away?" His vulnerability tugs at a heart I swore I was going to leave dead and buried.

I shake our joined hands. "Fine. Just let me go."

"I'm not certain I know how to do that, Laura," he murmurs as our fingers unlace.

Defiant, my hip cocks out. "You don't have a choice. Even if we were . . . what we were, I make my own choices, Liam. You have five minutes."

"I need to apologize," he admits, his voice laced with regret. "I want the chance to fix this, to fix us."

A storm of resentment and hurt swirls inside of me. I lash out, "Your words didn't just cut, they were designed to slaughter. I won't forget a single thing you said that night."

Desperation paints his features as he pulls his cell from his pocket. "I'm sorry. Let me make it right."

A text hits my phone. I sneer. "What is it? Another I'm sorry?"

"No, it's my files from Alice."

Despite my simmering anger, I waver. "You've been seeing her? Really talking to her?"

His head twists to the side. "What you're going to read isn't easy for me to admit. But as the woman I love . . ."

I hold my hand out to ward off his words as pain thunders through me.

Raw agony is visible in his eyes. "Just read the file, Laura. That's all I ask. Then, *if* you want my apology, it's yours. That's the bare minimum of what I want to give you."

"What do you really want?"

"To give you?" At my nod, he reaches out a hand. When I refuse to take it, it remains held out—like a plea. "Only my heart, my life, and our daughter."

The scab over my heart is ripped off. It begins seeping again. "I promise I'll read this, but you have to give me space, Liam."

"Laura . . ."

"Your apologies are just words. I need room." I can barely stand here and look up into eyes that I see in my sleep every night. I can't figure out what to do next based on a single apology.

"I understand. Just one request . . ."

"Liam," I begin, waiting for him to ask for something like an embrace—something to make me ache more than I already am.

"Will you please find time to reach out to Bailey? She's so confused."

"Bailey." I brace my hands on the rail surrounding the dock and try to drag air into my lungs. In my own pain, I isolated myself from her—from the fact she went through this trauma alongside me.

"She misses you, Laura. Every day."

I nod, the knot at the juncture of my throat unable to let me speak.

He lays his hands on my shoulders and brushes his lips across the back of my head. "Thank you." He hesitates before leaning forward to whisper, "I will always love you, Laura Lockwood, even if you can never forgive me."

Why did that feel like he was saying goodbye? My heart begins to thump frantically as his footsteps walk away from me. Spinning around, I call out, "Liam?"

I catch him dashing his fingers from his eyes. "We've made so many memories together—you, me, and Bailey. I just want you to be happy, Laura. Whatever happy is for you." With that, he turns and shuffles down the dock.

After he disappears from sight, I brace my forearms against the wood rail, thinking about everything he asked for and said. He loves me, and he wants me to talk with Bailey. He wants me to be happy. But he never tried to coax me to give him another chance. He left that entirely up to me.

"Darling?" My mother comes to stand next to me. Her arm slips around my waist.

"I thought I was prepared to see him."

"And were you?"

"Not even close."

She turns me to face her. "Do you love him?"

"Despite everything, I'm not certain I know how to stop. I just can't get the memory of what he said out of my head."

"Memories are like dreams, Laura. Something will happen in your life to shift them so they seem bittersweet instead of just bitter."

"Does anything replace the pain?"

"Of course."

"What?"

"Love."

"How did I know you were going to say that?"

"But when you love, replacing them—even when you're so livid with them you want to strangle them with your bare hands—"

I can't help but choke out a laugh at her description of how furious she was at my father.

"—isn't an option. They're a part of you. Trying to tell yourself lies to get through the pain of living without them just makes things worse."

She kisses my cheek before reminding me, "You're the guest of honor. Don't brood for too long."

"I'll be in soon," I promise.

But it's still a while that I stare at the water before I click the link Liam sent me. Then all I want do is sit down on the deck and read.

But I can't. I have a celebration to return to with people I know who love me.

And I'm not certain if that includes Liam.

From the Journal of Dr. Laura Lockwood

They say we get what we deserve, but if that's the case, why did you have to show up tonight? Are you serious about a second chance, or is this your opportunity to punish me forever? You said you want me to be happy, but how is that supposed to happen when what I want isn't but a few minutes away?

I listened to your sessions with Alice. What you went through—the fear and adrenaline pulsating through you, the similarities between incidents, Ashleigh's lies, and my withholding information. I get it now. Now, I'm crying all over again.

CHAPTER
Seventy~Three

Laura

I NEVER THOUGHT the chaos of the ER would ease the turmoil still roiling around in my mind, but it has.

"Take him to trauma room two," I order as I jog next to the gurney. When I feel a hand flail against my arm, I change to a sashay so I can focus on the patient. "What's your name, sir?"

"Hen . . . dricks," he manages just before he passes out.

I feel the life drain out of him and let his hand drop. Calmly, I order the team around me, "On my count, one, two, three . . ."

We transfer Mr. Hendricks from the EMT's board with ease.

Riyaz, our head nurse, says, "Gore's running this."

Inside, I'm reassuring myself everything is going to be fine. I demanded it was time for me to come back. I'm mentally ready. I can do this.

I can.

I didn't have Liam Payne at my back before this, and I don't need him in my heart now to be the best at what I do. I order, "Let's have a CBC type and cross match." Leaning forward, I listen to Mr. Hendricks's chest. "Call the OR and tell them to prep a room."

Riyaz quicks a brow. "Without having a chest X-ray?"

"Then you listen. His artery is completely blocked."

"I wasn't questioning you, Gore," she begins.

"You were. We don't have time for it. Every minute we stand here debating instead of acting—"

"Shit, he's flatlining!" Suarez shouts.

Riyaz lets out an expletive. She gives me the information I need without needing to ask. "No BP."

Rollins calls out, "No sensation radial or medial."

I yell, "Scissors. Get his clothes off. Inject an amp of lidocaine and start CPR."

Immediately Suarez and Rollins begin slicing through the T-shirt and jeans he's wearing. Riyaz draws the medication.

Suarez calls out, "He's arresting!"

"Charge the paddles to two hundred and continue CPR," I order. Once I'm handed the paddles, I call, "Clear!"

Everyone scrambles back.

It's a dance we've performed hundreds of times before, just with different partners. Even the victim knows the moves. Their body arcs in a bend they'd claim they never could consciously as the shock rips through their system while the devil rolls his eyes as we try to cheat death one more time.

Right now, it's not working.

"Charge me to three hundred."

"Charging," Riyaz confirms. "Ready."

"Clear!"

"Still in arrest," Suarez notes.

"Not anymore. Asystole."

Come on, come on. Don't do this to me on my first day back, Mr. Hendricks. Aloud, I call out, "How long have we been trying?"

"Thirty minutes," Riyaz confirms.

The cool wash of death starts to fill the room. Still, I give it one more try. "Charge to three-sixty. One hundred of lidocaine."

We all hold our collective breaths as we wait for a bounce, a blip. But after Suarez shouts out "Asystole" I know it's time to call it for my team, for the family.

For myself.

I look down at my watch and note, "Time of death, 14:24. Has his family made it here yet?"

Rollins murmurs, "We just got a hold of his wife. She's a schoolteacher."

I reach down and clasp his still warm fingers between mine and order the team, "Clean him up. Find me when she gets here."

Spinning on my heel, I'm about to burst through the doors to write down my notes while they're still clear in my mind when I hear Riyaz call my name. "Laura?"

My head whips around. It's so rare for my actual name to be used in the ER, I'm in shock. "Yes?"

"I can notify his wife," Riyaz says. At my silence, she goes on, "It's your first day back."

While I appreciate the offer, I need to cut away this last festering wound that's slicing me to the bone. "If I can't be there for the victims—whether the ones on this table or the ones in chairs—what right do I have to be back?"

With that, I slap through the doors, waiting for Mrs. Hendricks to arrive.

Fourteen hours later, I'm exhausted mentally and physically in a way I haven't been since I was an intern, but maybe the wound that's been gushing blood in my chest cavity is finally closing. I pause by the curtain where it all happened and check on the patient.

I whip out my phone and hesitate before I send a text to the person I know would most want to hear I went back to work today. Especially because I heard about a twenty-thousand-dollar donation to the victims' fund in my honor.

I have to thank him. It's only right.

LAURA:

Thank you.

Seconds later, I receive a response.

LIAM:

For what?

LAURA:

I heard about the donation. You didn't have to donate that much.

LIAM:

Yes, I did.

LAURA:

Why?

LIAM:

Your ER saves people's lives, Laura. You all sacrifice so much to do it every single day. The people who were hurt or died didn't fall in vain.

I stare at his text for long moments, trying to reconcile the man who screamed at me in such fury with the one who texted me. Realizing Alice is likely correct—that Liam channeled his anger at me since I was the person he was most closely bonded to in that moment in time, a person who had betrayed him—do I still have the right to retain my fury?

She says I can if he refuses to accept his fault in this. "You recall the event from two wholly different perspectives, Laura. Just because Liam said hurtful things in the heat of the moment doesn't mean you can't forgive him. It also doesn't mean you have to. Remember, you make the best choices for what your heart wants."

The question is, what does my heart want?

I hold on, praying for a lifeline, when I type out something benign and wait for his response.

LAURA:

It's my first day back.

LIAM:

Congratulations.

LIAM:

How does it feel? How do you feel?

LAURA:

A bit unsteady. I guess that's normal.

LAURA:

As for how I feel? Ask me tomorrow.

LIAM:

You've got this. I believe in you.

I believe in me too. I'm not going to fall, not again. Never again. Inside I know no man will ever drop me to my knees—physically or metaphorically—because I know the truth of what happened the night I stood here in this very spot. Time will help scab over my open wounds. I put away my phone and pull out the chart of the young patient presently in the bed Bailey occupied. "Looks like you took a nasty spill on a motorized skateboard?"

"Yeah," she moans.

"Maybe not today, but you'll feel like flying again one day soon."

"Promise?"

"Life's all about taking risks." I wink at her, reassuring her terrified mother.

Before I move, I pull up a different text string and send a quick message to the person who I'll always remember every time I stand in this very spot.

LAURA:

Hey, Buttercup. Hope you had a good day at school. XOXO

BAILEY:

I miss you, Laura.

LAURA:

I miss you too.

I miss your father too, but I bury that information deep inside where it can't hurt if I try to get up and fly again. Just like that little girl who tumbled head over feet.

I survived the loss of Liam, but I can risk everything by giving us a chance to start over. Or, if not, I'll figure out a way to live just fine without him.

Even if that means never falling in love again.

CHAPTER
Seventy-Four

LIAM

IF I'VE LEARNED nothing else in the last few days, it's neither words nor actions can speak exclusively for how a person feels. It's like saying every day can have a rainbow without both the rain and the sun.

No matter how many perfectly beautiful days I spent with Laura, the second the storm hit, I abandoned her. I didn't shelter her as she tried to protect me and Bailey. I let my hangups and dark past overshadow what could have been a beautiful path forward in our relationship.

I want Laura to be happy and from what I've observed, I need one crucial person in my corner.

The night of her party, I thought it would be easier to disappear from her life, give her a chance to move on from the vitriol I spewed at her.

Then, something happens to help me beat back the demons. A glimmer of hope.

She texted me.

I know I'm fighting for Laura on every front imaginable. But the first person I'm pitting myself up against needs to know the truth of what really happened that night.

After all, he's tied to her in ways I'll never truly understand.

I clutch the soft drink in between my fingers as I wait for Jonathan Lockwood to join me at a bar located in the World Trade District. O'Hara's stood long before 9/11 happened and opened its doors the minute it was granted authorization to post apocalypse. It's always been a welcoming place for cops and firefighters, which is why I asked Jon to meet me here.

I figure if he successfully murders me in front of witnesses, someone will read the note in my pocket that he isn't to blame. If that doesn't work, they'll at least bring Bailey to Laura to raise.

I study the scratches and nicks in the table, covered in a high gloss varnish in an effort to not worry he won't show up.

When a blond man with an unwashed mop of greasy hair drops onto the stool across from me, I almost bark at him to get lost. It's then Jon lowers his shades to reveal his natural eye color before raising them back into place in the dimly lit bar. I barely manage to catch myself before I gape at his disguise—he doesn't look even remotely like himself. Even his voice projects differently from the arrogant heir-apparent who strolled into my office. Grittier, he raps out a quick "Ya got info for me?" which has a pointed Bronx accent.

My lips part slightly. "Yes."

His twist into a nasty smirk before he leans over and admits in his normal tone, "Sorry, Liam. I was assigned a new case yesterday. I can't break cover, even for my sister." Sitting back and crossing his arms, his nasal-infused voice sneers, "Now, tell me how ya fucked this shit up?"

So, I do. Playing along with his cover, I start by confessing I never passed along the data he "recommended." Then I recap the events at the hospital from my point of view. Miserably, I conclude, "I'm certain you know the details."

"Sure as shit do, you piece of shit."

I cringe because that one came from Jon, the brother, not the man in character. "I want to make things right."

"Boy, you screwed the pooch on this job. I ought to have my boys fuck ya up."

Because he could mean either his family or Hudson's finest, I make only one request. "If you kill me, bring Bailey to Laura. I've already updated my will for that contingency."

Now Jon's face blanks with shock. He bellows, "You did what?"

"You're right. I fucked up. Royally. I said shit to the woman I love, using her as an outlet for my anger, which never should have been directed at her. I was furious at your father, at the Tiberis, hell, at the dead woman who birthed my child. But that doesn't mean I don't regret every bit of it. Bailey loves Laura. If something were to happen to me, I need to know she's with someone who loves her the same way I do."

Jon's jaw works back and forth so much I'm afraid he's going to dislodge the fake teeth he's wearing over his natural enamel. His head swivels around before his voice questions in his own tone, "I assume Laura has no idea."

I lift my drink and take a sip before I admit, "She asked for space."

"And you're giving it to her?" His voice bellows in its Bronx accent, incredulousness overlaid heavy so much over that heads swivel in our direction.

My hand slaps against the table. "What the fuck am I supposed to do?"

"Court her. Ain't she worth everything? Shower her with gifts—no, no, wait. Don't do that."

"Why not?" I'm now confused if he's in character or not.

"That cunt, Tiberi, may she rot in hell—did that shit. You don't need to be messed up with that."

"Right. No gifts."

"But you need to show your woman what she means to you—both of you." He chews on his knuckles a moment before leaning forward and giving me some ideas of the kind of things his twin would appreciate. Again, my hope rises tentatively.

"So, I have your approval?" I lay the question out there between us.

"You're redeemable, brothah."

"That's it?" I suspect him of holding back.

I wasn't wrong.

As low as his voice can pitch, he lets me have it with both barrels. "You had no clue of the heart you held in your hands, but you're not a complete fucking moron. You're trying to fix you before you attempt to repair what you broke. That doesn't scream out as someone who intends on hurting my sister again. Because if you did . . ." He lets the sentence hang.

I'm not stupid. There might be a second chance but there won't be a third.

He shoves to his feet. That's when I get a full look at him and want to chortle at the sight. Billionaire playboy Jonathan Lockwood is sporting a stained white T-shirt, faded jeans pulled down almost over his ass showing striped boxers, plus construction boots when the man proudly wears bespoke suits to the office. His words distract me as he pulls out a set of wadded one-dollar bills. Tossing a few on the table, he mutters, "In the end, if you do manage to get her to forgive you, I expect you to remember something."

"What's that?"

"Every day it should be your damn privilege to love a woman like her." With that, he turns his back and ambles out the back entrance to the bar.

What I didn't get to share is that even though we're as far apart as two people can be while still being connected through a thread of love, it already is.

Whipping out my phone, I text Laura.

LIAM:

I'm thinking about you. We miss you. I miss you.

LAURA:

Liam . . .

LIAM:

It's okay, Laura. You don't have to say anything back.

LAURA:

How's Bailey? I texted her, but didn't want to ask how she's handling her new schedule?

LIAM:

> Misses you in the afternoons. Irritated because she's not off her crutches yet. Done, tired, you name it.

There are little dots before a new message comes in.

LAURA:

> There will be something waiting for you both when you get home.

LIAM:

> Any clues?

LAURA:

> You won't need one.

Paying my tab, I leave Manhattan and begin the arduous drive back to Darien. I arrive just in time to pick Bailey up at her school bus stop so she doesn't have to hobble down the street. I'm treated to monosyllabic answers about how her day went despite what subject we talk about.

That is until I pull into our driveway and spy on the front porch balloons, flowers, and a familiar pink and red box. My heart leaps knowing Laura's been by.

Bailey's much more vocal about her demands. "Daddy! Carry me! I want to see what it is—who sent it!"

Because I want that as much as she does, I don't reprimand her. Instead, I carry her to the front stoop and ask her to sit. There's an envelope for each of us on top of the pastry box. Handing Bailey hers, I tear into mine.

And quickly find myself putting the envelope in my pocket so I can sit next to my daughter to gush over her back-to-school gifts from Laura— especially her buttercup cupcakes.

Enough, her card indicates, for her to share with her father.

Later that night, long after Bailey's open chatter leads to the most pleasant dinner we've shared in weeks, followed by dessert and bedtime, I slide the letter that's been burning a hole in my pocket from the envelope. Very quickly, I fall into Laura's emotional state.

Liam,

Are you serious about a second chance or is this your opportunity to punish me forever? You said you want me to be happy, but how is that supposed to happen when what I want isn't but a few minutes away?

I listened to your sessions with Alice. What you went through—the fear and adrenaline pulsating through you, the similarities between incidents, Ashleigh's lies and my withholding information. I get it now. Now, I'm crying all over again.

I texted you today to thank you—I never expected to do that after everything that happened. Your generosity almost makes me want to see you, but not yet. Still, I feel your worry, not just about Bailey. I want to let you know I'll be okay.

Someday.

Texting you doesn't mean I'm ready to welcome you back into my life, but it means I appreciate your gift to the people who meant the most to me. That is until I met you and Bailey.

When you texted back, I wanted to leap for joy, cry in a corner, and hurl my phone into a wall. Instead, I walked over to the cubicle where we ended. I faced my fears because you handed me the key to doing so the night I saw you at Tide Pool.

The memory of what you screamed at me still lingers, but slowly, it's being replaced by new ones—other patients I'm able to heal. Maybe I wasn't meant to be yours, or you mine.

Maybe we were meant to fall to know we could?

I don't know.

What I know is I can't push you out of my mind.

Wise people have shared that if I want to forgive, to move forward, I need to see beyond the landscape of pain. I'm working on that. I just don't know where it's going to lead me.

I'm adding this last part today before I leave this with you. It's only right after all this time. Celebrate, Liam. Every *milestone, every tear. Make certain Bailey knows she's the most important person in your life. Make sure she knows you loved her first and always will. It's what my father always said to me.*

She loves you eternally.

Take care. Be happy, no matter what it takes.

Love,

Laura

PS – I told Bailey the cupcakes, balloons, and flowers were from you so she doesn't get confused.

I shift the papers away so my tears don't drip on her outpouring of emotion that all stems from one feeling—love.

CHAPTER
Seventy~Five

LIAM

It's a few weeks later when my eyes finally get to feast on the woman I love after her cupcake delivery to my house. Bailey's dragging me forward into Bodega Taco Bar after she caught a glimpse of Laura. "Daddy, come on!"

"Bailey, I don't want to bother Laura." Okay, that's a damn lie. I do, but I promised to give her some space. I've sent her gifts Jon recommended, and a few I came up with on my own.

A framed picture from Bailey where I included a note.

> *Someone drew this especially for you. She wanted to hand this to you in person. You are missed every single day, Laura. You, just for being you.*

A travel coffee mug with a picture of the three of us emblazoned on the side of it.

This is where you belong—with us. By our side. I'm so sorry about what my selfishness did. Please forgive me.

Sheets of return address stickers with her name and *my* address, reminding her of where her home truly is.

Home is where your heart is. You left yours here. Come back, claim it. Please.

After each one, I get the same text.

> **LAURA:**
> Liam, you don't have to get me anything. <3

That's it. She could be throwing them in a box or setting fire to them in her backyard for all I know, but I need for her to know she's still part of our family.

And this family needs her.

"But she *said* I could. Anytime."

"Bailey, that was before."

"Daddy, that was her last text to me!"

I rear back as if I've been slapped. "Laura's been texting you?"

Bailey pulls out her phone and thrusts it in my face.

> **LAURA:**
> If we happen to see each other, Buttercup, I'd love a hug. I love and miss you too.

God, what I wouldn't give to have her text that to me.

I crouch down and capture Bailey's cheeks between my hands. "Bailey, you know what love is."

"Yes. You love me. I love you."

"And I love Laura," I inform her softly.

Instead of being upset, she almost takes out a few pedestrians when her crutches become bird wings in her excitement. "Woo hoo! Now, can we go see her?"

"Baby, it's not that simple."

"Why not?"

"Because . . ." Crap. How much do I tell her? *The truth.* "You know I said some not nice things after you and Laura were taken by the bad people. She was really hurt by it."

"Is that why she won't come over anymore?" Her lower lip quivers.

"Mainly," I admit.

Bailey bursts into tears. Immediately, I pull her into my arms for a hug. "I'm sorry, baby. I'm so, so sorry. I never meant to hurt you. I definitely never meant to hurt Laura."

"Then why did you say mean things?"

"Because I was scared."

"But you're not scared now."

"No, but the thing is, now she is." As I scan the busy street, my heart quickens at the sight of her—her aqua eyes meeting mine with a mix of surprise and guardedness before it they soften at the sight of who's next to me. Laura says something to her cousins, Kalie and Grace, before standing and leaving the bustling taco bar.

She approaches us and opens her arms, keeping her promise. Just like she always did when she swore she loved me. Like I should have when I said the same.

I wish that greeting included room for me, but the second my daughter rushes into them, Laura's arms close up tight. Keeping Bailey in, keeping me out. What's the damn difference?

"Hey," I manage, my voice betraying my longing.

Her whole demeanor softens as she holds the bundle in her arms even tighter. "What are you guys doing here?"

I swallow hard, the weight of my remorse threatening to suffocate me. "Just some school picture shopping."

"Oh?"

That's when Bailey blurts, "Daddy needs to apologize."

Laura twists one of her messy pigtails around her fingers. "No, he doesn't. He has already, Bailey. I just need some time to think it over."

"Laura . . ." I start.

"Liam . . ." she says at the same moment. We both slide our glances away awkwardly until Bailey shifts within Laura's embrace.

My chest tightens as memories of my outburst flood my mind—the venomous words I had hurled at her, the unjust accusations borne of my own unresolved pain. All the things I've been working through with Alice. Still, I drop my gaze to Bailey. Laura tips her chin in understanding. God, she's so careful with Bailey. How could I have even temporarily laid Ashleigh's crimes at her feet? "I want the chance to show you how much I —we—have missed you, not with a gift, not with a text. You deserve to hear it from my heart to yours. You deserve everything. That's what I wanted to say."

Her gaze softens, a flicker of vulnerability seeping through her defenses. Silence hangs between us, pregnant with fractured dreams. But beneath it all, there lingers a fragile glimmer of hope—a chance for redemption, for healing.

She murmurs something to Bailey before coming to stand directly in front of me.

"I don't know if I can trust you again," she whispers, her voice barely audible above the din of the weekend traffic.

"I'll spend a lifetime trying to earn it back."

"We'll see."

"Yes, we will."

Her face flushes and for the first time since that god-awful afternoon, I feel hope. After Laura says goodbye to Bailey, I stare after her as she makes her way back to her cousins. *One step at a time*, I caution myself.

One moment where she isn't pushing me away.

I'll do penance forever, so long as the journey ends with me on a path toward Laura.

CHAPTER
Seventy-Six

LIAM

SINCE RUNNING into her at Bodega, I've begun sending Laura a fresh bouquet of flowers that mimic the ones I handed her the night of the hospital gala. I've emailed her spa gift cards to use with her cousins. DoorDashed coffee to her on weekends.

Anything to keep the line of communication open between us.

Every second, I hope she's not going to tell me to get lost, or I'm not going to run into her with some other man. Christ, my heart—already in pieces—would be ash.

Dust.

But as each week passes, my hope dwindles. Bracing my hand against the window in my bedroom, I wish she knew how much I regret what happened to us.

"If I could turn back time, I would. I'd take better care of you, sweetheart."

Knowing that's an impossibility, I let out a large sigh before climbing into bed—a bed that feels far too large without her. Holding my buttercup pillow to my chest, I try to sleep so I don't wreck.

I have to take Bailey to the hospital for a physical therapy appointment tomorrow.

Maybe I'll get a glimpse of her even if it's on the damn hospital directory sign.

Outside of Greenwich Hospital, I lean against my car. *It's not going to get any easier, no matter how long you wait.*

"Daddy? What's wrong?" Bailey asks from my side.

"Nothing." *Liar.*

Her little hand slips into mine. "Is it because we might see Laura?" Her voice holds the same amount of hope my heart does.

I'd give anything for a chance to see her, to look at her. To tell her I love her . . .

But that's a chance I'm not likely to be granted. Instead, I set Bailey's expectations. Carefully, I squeeze her hand. "I don't think we'll see her, but yes, I'm sad because we haven't."

"But I heard you apologize." She frowns up at me.

"I've tried, Buttercup." *Over and over.*

We make our way toward the front of the hospital, my head drooping lower and lower as the site of my sins weighs heavily on my shoulders. Then Bailey screams "Laura!" and begins frantically waving her arm.

My head snaps up. Then I, too, see her as she emerges from the hospital front entrance. A mix of longing and apprehension washes over me. We're close enough that our eyes meet. In the silent exchange, there's longing and something else in her eyes.

It's not hate.

Or fear.

Could it be . . .

"Hey, Bailey." She drops to her knee and waits for Bailey to make her way over to her.

The second she does, any distance between them is immediately eradicated. Bailey throws her arms around Laura's neck. She mumbles something. Laura's eyes squeeze shut and her smile widens. "I miss you too, sweetheart."

She steadies my daughter before aiming a tentative smile in my direction. "Liam."

"Laura." Just her name, but in it is all the anguish I'm feeling.

Her smile waivers as if the sound of my pain hurts her. That has to mean something, right? I push my luck and move closer. "How are you?"

Her eyes meet mine and her ocean-colored eyes brighten. "Good."

I blink in surprise before I attempt my first smile not directed at Bailey in weeks. I start "Have you been receiving . . ."

For a second, a twitch of amusement lifts her lips. "The long term stay residents would like to say thank you for your generosity."

I'm confused before I yelp, "You've been giving away my flowers?"

Exasperated, she rolls her eyes. "Liam, you've sent flowers every. Single. Day. I'd be in anaphylactic shock if I kept that many at home. I'm sharing the . . . enjoyment with some people who don't have as much love around them."

"Oh." Then I think about her words, and my heart begins to beat faster.

She said love.

Immediately, I ask, "Is there anything else they need? Books? Magazines?"

Her mouth blooms into a real smile. A curvature of lips I never thought I'd see again. "As much as you've done for the hospital, there's no way I can ask that."

"What if I want to help . . . the hospital again?"

"If you want that information, see the charge nurse on six west." Just then, my phone beeps incessantly, reminding me of Bailey's appointment.

"I guess that's my cue to go," I explain.

She bends over and hugs Bailey again. "It was good to see you, Buttercup."

"You too, Laura," she chirps.

"Text me and let me know how the appointment goes," she makes Bailey promise.

"I will."

"It was . . . good . . . to see you, Liam."

"You too, Laura."

Giving me a quick nod, Laura strides back into the ER.

More determined than ever to win her back, to be on the receiving end of that smile and her love till the end of time. I urge Bailey inside. Casting a glance in the direction of the ER, I swear on my life I'll earn back her trust and prove myself worthy of her forgiveness.

Making our way to the bank of elevators, I smile down at Bailey. "Do you think you'll be up for taking Laura's suggestion after your PT?"

"Yes!" she practically shrieks.

"Good." Then we focus on Bailey for the next hour and a half. When we're done, we head up to the sixth floor to find the magazine subscriptions and sugar-free treats are out of stock.

Not for long.

CHAPTER
Seventy~Seven

Laura

I'M up on Six West a few days later, visiting a patient, when Felicity stops me. The first words out of her mouth have my jaw agape.

"Listen, if you don't want that delicious piece of man meat, can I have him?"

"No!" I shout, the idea of Liam with another woman infuriating me. Then I calm down. "What did he do?"

She drags me over to the kitchen and shows me the vendors restocking the kitchen available to patients.

"He really arranged for that?"

"He did, Gore. He renewed the subscriptions for the next five years and look!" She holds up a case of Sees sugar free candies and pops. "They were express mailed."

I had really meant to deter Liam from sending me massive bouquets of flowers, but what he did here touched me more than even one single petal. "That is pretty special."

"Also, look at these." Felicia shows me a folder of handmade cards.

At the sight of them, my heart takes me back to craft day when Bailey and I made cards and crafts I could hand out at the hospital. My emotions, riding too close to the surface, want out. Now. I manage "She's a doll" before I take off down the corridor.

"Now, how did you know she made them, missy?" the charge nurse shouts after me.

Because I know the family I'm in love with. But I don't answer.

I can't say anything.

I'm too busy wishing I was at home—my real home.

Later, just after my shift ends, I get a text that sends fear shooting through my heart and my SUV racing along the interstate.

LIAM:

Can you come over? It's kind of an emergency.

CHAPTER
Seventy-Eight

LIAM

"THANK YOU FOR COMING." I step back into the living room once she crosses over the front door threshold.

"Is Bailey all right?" Her breath comes out fast, as if she ran here instead of driving her car which is parked askew in my driveway.

I nod, even though the fact Bailey's her first thought fills some cold part of me with warmth. "Would you like anything to drink?"

Arms akimbo, she squares off against me. "Liam, I just got off shift. I thought this was an emergency when you texted."

I wince at her words. *Maybe I should have used a different phrase?*

Still, Laura isn't cruel. She rephrases, "I was worried something happened to Bailey."

"It sort of has."

Her mouth opens and closes a few times before she presses her lips together.

Moving over to the couch, I gesture for her to join me. When she does, I ask, "Bailey did something today at school, which I had no idea she did until I received a call about it. I'm hoping you won't be upset."

Laura frowns. "What happened?"

I shift forward and brace my elbows on my knees. Burying my face in my hands, the mistakes of what I've done haunt me more than ever. Knowing I have no choice but to admit this, I share, "She forged your name on a permission slip." Laura's visibly taken aback. I clarify, "As her parent or guardian."

"Excuse me?"

"That was the same reaction I had at first when the school called to verify your identity."

"What was it for?" Laura leans forward as well.

Scrubbing my face with my hands, I let them fall away. "Bring Your Parent to School Day."

Laura's lips part.

"I also think you should know before you react that I've pieced a few things together."

"Such as?"

"I took legal steps to make you Bailey's legal guardian. It is important to me that if something happens, I know she will go to the one person who loves her as much as I do."

A twisted sound of anguish slips past her lips. "Does she know this?"

"Not that I was aware of. I handled it all from the office."

She growls—actually snarls at me. God, she sets my blood on fire, but now's not the time to explore that. The time for that is after I explain why I made the decision I did and after I ask the biggest favor I ever will. "Love, especially the kind Bailey has for you, isn't just going to disappear."

"Was that before or after your gifts started?" she asks, fury in her voice.

"Before, Laura. One has nothing to do with the other."

I've flummoxed her. "Then . . . why?"

"There's really only one reason. Quite simply, it's because we love you. We always will."

"Liam, this is still something that you should have talked with me about," she protests.

Leaning forward until I've crossed the invisible barrier between us, I give her the truth. "Would you have said no?"

Agony and denial lace her voice but she still can't refute my words. "It's unlikely, Liam, but . . ."

Hearing my name when she's this close to me makes me want to lean forward and taste it on her lips. Instead, I limit myself to laying my hand on hers and feel the same sparks I felt the moment we first shook hands shoot up my arm. Judging by the way her eyes dilate, she feels the same. "Then please know I trust you, Laura, with the most precious part of me."

"It's everything." Two words, yet they mean the world.

"Then, let me ask you part two."

"God, Liam, there's a part two?" Laura doesn't bother disguising the fingers that dash beneath her eyes.

"Bailey would like her 'guardian'"—I don't dare use the word Bailey used when she begged me to text Laura and ask this question—"to speak to her class about her career as a doctor. She wants that more than anything in the world. According to her, it's important enough for her to erase wanting to run into DJ Kensington."

At that request, Laura's expression goes completely blank before a smile brightens her face—a smile I haven't seen since we imploded. "Yes. Absolutely, yes."

My heart is thundering inside my chest at the sight. I want to burst out with, *I'm sorry. I love you. Forgive me.* The words I want to shout are stuck in my throat, not that they'd be welcome. Instead, I tell her what I can about the event at school—which isn't much at all. "For this, I'll let Bailey call you. Right now, she's grounded, so don't be alarmed if she doesn't text you for a few days."

Laura's eyes sparkle up at me. I want my life to end with that vision, drowning in Laura Lockwood's sparkling gaze. If there really was an Amaryllis, she'll let me. "One assumes you didn't take it calmly."

"One assumes correctly."

Her fingers trail down and squeeze my hand with the compassion I know she's filled with. "It could have been a serious thing if the school didn't know to call you, if I wasn't someone you trusted."

I shudder at the implications. "I know. And having to explain all of that to her? That's why she's not out here right now."

Laura cocks her head in the direction of Bailey's room. "It must kill her to know I'm here."

"I told her we were going to talk, but *if* you wanted, you could stop in before you left." My voice comes out as sternly as I'd spoken to Bailey.

Laura's fingers tighten briefly around my hand. "I'm sorry. I'm so sorry for what my not sharing did to both of you."

Slowly, I drag my arm back until I've laced our fingers together again. I don't want to lose this connection between us—the first she's given me since I threw her out of our lives—to be lost. Holding her gaze, I give her the truth, trying to regain some semblance of the trust I lost when I shot our beginning to pieces. "None of this was your fault. I'm sorry for what I did to us. I *never* meant to hurt you, Laura."

Laura's eyes flare, her only indication she's absorbing what I'm saying. I realize my actions that night destroyed a connection to this woman I don't just need, I crave. She stares into my eyes before giving a tiny nod. "Do you know? I think I can finally believe that."

She pushes to her feet and I join her. "Thank you for all of this—for being there for Bailey now . . . and maybe if . . ."

She looks down at our joined fingers and applies pressure.

A miracle.

I can't let it go without taking a chance. "I'm sorry, Laura."

"I need to know for what, Liam. I will not accept a wholesale apology."

I begin with the heart of wrongs I hurled at her. "I know you would never have placed Bailey in any deliberate danger."

"No, I never would have. I had no idea the Tiberi family was seeking retribution, nor that my father was actively involved in investigating that."

"I'm sorry for accusing you of hiding that from me."

Her eyes glitter in acceptance. "You should be angry—just not with me."

I groan, "I know. Between your uncle and me, we've shared that with your father. I need to ask; is it too late for us?" *Please don't say no. Please, please.*

"Words can't be taken away, Liam. I'm always going to remember what you said that night—a night I needed the man I was falling in love with to be there for me too."

My heart withers hearing her use the past tense. "What would it take for you to give me a second chance, Laura?"

Her hands, inked with the delicate amaryllis flowers, lift and fall. "I don't know. What I know is I love Bailey. I am grateful you . . . trust me with her so I can still be a part of her life. What I know is I can't completely walk away from you."

"Would you if you could?"

Instead of answering me, she dodges the question. "I . . . I need to see Bailey before I head back to the house. I have an early shift."

My heart aches for the agony I've inflicted on us both. Still, I'll take her response any day of the week.

She didn't call her house home.

CHAPTER
Seventy~Nine

Laura

Just HEARING everything Liam shared with me was a new slice into my heart. I was up all night, thinking about the words he said, the ones he didn't.

The love I still feel for him.

I reach for the cup of coffee my mother offers me with a grateful, "Thanks."

She sits down in the chair next to me instead of behind her impressive desk. I've already shared with her everything that happened when I went to visit Liam yesterday. To say she was stunned is an understatement. She rubs the back of her neck. "Here I thought your father and uncles were the kings of grand gestures."

"Right? Mama, Liam is entrusting Bailey's *life* to me."

She holds out her hand. Placing my mug on the edge of her desk, I capture it between mine. "Laura, do you believe what Alice told you?"

"Yes."

"Do you believe he loves you?"

Up until yesterday, when he handed me the most important proof of his absolute trust, I might have wavered on the question. Now? "Yes."

"Then why are you hesitating?" Her head tips to the side. "Is there something else you're not sharing?"

I slide forward and take both of her hands. "I love him, Mama."

"Then tell him."

"I'm afraid."

She rears back. "Of Liam?"

"Of course not. It's just . . ."

"Just what, Laura."

"I don't know what happens next."

"Laura, you know I love you."

"Yes?"

"You were a wonderful student. You have a brilliant mind. You're an exceptionally gifted doctor."

"I sense a but coming on."

"Darling, that's the thing about happily ever afters."

"What?" After a certain point, I stopped reading fairy tales.

My mother kisses my cheek. "Everyone forgets that the story continues. It's implied the couple lives happily ever after. But the ever after is the best part."

"Even when you want to strangle them with your bare hands?" I remind her dryly.

"Exactly that."

I lean forward and wrap my arms around her, burying my face in her shoulder. "I love you, Mama."

"I love you too, Laura."

For long moments, I just absorb my mother's love before I twist my head and catch sight of the picture of me and my two brothers holding the balloon—a recreation of one of my mother and my Uncle Keene for a grandmother I'm named after taken close to sixty years ago. It was a genius gift, but I have no idea how to show the two people I love that I want to be a family. Unless . . . "Do you have any ideas about how I should let Liam know I'm ready to trust him again?"

My mother pulls back and presses a kiss to the top of my head. "No. But if we don't let your aunts and uncle help us plan, we'll never hear the end of it."

As if we conjured him with the word plan, my Uncle Phil pops his head into my mother's office. "Plan what? What's going on?"

My mother catches my eye and the two of us burst into gales of laughter.

"This isn't funny. We need cake. I'll just go get Ali, Em, and Holly and we'll meet you in the kitchen."

With a sigh, my mother reaches across and grabs her phone. She presses a button and Aunt Corinna answers. "What's up, Cass?"

"He's on his way and will be demanding dessert."

She hangs up just as Corinna starts threatening Phil. "And something else about love you'll learn?"

"What's that, Mama?"

"How to manage those you love to actively *avoid* strangling them."

With that, she stands and offers me her hand. "Now, let's go save your uncle from wearing a batch of Cori's frosting when we could be eating it."

Linking our arms together, we head downstairs just in time for Phil's screeching.

Filled to the brim with sweets, we migrate to Emily's workroom. Finally, I have the opportunity to bring up my idea to let Liam know I'm all in. My mother, who hasn't strayed that far from my side, wraps her arm around my shoulders. Pressing a kiss to the side of my head, she murmurs, "I love the idea of turning her into a princess here."

Emily has a faraway look in her eyes that only appears when she's designing. Sure enough, she's reaching for her family sketchbook and begins lazily drawing before she opens her mouth to contribute. "I need two days and I'm all set."

"What are you thinking, Aunt Em?"

Emily lips curve before she turns her sketch pad around and shows us the dress. It's a recreation of my gala dress—with a twist.

"Thank God. I was thinking you were going to whip out her gown," my mother says faintly.

"I wouldn't do that, Cass."

"I mean, it's not like you don't already have her wedding dress in the vault," my mother reminds her.

I try to find my voice. When I do, it comes out like a strangled squeak. "You what?"

Emily flaps her hand at me as if my question isn't of importance.

I turn to Corinna for some speck of sanity. But I should have known better. When my mother and her siblings are aligned, they're an unstoppable force. In a dreamy voice, she speculates, "I think there needs to be champagne. Plus our newest princess needs cocoa. Maybe we'll change her favorite buttercup cupcake into a tiered cake?"

"Oh, I love that idea," I enthuse, finally able to find something sane to get behind.

"Me too," Kalie admits from the floor where she's sitting at her mother's feet. "What can we do to help?"

Alison leans down and whispers in her daughter's ear. Kalie's head snaps up. "You think so?"

"I guarantee it. Just watch her." Alison jerks her chin in Emily's direction, who is frantically sketching.

"Right. So, I'm updating Aunt Em's copyright. What else?"

I yelp. "What else? There's more?"

Kalie just flaps her hand in my direction. "Don't you worry about that. Mama? What about you and Aunt Cass? Uncle Phil should do the flowers just like the ones Liam's been sending Laura."

Uncle Phil winks. "Already planned on it since the poor guy's been ordering in bulk."

A shiver of something runs through my body knowing the flowers Liam's been sending me have been made by my family. I beam at my titan haired aunt, who as usual, has her camera obscuring her face. "We all know Aunt Holly is going to be photographing the whole thing."

Alison smiles at Cassidy. "I think it's our job to get Prince Charming here on time."

"Prince Charming. You mean, Liam?" I exclaim. Everyone's eyes, including Emily's, jerk in my direction as if I've lost my marbles. My voice is unsteady. "If he accepts me after all I've put him through."

"Laura, do you not know how much that man is in love with you?" my mother shocks me by asking.

"I hoped. I mean, he's been giving me space, but after yesterday . . ." My voice dries up when I realize he's been doing exactly what I asked.

Giving me space, loving me from afar, and trusting me to love Bailey. I smack my palm against my forehead. Liam's been giving me everything while still reassuring me he loves me.

"What about getting him here under the guise of a father/daughter dance?" Holly pipes up.

My mother, aunts, and uncle fall on top of that idea immediately. My mother exclaims, "Oh, Laura. Do you remember your first dance with your father?"

Alison leans over and kisses the top of Kalie's head. "Five. You all were five."

Holly says dreamily, "It was kindergarten. They're some of my favorite photos to this day."

"I suspect you're about to make two people feel like they're living in their own fairy tale," my mother speculates.

"She said she wanted to be a princess," I remind her of one of Bailey's "Summer of Fun" ideas we never got to cross off.

"No, Laura," my mother corrects. "She wants the happily, because what did I say happens after?"

"The ever after," I tell my mother.

"Only you'll make it better than anything she ever could have imagined?"

"Exactly." Because I love them both.

CHAPTER
Eighty

I SHIFT BACK and forth while I wait for Laura to arrive with my daughter at the steps of Amaryllis Events.

LIAM:

It's today, right?

LAURA:

Calm down, Liam. She's almost there.

LIAM:

But no one's here. The doors are locked.

LAURA:

You tried the front door?

LIAM:

Of course, I did.

LAURA:

Trust me. You have less than five minutes.

Trust is something that's next to impossible to come by and so easy to demolish with a couple of carefully placed words.

Earning back Laura's has been next to impossible. It's consuming every waking thought I have when I'm not with Bailey. Still, it's the middle of a workday, hours after Bailey's done with school, and I'm waiting for the two of them wearing a tuxedo, wondering if they plan on punking me. All I was told by Caleb and Keene was, "Don't be late and cancel everything for the rest of the afternoon." And by each of them, "Be in formal attire."

"I swear I will make sure their annual tax bill gives them both heartburn if this turns out to be an 'oops!'" I grumble to myself.

That's when I spy a limousine pulling into the drive off Main Street. It parks directly in front of me before the driver alights. "Mr. Payne?"

"Yes?"

"Phew. Good. Your date is in the back." The young man grins. He leans forward conspiratorially. "I only took her around the block once we knew you were here because Aunt Cass and Laura didn't want her to be alone."

"What is going on?" I bellow, my patience at an end.

That's when I hear a *snick*. The mahogany door behind me opens, and my jaw drops at the sight before me. Dressed in a white, shimmering gown that's identical in cut to her gala dress, long locks of her hair twisted up, gloved hands cupping the tiniest wrist corsage I've ever seen, is a Laura I've only spotted in news clippings.

She's magnificent.

She's untouchable.

She's mine.

If I have anything to say about it.

It's been just a few days since she came to the house, but I've missed her with every breath of air I take.

Absorbing every inch of her essence as she moves in my direction, I don't miss the way her eyes roam me from head to toe. If it wasn't for the sparkle in her aqua eyes, I'd be concerned her full lips aren't smiling. Once she reaches the top of the stairs, she curtseys, as if I'm some kind of royalty, when all I want to do is haul her into my arms. "Liam."

Just the sound of her raspy voice sets my nerve endings alight. A fire begins at the base of my spine even as I notice an honor guard has formed behind us—all decked out as if royalty is about to be unveiled. "What's happening?"

Laura lifts her skirt and begins to descend the steps. Immediately, I step forward and take her free hand so she doesn't fall. With a quick nod, she aligns herself next to me before calling out, "Mike, can you prepare to open Bailey's door, please?"

"Will do, cuz." The young man snaps to attention before leaping from where he was stationed near the steering wheel. It leaves Laura and me a few precious seconds alone.

Laura spends that time straightening her skirt. When her hand accidentally grazes my thigh, I capture it, never wanting to let go.

Her eyes lift to mine. In them, I find a torrent of emotions—excitement, nerves, both overlaying some other emotion I can't quite pinpoint. I cock my head and ask her directly, "What's going on, Laura?"

Laura takes in a deep breath, collecting herself. "It started because Bailey asked as part of her . . ." Laura swallows hard before she continues. "There were items on her summer wish list we didn't have a chance to finish. One of which was to feel like a princess. I brought the idea to my family and it evolved into this."

"What's this?"

"Making Bailey feel like a princess."

My whole body seizes. My voice is hoarse. "What?"

A trace of a smile graces her lips. "Of course, Bailey's transformation is being hosted by Amaryllis Events and Company."

My heart trembles as I turn back toward the mansion behind me. "Your family did this?"

"Uh-huh."

"For Bailey?"

Laura gives me a non-committal response as she passes me the corsage. On auto-pilot, I take it. The second I do, Laura steps away from me. I immediately miss her presence by my side. Instinctively, I hold out a hand. Pleasure rips through me when she takes it and gives it a comforting squeeze. "Now, as a former member of her medical team, I've been advised Bailey can dance on her legs for one dance if you bear the brunt of her weight, Liam."

"All of this is for one dance?" I'm astounded.

"All this and more."

"Laura . . ." Words fail me.

Shocking me, she leans forward and presses a lingering kiss near my ear before murmuring, "Just wait until you see what we have inside. Now, why don't you get Bailey out of her ride. I know a good deal of time was spent making sure she looks perfect."

Laura turns to climb the steps again. I want nothing more than to follow her, to let me hold her and dance with her, but I have a date to greet first. I wait while Mike opens the limousine's back door.

My head spins.

My heart stops.

Bailey carefully alights from the vehicle wearing a sleeveless A-line satin dress with crystals sewn around the armholes and collar. She's also wearing a tiara.

She looks like a princess, but more than that, she's openly beaming with joy. I never want to see that look disappear from her face. In the farthest region of my mind, I hope her grandparents can see her. A part of me, a tiny unselfish part, even hopes Ashleigh can despite not deserving to witness the beauty her daughter has become.

Pulling myself together, I bend over my daughter's wrist and slip her corsage on.

It's then I realize it's made of white roses and buttercups.

I step back and admire my daughter's long curls, carefully arranged to be just like Laura's. The light dusting of blush and lip gloss. Just enough to make a seven-year-old feel special but not too much to hide my daughter's budding beauty. Tears clog my voice when I tell Bailey, "You look beautiful, sweetheart."

"Thank you, Daddy. Laura tells me I have to ask you to be my escort inside. So, will you?"

I scoop her up so she doesn't have to bear any more pain than necessary. "It would be my honor, Buttercup."

"Mike, will you get Bailey's crutches?" Laura reminds her cousin.

"For our newest princess? Of course."

Bailey giggles as I walk up the ramp with Laura and her cousin behind us. Once inside Amaryllis Events, we're both shocked by what awaits us.

CHAPTER
Eighty~One

LIAM

"What was your favorite part?" I ask Bailey on the drive home. I declined the "limo service" Laura's cousin offered in favor of driving my daughter back to our own home.

Bailey's voice pipes up from the back seat. "Dancing."

My voice chokes when I agree, especially after I realized Laura wasn't helping run the event but was a guest herself.

The guest of honor, it turned out.

We had customized menus that explained our schedule. First on the agenda was Dessert for Three that consisted of hot chocolate and a tower of other delicious desserts. Cassidy approached from the shadows at one point when Bailey's face dropped in tragedy at being unable to eat more—causing both Laura and me to laugh. She told us not to worry about finishing our sweet smorgasbord. "We're already creating special to go boxes for you."

With a wink, she recommended we read the next item on our agenda. It was a special father/daughter dance. Bailey's lips parted in anticipation. "Daddy, am I allowed to dance?"

Just then, the opening strain to Paul Simon's "Father and Daughter" started playing. I laid my napkin aside and held out my hand. "Just trust me, Buttercup. There's nothing to be afraid of. I won't let you fall."

She giggled when I swooped in to lift her from her seat. Taking her little hand and holding it against my heart, I sang every word directly to Bailey —a vow. A promise to protect her precious heart. In my heart, I know I will do everything within my power to prevent my daughter from feeling an ounce of pain ever again.

It's a vow I planned on making to Laura as well if she'd let me.

Every time I spun her around, I caught a glimpse of Laura's eyes. Cassidy stood behind her, squeezing her shoulder. At one point, I caught her leaning down and whispering something in her daughter's ear.

Laura nodded frantically.

When it was over, I wasn't certain if my stomach was churning because of the amount of delicious desserts we'd consumed or because of the look on Laura's face while we were dancing. But that eased when I spied a mini three-tiered cake designed to look like a field of buttercups had been placed in the center of our table.

I couldn't help but notice the shape was a wedding cake. But I had no idea what it meant.

That's when the song changed.

My heart flipped over in my chest when Laura stood up and glided gracefully around the table. It was as unsteady as the down beat of the timpani drum featured in the song playing.

When Laura reached for my hand and asked, "Liam, would you like to dance?" I couldn't answer her, not verbally. All I could do was bypass her extended hand, slip my arm around her waist, and tug her flush against my body before I sent a prayer to whatever god was working the sound system that they'd play the song on repeat.

For eternity.

Laura picked out the perfect song for us to dance to. Chaotic emotions entwined with a love so strong neither time nor death could pull it apart. Harsh words, separation, they slipped away from us as I held on for dear life. Pulling her even closer to my body, I dropped my head and whispered, "This is exactly what you've made me feel since the day we met."

Her head tipped back and I was shocked to find my own emotions reflected back at me. "I've felt the same way."

"Laura, do you trust me?"

"For what, exactly?" she hedged.

"To love you. To cherish you. To take whatever steps I need to, to avoid making the same stupid fucking mistakes that broke us. To support you, to be by your side every moment of every day."

She was quiet for just a moment. "Those sound an awful lot like vows."

"I'll keep every one of them."

That's when Laura stunned me. She pulled out of my arms. Right before dropping to one knee, taking my left hand in hers.

Shock rendered me immobile, but my mind was racing. *I'm dreaming. This can't be happening.*

The music lowered to a low buzz, or maybe that's the buzz going on in my head.

"Liam, I want you to think carefully about what I'm going to ask you."

I open my mouth to shout my answer to the entire town of Collyer, but Laura squeezes my fingers to stop me. "This isn't a small change, I'm proposing . . ."

"You're not proposing anything," I pointed out, what I believed to be helpful.

She glared up at me. "That's because you're interrupting."

There were giggles from the table. I twisted my head in time to see Bailey standing on a chair supported by Cassidy—who winked at me, approval stamped across her every feature. My head swivels back to Laura wearing the same expression I'm certain is on my face—love. Love for each other, love for our family, her family. She cleared her throat. "You, Bailey, life is different without both of you. Don't get me wrong, I could go it alone . . ."

The growl that erupted from the back of my throat makes her laugh. "But I don't want to. I could be satisfied with safety—never worried about being hurt—"

I finished for her, hauling her up against my body. "Or you could tell me you love me and take the fall, knowing I'll be right beside you there the whole way down."

"See, that's the problem with you rushing me."

My fingers stroked her cheek. "Oh?"

She nuzzled her face into my palm. "I don't think we're going to fall if we leap together. Together, we're going to fly—you, me, and Bailey."

My forehead crashed down to hers. "You're absolutely right."

Just then, we pull into the driveway at my house with the car that's been following me pulling in behind us. Bailey's words slurred as we approached the house, so it was no surprise to find her conked out. Carefully, so I don't wake her, I lift her from the back seat.

Laura approaches from the side with the goodie bags her Aunt Corinna prepared for us. "Do you need help with her?"

A glint reflects off the platinum band I'm now wearing on my left hand. "No, *fiancée*. I'll put her down."

Fiancée. Laura proposed. Right then in front of her family and the employees of Amaryllis Events and Company. As I carry Bailey to her room, each step has me recalling Laura's words as I clutched her to my chest in the foyer of Amaryllis Events. "Liam Payne, I want my heart to come back home. That's here." She laid her hand on my chest. "I don't want you to let me go. I don't want to be let go. There's no safer place for me to heal than right at your side."

My breath came out fast.

Then she laid her lips against mine and the loneliness caused by my carelessness evaporated. "Marry me. We'll take our time to make certain Bailey's comfortable after everything, if you're concerned about that but—"

I interrupted to give her my response. "We can be engaged until tomorrow or for as long as you want. I just want to know one thing."

"What's that?"

"How can you still love me after everything I put you through?"

Laura's smile broke across her face. "I never stopped, Liam."

After I press a kiss against Bailey's cheek, I receive an incoming text.

> LAURA:
>
> Open the boxes in the kitchen. There's something special in them you need tonight.

Huh. Assuming the items may have to be refrigerated, I decide not to wait for Bailey. After I see the half a dozen Amaryllis pastry boxes on the counter, I start unwrapping them. "I hope something the bakery decorated didn't fall over. Bailey will be heartbroken."

In the final box, I find what Laura intends for me. There are three wrapped presents. Opening the first, I'm gobsmacked when I find an engraved silver frame with a black and white photo of me and Bailey. I'm holding Bailey as I swirl her around the room to the first strains of Paul Simon. Her eyes are sparkling as much as the crown nestled on top of her hair. And me? I've got half of my world in my arms.

Lifting the frame, I read what's engraved on the bottom.

LIAM AND BAILEY—2024

Beneath it is a flat package that reveals a photographer-grade acid-free paper. I immediately flip it open. In Laura's perfect penmanship are moments cataloguing the entire day with Bailey—from the moment Laura began curling her hair to the time both of "my girls" got dressed. A wink and thumbs up they each gave the photographer once they were inside the car to drive to Amaryllis Events. There's one of Laura, crouched next to Bailey and her cousin, giving them last minute instructions seconds before my car pulled into the empty lot. I relive each and every moment of the event from the time Laura made an appearance to our final goodbyes and it makes me realize something.

I could apologize for the next hundred years, and I'd never be able to humble myself enough to be worthy of this woman.

"I can't believe how much planning you put into this," I murmur.

"Well, I had a little help from a few people, to be sure." I whirl around and almost drop the second package when I get a load of my bride-to-be barely clad in see-through lingerie she must have been wearing beneath her white dress earlier. Her eyes dart to the second package. "You should open that."

"Instead of taking you?" I ask incredulously.

She runs her hand from her chest to her hip. "This will still be here."

Darkly, I inform her, "Not for long."

Her throaty laugh makes my heart sing. "Open the package, Liam."

The second package contains a journal. I frown at it until I flip it open and what's inside causes my shoulders to immediately shake. I flip through the pages to make certain I'm not wrong.

Then I reach the flyleaf and see in her curiously perfect penmanship.

The Journal of Dr. Laura Lockwood

I clutch the binding tightly, wondering what emotions I'm certain to find inside. Dr. Laura Lockwood was meticulous at her studies and she certainly would be in cataloguing every thought leading us to this moment.

"Flip to the tabbed page, Liam," Laura orders me, approaching me in stocking feet.

I do. When I start reading, I'm grateful for the counter, as my legs almost give out.

It's the reason she forgave me.

Laura takes the book from me. She runs her finger back to the beginning. Then she reads her own words aloud. *"They say love is unconquerable. But it takes more than that. Like all other things that require life, love requires passion, air, feeding. But people don't give the same thoughts about love requiring that same love and care.*

"Liam has. Some might say too much so with too little effort on my part.

"But unless you lived our story, is that a fair assessment of our wounds, our injuries?

"Maybe, maybe not.

"I know in the last few weeks, I've realized being without him has made all the little things I used to take for granted in my life fruitless. I don't want to make meatballs. I have no desire to see the beach. I'm constantly chilled and nothing gets me warm except those brief glimpses of him.

"Is that enough for forgiveness, mind? Because my heart forgave him before I shed my first tear.

"Oh, sweet mind, we talk ourselves out of so many life experiences out of fear, but why do we sabotage our own happiness? I asked my mother about that. She said there's a quote about not trusting people who sabotage your happiness. So, is it Liam I don't trust, or myself?

"Liam opened his home to me. Shared the burden of my personal pain while opening up about his. He accepted the fact I withheld pertinent information. He understood my withdrawal and still persisted in letting me know he was sorry for wrongfully attacking me.

"Tonight, he gave it all back to me and he doesn't know it.

"I have to show him how much his trust means to me.

"I didn't leave tonight to run away from the man I gave my heart to. I left to plan so I could refuel our love with the energy he's been feeding it this whole time we're apart. He never took the coward's way out when it came to winning me back. He loved me.

"Now it's my turn to show him I **saw** *what he gave me—fire. Passion. Dedication. Sensitivity.*

"He created a heartbeat from ashes when dust may be the only thing we had left.

"It's Liam. It's me. And we're not letting go.

"So, I'm going to fight for him and hope he says yes. Because this time, I'm not going to let him down."

By the time her final words form, I'm already picking her up and lifting her to the counter. She yelps when her skin kisses the cool Corian, but her face nestles into the crook between my shoulder and my neck. She murmurs, "I love you, Liam."

"I love you too, Laura. Never, ever, forget that again, even when I'm a complete jackass."

She nods. "Only if you remember I'll never hurt our family."

I pull back. "I know you won't. I especially know you will never hurt Bailey."

Relief washes across her face. I press her face back against my shoulder and she nuzzles in, wrapping me up tight.

I slide my hands beneath her rear and boost her up. Her legs wrap around my waist. I stride up the stairs and down the hall to my room. Kicking the door shut behind me, I lay her down on the bed and brush my lips against hers.

Once.

Twice.

Laura's hand slides behind my neck and she pulls my head down. "Come here, fiancé."

That's all it takes to snap the control I have. I roll the two of us so she's on top and I can unclasp and tear her lingerie off her body. I'll need her. More importantly, I'll love her.

Now.

Forever.

'Til death do us part.

Epilogue

THREE YEARS LATER

LIAM

I LIFT my phone to admire the picture of Laura and Bailey giving identical winks and thumbs up to whomever snapped this photo and feel the rightness deep in my soul. Leaning back in my chair, I think about everything we overcame to get to where we are today. My girls are off to get their hair trimmed with Grams—something Bailey immediately started calling Cassidy after Laura and I got married behind what her family affectionally refers to as the Farm two years ago. After the night Laura proposed, we came together in a tangle of love making that still makes my dick hard all these years later, both of us needing the physical connection to reassure one another we weren't imagining the other.

Then we talked until sunrise.

In addition to needing time to finish her residency and to rebuild her relationships within the ER, Laura said we should "Wait to get married.

It's what's best for Bailey and for us."

I didn't reply, just stroked her hair off her face while she gathered her thoughts together. Then she concluded, "We three need to time to heal, Liam. And a party doesn't make the last few months go away."

Pulling her against the length of my body, I agreed with her. "We collapsed because we never fully let our wounds close—on both sides."

"Exactly." Through the moonlight, her eyes probed mine. "I want this to be right for you and me, but most especially, Bailey. Her heart has been through too much."

In agreement, we decided on a long engagement. It was a year to the day she proposed, a Saturday of the following year. Laura was attended by her two former roommates and our now eight-year-old daughter as flower girl. I had her brother Jon, who I'd become close with, and Keene by my side as Caleb escorted Dr. Laura Lockwood up the aisle to become Dr. Laura Payne in front of about one hundred witnesses.

When she flung the bouquet and it landed in Kalie's hands, her cousin let out a feral snarl before she began to attack the bride with it. Laura, cackling, wrapped her arms around Kalie's shoulder and whispered something in Kalie's ear. Their heads immediately snapped in Grace's direction, who had returned after the bouquet toss to continue her discussion about body parts with one of Laura's ER residents.

Then in unison, their faces broke out in malicious smiles when they located a set of male eyes glaring at the back of the cool brunette. I shared with my wife and her cousin, "You both scare the crap out of me."

Their "Good" made me laugh as I pulled Laura against me. And I laughed harder when Phil, with his husband Jason watching on amusedly, was the first to kick off the tradition of silverware tinkling on glasses. For once, we both were happy to comply with his shenanigans, as Laura called them.

Still, I was stunned when Laura and Bailey cackled at me few months later during the white elephant gift giving during Christmas. Holding up an object I'd swear in court a four-year-old made in art class, I roared, "We're supposed to be on the same team."

Hearing the giggling from both my girls as they said in unison, "No one is safe until Christmas is over!"

I can still only be grateful Laura still had some retribution left in her and targeted her father with a gift of a five-pronged candlestick holder made out of coquina shells, bamboo, and brass. Cassidy held up her hands and accepted defeat gracefully. "Laura, that is truly atrocious."

"I know, Mama. I've been saving it."

"Christ, Cass. Where are we supposed to put it?"

"That, my dear husband, is up to you." Cassidy shoved the shelled disc holding the sticks back into Caleb's chest. Then she gave me a warning. "Liam, we'll be out for retribution next year. Watch out."

I drop by HomeGoods on a regular basis now—just to keep an eye out for things that might help our cause.

Well before any of that, Laura and I concluded we should have a few sessions with Alice so we never got back to where one of us was trying to talk and the other refused to listen. Together and apart, we'd sustained the blows of some harsh realities we needed to be able to navigate. Our past wasn't going to disappear, and we needed to be able to dissipate shadows that appear throughout the years—which, inevitably they do.

But the idea was to be able to discuss them and not sweep them under the rug, so the dust is so insurmountable you can't get over it to the person you love.

Not only did we talk about the criminal aspects of what we'd both endured, dating back to Ashleigh through to the Tiberis, we talked about parenting strategies. We talked about how many children we wanted. We talked about boundaries and that's where I laid down the law about a few things because, Christ. My future wife was due to inherit *how* much money? I thought all of that was just rumors. And put my inheritance to shame.

Laura just shook her head woefully. I'm certain I looked at all my future in-laws differently for a few days after that session.

Fortunately, we quickly realized not only were Laura and I copasetic in so many ways on a personal level, but we harmonized on the important ones that could cause friction years down the road.

As we made our way to the car one afternoon, I remarked, "Now, I know why so many people advocate pre-marital counseling."

She agreed with my assessment. "It's to open up lines of communication. Our hospital recommends it because of the amount of stress we're under doing what we do."

Now, when we really need to have the other person listen in the hectic jumble that's our lives, we schedule time to listen. It's our chance to let one or both of us vent so the other can clarify, reflect, and show we're listening by asking questions or summarizing the other's concerns. We do this out of Bailey's earshot. I expect we'll do it soon with our baby's monitor gripped in one of our hands, half asleep. Okay, so the question and summarizing part might take a bit longer. My lips quirk when I reminded Laura recently that sleep deprivation is a perfectly understandable reason for one spouse to not get it right away.

She rolled her eyes and said our sex life causes sleep deprivation and I can't use it as an excuse. I roared with laughter before kissing her senseless.

That being said, just because we work to ensure there are more days where our home is filled with sunshine and laughter than clouds and tears, doesn't mean there aren't any. Laura loses patients. I have days at the office where I want to strangle my bosses—her father and uncle. Bailey has residual pain we need to cope with. Ever after isn't perfect, but it's ours.

Knowing I'll spend it with Laura makes me feel like I'll never stop falling in love.

One night, lying in bed, my hand resting over the bump of our unborn child, I shared that with her. Her smile beamed at me. With her already straddling my lap, she leaned down and pressed her lips against mine. "That's how I feel every time I wake up with your arm around me."

A grin breaks out across my face just as Caleb saunters into my office—his own face relaxed and happy. "Did you get the picture of my girls?"

My brow wings upward while my thumb twirls my wedding band around. It catches the overhead light, but no matter how much it shines it doesn't compare to the light Laura's brought to my life. "Your girls? Caleb, wrong determiner. Laura and Bailey are mine."

Stubborn fool he is, he growls, "I loved her first."

I lean forward and meet my father-in-law's gaze head on. "I'll love them forever. All three of them—Laura, Bailey, and our new little one."

His smile bursts free at the mention of our daughter, due in about eight weeks. "Did you decide on a name?"

I snort. "Like I'm going to tell you? Please."

He objects vociferously. "I know how to keep a secret."

"One of this magnitude? From Cassidy? Do you want to be in the doghouse with her again?"

Morosely, he gives in. "No."

"Because if you tell Cass, the whole family will know. Then *I'll* be in the doghouse for sharing. Trust me, that's the last place I want to be."

"Because you're afraid I'll kick your ass?"

"Because I'm terrified your daughter will come after me with a scalpel."

We both snicker, knowing it's the truth. A few more minutes of banter back and forth occurs before Caleb gives up on his fishing expedition. I reply to Laura's text.

> LIAM:
> Sorry, love. Your father was in here.

LAURA:
That's okay.

Mama's badgering me to find out what we're naming her.

> LIAM:
> Your father was just in here doing the same.

LAURA:
Think we should tell them?

> LIAM:
> That's entirely up to you.

LAURA:
If we do, I want to do it together.

> LIAM:
> Like . . . family dinner? <horror>

LAURA:
Of course. I mean, can you imagine their faces?

> LIAM:
> I think if we do, we're going to need tissues.

LAURA:
That's it, Liam! We'll pass around pink tissue packets with her name on them.

LIAM:

Think your mother's going to be surprised?

LAURA:

That we're naming the baby Cassidy Amaryllis
Payne? She's going to sob. She's going to need
six or seven packets of tissues.

But since she named me after my grandmother, I
don't know why she hasn't thought of it.

I think back to the story Laura shared with me about Cassidy and Caleb.
How they got together and their shared past they didn't put together until
it was almost too late. Then I think of the oil painting hanging in Keene's
office and my smile widens realizing what a sentimental bastard her uncle
really is.

LIAM:

You might want six or seven packs per relative.

LAURA:

Good point.

Got to go. We just pulled in.

LIAM:

Be careful. My whole world is in that car.

LAURA:

We will.

LIAM:

I love you, Laura.

LAURA:

I love you too.

I slide my wedding band off my finger for just a moment so I can read the
inside inscription. *L & L.*

Most people think it means Liam and Laura but between us, we know the
truth—it's our vow. Leap and love. *I don't think we're going to fall if we leap
together.*

Sliding my ring back on my finger, I focus on what I'm doing so I keep up
my vow in return—to love her 'til death do us part.

Want to Fall More?

BONUS SCENE

BAILEY PAYNE'S "SUMMER OF FUN" list wasn't quite complete at the end of Free to Fall. Dr. Laura Lockwood is determined to make certain the little girl who changed her life has everything her heart desires.

Read about how Laura arranged for her to meet her idol, the infamous DJ Austyn Kensington.

Click here to have the bonus scene sent to your device. Additional information may be required to gain access to the file.

Where to Get Help

THIS IS as real as it gets. I suffer from anxiety.

Anxiety can be triggered by events in your everyday life—a doctor's visit, a relationship that's not on track, or financial difficulties—or it can be generated internally through thoughts of real or imagined threats.

There are different types of anxiety—generalized, social, phobias, and what I suffer from, panic attacks.

I'm fortunate in that I have been able to control my anxiety, for the most part, through a combination of lifestyle and behavior changes. I rarely (if ever) drink caffeinated coffee and avoid spicy food, as I know both trigger my attacks.

In being able to manage my triggers, I manage that absolute tidal wave of fear that tried to drown me and often succeeded.

I'm not a doctor; I can't say whether or not there's a future for me without anxiety, a world without panic attacks. What I can say is people are willing to help. In the United States, the National Institute for Mental Health provides ways for you and your loved ones to get assistance.

Remember, your beauty can rise out of ashes.

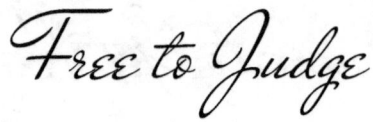

Free to Judge

IF YOU LOVED Kalie Marshall in Free to Fall, you'll love here even more in her own story, Free to Judge.

Coming Winter 2025.

Sign up for my newsletter to be notified of the exact release date!

Keep reading for a sneak peek at Kalie's opening argument.

Kalie

If I had a do-over and paused to look past his face, would I have cursed first and hit second instead of the other way around? I'm not sure. Either way, I'm confident the result would be the same. Struggling against the officer, I screech, "You're putting these on the wrong person. He's the son of a bitch who hit my niece."

That gives the officer a moment's pause but doesn't deter him. Crap. Then I spy a familiar face across the breezeway and shout, "Jon! Get this goon to take these cuffs off me!"

My cousin's eyes narrow before he leaves the group of people he was conversing with to bolt my way. Not even breaking a sweat in his bespoke suit, his "What the fuck, Kalie?" is heard by every person in the small circle around me, many of whom have cell phones up since the sinfully rich and equally gorgeous Jonathan Lockwood is in their presence. I roll my eyes. This ridiculously handsome playboy is the same child my cousin Laura and I would force to eat our mud pies. One would think they'd be more impressed that a dainty brunette in four-inch heels managed knock out a man who is built like a linebacker with one solid punch.

Not.

I can thank Mama and Daddy for my pugilist skills. They made certain all their "girls" could protect themselves in any situation. Whether it was running or self-defense, one of the Marshall clan's more annoying tendencies includes a never-ending competitiveness.

Those feelings festered and flourished in me—the first-born daughter to a man who openly admits he was born into a family that encouraged his being a sanctimonious prick. I heard it wasn't until he met and married my mother that his attitude changed—at least for those he loved. Not that I can blame my parents for my current predicament. I shake my wrists, feeling the cold steel against them—not a good look with the vintage Valentino suit I'm wearing for court.

A groan from the floor alerts me to my behemoth awakening. Glaring at me, Jon—the traitorous jerk—leans down and offers the prick a hand. I'm not sure my mouth can fall open any farther when the son-of-a-bitch clasps my cousin's forearm and says, "Thanks, buddy."

"Excuse me? What the hell is happening right now?" I snarl at both men.

That's when furious chocolate brown eyes bore into mine before my victim snaps, "That's what I'd like to know."

Free to Dream

Have you read the about how Caleb wooed Cassidy into giving love a chance?

One-click Free to Dream on Amazon/KU!

Read on for an excerpt and begin your journey into the Amaryllis Heritage family tree.

Caleb

My brother is damned lucky I love him as much as I do. Otherwise, I might toss his newly engaged ass off the rooftop deck where we're sitting.

The cool snap of fall came quickly, so the deck opposite ours is empty. It's like these people who live year after year in this climate don't appreciate the fact that this will be one of the last times they'll have to use their magnificent spaces before winter comes, bringing snow and frigid temperatures.

The streets of Tribeca are alive below us, but we're high enough up that the noise and bustling crowd doesn't feel like it's closing in. I still want to pitch my baby brother over the safety rail, but I have to give him credit. This condo he scored for us in the historic Powell Building is amazing. City living wasn't what I'd expected when I came home from years overseas. But Ryan made the argument with both of us working in New York, putting in insane hours, it made sense to have a place to crash while we were here. At least we'd be able to catch more than just a few hours of sleep a night.

It's been more home here than the mausoleum we had grown up in. I'm going to miss it here. When he gets married in a few months, I'll be moving out.

It was easy to make the decision to move to New York once I knew Ryan didn't intend on making the family home he inherited his home base. I had no real emotional ties to the place since my father died before I joined the Army, and Ryan moved out shortly thereafter. Lord knows, my mother is as frigid as the glacier that sank the Titanic. How Ryan could bear to let her live there is a whole different matter.

I halfheartedly scowl into a face that's almost an angelic, younger version of my own. Christ, did I ever look that innocent? Maybe back in the early days of college, which is about how old Ryan looks this morning in his T-shirt and lounge pants. With our matching dark hair and eyes, our family resemblance is striking.

A woman I once slept with said she'd planned to seduce Ry into her bed because at least he had a heart. As I rolled out of her bed and pulled my pants back on, I told her she was welcome to give it a try, but that my brother didn't go for my seconds. He never had. I smirk at the memory.

The irony there is that two weeks ago, Ryan ecstatically got engaged to Jared.

Picking up the coffee in front of me, I take a large drink. "So, let me get this straight. Because of media problems in the past with large events, you want me to go to the office, on a Sunday no less, to do a background check on a wedding planning firm you and Jared are thinking of dropping a shit ton of money on for your wedding? You do realize that's five minutes of my time and way below what I actually do, right?"

Ry smiles at me. "I didn't think it would be such a big deal. I actually figured you could do it from here."

Normally, he'd be right. But the investigations my firm runs and the systems we access are either cleared at levels I can't discuss or not always legally obtained. I refuse, for both legal and security reasons, to use our home computers for work. "It's in the shop." I wait for his laughter because he knows I feel helpless without my laptop.

"Why do you have to have it today?" I argue as I stretch out my legs to get comfortable. I had planned to go to the gym to work out. When I was in the Army, following traditions that could be traced back to the Revolutionary War, I worked out daily. I'd tried to maintain the habit, but I manage instead with four hard workouts a week.

"Because I'm meeting with one of the owners over dinner tonight." He reclines in his chair, doing some relaxing of his own. He knows I would do anything for him, including this.

"Way to wait until the last minute, brother," I grumble, kissing my long workout goodbye.

Sitting up, I start to stand when Ry motions me back down. "Relax. This shouldn't take you all afternoon. I wanted to talk with you about the wedding anyway."

"Uh, Ry. You realize you should be talking with Jared, right? I mean, I know I have pretty decent taste, but it's his wedding too," I tease.

He rolls his eyes at me and mutters "asshole" under his breath before taking another drink of coffee. Setting down his mug, he looks me in the eyes. "Stand up for me, Caleb. Be my best man." He smiles and my mind goes blank. I'm unable to answer him. "You're already the best man I know. But stand with me when I marry the man I plan to be with for the rest of my life." His complete trust and faith in me is overwhelming.

I swallow hard. Jesus. This is like a sniper attack—one shot and I'm down.

Rolling myself into a standing position, I walk around the table and pull my brother to his feet. Since he had his mug of coffee in his hands, it predictably went sloshing everywhere. As he's sputtering about the mess, pulling his wet T-shirt away from his stomach, I nab him for a one-armed hug. "Nothing would make me prouder." My voice is barely a whisper because I can't swallow over the knot lodged in my throat. "I love you, Ry. And I love Jared for you."

"Thanks, Caleb." Looking into eyes that mirror my own, there's something there. I've seen it for the last few years—a secret he can't or won't share. I know he's hiding something because the same look reflects back in the mirror every morning when I shave.

My thoughts and memories are wrapped up in government clearances that can never be shared.

"And as my first act as best man, I will forsake my workout," I joke to lighten the mood. "I'll go to the office on a sacred day off to research this firm you want to hire."

Ry laughs. "Right. Like if your laptop was working, you wouldn't be on it today."

Busted.

Ignoring the comment, I ask, "What's the name of the firm?" Now, I'm actually curious. I knew Ry had planned on proposing to Jared for some time, so I figured he'd been giving this some thought. Our family is wealthy and well-known, but I could not imagine a wedding planning firm requiring a deep level background check unless it was on an employee.

"An event planning company in Collyer, Connecticut. Amaryllis Events," Jared, Ry's fiancé, says from behind me as he makes his way over to Ry. The two of them share a kiss, murmuring their good mornings to each other while I lose myself in thought.

Amaryllis Events. It conjures up ideas of elegant tea cups with pinkies out, not the psychological warfare combined with lion taming required for events like this wedding is going to need...wait. Did he say Connecticut?

"Connecticut? Fucking Connecticut? Are you serious? You're going to have the wedding there?"

Ry turns from his fiancé to face me with steel and determination in his eyes. And if I'm reading my brother right, vengeance. "I refuse to let her keep me from doing what I want. And if Mommy Dearest doesn't like it, she can get her ass the fuck off my property. Despite the fact I've never wanted to live there, I do own and pay to upkeep the place."

"And you're hiring a company called Amaryllis Events? You should be hiring armed guards, Ry," I fire back.

He sits back in his chair, where Jared wraps his arm around his shoulders. "Everything I've heard about this company tells me this is the way to go. The CEO and event planner apparently could negotiate a truce in the Holy Lands and make them think it was their idea."

Humored by his response, I ask, "How'd you hear about them?"

"Remember Austin's wedding? Right after his dad married his personal admin?"

Austin is one of our friends from high school. I nod as a snort escapes me. "You're kidding. They organized his wedding?"

I remember how stressed Austin had been about that wedding. There was talk of sex tapes being released to the media by Austin's vengeful mother. Board members threatened to vote his father out as chairman of their company, and the press circled like vultures. About a month before the wedding, it was like someone had given Austin a Xanax salt lick.

"Hell, why do you need the background investigation? Hire them. That wedding was a catastrophe waiting to happen and you would never have known it." Literally, I attended with multiple pairs of handcuffs, thinking I might need them to keep the peace. But it went as smooth as honey.

Ry and Jared exchange a look.

"Wait, *was* someone drugged?" I demand.

Jared laughs, while Ry says, "Nothing like that. I just happen to have an indirect connection to the owners. Before we sink twenty-five percent of the cost of the wedding with the potential for acrimony, I'd like to know more about the business."

Twenty-five percent? I'm thinking even I don't charge my clients enough when the rest of his sentence penetrates. "What acrimony?" My eyes narrow on my brother, trying to siphon the things out of him that he's not telling me.

"I'll let you know after tonight's dinner, if there's one at all," Ry waves off my concern. "So, could you run the background check?"

I sit for a moment and think it over. "Yes. I'll head downtown in a while. It shouldn't take too long. What time is your dinner?"

"It's at five."

"I'll call you if it's a no-go."

I manage to get in a run and a boxing workout before hitting the showers to head into the office.

Standing beneath the warm spray, I brace my thick legs apart as the suds slide down my body, over my abs, and around my cock. Letting out a low hum at the sensation, I realize it's been way too long since I've gotten laid. To be honest, a woman didn't seem worth the effort when I could rub one out a hell of a lot quicker.

To me, women came with one of three problems—they want my money, my body, or my face, and pretty much in that order. I need one who not only has her own success, but is a challenge. Beautiful, but doesn't live or die by the need to look into every reflective surface she passes. A woman who wants to be held as much as she wants to be fucked.

In other words, I want a fucking unicorn.

Slipping on a pair of well-worn Levi's, a thin cashmere sweater over a T-shirt, and my steel-toe boots, I quickly toss my dopp kit into my gym locker. Shrugging on my leather jacket, I walk the mile-and-a-half to my office near Rockefeller Center.

Sundays in New York are unlike any other day of the week. If you want to know why a person would live in the city, explore it on a Sunday. Sure, there are tourists. I mean, it's New York, when are there not? But there are also random people finding what little green space there is for a nap, lines for people waiting to eat brunch wrapping around a city block, and random street fairs fucking up traffic. I stop at one of the street fair booths and order a Gyro to eat as I make my way toward Rockefeller Center.

Thirty minutes later, I'm behind my desk at Hudson Investigations, having tossed my assistant a quick wave on my way in. I shake my head as I pass. Time and again, I let my assistant know Sundays are not required as part of the job. I've given up trying and just caution now against burning out.

When I left the Army, I knew I could live the rest of my life on my inheritance, but that's not my style. I knew I would be bored within two-point-five seconds if all I was doing was playing golf. I knew I would need something in my life to give me a challenge. I wasn't like the pampered society darlings my mother kept tossing at me, who wanted to fuck and produce Lockwood heirs. Seriously, the idea of settling for one of those dumb bimbos bored me. If I had to go through life as a bachelor, buying lube so I didn't chafe while taking care of business, I didn't care. I refuse to settle.

Instead of what would amount to buying a relationship, I put my time, effort, and soul into the investigative agency I bought out three years ago. The former owner, Laskey, had a solid business, but he was ready to retire. To me, compiling competitive intelligence and digging into companies to look for things like fraud was better than a woman scraping her false nails up the inside of my thighs. Protection details with the occasional high-level missing persons case could send a chill up my spine more than hips swaying in the right dress. Helping fend off corporate espionage was better than a night of hot sex.

I want the things in my life to require some effort. I want my life to have meaning. I was born with the proverbial silver spoon in my mouth. I think I spit it out within minutes of it being shoved there.

I like puzzles. I love a challenge. I crave the high I get from figuring out a mystery. It's probably why I excelled when I was in Army Intel for eight years. Give me a good case to dig into and I'm like a dog with a meaty bone. I don't rest until I own all the answers.

While I'm waiting on the basic financial report and background check I requested on Amaryllis Events from one of our new analysts—mostly to disclaim my suspicion the business didn't drug anyone—I receive a knock on my office door from my head of missing persons and protection services. He's carrying a thick file under his arm, a file I don't recognize.

First, it's paper. Second, I would recall authorizing its creation. "Charlie, what are you doing here on a Sunday?" I stand, my eyes dropping to the folder now in his hands.

"You requested the Freeman file, Caleb. I need to know why." No nonsense and to the point, Charlie Henderson shakes my hand before sitting down in one of my guest chairs. He places the thick file on his lap, his hand absentmindedly tapping it.

Dragging my eyes away from the file, I find him looking at me with his head tilted. His expression is serious. "The Freeman file? The only thing I've asked for today is a business check on an event planner for my brother's wedding, Charlie. A company called Amaryllis Events."

His eyes don't leave mine. He doesn't say a word, just continues to stare me down.

I say slowly, nodding to the file, "And I take it the file you're holding has something to do with that request?"

Nodding his head, his hands stop tapping Morse code on the hard copy. He shifts in his chair, but doesn't speak immediately. I wait patiently, because I know Charlie. He's not deciding on whether or not to tell me, he just needs to organize his thoughts.

When I purchased the investigation firm, I inherited Charlie. He's a rare, raw, tell-it-like-it-is, pain in the ass that needs the right hand holding. He had turned in his resignation when I first met him. Now, he's one of my best assets.

I trust his instincts.

Giving him the minute he needs, I stand and walk over to the wet bar in my office. Grabbing two bottles of water, I place one in front of him before I sit at my desk again. Twisting off the cap, I wait.

"About eight years ago, a group of kids came to the office. Unusual case. They wanted a background investigation run."

I'm not sure what's odd about that. Parent who left them? Parents, plural, who left them? I tip my head as I take another drink. His next words do surprise me.

"The Freeman children wanted us to investigate them. There are six of them. They wanted to know how hard it would be for anyone to find them, and they wanted to know if the people in their previous lives were alive or dead. They were all hoping for dead. By the end of it, so were we." He shudders.

Charlie Henderson has seen a lot over the years, but I've never watched him visibly shudder.

"Those kids, the Freemans..." Charlie takes a deep breath. "They own Amaryllis Events."

Slowly putting down the bottle, I sit up straighter. Ry, you ass. What the hell did you get us involved with?

"It's all in there?" He nods. I reach my hand out for the file, and just as I'm about to touch the thick folder, Charlie puts his hand on top of mine. "Caleb." My eyes lock onto his. What now?

"Ryan came up as part of the investigation. There might be things; you know...things you don't know. I have no idea. But from the look on your face, I'm guessing the second." He releases the file as I sink in my chair. The file is easily six inches thick.

"I put the flags on the family so I could let them know if someone was trying to hunt them." He gives me a hard look that tells me if it was, I would easily be facing an aging ex-SEAL in a grudge match. "But based on what you just said, I'm assuming your check has nothing to do with that."

I'm left holding what may be the equivalent of a paper bomb. I can't take my eyes off of it.

I know instinctively if I handle what's inside wrong, my whole world is going to implode.

Charlie turns and walks to the door. With his hand on the knob, he turns and says something odd. "If I lived through what the people in that file lived through, it would be hard for me to choose dedicating my life to 'happily ever after' day after day." He takes a deep breath and slowly lets it out. "That's the only copy. Nothing's digital. I want it back in my hands by the end of the day."

Nodding at me, he leaves my office, closing the door behind him.

I set the file down in the center of my desk. Bracing myself, I flip past the initial confidentiality pages and get to the table of contents. Scanning it, there are names I am sure I'll become very acquainted with: Phillip Freeman-Ross, 32, Cassidy Freeman, 29, Emily Freeman, 29, Alison Freeman, 27, Holly Freeman, 27, Corinna Freeman, 27, and Jason Ross, 35 (with a notation that he is Phillip's husband).

Then, names that make my gut churn.

Ryan Lockwood, 29.

Mildred Lockwood, 62.

What the fuck does my brother and mother have to do with the Freeman's request?

Pressing a button on my iPad, I engage the locks on my office door and begin to read.

Hours later, my world has shifted on its axis and I know two things.

One, that cunt will never again be called my mother.

Two, I need to meet the Freemans.

I pick up the phone, call Ryan, and tell him he's a go for the meeting with Amaryllis Events, setting their plans in motion. There's just one caveat. I want to meet the Freemans. As soon as possible.

Ryan is outraged. Especially when I won't share the reason why I feel this need to do so. We argue on the issue back and forth the entire time he and Jared are in transit to the restaurant in Westchester, resulting in Ryan hanging up on me.

Hours pass. After trying to clear up some issues I'll need off my plate for a trip out to Connecticut in the morning, I find myself unable to think about anything but the contents of that file. I stand in front of my office window, long after the sun sets, not seeing the beauty of the Manhattan skyline. The sky transitioned from a deep color that can only be found over the Hudson in the fall to a deep murky ink color when my phone rings. After a terse call from Ryan confirming I'll be meeting with the Freemans in the morning, he hangs up.

I let out my slow breath. I have my time to meet them. What I'll do with that meeting, I have no idea.

I'll use my instincts and figure it out in the morning.

Cassidy

IT TOOK me forever to figure out what to wear this morning.

I wanted to dress to give the impression I wasn't nervous about the Lockwood meeting, but I wanted to carefully showcase the success our company has attained.

Looking down at my outfit, I'm satisfied with my decision—casual elegance with power thrown in. I figured my mulberry colored cashmere sweater dress, ending right above my knee, paired with high heeled black leather boots conveyed that. Hanging behind the door was a matching cashmere jacket in black that would graze the bottom hem of the dress if I needed to toss it on.

I can hear Phillip's words from last night. "But you're the face of this company, Cass. There's no one we trust to do this more than you." I can't imagine how he could think that.

My gaze travels over to Phillip and Jason's wedding photo. Both of them are beaming at the camera, with the rest of our family clustered around them. I hardly spare myself a glance, bypassing my image for those far more important in the photo.

When Holly showed me the photo after she developed it, she asked me what I saw. I told her immediately, "Golden beauty. I mean, just look at all of you." My compliment was sincere.

Holly had cocked her head and said rather enigmatically, "You don't see it at all, do you?"

"See what?" I had asked her, confused.

She patted my hand, took the picture from me and hung it on the wall where it resides today. "One day you will. I just hope I'm around when you do."

I shake my head and glance at the clock—it's 7:50. Perfect. I have enough time to run down the street for a cup of coffee and make it back in time to review the Lockwood notes Phil had tossed on my desk earlier. Phil generates event profiles before clients come in for their consultation.

After yelling at Phil's needy ass that I would get him a large, extra skinny latte with whipped cream, I grab my phone and wristlet, and duck out the side door into the crisp morning air, mentally wishing I had grabbed my coat. Fall is going to hit early in our little southern Connecticut town.

Other than my dreams, my life has become monotonous. My greatest stress comes from what I'll wear to the office. My complacency hasn't escaped me.

Pausing on the street, I take in the former gingerbread mansion on Collyer's Main Street, which now houses Amaryllis Events. I let out a wry chuckle. Who would have thought that six of the most cynical people— when it came to love and relationships—would become some of the best wedding and event planners in the Northeast? Not this woman, that's for damn sure. Each of us use our individual strengths for each event, providing unique moments crafted with elegance, considering everyone's wishes. We even incorporate input from the spinster aunt that no one wants to listen to. We all know feelings matter. Feelings count. Feelings can destroy souls, and an event as important as a wedding. We work to show people that, and people pay us damn well for our attention to the details.

Strolling down the street of the closest thing to a hometown I have ever known, I nod at several store owners unlocking their front doors minutes before their eight o'clock store openings. I shake my head, not knowing how people can stand to be rushed in the morning. The feeling of never having enough time to take a deep breath, let alone get coffee, before dealing with the good citizens of Collyer, it would be akin to a terrorist attack to my stability.

Passing by the dance studio and candy store, which I know will be filled with high school students later in the afternoon, I duck down the alley between the Colonial-era buildings to head toward The Coffee Shop.

Ava and Matt, the owners and my trusted confidants, look up as I enter. Matt frowns while Ava scurries over with her arms outstretched.

"Cassidy, darling. Why don't you let us bring you your morning coffee?"

"Ava, if you did, I would never leave the office," I reply, leaning down to give her cheek a quick kiss. "Besides, it would give Phil a reason to say we never do a damn thing for him."

"Mouth, Cassidy!" Ava scolds me, gently thumping my arm. Ava is a little bit motherly toward me. Toward all of us.

"Should have heard him this morning while he was whining about not having his extra skinny latte already, Ava. And how can one suck more skinny out of the already skim milk? I told him to stop lying around on his ass and use the treadmill he made Jason buy him, and maybe he wouldn't be worrying about those washboard abs of his." Ava tries to hold in her laughter. She finally gives in, and by the time she stops, she's wiping the tears of laughter from her eyes. "Besides, he wants whipped cream. You should have heard what I said about that." I smile and wink at Ava because Phil is beyond ridiculous about his coffee demands and we both know it.

Ava lets out one last bellow of laughter, throws a smile at me, and begins making coffee while talking to other customers.

Matt ambles out of the heat of the miniscule kitchen, resting his arms on top of the counter in front of me. "Not sleeping again?"

A former VA psychologist, I found I was more comfortable talking to Matt about my past than any other doctor before. Maybe it's because he'd gladly take one of his viciously sharp meat cleavers to anyone who would try to hurt me. I think it's because he understands I feel I'm at the end of my rope.

My childhood was stolen, and that made my future feel bleak. I feel like I'm alone and always will be.

Matt can sense my isolation and reaches forward for my hand. "You're not alone, Cassidy."

I laugh derisively as I try to pull my hand away from his large paw.

"You're not," he insists, holding onto my hand.

I lean forward, my braid falling over my shoulder. "Then why does it feel that way when I wake up crying and alone, Matt? No one wants someone that's ruined or damaged." I pull my hand away as Ava comes bustling over with my drinks. I stand up and smile at Matt. "I'll always be alone."

I drop a ten-dollar bill on the counter and tip my lips at Ava. Matt can't hide his concern, which I choose to ignore as I head out the door.

Holding our coffee slightly away from my body, I meander down the tree lined streets, back toward the office.

Em wasn't wrong. Something was going on with me. What I felt, I couldn't put into words to help my siblings understand.

I always recognize when something is losing its course in my perfectly organized life.

"Here's your extra skinny, practically water latte, with fat-laden whipped cream." I hand the coffee over to Phil.

"Don't you start with that mouth today, Cass," Phil warns, like I'm nine years old again and not twenty-nine. "I'm in no mood. My abs are just as washboard as the day you met me."

"It's not me who has to see them every night. That would be Jason. And I have no idea why you're freaking out over this, since you look the same as the day I met you. Most days, you act the same way too," I quip, sipping my cappuccino.

Phil stares at me for a minute before he puts the coffee down and places his hands on his hips. "I swear to God, that mouth of yours is going to be the death of you one of these days."

"What did you say to set him off this time, Cass?" Ali calls as she passes us, walking into my office.

"Phil, if you took after Ali and worked for those abs, you wouldn't be worrying about ways to filter out the 0.01% of fat out of skim milk," I taunt.

"Ohhhh," my sister drawls out as she pauses, her Southern accent making it a five-syllable word. "Should have run with me. I got up when y'all did and put in five miles. Maybe I'll go get a mocha with some extra whip from The Coffee Shop."

"Keep out of it, Ali," Phil huffs. He raises a perfectly sculpted eyebrow, challenging her to step into our argument more than she already has.

"Seriously, Phillip, what's wrong with you?" I ask. "We're actually here for a reason this morning. You know, a quick briefing before a potentially lucrative client walks through the door in about fifteen minutes."

Phil looks at us for a moment before speaking. His eyes, which are so incredibly blue and filled with a raging regret, begin to soften. "If I said nothing, would either of you believe me?"

In unison, Ali and I both say, "No."

Sighing, Phil follows Ali and sits in one of the chairs across from my desk. I join them, crossing my legs and folding my hands over my stomach as I lean back. "Okay, out with it. Why have you been a douche this morning? More so than normal? We have our first appointment coming in"—I check the clock—"in seventeen minutes. Out with it, and do it quickly."

"So, about that first appointment," Phil starts. I slowly uncross my legs and sit forward.

"Yes?"

"There's something you should know."

I'm going to throttle my brother. After all our years of working together, if he left out telling me any minute detail about this appointment, I'm going to lose it.

Knowing Phil, this could be anything from the appointment was supposed to be at the Lockwood company headquarters in Manhattan or their family compound in Greenwich. If Phil suddenly springs on me that he forgot to tell me the client's expecting to have a champagne catered breakfast ready, I'm going to give up on keeping my legendary control, take my scissors and straddle him while I cut off all his hair in massive chunks. He won't be able to stop me because he'll be too busy choking on the extra-skinny, watered down latte he just made me pick up.

In my calmest voice, I ask, "What about it?"

Ali whispers "Uh-oh" under her breath.

Phil looks at his hands, then at the clock. Another minute ticks by. Sixteen minutes until this appointment. He looks at Ali, who just stares back at him with a mean look. He looks back down at his hands. Silence. Fifteen minutes.

From the doorway, Holly pipes in with "Did you fuck the groom or something?"

Ali starts to laugh as I gasp. Standing in the door, Corinna, Em and Holly are standing in varying states of arms crossed, waiting for Phil's answer. Em just mean mugs Phil. I check the clock again. Fourteen minutes.

Phil sighs and looks at me with guilt on his face. That was my only warning.

"No, but Jason was engaged to him about ten years ago and broke it off to be with me. Or so the story goes."

Chaos erupts in my office. In my disbelief, I make a few mental notes. First, Phil is prohibited from doing any further client event profile forms. I also give myself a mental reminder to review all his other forms for new clients for the rest of the week. How could he not think this information was important for me to know, especially now, having more than mere minutes before the Lockwoods come through my door?

As I sit back, listening to my siblings yell among each other, I try to regroup. I have no time to call Jason to discreetly find out what occurred.

I now have five minutes to get this under control.

Forget who fucked who or who fucked whom over. This is not how we built this business.

Phil. Might. Die.

Slowly.

Blunt force trauma caused by my planner. That's a delicious thought.

But later.

I'll enjoy planning it in detail, after I deal with damage control.

"All of you, get out of my office. RIGHT NOW!" I yell at my siblings. "I have exactly four minutes to figure this out. I think you all might be depraved lunatics, and how I know this and continue to work with you all on a daily basis is eluding me. This is not the impression this company will give under any circumstances, short of the building catching fire. Find your offices and have your meltdowns in there."

Then I hear it. That fucking bitch Fate. Three goddamn minutes early. Of course.

"I happen to agree with Ms. Freeman. She and I have an appointment on behalf of my family."

I find myself staring briefly into a set of the most gorgeous, chocolate brown eyes I have ever seen, before they drift away, looking around the room.

My stomach turns. My skin tingles. My heart flips in my chest.

Holy Shit. Is this the groom?

Of course, it is.

Fate, throwing the first man at me that I find remotely desirable and absolutely can't have.

Caleb

I STARE AT THE ENSEMBLE, every one of them frozen in front of me. I decide if the Freemans entered a mannequin challenge, they would likely take first place. Not just for standing completely still, but for the shock and awe on all their faces. Internally smiling at the humor of catching the notorious family in one of their battles, I let my eyes roam around the room.

Since I'd done my homework on them—frankly, I'd read everything about them—before I walked into the door, I'm way more amused than shocked at the scene unfolding before me. While my original intent was to make sure my brother didn't get swindled by these people to create his dream wedding, I was compelled to meet this family after what I read yesterday. I ran the background check for Ry, then carefully manipulated him and Jared into letting me handle the preliminary meeting today on their behalf. They're convinced the Freemans will create the perfect wedding and reception based on recommendations from friends and colleagues.

I think I just saw the reason why.

It's not the youngest, Corinna, whose cat eyes and curves likely have most men fainting before they ever took a bite of the cakes she baked. It's not Allison, whose devastating blue eyes and severe mouth could slice you in half. It's no surprise to me that she's the corporate financial officer and attorney, and didn't deal with the day-to-day wedding events.

Emily and Holly are both knockouts as well. Emily has her blonde hair pinned up, dark blue eyes flashing behind her dark glasses, and her red lips pursed, ready to spring to the family's defense. Her sharp style matches her sharp gaze. I could easily see Emily dressing Ry and Jared in appropriate wedding attire and not taking any bullshit in the process. No one was going down the aisle in gold brocade if she has anything to say about it. Holly, well, she's the dreamer. I nabbed her checking me out, as if she had her camera in her hand, trying to find the best angle to take one of her illuminating shots. I can practically see the wheels in her head spinning as she gnaws on her full lower lip.

Then there's Phillip, the older brother. Jason Ross' husband. The one who had fallen into Jason's life, breaking up my brother's sham of an engagement, the results of which left Ry reeling for a while. The Golden Boy, as Ry used to derisively describe him over Skype while I was overseas, and according to the file I read. He's probably afraid I'm here to upset his happy world order and ready to beat the shit out of me if I do.

The man standing in front of me took in five girls when he was barely a teenager himself, none of whom were related to him, and helped raise them to be the highly successful women standing in front of me. Regardless of what had happened in his or my brother's love lives, he has my respect for that alone.

I ignore the occupant of the room, the one I'm dying to look at, and reach my hand out to Phillip first. "Caleb Lockwood. A pleasure."

"Phillip Freeman-Ross. I apologize for…"

Now I let the smile cross my face. "No need. You should have heard the battles that would happen in our house as kids. And there were far fewer of us."

A bark of laughter leaves Phillip's mouth. He glances over my shoulder like he's been distracted by movement. I imagine daggers are shooting from the gem-colored eyes of the oldest Freeman sister. "As my sister stated appropriately, at Amaryllis Events, this isn't the impression we like to provide to prospective clients. We like to save the crazy for meeting three, at least."

"Phillip."

His name is said in a calm voice. She's too calm if I go by the number of choked sounds, accompanied by phones and hands raised in front of the mouths of the four sisters to muffle their snickers.

"Right," Phillip says. "I'll be leaving now. Say, Caleb, can I grab you a cup of coffee before you meet with my sister?"

"Phillip," the voice behind me says again. Calm. In control. "Get out. Now. If Mr. Lockwood would like coffee, I am more than capable of obtaining it for him. However, you may choke to death on yours and it will be the last extra skinny latte you ever taste. Now, do you want to press your luck and continue to speak in front of me another minute more?"

The sisters can't control their laughter any longer. They all offer their welcome, quickly introduce themselves, and leave Cassidy's office. Phillip doesn't say anything else, but shakes my hand firmly, his eyes meeting mine directly. His expression clearly says, have an issue with me, fine. Don't fuck with my family.

It's an expression I'm familiar with, as I wear it often.

As the door closes softly behind him, I turn to face Cassidy Freeman, CEO, event planner and distraction extraordinaire. Fuck, if I don't like what I see. I let out a soft breath. From the moment I walked in the room, I deliberately ignored her. I now get the full impact. From the top of her head to her booted feet, everything about her intrigues me.

Sweet Jesus, she's a knockout.

Easily the shortest member of the Freeman family, Cassidy's petite size doesn't take away from her presence. Fuck no. A face that is bewitching more than classically beautiful, with long curly hair pulled back in a braid, and the brightest blue-green eyes framed by the longest lashes. Her lower lip, painted a deep burgundy, is thrust forward, and her hands are on her hips, stretching the fabric of her sweater dress across her breasts. Shit, she's tiny. Even wearing boots with a three to four-inch heel, she only comes up to my chin.

During my discreet perusal of her, she takes a deep breath and turns her head toward the window, clearly regrouping. I glimpse the side of her neck where her amaryllis tattoo, the Freeman family logo, peeks out from beneath her heavy mane of hair. Damned if I needed yet another reason to be turned on by her.

She's a brilliant, badass puzzle in a package built for every fantasy I've ever had about a woman.

I don't know if I let an incontrollable sound escape, or if her self-preservation instinct kicked in, but suddenly her gem-colored eyes turn and lock on mine.

I'm standing at least four feet from her, and the delicate pulse in her neck is fluttering visibly. Mine starts to synchronize with hers—a little fast-paced and agitated. I'm not the only one affected, but I might be the only one who understands why.

Nothing I read about her yesterday, no picture I saw, could have prepared me for the impact of her on my senses. She's an enigma.

"Mr. Lockwood, I'm Cassidy Freeman. Again, I would like to offer my apologies for the circus you walked in on when you first came in. As I'm sure you likely overheard, my brother failed to provide me with the details of your appointment in enough time for me to fully prepare for our meeting. It's our preferred approach to be prepared well in advance in order to anticipate your needs."

"I don't think there's any way you could have anticipated what your brother had planned on telling you, Cassidy. It's fine. The most important thing is making sure Ryan has the wedding he's always dreamt of with no flaws."

The professional she is, she squares her shoulders, gesturing to the chair Phil had vacated earlier. "May I take your coat?" I gesture to her I'm fine. "Please take a seat then. Can I offer you that coffee Phillip mentioned earlier? Tea?" I shudder in revulsion. "I'll take it that is a no. For both?" A light laugh trickles out. "A Coke?"

"Please."

She reaches into a refrigerator nestled in the cabinetry in front of her. When she turns, she's holding a familiar red and white can and makes her way back to me on those fantasy-inspiring boots. Handing me the can and a coaster, she sits elegantly behind her desk.

It appears my girl's a bit obsessive about neatness. My girl? Whoa, boy. You just met her. Just because you know everything about her, doesn't mean she would be interested.

In fact, if I read her file correctly, she would never be interested.

Damn, if that isn't a deflating thought.

"So, tell me more about the groom," she inquires, picking up a cup from The Coffee Shop. Taking a sip, she scrunches her nose and puts it aside. Pulling her wireless keyboard closer to her, I glance around for the screen and realize she has it submerged beneath the profile of the desk. Efficient. Cassidy can take notes and not lose line of sight with her clients. I may need that setup for my office.

"Ry's fantastic." I can't help but laugh. "He's probably the most romantic bastard there is in the world. When he proposed, I know for a fact he bought out three nurseries of primroses to make the rooftop deck of our house a virtual Garden of Eden. You know the meaning of primroses is, 'I can't live without you,' right?" Waiting for her nod, I continue. "He took the day off work, got everyone we know involved in arranging them just right. We have a condo in the Powell Building with an outdoor roof deck in the city. Ry spends all day stringing lights all over the place, moves the speakers outside, and what happens? It starts raining! Not like it mattered, of course. Everything ended up just perfect for Ry."

Cassidy says nothing, but offers a polite smile I don't quite get. She looks down and begins typing. Did I miss something? Didn't she ask about Ry?

"Have you discussed what kind of wedding you two are thinking of? Something large, or small and intimate?"

Wait. What the fuck did she say? Ry and I? Married?

From the moment I walked in the door of Amaryllis Events and heard the husband of my brother's ex being ripped a new asshole by his five sisters, and having my dick turn semi-hard from my first glance at Cassidy Freeman, to now being asked what I would like at the wedding she thinks I'm having by marrying my brother, this morning has been nothing but a comedy of errors.

I toss my head back and laugh from the depths of my soul. I can't wait to replay this entire morning later in bed, while thinking of blue-green eyes and dark hair. I lean back in my chair and cross my legs at the ankles, putting my arms behind my head. I notice Cassidy's eyes do a quick bit of wandering themselves. So, the pixie at least likes what she sees. That's a good start.

"No, Cassidy. Ry and I have not talked about the wedding at all. However, I know he and Jared discussed it in detail the other night without me before I got home from a business trip. Since they have since shared their decisions with me, I have a fair idea of what's needed."

I think Cassidy gets whiplash, her head comes up so fast. Her left arm flings out, knocking her coffee cup off her desk and right onto the floor. As she jumps up, her office chair flies back and slams into the wall.

"Shit!" she yells, before her face turns to me in horror. Racing over to the cabinet where she got my Coke, she grabs paper towels from another one of those hidden cabinets, muttering under her breath, "Phil...Won't live to his first anniversary... Scissors...Hair" as she cleans up the coffee spill from the hardwood floor and her desk.

I make no move to assist her, because frankly, I'm enjoying the tight pull of her dress over her ass too damn much.

She stands, throws out the mess of towels and washes her hands at the wet bar. She appears to be doing some sort of deep breathing exercise that shows off her magnificent breasts.

Jesus. A woman like her needs to come with a warning label.

After the eighth or so breath, she has herself back under control and is apparently ready to deal with what she thinks will be my marriage to two men, one of whom is my brother.

I sit back with a shit-eating grin, ready to enjoy the hell out of this appointment with the fantasy-inspiring Cassidy Freeman.

"Again, I apologize, Mr. Lockwood—"

"Please, call me Caleb, Cassidy," I say with a huge smile. "After all, we're going to be working very closely together for the next few months. By the end of this, I imagine we'll know each other so well, we'll be exchanging holiday cards every year, at the very least." I toss in the last part for good measure.

Her eyes widen slightly. "Well, Mr. Lock—I mean, Caleb. In all my years in the business, I have never met a family member with as much... enthusiasm as you have. I'm sure we'll enjoy our relationship quite a bit."

Oh, Pixie, if you only knew.

Biting the inside of my cheek, I train my expression to be as deadpan as possible. "As much as I want to talk about Ry and Jared, and could do for hours, I do have a limited amount of time today, Cassidy. Let's get down to the nitty gritty. What do you need to know so we can get this under contract?"

Straightening, Cassidy gives me her professional smile and begins firing questions at me. Do I want to use all services offered in-house? Of course. Amaryllis Events has an enormous reputation for being the best at everything. Even if they didn't, I want it to be Cassidy's job to corral my mother's ass. I don't mention that point to Cassidy just yet. Do I have a preferred location? Our family home in Greenwich. I can't get Ry to budge on that. What is the date of the wedding? I ask if Thanksgiving weekend is too soon since the location is a private residence.

Back and forth on the questions. I think the only two items that even mildly threw her for a loop was when I dropped that there would be well over 500 guests in attendance, Thanksgiving weekend or not, and that we wanted unfettered access to her anytime, day or night, due to the scale and significance of the wedding.

Cassidy quickly sorted many details with an efficiency that, had I actually been planning my own wedding, would have impressed the shit out of me. Mentally shaking my head in wonder over how her brain works, there's a knock at the door.

Shit. Ryan and Jared are here.

"One moment, please," Cassidy calls out. "Caleb, I do believe we have about seventy-five percent of the major decisions made. You appear to know what Ryan and Jared are looking for with the wedding. I may make a few suggestions and recommendations for enhancements along the way, but nothing to detract from the vision coming together."

"Cassidy, there's one more thing." I look directly into her eyes. I want that physical connection between us before that door swings open. There's something between this woman and me, and I need more time to figure out what it is. I stand and hand her my business card. "I'd like to continue this conversation later, but I need to get going. That's my number on the card to reach me any time."

"Of course. And here's mine. Let me write my cell phone on the back for anything you might need. After all, once the contracts are signed, you'll need this if any of you have questions that arise in the middle of the night."

As she hands me her card, I feel my body already yearning for the connection to hers, which I know is about to be severed in just a few short moments. I continue to stare into her amazing eyes. I figure I have less than thirty seconds before my brother and his fiancé come in to wrap up this appointment, sign the contract, and the stunning pixie before me starts making a list of who to kill first—her brother or me.

"Cassidy? There's something I need to tell you," I say, as the door swings open, revealing Phillip, Ry, and Jared. Right on time.

"Yes, Caleb?"

"I'm not one of the grooms. I'm Ryan's brother."

Acknowledgments

Nathan, I love you. You are my ever-after.

To my son, if I had a single wish for you, you would fall in love and fly to the stars.

Mom and Dad, thank you for showing me what love was meant to be.

Jen, now you have your own HEA. I couldn't be happier. I love you.

My Meows, my inspiration, my family. I love all of you.

Amy, Kristin, Dawn, and our missing butterfly—the Fab Four—always. I love each of you.

To Missy Borucki, thank you for the Stranger Things love notes in this edit. I needed that, LOL. XOXO.

To Holly Malgieri, thank you for looking me straight in the eye the first time you met Cass and giving me the honesty you knew I needed. Look at where she is now!

To photographer Wander Aguiar, Andrey Bahia, Jenny Flores, and Donna Lathan, je vous aimez toujours! And to Gianni Militello for being an absolute sweetheart!

To my cover designer, Deborah Bradseth, for the tiny tweaks that made the next generation even better than ever! XOXO

To Gel, at Tempting Illustrations, amid everything, you still rose from your ashes to give me beauty. I'm honored to be a part of your world.

To the team at Foreword PR, thank you for your love and heart and for being there for every moment.

To Claire Hastings. I'm still smiling. You make a fabulous "pilot" of my Amaryllis crew.

Linda Russell, for always having my back, my front, and watching my six. For loving me enough to help me juggle my sanity, my crazy, and my excitement, I love you right back.

Finally, my readers, I am overwhelmed by your love of Amaryllis. I hope you know how much I adore your emails, comments, and reviews. I love hearing from every one of you. Thank you for your support and for choosing to read my words.

About the Author

It began when Tracey stayed out for hours and making up stories in her head as she biked around her neighborhood in Connecticut. Writing, always a passion, started interfering with her life when she started rewriting ends of books instead of finishing papers during college. After all, what was more important, a happily ever after or Greek mythology?

Eventually, she combined both when she wrote the Amaryllis Series.

With over 125,000 copies of her work worldwide, Tracey's collection of contemporary romance and women's fiction is available on Amazon.com and free on kindleunlimited. This includes her best-selling Amaryllis Series, Midas Series and Glacier Adventure Series. She has over twenty-five books in print and has participated in several anthologies for reader pleasure as well as charity.

Tracey is dedicated to her own happily ever after, having been married since 2007. She and her husband have one son who is as addicted to his Fortnite as his mother is to Starbucks.

When she's not busy with her family or writing, Tracey can be found in her home in north Florida drinking coffee, reading, training for a runDisney event, and feeding her addiction to HGTV.

www.ingramcontent.com/pod-product-compliance
Lightning Source LLC
Chambersburg PA
CBHW072018020726
47501CB00006B/1858